MIDNIGHT LAMP

MIDNIGHT LAMP

GWYNETH JONES

GOLLANCZ

LONDON

Copyright © Gwyneth Jones 2003
Frontispiece © Bryan Talbot

All rights reserved

The right of Gwyneth Jones to be identified as the
author of this work has been asserted by her in accordance with
the Copyright, Designs and Patents Act 1988.

First published in Great Britain in 2003 by

Gollancz
An imprint of the Orion Publishing Group
Orion House, 5 Upper St Martin's Lane,
London WC2H 9EA

A CIP catalogue record for this book
is available from the British Library

ISBN 0 575 07470 1 (cased)
ISBN 0 575 07471 X (trade paperback)

Typeset by Deltatype Ltd, Birkenhead, Merseyside

Printed in Great Britain by Clays Ltd, St Ives plc

Acknowledgements: Many thanks to Jo Fletcher, Malcolm Edwards, Nick May, Bryan Talbot and Anne Sudworth, and my agent, Anthony Goff. Thanks to Peter Gwilliam and Gabriel Jones for full life support, to Stan Robinson and Karen J. Fowler for Californian hospitality, and to many other Californians who took the time to talk to me. Thanks to the community of Darwin, Inyo County, for standing in as Lavoisier; and to the Viridian Pope-Emperor for more information than you would believe possible. Grateful acknowledgement to the master filmmakers, especially John Huston and Ingmar Bergman, and to the Red Hot Chili Peppers, for a roadmovie soundtrack. This book is dedicated to all those who burn the Midnight Lamp.

For full credits, lists, pictures, anecdotes and the annotated *Midnight Lamp* see:
http://www.boldaslove.co.uk

From: Harry Lopez
To: Marshall Morgan
Cc: Julia

Hey, Marsh,

   Thanks for lunch, thanks for the green light, and you want something in writing. Look, this is not a pitch. I don't do pitches. I want to tell you a story. Have patience if I ramble.

In the beginning there was the crash (which is my Big Bang, I cannot know what was before). Over here, our problems were and remain plain old economic. Anyone over twenty-five thinks the price of gas is a crime against humanity, and poor people try to club you to death as you scurry from your cab into the airport. In Western Europe it went into a runaway chain reaction. They had penniless crash victims, mom and pop types included, *hordes* of them, turned nomadic, wandering around like lemmings. They had the anti-capitalist, anti-GM, pro-Gaia, pro-paganism, magic-murky, Save Our Planet thing growing into a monster *volk* movement: shaping up to be the green nazis. They had lootin' and a-shootin' and mad dog migrants from the poisoned lands. Governments fell. Armed forces and teachers and other useful persons just upped and quit. That's the bgd.
   Then the story begins. It's the story of the man who would be king. He's called Ax Preston. He was recruited, along with several other rather amazing people, to what the British government called their Countercultural Think Tank. He was a guitarist, at the time, with a chipper little band called the Chosen Few, from Taunton, Somerset (=*deep* in the sticks). He was twenty-six. Next thing you know there was a blood-spattered coup, a veritable massacre in one of the royal parks, and Ax and his pals were hostages of the deranged hippy régime that had taken over England. They were kid rock musicians. One minute they were dreaming of a record deal, next thing, they were doused in the blood of revolution. But they were patriots. Ax told them they could use the music, and turn the awful situation round. And they did it! The catalogue of disasters that they beat would be unbelievable except it was all part of the same thing: collapse of the card house. It took Ax two years. When he was twenty-eight he was the ruler of England, by the will of the people. I want to tell the story of how that happened. Ax Preston is a phenomenon of our times. I want to show him

I

making hedonism and free will work, in a tsunami of brutish violence. But what makes it **fabulous** is that it was all done with the music.

Ax would be king: but there's more. There's Fiorinda, the scary-smart babe-rocker with the abusive megastar dad. There's Sage Pender, aka Aoxomoxoa, who needs no introduction. (Okay, you twisted my arm: introducing Sage. He's the demon techno whose very existence **irradiated** my youth. He's regarded as the Antichrist in many parts of the USA. He invented immersion code. He's God, in my opinion.) There's the relationship between these three, which is very slippery. Suffice it to say, the guys compete like wolverines disputing a kill, they share the girl and that's not all they share. I love it when beautiful guys love each other passionately, but they're not gay (this is not a proposition, btb). It's very rock and roll, very glamorous and it gives me an immense Jungian thrill, a masculine romance **with girls in it**.

And with guitar!

No, we're not going to go into what happened to them last summer. Nor what's happening in England now. I want to end on a note of valedictory glory, a triumph that foreknows its fall, a sense that great deeds are evanescent as a dream, and that's the way greatness should be. The Japanese have a word for it, Bushido. Ax's England blossomed and died, it was brief and perfect.

I'm sending you **Unmasked** and **Yellow Girl** and **Sweet Track**, Ax's only solo album, and not easy to get, even tho' the fucking data quarantine has supposedly given up trying to isolate us from European Revolutionary Culture. (I've sent them, they're on this letter, just press and play.) You also have to hear the Aoxomoxoa and the Heads mix of **Little Wing**, which came about because one day Sage said to Ax, the reason why Jimi Hendrix is not revered like Beethoven is because the mass market has to be turned on to something or it doesn't survive, and you can't dance to 'Little Wing'. It is **BLAZING**. It explains our whole global culture.

Please, Marsh, let me make this movie in style, no scrimping, c'mon, c'mon. It's surefire, fantastically goodlooking, and the best idea I ever had.

Yours, most respectfully and sincerely,

    Harry

Enrico Ernesto Fortunato Curtis-Lopez de la Concha

From: Harry Lopez
To: Marshall Morgan
Cc: Julia

It's not a problem. I know he hasn't returned a call since he resigned. I'm onto it. I can get hold of him. Don't ask me how, because I can't tell you, just trust me. Mr Preston is coming to Hollywood. It can be done, it will be done. I have an offer he can't refuse, right here in my pocket.

Harry

1

Something In The Way

On a beach on the Pacific coast of Baja, Mexico, two small boys were exercising the tourist-horses. Shore birds in bewildering variety played chicken with the waves, racing in and out above their reflections in the wet sand; over the dunes a turkey vulture coasted on broad black wings. All else was lost in a shining, opalescent haze. Into this stainless world there came a young woman, emerging from the mist as a stick-thin figure with a raggedy cloud of red hair, yellow suntan that gave up at the base of her throat, and an expression of dogged, mutinous calm. The boys galloped towards her, shouting in Spanish as they drew level, did she want a ride? 'No!' she shouted back, in English. 'Not now, and not the other fifty times you asked me.' The boys laughed, the big brown horses danced on the spot, wheeled around and thundered away.

Fiorinda continued her promenade, noting sandpipers, sanderlings, busy little dunlins, elegant terns, whimbrels, dowitchers and curlews; ooh, possibly a marbled godwit. The mist, parting ahead of her, disclosed three fishermen in shortie drysuits and parkas, hauling on a net. A handful of flip-flopping things glittered in the long expanse. *Plenty more fish in the sea*, she thought, is a concept to bemuse the children of this century.

Ideas and memories rose up and fell away like the spindrift. The pale sweep of the sands reminded her of Tyne and Wear, the cold north-east coast of England, where she had found friends, acceptance, a reason for living, after she had escaped from her hateful childhood. But this beach at the end of the Western World was more beautiful and more desolate: and there go the pelicans, one, two, eight, fourteen of them today, in stately procession just above the blunt sawteeth, out where the ocean turns navy blue and solid. South in the morning, north in the evening, regl'r as clockwork. What do they do down there? When I've lived here a thousand years, I'll take my shoes and follow them. But now she'd reached the upturned, derelict fishing boat which marked the end of her habitual stroll. She sat down in its shelter and rubbed her cold bare toes.

So here I am, back in the modern world, after seven years in fairyland. Traffic fumes, cable tv, air travel, internet connections, swimming pools, movies – and everything that happened to us in those strange days vanishes like a dream ... I think it was a dream. My boyfriend was never the king of England. The European Crisis was a global-economic-meltdown sideshow. My father didn't rip Sage to pieces, on the beach at Drumbeg.

Some events hadn't vanished with the spindrift. It was still true that Ax Preston the guitar-man, radical rockstar, had become a significant figure in the Crisis, and that he'd been kidnapped by terrorists while on a mission to the USA ... Must be, because she distinctly remembered coming here to Mexico in a big aeroplane (first time she'd been on a big plane in her life), and going to Mexico City so that Ax could make a deposition, which had not been comfortable, because some of the gang were still at large. But the Justice Department had needed Ax to come over in person, and said they'd pay the fares: a convenient offer. The former rulers of the Rock and Roll Reich had been wanting to get away, and they were very broke. The deposition business hadn't taken much time. So now they were on the Baja, having wandered right across Mexico because Sage remembered surfing on this coast, long ago. There was no surf at this season, and no swimming, because the water was ice-cold. No scenery either, and April weather barely distinguishable from a chill spring in Margate, apart from the fearsome UV.

But here they had come to rest.

The flank of the old boat was warm against her spine, as if it had already sucked up heat from the morning sun, though the air was still cold. She leaned back, with a sigh of deliberate content. A glimpse, out of the corner of her eye, forced itself on her attention. She must turn her head. She must see a hole in the sand, which had been smooth a moment before. Something was lying in the bottom, in a crumpled heap. It was her green and white kimono, the kimono she'd worn the night she gave herself to the dead man, in trade for her friends' lives. She was sure that gown had been burned, but there it was, sand clogging the skirts. The sight of it made her feel as if someone was pouring concrete down her throat.

Fiorinda gazed, stubbornly. The hallucination was nothing, except for the choking feeling in her mouth. But the kimono turned into another beach, under a dark sky. She could feel the weight of Sage's broken body, dead in her arms. A hundred perceptions rose up: a thousand, uncountable, each with its specific freight of sensation and emotion; many of them vile, horrible ... and oh, God, I'm not really in

Mexico. Oh, God. The very bad thing could be happening to me, *right now*, and me blanking it out.

She set her teeth, breathing shallow, until the kaleidoscope steadied and the sea and sky returned. But the world was made of paper, it felt like nothing. If she moved her head, it was like trying to see into the corners of a room in a dream.

She wasn't sure when she'd first realised her happy ending was fake. She knew there'd been an incident at Tyller Pystri, when Sage had been well enough to travel and they'd gone down to Cornwall to complete his convalescence. Something had happened, the illusion had been shaken, and since then she'd been living in paper-world. What did I do? I know it was wicked, but I don't remember . . . She was afraid to study the immediate past too much. There were gaps in it into which she might fall, and lose her grip completely, *completely*. She had enough trouble tackling the episodes that came of their own accord, and broke the scenery up, and forced her to face the truth—

When she was thirteen, in the first really terrible year of her life, Fiorinda had discovered, or invented, a place inside herself: where she could go to escape and recover her strength, hiding in the aeons between one moment and the next. She'd tried in vain to do that trick since she'd found out she was in paper-world. Something blocked her, and dimly she remembered she had made this bargain with her father, *you must not leave your body*. Apparently the promise had followed her, on her flight from reality, and thank God for that because—

So this is where I am. Sage is dead, Ax never came home . . . and I am in hell, with the dead man fucking me. But I am keeping my father sweet, and protecting my people. I will go on fighting, she thought, gazing at sea and sky. One day I will wake up from this, in bed with your carrion disguise, dear Father, and only seconds will have passed. One day you will defeat me, and take us all to hell. I know that. But until then, *fuck you*.

Ha. Other alternative: I'm just a little mixed-race girl from Neasden, whose rock-god absent father came home to make her pregnant, and she ended up in a padded cell—

She stood up and started walking back, reflecting detachedly that she didn't believe and couldn't make herself believe the padded cell option. Was this a plus or a minus, she wondered? She felt it was a plus . . . All you can go on is what makes a situation bearable. I think I'm better off convinced that I had lovers once, and that I'm serving a cause.

The fishermen were gone. Three dolphins were leaping where the nets had been. She paddled in the punishing cold water, and what's this?

What's this round flat purple furry thing? Hey, *it's a sand-dollar!* This is what they look like when they are alive! She picked it up. The purple fur was made of tiny wriggling tentacles. It's like a . . . a flattened-out sea urchin, a fused starfish. How cool! A myriad bewildered little fingers wriggled. She set the creature back in its watery home and watched it drift down to the sand feeling like a gentle god.

I must never tell them. If they are dead, at least my darlings don't have to know it.

She straightened, and looked up: and *there*, not on the painted sky but far, far off in the darkness of her soul, she glimpsed the shining limb of a different answer, which for a moment she knew was real, absolutely *real*; but she could not reach it.

Something in the way—

Ax had been talking to Smelly Hugh about Para, Smelly's oldest daughter (named *Paralytic*, as that was what her father had been the night she was born). She now called herself *Paradoxa*, sensibly enough. She'd dropped out of hedgeschool baccalaureat and announced she was joining a hardline Gaian group; she would no longer be using clothes, or articulate language. She'd told her bewildered parents she wanted to recover from the disease of being human. 'She loves animals,' said poor Smelly. 'An' she's dead clever. Me and Ammy, we thought she might be a *vet*. But I don't get this. We're the leaders of the Rock and Roll Reich, we're supposed to set an example. I'm not bein' a fascist dad, Ax. I jus' want her to do somethink worfwhile, not sittin' on her bum—'

Ax knew Para quite well, and doubted if anything would deflect the young woman from her course, but he'd made soothing noises, and the hippy paterfamilias had seemed comforted before he winked out of sight. Smelly Hugh's a punk philosopher. He doesn't think twice about the miracles of technology. He zooms over to Mexico on the astral plane, smells the ocean, and zooms right back to London—

'You din't mind me calling? Ammy said I shouldn't. She says, they're on holiday, leave them in peace. But I thought, Ax won't mind—'

Smelly's old lady was sharper than her helpmate. Thanks for trying, AM.

Alone on the water margin he sat turning the b-loc headset in his hands, wondering if he should chuck it in the sea. Hugh's earnest, fractured groping after Utopia brought back too vividly the multitude of others, the people Ax had served, the forty million lives he had tried to hold in his hands . . . The taste of failure was like bile in his mouth. He felt that he would never be free of it. Back in England now, the suits had finally accepted that he was not going to change his mind. He had been dictator, a temporary measure for a very rough patch. He was not going to stay on as a rubber stamp for the neo-feudalists. Ax knew that the secret rulers had approached his brother Jordan. They fancied another rock musician Green Head of State: an easier model, who would take the perks and shut up. Jor was reportedly tempted by the job. He'd already taken over the band. All their lives, anything Ax had that looked good, Jordan had to muscle in and grab it . . . Reportedly, he was holding out for his big brother's approval. Ax was determined to avoid that conversation, but—

He had to choke down the pain and fury, because Fiorinda had appeared in the distance. They walked towards each other, herding scurrying birds between them, until they met in a whirling crown of silver wings.

'Hi,' she said, with the faraway eyes and otherworldly smile that cut his heart in two. 'What are *you* doing out so early, mister?'

'Smelly Hugh decided to give us a wake-up visit. Sage was asleep, so I came out here. Fuck. I told them, don't call us: we'll call Allie *once a week*, to prove we haven't been kidnapped. I should switch off incoming, we wouldn't miss it.'

The bi-location phone was a spin-off from the Zen Self quest, what they called fusion consciousness science over here. The technology was unknown in Mexico, so the phone was useless for anything except satellite-phreaking: but that was no loss. They didn't have anyone they wanted to talk to in the New World.

'Don't do that. There might be a real emergency and we wouldn't know. You should have come beachcombing. I found a live sand-dollar, and I *think* I saw a marbled godwit—'

'You're kidding. Sure it wasn't a Common Loon?'

They followed their own footprints through the dunes to the fishing camp called El Pabellón, where they'd been staying in one of the cabins for a week or so. It was off-season, and sports fishing in steep decline: hard to say what most of the people were doing here really, except maybe hiding from creditors; or the police. The painter lady was under her striped awning, catching the morning light like Monet. Nothing moved in the township of middle-aged bikers. The little tent belonging to the teenage runaways had fallen down again, leaving them asleep but shrouded like dead bodies. The Clam Diggers, (not genuine campers but locals, here to harvest shellfish for the restaurant trade) were at work, monopolising the standpipe. Nevada and his old lady, proprie-tors of a wagon-ring of strangely assorted, half-derelict vehicles, were

9

up and about, toting shotguns. The kids were not in sight. The Nevada dogs stood up and woofed.

'Hi, youse guys,' called Nevada's buckskinned and gypsy-bloused old lady. 'You been on the beach already? How's the world looking?'

'Same as yesterday,' Fiorinda called back. 'Sand. Birds. Sky. Sea.'

'She's a poet, and she don't know it,' remarked snaggle-toothed, draggle-haired Nevada, grinning his shit-eating grin. 'Hope she don't blow it. You guys coming to the shindig tonight? You'd be very welcome.'

They laughed, and said maybe, and passed on.

When they reached him Sage was reclining on the cabin's only sunbed with a sketchpad: but he'd made the coffee and cooked the eggs. They berated him, and agreed between them silently he *mustn't* be left alone. The moment you leave him alone he starts doing too much. And so another quietly busy day begins. That's the last of the cinnamon buns: better review the exchequer. Would you care to initial these accounts for me, Mr Preston? Why certainly, Ms Slater . . .

Later, Ax walked up to the Transpeninsular Highway, to the little shack-store beside the Church of the Holy Family. The cinder cones of San Quintín floated over the north-west, the cows in the beaten-earth field by the track were contemplating a vivid load of surplus tomatoes that had been dumped for them. Now that's something you don't see every day . . . Wonder if they like the taste? Of course, if you tried to buy tomatoes for human consumption around here, it cost an arm and a leg. The death-wish contortions of post-modern agribusiness were no longer Ax's concern, thank God, but he stopped to stare: thinking about a yacht called the *Lorien*. What a boat, thirty knots under sail, and endless other passionate details, whispered through the long hospital nights (the intensive care unit in Cardiff, that was the setting he remembered) . . . I want Sage to have his yacht.

I'd buy you a jet-plane, baby, I've had it with green austerity—

But they had no money, and soon this was going to be a problem that Ax must address. Sage and Fiorinda must never be asked to go on stage again. They must never be asked to *work* again. Ax would have to make a living. What are my skills? Ex-dictator, former rockstar, horrendously in debt . . . This needs thought.

Make a list: One pack flour tortillas (NB, not the brand that tastes of soap). Maize meal for Fiorinda's excellent stove-top corn bread; eggs. Veg, whatever they have fresh. Tinned fruit, any kind but pineapple which we all hate, the cinnamon buns she likes. Little elastic bands to mend the Nevada kids' stunt kite. What's the Spanish for that?

I wonder exactly how much a boat like the *Lorien* would cost?

Fuck it. We won't starve. We can live on clams and steal the cows' tomatoes.

It dawned on him that he'd started to think in terms of never going back to England. What, *never*? What, just vanish from the screen . . . ? He turned his face, to avoid getting choked by dust as a blue off-roader compact rumbled past him, and looked after it; idly curious. US plates, surfie stickers in the rear window, longboards on the roof. There aren't any waves, he thought.

New campers? They better fit in with the ambience.

The driver of the compact pulled up at the entrance to the fishing camp and got out. Above the gateway, which possessed no gates, a marlin leapt in blue and white mosaic, leprous with deleted pixels: flanked by red and yellow butterflies. A hand-painted sign advertised cabins, RV hook-ups, cocktails, firewood, surf-fishing, drysuit hire and HORSE rides . . . Beyond the gateway a row of battered *talapas*, straw-thatched beach umbrellas, stood outside a flat-roofed, pastel building, possibly a bar. Nothing stirred when he peered into the dark interior.

'Anyone home?'

No answer, only the sound of the ocean.

Cautiously, he explored. The scurvy RV camp was noontide silent. There were dish-aerials, most of them big enough to be illegal; a recycling plant beside a midden of scrap plastic and metals. Stacks of dessicated clam shells, pyramids of beer bottles, a skeletal *thing* made of thousands of old pens: ballpoints, felt-tips, gel-tips, rollerballs. A large grey iguana stared him out, sideways, from under one of the trailers; everything had an air of post-futuristic dereliction and outlawry. Two of the dogs in the biggest compound (command post?), stood up, rattling their chains: a German Shepherd and something like an Irish Setter, but bigger, with deeply malevolent yellow eyes. He retreated.

Beyond a mutant tamarisk hedge, festooned with sun-drained rainbow pennants, he found a row of cabins. The first had a shiny jeep and a boat-trailer outside. The rest were padlocked and clearly unoccupied, except for the one at the end. He listened, glanced around and moved closer. There was a towel hanging from a line, a dishpan of murky water, full of submerged underwear. A sketchpad, held down by a slab of plastic-cased hardware, lay on a trailer-park sunbed that had seen better days.

Doubt assailed him. Why would they be living like this?

He bent over the pad, careful to touch nothing. On the top leaf there was an unfinished portrait, male, half profile ... and the hardware, he realised, was a portable videographics desk, of alien but hi-spec design. Oh yes. What do the English say?

Gotcha.

Out on the beach, beyond the gap in the dunes, there were figures in the landscape. Kids ran around; local people were digging clams. He tipped his straw hat onto the back of his head and strolled. Below the tideline a tall, very slender white guy was playing a ball game with a young woman whose ragged red hair whipped to and fro, like the pennants on the tamarisk hedge. She was wearing a body glove and knee-length denims. The man wore a loose white shirt and pants that accentuated his willowy height and languid movements. His hair was cropped yellow curls, eyes invisible behind aviator shades. Each of them wore a ring on the third finger of the left hand, but he couldn't get a good look. He watched the game.

They ignored him, but not in an unfriendly way.

'D'you mind if I ask a question?'

The young woman turned on him a mask of beaten gold, pierced by a pair of eyes like clear grey stones – so like the cover image on her second solo album that his mouth went dry with excitement. Yellow Girl. It's really her!

'Go ahead. It'd better not be difficult. We have no brains.'

'Why are you playing cricket, with a softball and a baseball bat?'

He was pleased with himself for spotting the game. That should have an effect.

'Oh, tha's easy,' said the languid giant, planting the bat in front of his stumps – which were stalks of bleached tamarisk root, capped by clam-shell bails. 'We don't have a cricket bat, an' if we used a smaller ball I would never hit it. I'm useless.'

'He's lying,' said Fiorinda. 'We found the bat. We had a proper baseball, which we bought in Ensenada, but our demon bowler, er, pitcher, managed to bury it in the Pacific. It's over there. If you'd like to fetch it for us, we'd be grateful.' She pointed out into the ocean, smiling at him with great charm, and chilling strangeness.

'You guys are English, aren't you?'

'Yes.'

'I recognised the accent. We haven't seen many tourists from Crisis Europe the last few years. Things have quieted down over there now, I guess?'

'Much quieter,' she agreed. 'Practically back to business as usual. Except for Italy and, um, a few other hot spots.'

'England's still revolutionary, though, isn't it? But you're allowed to travel—?'

'As long as we promise not to eat at McDonalds.'

'Okay—' he said, nodding politely. 'The name's Harry. Harry Lopez.' He held out his hand. They smiled, but didn't take it. They didn't offer their own names.

He went back to the campground and looked into one of the toilet blocks. The showers and the stalls had plastic curtains, no doors, but everything was clean. He tried turning on a faucet and leapt back, cursing. The water was *boiling*. A little Mexican girl had appeared at the uncurtained door to the outside, a black and tan puppy in her arms. She stared at him, scandalised.

'These are dire and troubled times,' he said to her, shaking his scalded fingers. 'This could be the end of days. Do you believe that?'

He tried the other faucet. There's something about F and C . . . Fuck! Also boiling.

'This is the *ladies'* room,' said the little girl, in Spanish.

'Do you have an office? *Oficina?*'

'Strange bloke,' said Fiorinda, meaning the man in the straw hat. She had called a halt. Sage was obediently lying down on their rug, while she sat beside him on the sand. They watched the world go by.

'I dreamed of Fergal again last night.'

'Oh yes?'

Sage didn't know what to make of this development. Fergal Kearney, the Irish musician, casualty of the lifestyle, was the man whose dead body had been used by Fiorinda's father as his instrument of torture. She refused to talk about the horror she'd suffered: she had never known the real Fergal, why had she suddenly started talking about him?

'He was sitting by my bed,' said Fiorinda softly. 'I didn't *see* him, but he was there, in my mind's eye. It wasn't a nightmare, Sage. I felt that he was on guard, keeping bad at bay. The strange thing is, I still thought he was my father, same as before: and in my dream I didn't mind. You know how all the people around you are really just patterns created by firing neurons in your head?'

'Mm,' said Sage, carefully neutral.

She laughed, cold and sweet, and took his hand with chilling deliberation. 'Hey, I'm not saying you don't exist. I'm just saying, obviously that's what ghosts of the dead must be, too. Phantoms of the mind. My father is dead, and I killed him—'

'Er, as I recall, *I* killed Rufus, babe—'

'I helped to kill him, and I bloody well think I had a right. But I believe I want him to forgive me. I think when I imagine Fergal by my bed, on guard, it's my mind's way of telling me we did okay, that night at Drumbeg. We rescued Fergal from hell, and he's grateful, and we even did Rufus some good, somehow. Is that very soppy?'

'Fee, you are amazing.'

'Thank you so much . . . Sage, what'll I do about not wanting to be famous any more? All the time we were trapped being leaders of the revolution, I was secretly thinking, *fuck this, I need to tour Japan*. Now I can't stand the idea, and it's not just a career problem. I need to redefine myself. I'm scared to have no grand plan. I think I'll fall apart.'

'Nyah. Remember what you told me, about never being Aoxomoxoa again? People talk a lot of crap about facing up to big life changes. Why bother? Spend a few years in denial. Then you can tackle accepting the obvious when it's old news, and hurts less.'

'Did I tell you that? I am a vicious brat . . .' She sighed. 'Well, benign neglect, that's how I'm dealing with the *other* major problem, about never having a baby. But—'

Fiorinda had been sterilised without her consent when she was thirteen, after she'd given birth to her father's child, the little boy who had died at three months. The treatment had been meant to be permanent, but reversing it might be possible—

'You don't know you're never going to have a baby.'

'Yes I do, Sage, because I'm never going to try. How could I have a baby? It was okay when I thought my father was just some bastard of a megastar who didn't mind seducing his own daughter. Now I know what kind of weird monster he really was, how could I possibly want to pass on those genes?' She frowned at the sparkling ocean. 'Unless, um, unless as I sometimes think, I imagined the whole thing? I don't mean the Crisis, or running the revolution, I mean, the rest of it—?'

She'd let go of his hand. He took hers, ready to back off the moment she flinched. But she would not. His touch seemed to comfort her (a handclasp, arm around her shoulders). He hoped that was a good sign.

'Sorry, babe. You didn't imagine it. It was all real. I was there, trust me.'

'What crocks we are,' said Fiorinda, after a moment. 'The three of us. Me with my gross memories and my monster of a dead dad. You, had to come back from heaven and never going to be the big strong king of the lads again, and Ax, with his post-hostage stress; and what's worse, he doesn't believe in saving the world any more. Oh, Sage, do you think we can ever make him happy? Just you and me?'

'Yes.'

'Did I say, also completely penniless?'

'Hahaha. I don't mind being broke. I like it.'

'Oh sure, my one-bowl, one-robe pilgrim. What about the yacht, hm?'

'Tha's different.'

She smiled at him tenderly and tugged his hand to her face, rubbing his knuckles against her cold cheek. Ah, my darling, he thought. My sweet girl. You make such a brave show, but you don't even know I'm here.

They folded the rug, collected their bat and the softball, and went to look for Ax.

On quiet nights they would play and sing on their terrace, after dark, for their own amusement. The shindig drove them indoors, but then the hermit crab, which had been lost in the cabin for days, started to make excruciating ragged-claw noises. The Baja heaves with geo-thermal power, but the fishing camp electric light was low and peevish. They searched under beds and in corners with their wind-up torch, to no avail, and decided to go back outside. The Clam Diggers chorus was rendering Beatles' Greatest Hits, backed by a miserable machine-beat bassline, and constructive interference from the old bikers' Jazz ensemble. The communal bonfire painted orange shadows above the tamarisks, the Nevada dogs howled, the Pacific sighed. The former rulers of England sat shrouded in rugs and watched the bold cactus mice from the hedge hunt for scraps.

'I don't know where the fuck it hides,' grumbled Ax. 'We haven't *got* any furniture. Oh, look at that one. Commando mouse—'

'We should build them an obstacle course,' said Sage.

'We should join the shindig,' suggested Fiorinda, cheerfully, 'since we're going to get the benefit of it anyway. I bet Mr Strange with the straw hat will be there. The Nevadas are always looking for new blood.'

'I'm tired,' said Sage. 'Don't feel like it.'

Ax caught his eye in the light of the camping lantern. Silently, they'd agreed not to worry about the man in the straw hat. Say nothing to make her anxious. But fear brushed him with a stealthy hand, and suddenly he realised what unbelievable good fortune he still possessed. Just to be with them, to be *alive*, and loving them—

'Nah, me neither. Let's get indoors. The claw's probably asleep by now.'

Every dusk the firewood arrived, in a red pick-up. Campers gathered in the town square, an open space with a ring of logs and stones around the bonfire site. The horse-boys and their sister tossed out bundles of hardwood root and scrap timber. Señor El Pabellón, a square-built man with a handsome moustache, got down to take the money. His wife (presumably), who ran the campsite office, stayed in the cab with the old lady who was (probably) her mother-in-law, and made critical observations, in a rapid but none-too-discreet undertone. *The hippy woman is too old to wear her hair down her back, she looks ridiculous, and her children are brats. The painter is a stupid old lady with no talent. That young man in the straw hat is a strange one. He looks like a debt collector.*

'No, you don't want that one,' said Señor El Pabellón to Fiorinda, in English, 'there are nails in the wood, take this one, it's heavier . . . You'd like a horse ride tomorrow?'

'Caballo no me gusta,' said Fiorinda, 'caballo demasiado grande, soy pequeño.'

Señor El Pabellón laughed, and winked at Ax. 'Ah, she's learning Spanish! The horse is big, and she is small, yes: but my horses are gentle, eh. Tell her that.'

Fiorinda could ride okay, but she didn't like horses. *She sleeps with the blond,* said the wife. *Nah, she sleeps with neither,* said the mother-in-law. *El guero is some kind of celibate priest, and the Indio is like her brother. It's a mystery.*

True enough, thought Ax, paying for the bundle without the nails. *And you two mean old bats know fucking well I can understand you.* But he wasn't really offended. He'd lived in the public eye a long time: you develop a tolerance.

'Hey, are you coming down tonight?' asked Nevada's old lady, heaving up her bundles. 'Free food. We're laying on barbecue,' she added persuasively.

Fiorinda looked at Ax. 'Shall we?'

His premonition had faded, and he hated to be the control freak. *Whatever she wants, she should have.* 'Okay by me. Let's ask Sage.'

Harry had discovered that they were known as Red, Mr Guitar and Blondie. They were liked, their musical talents had been noted, but they were hard to get. By their lahdidah accents they came from 'New

England' – which to the campers meant the north-eastern seaboard of the USA. Or else they were Canadians, or even Australian, but not Irish. Red and Mr Guitar were seen as the couple, with Blondie tagging along, but there was a minority in favour of Guitar and Blondie, with Red as their 'beard'. One romantic variant had Red an heiress hiding from the media, Blondie as her dissolute and wasted brother dying of AIDS, and Mr Guitar as the trained assassin bodyguard.

I'll file that one!

In the *Oficina*, for a small cash payment, he'd had sight of a single European Union passport, suspiciously fresh and new, issued to a Daniel Brown. Like hell.

He was astonished that nobody had recognised those three faces. It made him doubt the evidence of his eyes, and of the technical data. Maybe you could pass Fiorinda on the street, if she was dressed down and not deploying that terrific stage presence. Maybe you could pass Ax Preston (though you'd sure as hell remember him). You might not spot that the willowy blond in aviator shades had once been muscle-bound techno-wizard Aoxomoxoa, of Aoxomoxoa and the Heads ... He of five Grammys the year before last, the inventor of 'immersion' code: rock *auteur* of a horrific, hallucinatory string of albums, banned in twelve states. But together! How could anyone miss them?

Briefly, he'd felt crushed. No one knew about these people, no one cared, his big idea was a dog ... But the denizens of the caravanserai were wilfully ignorant, self-selected out of so many loops; whereas one of the people who shared Harry's delusion was Kathryn's Uncle Fred ... Maybe he need not worry. Maybe what he had here was not a private obsession, but *an untapped mother-lode*.

'There will be wars, and the rumour of wars,' he muttered, loitering by the trestle table where the barbecue was laid out, eating coleslaw from a paper plate and eyeing the inexplicable thing built from worn-out pens: which stalked in the shadows, dangerously unstable. The bonfire was lit, the crowd moved over. He saw Ax and Fiorinda arrive, with guitars. Sage was already here, talking to the pen-thing's keepers, a young guy-couple who looked like slumming MIT mavins.

This is it. How unbelievably romantic.

He found a place on a log of driftwood, between a grizzled Hell's Angel and the spooky, spectral teenagers. Ax had a semi-acoustic. Fiorinda was handling the legendary Ax Preston Les Paul. (Harry was no guitar buff, but a classic Gibson he could spot.) They had those futuristic little Oltech amps patched on the soundboxes, hm, well-up on the high tech, these three vagabonds ... Without any fuss, Ax started to play, and it was 'Riq', a very sexy instrumental from the glory days of the English Dictatorship. My God, Harry thought. Can anyone beat this? I'm listening to Ax Preston, *live*, in a Baja RV camp, surrounded by pension-stretching nomad seniors!

The campers chatted through 'Riq'. Then they seemed to realise they'd got something good, and started yelling for their favourites. They wanted 'The Boxer', they wanted 'Mr Tambourine Man'; Harry could have killed them. The Triumvirate simply complied, with a set of Reader's Digest Favourite Twentieth Century Folksongs (someone's got a thing for The Beatles . . .) relieved by Sage and Fiorinda duetting on an unplugged version of 'Stonecold', the *Fiorinda* punk anthem which had become a standard even in the New World. In 'Stonecold' Harry ruined the experience for himself by realising he had a chance to stare without being noticed. He gave the side of his head a discreet tap, blinking to focus his gaze. He was wary of making it obvious. Eyesocket digital devices might be okay, but he could be surrounded by eco-maniacs. As a rule of thumb, Harry had observed that the fewer houses you can see, the higher the concentration of lunatics.

Close up, *of course* it's Fiorinda, and *of course* that's Ax Preston, the rockstar warlord with the boy-next-door charm. He lingered over Sage, the one of the three who'd been global before the UK collapsed. Aoxomoxoa and the Heads used to wear digital skull masks, not just on stage but on all public sightings. Sage Pender, aka Aoxomoxoa, had worn a designer 'living skull' model that he'd coded himself. He'd kept his hands masked too, to hide the fact that he'd lost several fingers to infant meningitis.

There wasn't a sign of reconstruction, regrowth or scar tissue on the naked hands and wrists that Harry studied now, not at any magnification. And the technical data says that's no kind of digital veiling, that's flesh and blood.

The hairs on the back of Harry's neck prickled.

What the hell happened to you? he thought. *What was it LIKE, Sage?*

The rings intrigued him: Ax had one too.

The Angel next door nudged him with a quart of mezcalito.

'This is incredible,' whispered Harry, fumbling it back untouched.

'Shit. Guess you're too young to have ever been at a *Yes* concert. Still,' the geezer downed an inch or few of rotgut spirit, 'they're good . . . Are you a talent scout?'

Harry furtively tapped his head, restoring normal vision. 'Uh, you could say so.'

'Well, walk on by, mother. What can you give them that they ain't got? Don't fucking ruin their lives. Those,' he gestured with the quart, 'are free people.'

You are as wrong as you can be, thought Harry. But you are so right. I'm the last person they want to meet. For a second or two he felt like a butterfly hunter, greedy and guilty ... But the three were saying they'd do one last song and goodnight. It was 'Heart On My Sleeve', the Aoxomoxoa and the Heads dance track, a major European hit at the time of the Floods Conference; album release on *Hedonastick*. This was an *a capella* version, the three voices blended in mesmerising harmony. The campers went utterly silent. Chills crept up Harry's spine at the purity of that homage.

He probably didn't draw breath himself until the music ended.

The Angel dug him in the ribs again. 'Couldn't help but notice you have a concealed weapon, sir. Don't you know an alien carrying a firearm is illegal in Mexico?'

'Yeah, but I have a ... Hey, I'm just doing the same as everyone else.'

Outlaws are all alike. He was morally certain there'd be enough illicit weaponry in this seaside dug-out to mount an assault on Camp Bellevue.

'But no one else is wearing a hat like yours. You've been acting kind of suspicious, young man, and those are neighbours of mine.' Suddenly the old guy had fixed a hefty grip on Harry's shoulder. 'Tell me straight. Are you the law?'

The three were leaving. They were walking away, laughing and shaking their heads at the applause, Ax and Fiorinda shouldering their guitars. Shit!

'I am not the law! I'm their biggest fan! Lemme go!'

He dashed around the fire, in time to cut them off.

'Hi! My name's Harry Lopez and—'

'Hi,' said Ax, in a cool, negative, English tone of voice.

'I wanted to say, uh ... Did you, was that your own arrangement on "Heart"?'

'Yeah,' said Sage, in the same tone, but frostier.

'It was, uh, excellent. Very, um, original idea.'

'Thanks.'

Fiorinda, between her bodyguards, was almost invisible in shadow. If I tried to touch her, he thought, reeling before a blast of inexplicable, over-the-top-hostility ... If I even look at her hard, they'll rip me to shreds. He was terrified. If he let them go, he might never dare to get near them again.

'Have you ever been offered a recording contract? I mean, in the US?'

'Can't say as I have,' said Mr Preston. 'Excuse us. It's late.'

Sage was officially allowed to work for an hour in the afternoons. It was still the immix tracks for *Unmasked*, which he'd been tinkering with for too long, sometimes convinced he was doing something new and brilliant; sometimes bored by the relentless difficulty of the task. After forty minutes – weaving the loom of firings and partial firings, edge and hue and limbic routed emotion – he knew he was flogging dead meat. He kept going, obstinately, until the hour, zipped down the code to be fired off to his collaborator when the satellite window opened, and dressed for a cold swim. His collaborator, Peter (Cack) Stannen, didn't like to use b-loc, which was fine. They'd never worked in the same office. Poor Peter, some things you just can't explain to him, like why did the boss go away, and if we beat the bad guys, why isn't everything like before—

He missed his band. He missed England, and the Atlantic. But here is an ocean that makes the Atlantic look *parochial*. Out in the California Current he dived: into the blue, into the immense smooth masses of movement. I have to get them down here, he thought. It is NOT too cold. A decent drysuit is all you need, and the rental ones here are good. A pod of dolphins barrelled up and he broke the surface with them, in a rush of bubbles; gloriously, momentarily, completely himself. But he'd swum too far. He plodded back, stroke by stroke, stumbled out and fell crushed on the slope of a dune.

Ax, who had been running, came up and sat down, shaking his head.

'I saw that, you lunatic. Are you *trying* to set yourself back?'

'Fuck off,' mumbled Sage. 'I'm okay.' He forced himself to sit up. 'I get *tired*, that's all. I'm not sick, nothing hurts, I'm just *fucking exhausted*, the whole time.'

'Doctor, doctor. I had my liver and half my right lung torn out ten months ago, and now I can't swim a mile in freezing cold water without feeling poorly.'

'Half a mile.'

'Yeah, really? A country half-mile. Sage, you're unreasonable … How's "Relax"?'

The *Unmasked* concept was brain-burning techno-wizardry applied to golden oldies, a simple idea that had turned out to be a bugger to implement.

'Not,' said Sage, gloomily. 'I should call Holly, tell him it isn't going to happen.'

'Nah, don't do that. You'll get there.'

The mist had descended. Fiorinda, the Nevada kids and the Pabellón kids played rounders down along the shore, dim figures wavering in cloud.

'What do you think of her now?' asked Ax, quietly.

'She's . . . okay. No better, not much worse.'

'I think she's better, Sage. Look at her, she's *playing*. It's like the childhood she never had. I think she had a nervous breakdown and she's coming out of it.'

On the beach at Drumbeg, Fiorinda's father had used his last breath to promise Sage that neither he nor Ax Preston would enjoy his daughter again. Sage had been convinced, as the supernatural power he had borrowed for that duel drained away, that the curse meant he would die, and they would blame themselves and break up; or he would linger as a hopeless invalid, ruining his lovers' lives. He had chosen mortality. Health and strength weren't necessarily in the deal. But Sage had returned from the brink, it was Fiorinda who was lost.

No one at home knew what was behind this flight to Mexico. At least, no one knew what had happened at Tyller Pystri. Probably everyone who knew her had seen Fiorinda was in trouble. Fear for Sage's life had kept her brave and calm; she'd begun to fall apart as that fear faded: quietly, day by day, until there was nothing left between her and the foul things that bastard O'Niall had done, or the foul things the *fucking English* had done to her . . . and at last the collapse had come. It was natural, maybe even cleansing—

'She isn't having a nervous breakdown,' said Sage, breaking in on Ax's hopeful reasoning. 'Psychologically, she's in amazing shape.'

'What—? Are you *kidding*?'

'I am not kidding. Her bastard of a father raped her for seven months in the body of a dead man, then the English tried to burn her for a witch, and she came out of that with her colours flying, emotionally intact, because she is our babe, and there is no one like her. I mean, the damage is hardwire.' Sage sighed, pulled back the hood of his drysuit, and rubbed at the drying salt on his forehead. 'She has frontal lobe damage. I'd need a scan to give you the details: but it wouldn't make any odds, there's nothing anyone could do. Fiorinda's brain is too weird, nobody would dare to contemplate surgery.'

'What are you saying?'

'I'm saying, prolonged mental or physical torture will make people schizophrenic. It will do that. It's a syndrome, not a disease, and once the damage is done, doesn't matter a fuck how it was induced.' He held out his tanned right hand and spread the long, strong, square-tipped fingers. 'You know the world is nothing but virtual particles, popping in an' out of existence, don't you, Ax? You know technically you could be dreaming, right now, because everything you perceive is just firing neurons? It doesn't bother you, it feels okay, because of a trick your brain does. That's what Fiorinda has lost. She can't distinguish internal and external stimuli. She's lost the illusion of a single reality, and horrors rush in to fill the gap.'

'You're telling me that Fiorinda is crazy.'

'No, I'm telling you her brain chemistry is fucked. But in Fiorinda's case there's an extra twist. She knows what she is, she knows what her father was. It's not just that the world around her doesn't feel real. She *knows* that she can change the world, that it is malleable as software, in certain circs. She's done it: and so have I, or I wouldn't be here. I can deal with the situation, because of the – the route I took to reach the Zen Self. She doesn't have the protection I have. It's no wonder all the anecdotal evidence says people with magic power are unstable. It's a fucking shaky psychological platform.'

If Sage had been taking the news with Buddha-like calm, Ax would have hated him. But no, that was not what was happening. They looked at each other, and quickly looked away: ah, God, unbearable. Fiorinda ran and laughed, playing with the children—

'Is she dangerous?' said Ax, at last.

He had encountered Fiorinda's magic, that night at Tyller Pystri. He didn't remember much, but he had a feeling he was lucky to be alive—

'No!' Sage recovered. 'She's not dangerous because she's still *our babe*. I couldn't help what happened in Cornwall, I was too weak and it caught me off guard. In future we'll always be looking after her—'

'I did this,' said Ax. 'I set off the bastard's time bomb.'

In a moment of weakness, Sage had eventually told Ax about Rufus O'Niall's last words. He wished to God he hadn't. He shrugged. Pleading with Ax not to blame himself would just have them both sobbing. 'Nah . . . Forget it. There was no curse. Rufus said that because he knew what he'd done to her. And because *even then* he was trying to fuck me up . . . what a guy, eh?'

He had decided to withhold Fiorinda's ghost story. Enough is enough.

Ax reserved the right to hate himself, but he wasn't going to argue. 'So,' he said, 'okay, let's engage. What are we looking at?'

'We can't hand her over to the whitecoats—'

'God, no. She *hates* doctors, she'd be terrified. We can't let them lock her up.'

'Good, I'm glad we're agreed. And no medication, likewise; but that's okay. A lot of opinion says the drugs don't work. Well, untreated schizophrenia . . . It's doable. With luck we're looking at an intermittent fault. I think we can forget about sex, or children—'

'I'd worked that one out, thanks.'

'Not because of the damage, more because of how she feels. I'm afraid things are almost certain to get worse, but . . . Okay, we keep her quiet, nurse her through the bad patches, a stable routine, all our love; these things help. We could hope for periods of years, maybe, with her as calm as she is now—'

'And other times when she's in hell, and there's nothing we can do to help . . . .'

The mist had closed around them. Children's voices were like seagulls' cries; the great ocean almost silenced. They looked at the life ahead of them, and shouldered the burden gladly. But what did *Fiorinda* do, to deserve such a fate—?

'Hey. *It isn't going to happen, Ax.* I won't let it happen. I can break her out of this, I just need to be a little *stronger*, get rid of this fucking stupid *tiredness*—'

Ax nodded, compassionately.

'I can take her. You don't believe me, but I can. I'm no magician, I can't fix the damage, but I can make it okay. The problem—' Sage had to stop and knuckle his eyes; he tried again. 'The problem is that she'd have to trust me, absolutely, with her life and sanity. And I'm the bastard who left her to face Rufus O'Niall, all alone.'

'No. We both left her. *We* are the bastards who left her all alone.'

Ax reached out and gripped his friend's hand. They rarely touched each other now, because they'd been lovers and that was over. The bisexual threesome had always been for her sake. They both knew this, though there'd been no discussion; and it was fine, but the past, at this painful moment, rose up unexpectedly—

Someone was coming out of the mist. Fuck, it's the A&R man.

The handclasp was dropped, abruptly.

'Shit,' muttered Sage. 'Are we going to have to leave?'

'No way,' said Ax, through gritted teeth. 'We're staying, he's going. Fiorinda *likes* it here. Hey, I have friends. The Justice Minister says he's a great admirer of Ax Preston: he should be good for a few parking tickets, or making the bastard in the stupid hat vanish. I have no shame. I'd hustle a favour from the Emperor, if I had to.'

'The Emperor' was Fred Eiffrich, President of the United States, one of the useful personal contacts Ax had racked up in his glory days. But meanwhile the bastard in the stupid hat was coming up fast. Ax gave Sage a guilty look.

'Well, I'll do another couple of miles. See you back at the cabin.'

Ax jumped up and bolted. The A&R man stopped, nonplussed; then came on again. He was wearing black golf shorts, a mauve Hawaiian shirt and a football jacket, and of course the hat. He was very young: his complexion amazingly soft and pink, with a tiny moustache like a line of felt-tip. He sat down, a slight, respectful distance away. The rounders game had broken up, the children had vanished, there was no one else in sight. Sage and this gadfly were as if alone on a mist-shrouded sandbank.

'How does it feel to come back from the dead, Aoxomoxoa?'

'I don't know. I've never tried.'

'Now put me into the barge, said the king,' remarked the soft-faced young man, frowning as he took care to get it right, 'and there received him, er, three queens, with great mourning . . . and so they rowed him from the land, and Sir Bedivere cried: Ah my lord Arthur, what shall become of me? Comfort thyself, said the king, for in me there is no trust for to trust in; for I will into the vale of Avilion to heal me of my grievous wound . . . How is the king, Mr Pender? Has he recovered of his grievious wound? I heard he was pretty fucked-up, after the hostage thing, and the way he had to invade England to get rid of those Celtic guys—'

'Greevus,' said Sage, 'it's *greevus*, next time you say it in public. The king is doing fine. If you have something to pitch, pitch it, Mr Loman.'

'It's Lopez.' He reached inside his jacket. *Oh, shit, one of those.* Instead of a firearm he produced a gracious-looking square, cream laid envelope. He held this with a curious reverence (maybe he just liked quality stationery). 'Harry Lopez. What I said last night . . . I would love to offer you a recording deal. The three of you, it's a fantastic concept. But actually this is about a movie.'

Ah, so that's it. Sigh. 'Oh really?'

'You do know about the movie?'

They knew about the movie. Some virtual-movie company was making a feature about the Rock and Roll Reich. They didn't need permission, the story was public domain. They'd tried to get co-operation, they had been told to piss off. The Few and friends, Ax's

24

core organisation, weren't mad about featuring in a cartoon; and if there was money in it, the fucking Second Chamber government would get it.

'No recording deal, huh? Just the Bugs Bunny thing? Damn. You had us all excited.'

'Sage,' said Harry Lopez, with dignity, 'er, Mr Pender . . . I'm a great admirer of your stuff. But with total respect, you've been stuck in data quarantine for years. Big things have been happening, out in the real world. You don't know what you're turning down. Cartoon is a genre I admire, but a virtual movie is nothing like the same thing. I'm the producer. I have my heart and soul invested in the project. If you'd let me explain what—'

Sage was looking over Harry's shoulder. Mr Preston had reappeared: the ex-dictator of England in shabby running shorts and a singlet, the sleek wings of his dark hair bound back by a red headband and pearled silver by the mist— 'Sorry,' he said, sitting down beside Sage. 'Momentary fugue. What's the damage?'

'None, yet. Mr Loman here is from Digital Artists. He wants to put us in the movies.'

'It's Lopez . . . You wouldn't be acting. It's a one-off, uh, recording. The studio would make virtual masters of you guys, and the Few. We get them over, all expenses. That would be it. Of course we'd *prefer* you to do promotion. But before we get to terms—' Harry reached into his jacket again. He stopped dead in the act, and said carefully. 'I am not taking out a firearm, Mr Pender, sir. Or any other kind of weapon.'

'I'm sure you wouldn't.'

'I am taking out this small electronic device. It's a signal jammer. I'm setting it down here where we can all see it, and turning it on . . . Now, in case anyone was eavesdropping, which is possible anywhere, these futuristic days, we've moved into a secure area, very reasonably, for our business meeting.'

Sage and Ax looked at each other.

'I had no idea the movie business was so paranoid,' said Ax.

'This part isn't movie business,' said Harry, dead straight. He held out the cream laid envelope. 'I have a letter for Mr Preston, from Kathryn's Uncle Fred.'

Sage took the envelope, opened it; held it for a moment without looking at the text, then passed it to Ax. Harry blushed and nodded. The king doesn't accept anything from a stranger's hand, that's risky, that's how he was taken hostage. Ax read the letter, which was short, and handed it back to Sage, raising a quizzical eyebrow.

'How do you know Kathryn, Mr Loman?'

Ax had met Kathryn Adams, the President's niece, at the Flood Countries Conference in Amsterdam. She was the one who'd brought him over to do the data quarantine deal. She'd also been mainly responsible for the persistence of the search that had located him and rescued him, after a year held hostage in the jungle.

'Lopez. I've known her all my life. We were in kindergarten together.'

'Ah,' said Ax, with a faint smile. '*Right* . . . Do you know what the letter says?'

'Yes,' said Harry. 'It says Fred wants to see you. He wants you to do the movie promotion, because it's a worthwhile project, and he believes in my work, and it will raise your profile in the US. It'll also give him the chance to see and talk with you again, as a friend. I'm here to tell you a couple of things that were better not written down.'

'Oh yes?'

'The Pentagon is running a Zen Self Weapons Project, which you Europeans believe is not going to work, but you could be wrong. Mr Eiffrich doesn't want them to succeed; in fact, he wants them taken off the air. As you know, he's in principle, and publicly, against the development of fusion consciousness science, while in practice he accepts the neccessity of deterrence. But he's found out that it's possible there is a Fat Boy candidate. It's possible they are on their way to the "It's a *Good* Life" scenario.'

The young man paused, to see how they were taking this: stone faces.

'Mr Eiffrich wants you to help him stop them. The movie project is going to get you into the US, and it is personally vitally important to me, but . . . it's Fred who's asking.'

'I thought you said you were a producer,' remarked Sage, mildly.

'I am. But this is a historic-level weird situation and there's no orthodox way to deal with it. The President of the United States can't accuse the Pentagon of . . . of trying to create another Rufus O'Niall, not without unimpeachable evidence. You guys have the experience. He wants you to help him get the goods to close them down.'

Stone faces.

'If I understand anything,' said Ax, 'there's some basic misreading of the Zen Self premise in the US military project. Are you a weapon of mass destruction, Sage?'

'Not just now.'

'This is not about Sage,' said Harry. 'It's not about the mystical aspect, and it's not about Europe. I don't agree with them, maybe Fred doesn't agree with them, but our military considers what's happened to

Europe a sideshow. They see a new superweapon, which our enemies could develop or get hold of, and therefore we need to have ours. To an extent, it's a valid point. That's my opinion, by the way, I don't speak for Mr Eiffrich. But the military could be way over their heads, vis-a-vis fusion consciousness science, without knowing it, it's all so new, and maybe they are being poorly advised.'

They watched him, noncommittal as two timber wolves.

'Okay, I'll shut up. Mr Eiffrich will talk to you. We want you to come to California *norte*. I have a car waiting ... Mr Eiffrich thinks you'll like the car, Ax. He knows you like cars. There can't be an official meeting, that would work against us. But you would meet privately with the President—'

The deadpan reaction shifted: Ax showed a trace of sardonic amusement.

'We know Sage killed Rufus O'Niall,' said Harry. 'And we know why. He was an American citizen, no matter what else he was. Did you think about that?'

Stone face from the assassin, very faint sardonic smile from Mr Preston.

'Let me recap,' said Ax. 'We're to come with you to California.'

'Hollywood. You'd be coming to Hollywood.'

'Right. Where they don't make real movies anymore, and haven't done for decades. We're to pretend we are promoting a cartoon, so that I can meet the President on the back stairs and discuss whether the Pentagon is financing something loony. Meanwhile Sage is arrested for murder, in a state that makes liberal use of the death penalty, last time I looked. And we get a free car. No offence, but this is your best offer?'

'Virtual movies *are not cartoons*. I shouldn't have mentioned Rufus like that. I'm sorry, it was a misstep. I meant, forget the ignorance of global affairs for which we are famous, the US does have something called intelligence, and US Intelligence knows what happened, we know what you guys did and why. We know why to be afraid. I'm saying, please. Of all the people in the world, you three know the fathomless, endless nightmare we could be falling towards. You know why you should listen—'

They let this impassioned plea hang for a while.

'I see a difficulty,' remarked Sage.

'Uh, right. I want to hear it.'

The Zen Self champion held up his hands, palms forward. 'These. There'll be people who remember about Aoxomoxoa's fucked-up hands. I won't be masking them. I thought your government wanted to keep the, er, spooky aspect of fusion consciousness science very low-profile. What do you suggest?'

'It's been ten months,' said Harry, at once. 'You went to Japan, you had reconstruction. Okay, it doesn't look like any recon surgery or regrowth known to man, but the term Pac-rim is magic, er, to coin a phrase. Anything can happen there.'

'We'll think it over,' said Ax.

'Okay,' Harry nodded, intensely relieved. 'Okay, that's all I ask. So, well, I'm going to stick around for a day or two. We'll talk again . . . Uh, there's a couple of things from the studio. I should run them past you, because they may influence your decision. Mr Preston, you're a Muslim. We have to be careful how we use that. If you were promoting the movie, would your faith have to be in the foreground?'

'What's the other thing?' said Ax.

'Please don't take this as an intrusion, but the relationship. The ménage à trois. I'm not asking for a personal confession, I'm clarifying what we say to the public. Is it just you share the girl, or is there an actual sexual relationship between you two guys?'

'No,' they said, in the same breath.

He seemed disappointed. 'But there could be ambivalence?'

'Oh yeah,' said Sage. 'Ambivalence is fine.'

'We can do ambivalence.'

'Well, that's it . . . When you discuss this with Fiorinda, could you tell her how much I love *Yellow Girl*? I think it's the best female solo album ever recorded.'

'She'll be thrilled,' said Ax.

Harry got to his feet and hovered in the pearly gloom, as if baffled by protocol. Maybe he thought he should retreat backwards from the king's presence. 'Sage,' he burst out, 'I know what the Zen Self is. I know that *you* are not a weapon, I know something about how it works. If you can change the world for the good, if you can end some of the horrors in it, *why don't you do that—*?'

'You don't get it, Harry. Why don't you eat your hat?'

'Brace yourself, kid,' said Ax. 'To the Zen Master here, this is the best of all possible worlds, just the way things are. It's not a bad idea about the hat though.'

There was a piano in the back room of the disused bar. Fiorinda had found out about it from the kids, and had been given a key by Señora El Pabellón, so she could practise. They locked themselves in there the next day to discuss the unwelcome development. The room, lit by dusty sunlight falling through a row of Moorish arched windows, had the air of a small, despondent, English village hall. A stack of Seventh Day Adventist leaflets lay on the cocktail bar in the corner, getting flyblown.

Fiorinda was at the piano, her ragdoll head bowed over the keys. She had not brushed her hair for a month, and was oblivious of this. She refused to let them touch it. She would not eat, unless you put the food into her hands. Little things gave her away, though she so valiantly tried to pass for normal ... Little things like the neglect of her own body, and the look in her eyes. They had told her Harry's story, because they would never shut her out. She had taken it calmly, but today she was very withdrawn.

They sat at a bentwood table, glancing at her often; talking it around—

'It was the b-loc,' said Ax. 'Fuck. I knew I should have thrown it in the sea.'

The bizarre b-loc signal, unknown around here, would have pinpointed the English like a radio beacon for anyone who knew what they were looking for.

'Don't beat yourself up,' said Sage. 'They'll have tracked us since Mexico City. Shit, Harry's probably listening right now,' He poked a dead fly with his finger. 'There you go. Surveillance is everywhere,' He felt Ax recoil, remembered post-hostage stress, and quickly changed his tone. 'Hey, it's not worth worrying about, babe. Let them listen. Fuck 'em. Insult the flag.'

'I don't think that's going to help.' Ax read the letter over. 'Call me paranoid, but I start wondering if Fred Eiffrich arranged for me to be summoned to Mexico City so he could pull this. I know he was pissed off when I resigned. He wants to recruit me as his goodwill ambassador in the fuck-up that is Crisis Europe: he thinks I'm the pick of the mad dogs, which I do not consider a compliment.'

Sage knew not to get into that conversation. 'Well, we can't stay here.'

''Fraid not. Maybe we can make Harry Lopez go away, but we'd just be waiting for the next gadfly. It makes you realise how atrociously vulnerable we still are—'

'It won't last. We'll be old news soon. We just have to weather it.'

They looked at Fiorinda. She plonked a piano key, and didn't look at them.

'What do you make of his story, maestro?'

'Well, it's true there's a team of US military-financed neuroscientists trying to build a human weapon, at a place called Vireo Lake, out in the desert in Southern California. Olwen's been tracking their progress, through some Irish contacts—'

Olwen Devi, the Zen Self guru, had been Ax's chief scientist in the days of the Reich; while also pursuing the goal they called *fusion* out here in the real world. Sage had been the first to achieve the Zen Self, and to prove that the wildest of post-modern scientific ideas was absolutely true. It was possible to break consciousness out of time and space, and fuse the four-dimensional subset that was a human self – past, present and future – with the whole of the information. Briefly, after he'd been in that state, Sage had had the power to change the code of reality, and he'd defeated Rufus. The US theory was that if you could stabilise fusion and make it sustainable, you'd get a phenomenally powerful, clean and humane weapon.

'Yeah. This I know. But no one in Europe thinks it can be done?'

'Mm. Bearing in mind "no one" means a handful of people, theorising right out on the edge . . . If you want my personal opinion, I think they wanted to do the work, because fusion consciousness is incredibly sexy, so they emphasised the clean, green mass destruction idea, and they got Defense Department funding. It may not be the most ethical route, but it is well-trodden. They have the biggest, fastest hardware, they have license to whack a team of military volunteers full of nasty, scary, wrecking-ball neurosteroids. I expect they're getting somewhere, but probably not the Neurobomb.'

'D'you think it's true that they got hold of Rufus's head?'

The 'green nazi' European Celtics had planned for Rufus to decimate the population of Europe. When Fiorinda and Sage had brought the magician's severed head back to England, and presented it to the enemy, the bastards who'd taken over in Ax's absence had found the defeat of their superweapon a convincing argument. Resistance to Ax's come-back invasion had collapsed, peace had ensued: but the severed head had vanished in the shuffle.

'Yeah.' Sage glanced at Fiorinda. 'I don't think it will have done them any good.'

Maybe they'd been fools to think they could cross the ocean and leave it all behind: but they were deeply disconcerted. In Europe, the death of a senior Irish/American celebrity (known 'green nazi' sympathiser) on his private island last summer had been quietly buried, by everyone including the Irish police. We know how to handle these things, what's this Harry Lopez doing, doesn't he know when silence is best?

'I remember a Fat Man,' said Ax, after a pause for thought. 'It sounded familiar, and it comes back to me . . . Wasn't that the nickname they gave to one of the first atom bombs, devices, whatever? And there was a Little Boy, too. But Lopez said, *Fat Boy*—'

'It's a nickname. It's what the Celtic "druidic science" lunatics were aiming for with Rufus. Fiorinda knows . . .' They looked at their babe, but she was still idly plonking keys— 'You take a major natural-born magic psychopath, of which, thank God, so far Rufus is the only example. You pump up the volume with the rocket fuel he gets from human sacrifice, and he goes critical, like a nuclear pile.'

'What about "the 'It's a *Good* Life' scenario"?'

'Same. "It's a *Good* Life" is a classic science fiction story. It's about a little boy, born with a mean mutant brain. Whatever he wants, he can make it so. Everybody has to grovel to this kid, because if he tells you to turn inside out, then you will. If he tells the sun to explode, then it will. It's what happens when the Fat Boy's up and running. It isn't proven, it's just a weird possibility.'

'I'm glad to hear it.'

'Well, there you go. Fiorinda and I thought we were assassinating Adolf Hitler, to prevent the Holocaust. It turns out we were making a futile attempt to suppress the discovery of nuclear fission. What a bust.'

'Shit. And here's me thinking Rufus was our *private* nightmare.'

'The nightmare's private enough. There are millions or billions who know about Ax Preston and the Reich, my dear. Very, very few people understand what happened to the world last summer; or what's going on right now at Vireo Lake—'

'And a kid cartoon-movie producer is one of them. I find that most bizarre.'

Sage nodded. 'Most bizarre.'

'Can't help wondering what's behind it.'

'I suppose we'll find out what's behind it when we get to Hollywood,' said Fiorinda.

Both men started, and turned to her, shocked and guilty.

'Oh, no, sweetheart,' protested Ax. 'That's not what we're discussing.'

'No, no! We aren't thinking of *taking* the gig, we're just talking—'

'For fuck's sake.' Fiorinda brought both hands down on the keys with a jarring clangour. 'You want to go with your Harry Lopez, I can hear it in your voices. You just don't want to take me, because I'm in a bad state. I killed my own father. I used my m-magic (God, how I hate that word), which I had vowed and sworn I would never do. How can I live with myself, if that was all for nothing, if there's another monster—?'

'Fiorinda, hey, there isn't another monster—'

'Oh? You told me the man in the hat said the Pentagon is building a Fat Boy.'

'He said something like that,' admitted Sage. 'It can't be *true*. You'd need to start with a phenomenal natural magician—'

'*I know*,' snapped Fiorinda. 'I haven't been in a coma—' She stared at them, pushing back the clotted masses of her hair with both hands, the pupils of her grey eyes wildly dilated. 'I've been trying to protect you,' she said, wonderingly. 'But I could not get there ... Oh my God, and maybe now I know why—'

Electrified, they realised it was *Fiorinda* looking at them, speaking to them. *Fiorinda*, back from wherever she'd been wandering—

'You don't need to protect us,' said Sage, intensely still, as if an unwary breath might send this bird out into the dark again, 'it's over, babe. You did it. You protected everybody. You did *brilliantly*, and now you're safe with us.'

Fiorinda's eyes snapped back and she let go of her hair.

'Safe ... ?' The clipped, crystalline vowels of her childhood, always well to the fore when she was exasperated, had never sounded so sweet. 'Is that what you call it? *Look*. Ax can never touch me sexually, because next time I might *strike him dead*. I don't believe I could harm you, Sage, but I'm not mad about the idea of therapeutic rape, and I think you know it. We should go to Hollywood. What's the alternative?'

'We don't have to go back to England,' said Ax, quickly. 'We'll find somewhere—'

'What, another beach where we can be nice to each other, get excited about shellfish and tick off the bird book? How long's that going to last? You two feel sorry for me now, but you'll get bored, you'll dump me and run away, like you did before—'

Ax was horrified. 'Fiorinda, how can you say—? I *did not* dump you. You were miserable, Sage hated me, I was in the way. I left because I wanted you two to be happy.'

'Did you fuck want us to be happy. You wanted us to come running after you, and it backfired, because you'd forgotten you had us so well trained we would never dare ... All right, you couldn't have known you would be kidnapped, but walking out like that was a cry for help, in an *unbelievably* stupid form—'

Sage was staring at Ax in naked hurt. 'I'd follow you anywhere,' he said. 'I'll do whatever you want me to do, be whatever you want me to

32

be. I . . . Fiorinda was unhappy, that's all I knew, that's what you saw in me. I never *hated* you—'

They remembered, shocked at themselves, how fragile she was—

'Could we stop this?' said Ax. 'Please could we stop this? It does no good.'

'We could stop,' offered Fiorinda, after a moment.

She crossed the room, pulled up a chair at their table: took Ax's hand and reached out to Sage. The rings they wore, of braided white and red and yellow British gold, gleamed in the dusty sunlight. They'd been Ax's idea. They weren't wedding rings, perish the thought, but they were a declaration. We are not going to break up again. We've tried that solution, and it is worse than the problem.

'I've been giving you hell, haven't I?'

'No!'

'You give us heaven,' said Sage, passionately.

'Idiot . . . I know I'm in a bad state, all right? But I think we have to say yes. We have to go to Hollywood. Look at it this way.' She smiled, shakily, 'Our pension fund is fucked, and we can't live happily ever after. We might as well get back in the game.'

'You'd better tell Harry,' said Sage to Ax. 'He'll be thrilled.'

There were two beds in the cabin, a single and a double. The single was Fiorinda's. Sage and Ax slept on the double in their sleeping bags, like soldiers in a bivvy. On the shelf by her head, Fiorinda could see the outlines of her best shells, and the 'Ax 'n' Sage 'n' Fiorinda' miniatures that Ax had bought when he was last in the US, which had been returned to him, along with his other belongings, after he was rescued. Her heart jumped, because her saltbox wasn't there: then she realised it was beside her. She tucked her hand around the polished wooden apple, the talisman of her magic, which she did not dare to part with, how irrational can you get? But where's the light coming from . . . ? The door of the cabin was open, and Sage was sitting there. Moonlight gleamed on his close-cropped head and caught the wide, pared-down angles of his cheek and jaw.

'Sage?' She wrapped a shawl over the big T-shirt she was using as a nightgown and went to join him. 'What's the matter?'

'Couldn't sleep. I thought I'd sit up, in case Fergal needed back-up.' He leaned his head against the wall. She saw the glint of tears in his thick golden lashes.

'You believe in Fergal?'

'Yeah, why not? The world's a strange place.' He sighed. 'Our Willy

33

Loman is afraid of me . . . ain't that a joke. I don't know what he thinks I'm going to do.'

'You could use sarcasm,' said Fiorinda. 'You're good at that.'

She wanted to tell him that he was beautiful, and strong, without the bulging muscles, and she loved him just as much. She knew he wouldn't listen. They were all clinging to their separate hurts, even the bodhisattva.

'I'm sorry about *therapeutic rape*. That was horrible. Forget I said that.'

He wiped his eyes. 'I'll try to put it out of my mind.'

They watched the moonlight on the tamarisk hedge, and listened to the ocean.

'I will never forget El Pabellón,' whispered Fiorinda.

'Fiorinda, listen to me. I know what's happening to you, and I can help.'

'Don't.'

'Listen. I know what it's like to be aware that all the horror is still going on, and you are still there in it, still doing the worst things you did, and bearing the worst things you had to bear. And I have done some bad, bad things . . . I can help you get to the other side, I can take you to *guai-yi*. It's the only way, my baby. You've travelled too far. You have to reach shelter now.'

'I keep trying to remember things from *before*,' she said. 'From a time when I was sure magic didn't exist. I keep thinking if I could remember being normal, I would get better from being . . . being in a bad state, and we would be happy. It doesn't work, because one thing I always know is that if magic doesn't exist then you're dead, Sage. You died on the beach at Drumbeg . . . I go round and round, I have some hateful imaginings, but it doesn't matter how I figure it, none of this is real. It's a toy I made. That's what I have to learn to live with.'

'Fee.' He took her hand. 'That's *not* how it is. You've forgotten. Let me show you.'

There was a pulse in the air, stronger than the murmur of the Pacific. She found herself thinking, dare I take my life from this man's hands? Dare I let him pick me up and carry me? It's not for nothing that one of his best mates, *his collaborator*, has Asperger's so bad that . . . Peter Stannen couldn't survive in the normal world without the Heads to look after him. And it's not just that he's male to the point of screwy. Sage was strange before he went near the Zen Self: liable to go off into obsessions, and drug himself insensible because he can't resist the way it soothes his racing brain ... The more she thought of his strangeness, the more she pitied him; and the more she loved him.

But oh no. I want my life to be my own.

'Oh no,' she said, smiling into his eyes. 'No you don't, Sage. You are not going to talk me down from this. I will make my own way. This is mine.'

'Okay,' he said, 'I will respect that, but I'm here. Whenever you need me.'

Ax stirred, and sat up. 'Are you two okay?'

'Yes,' said Sage.

'Very okay,' said Fiorinda.

'Come back to bed.'

They kept Harry waiting a day, and then they wanted to leave at once. It was agreed that they would drive down to El Rosario, the rockstars in their Mexican hired car, Harry in his compact. They would meet there, do business, and Harry would explain about how they were going to cross the border. They did not have visas. They had not intended to visit the States. For the former rulers of the Reich to try and get into the US as tourists would have been embarrassing all round. But that was all fixed, apparently.

Ax and Sage kept asking each other, in glances that they hoped she didn't see, *are we doing the right thing?* But Harry's news had snapped her back into herself, and anything that does that has to be pursued. If Hollywood turns out to be a bad move, then fuck it. We'll have three first class tickets home, please ... They didn't think very hard about Harry's pitch. It wasn't in the least relevant to their real concerns.

They packed up early in the morning. Fiorinda found the hermit crab and took it down to the sea. *Bon voyage*, little ragged claw: and there go the pelicans ... one, two, and goodbye. I'm going to the USA, she thought, frightened because she knew Ax and Sage were not frightened, and they ought to be. Maybe America will make me free.

Harry came to the cabin while Fiorinda was on the beach and Ax was at the *Oficina*. He was still wearing the hat, but with a visible air of defiance. Sage had a mean impulse to start on the moustache. He had to remind himself that this pink-cheeked young man had no idea what he'd done to offend. He knew nothing about Fiorinda's state of mental health, and he wasn't going to find out from Sage; or Ax. *She* won't break down. She's a trouper. What's going on with her will be our private nightmare.

35

'Sage,' said Harry, 'I should mention to you about the back-up. There'll be an escort. The men will be discreet, but they'll never be far away from now on.'

Sage was absurdly pleased to have been cast as the hulking minder. But no thanks, Harry. We don't like to have other people's servants hanging around us. Especially not if they're armed. 'We don't need that. Call them off.'

'Huh?' The A&R man stared. 'Look, there's not going to be trouble, but the studio would feel better, it's customary on a journey of this kind.'

'The times we live in. I said no. It's not the right message, we're supposed to be pacifists, are we not? We drove across Mexico alone, we're not frightened.'

'Okay,' said Harry, 'well, that's, I guess that will be all right.'

He looked in bemusement at the Triumvirate's backpacker bundles, and around the bare cabin. There were some sketches still taped to the back wall. Sage had decided to leave them there; they weren't good enough to keep and he hadn't the heart to throw them away. Harry stepped over and carefully took down a Costa's hummingbird.

'May I keep this?'
'Sure.'
'Will you sign it?'
'No.'

London, without Ax

The Rock and Roll Reich was over, but the organisation struggled along, hampered by mainstream government 'assistance'. They looked after the drop-out hordes, the frightening masses of people who had simply given up, in the economic crash or later on: taken to the roads and never gone home. They had a means-tested, first class arts and alt.tech hedgeschool education scheme, for the Countercultural nation and anyone else, young or old, who could meet the criteria (or blag their way in). They were committed to running a joyous programme of free events, not exclusively but predominantly rock and roll, known as the 'Crisis Management Gigs'; which had become a beloved tradition, vital for public morale. They had to keep doing it all. This was the responsibility that Ax had bequeathed to them, and it was all they had left of the place they'd once lived: up high, electrified and terrified, on the wings of the storm.

They couldn't think of anything else to do with themselves.

One wet morning in a grey and thankless springtime, Allie Marlowe arrived first in the Office at the Insanitude, and swopped the bowl under the leak by the balcony doors for an empty pan. The windows rattled in their peeling frames, the blossom streamed away from the trees in St James's Park. She looked out on the Victoria Monument. Well, here I am in Buckingham Palace, running a rockstar charity for the government. It wasn't where she'd thought she was going to end up. The room was freezing, and for no particularly green reason. They were well in the black on the Central London energy audit; it was just another petty ordinance. She wrapped herself in an old cardie of Fiorinda's that she kept at the San for this purpose, sat down and switched on her machine.

—the minor donations; the surviving on a shoestring—

Sometimes she thought it would be better if the original Few, the handful of people who had been with Ax since the absolute beginning, were to quit. Allie Marlowe, whose previous career had mainly involved going to the right parties so that she could promote the coolest clubs, had been the chief administrator of the Reich. She had been Ax's Lord Chancellor, for fuck's sake ... We're not the best people to be dealing with this government, she thought. We should go, let the second generation take over. More would get done. We should go before they appoint a new President. If it's Jordan, I can't stand the idea anyway. How dare he ... She didn't believe it. She knew she didn't have the resolution to walk away.

The second generation ambled in, put something annoying on the sound system and settled to their work. Allie hit the scan of a dog-eared, funky, Cornish holiday postcard in her personal email: a cartoon of a bearded seaman in a sou'wester.

> **Fishin' Scat,**
> > **Farmin' Scat,**
> > > **Tourists Scat ... Back To Wreckin', Me Hearties!**

She flipped the card over as she checked its provenance. It had been scanned in Mexico. Anonymous transit. Something wrong with their phone? she wondered, anxiety leaping. She'd been afraid since the day they left the country: that they would be kidnapped the way Ax had been; that they would die in an earthquake. She had separation anxiety. It was Sage's handwriting, cuneiform, and barely legible. Apparently being hard to read was natural to Sage; the new hands made no difference. I'll go along with that, she thought. She was an Ax and Fiorinda loyalist, and always would be.

Hi Allie, she made out. *We're on our way to Hollywood. Talk to you soon.*

Nothing else, except a threefold monogram.

The monogram was in the form that said: trouble but nothing that we can't handle.

The rain beat on the Victoria Monument; post-Ax pop-music ravaged the Office air.

2

Bears Discover Fire

When they'd parted company from Harry they left the Mex1 at the first opportunity and found a place to pull off, on a country road in a valley chequer-squared with grapevines, bright with new leaf. They'd eaten lobster burritos at a restaurant once favoured by Steve McQueen. They'd graciously accepted Digital Artists credit cards; they'd insisted on making their own way to the border, and arranged to meet with Harry there in a few days' time. *A few days* was arbitrary, they'd wanted a last taste of freedom.

They were suspicious about the ease of all this.

The free car was not instantly impressive. It was a chunky off-roader, squashed-down SUV, on the same lines as Harry's compact, in light brown, with a scarlet trim and silver wheels: called a Toyota Rugrat. It was box-fresh, hinting at machinations behind the A&R man: no one had *driven* this car from the US. They had personalised it, eyes, voiceprint, touch, but that didn't guarantee they were the master's voice.

'Okay,' said Ax, 'let's check it out.'

Fiorinda reserved the right not to touch anything mechanical or geeky when Ax and Sage were around. There have to be some advantages to being the girl. She sat by the roadside and dissected the US English language newspapers they'd bought in El Rosario. California *norte* is having a water crisis (you don't say). Also a power crisis, but that isn't real, it is trumped up by monopolies (well, what changes?). Mr Eiffrich is widely held to be set for his second term, in spite of continued Downturn – meaning, crash deeper than the nineteen thirties, when 'Depression' was the favoured euphemism. She read a learned article about how in hard times the country likes a Democrat in the White House, but Republican control of Congress and the Senate, and an essay on the psychology of the Oil Wars ... A Big Name's new album signals he is heading for politics (copycat!). Top moviestar has double platinum hit with novelty song. Tuh. Never heard of her. There was nothing about the project at Vireo Lake: witchcraft and magic were dealt with pleasantly under Lifestyle.

She read the cartoon strips, *the funny pages*, until Ax and Sage came to join her.

'If the car's wired, we can't find it,' said Sage, flopping down on the stony ground. 'Couldn't find the weapons cache or the drugs either; it's a piss-poor rockstar mobile. But we have camping gear you could use on Mars, *and* a water distillation plant.'

'*La mordida reina*,' said Ax, mordida being a bribe, 'it doesn't look like much, but I have to admit it drives sweetly, for a brick on stilts. We've disabled the nauseating baby voice, sorry Fio. Thank God it has a steering wheel. I don't see driving by holding fake conversations with a car's software. It's a ridiculous idea.'

'You'd feel different if you'd ever had fucked-up hands.'

'Harry said it was a fat ride,' said Fiorinda, 'meaning wicked, I presume, same as in England. How clever is it, really?' They looked at the Toyota. It was definitely *watching* them, with the red cam-eyes above its headlamps. 'Can it understand us now?'

'It can hear us,' said Sage, lying back and gazing at the sky. 'It recognises some words; I'm not sure what it understands. I don't think there's anything going on to upset the Turing Police, but it's emotional. Maybe like a dog or a cat.'

'Now that's something we're missing out on in Crisis Europe,' remarked Ax. 'The emergence of consumer durables as an oppressed underclass.'

'It could have the sentience of a grey parrot. Or even a small child.'

'I hope you're kidding,' said Fiorinda. She thought of Serendip, the mainframe computer Olwen Devi wore as a jewel in a ring on her finger. But Serendip was a divinity, not a prisoner.

'Can we turn the feelings-feature off?'

'No, that would make it dead. Too bound up in the motor cortex.'

'Fred Eiffrich was planning to give limited AIs animal welfare rights,' said Ax. 'I don't know what happened to that. We better treat it nicely, or we'll get pulled over.'

'Maybe we should give it a name.'

'Right of veto,' said Ax. 'I will not ride in a car called Tiddles.'

Sage grinned. 'Ruggy the Rugrat it is then. Ax, I don't think we're under surveillance, except in the strictly formal sense that you never can tell. Could we forget about it?'

'I hear you. I'll be grown-up.'

Sage reached over, and they slapped hands. For a year, Ax had never been alone except in the dark. The constant feeling of being watched still plagued him.

'What shall we do now?'

'The hired car wouldn't do back roads,' said Fiorinda. 'Let's explore.'

Their country road headed into the mountain spine of the peninsula. It quickly became abominable, but the Rugrat danced over washed-out river-beds and floated over boulders. Ax started to grin. Sage and Fiorinda, beside him on the front bench, stopped thinking that the crash bar was absurd nannying. When the road gave up entirely, without warning, in the middle of an uphill corniche switchback, Ax just laughed, shifted the stick and the Rugrat hit the chasm brim careening along on half its wheelbase, the bench and bar morphing to compensate, Sage and Fiorinda yelling—

'That's rugged terrain extra,' said the demon behind the wheel, placidly. 'Mind if I put on some proper speed?'

At a high pass they stopped: alone in a sun-seared, wind-ripped landscape of rocks and fragile flowers. 'You know what,' said Fiorinda, when the adrenalin had let go of her windpipe, 'every family in the American suburbs has one of these, and they use them to drive to Asda and back.'

'Walmart,' said Sage.

'Wear your anorak with pride.'

'But you're absolutely right. What a crime!'

'Anyone else want a turn?' asked Ax, nobly.

'Hahaha. No, no, my dear. This is *your* present.'

'Tomorrow,' Fiorinda compromised, 'we take turns tomorrow.'

The jagged landscape fell away, wilder and wilder into the distance on every side: painted shades of red against a parchment haze; a sharp-edged, impossible and dreamlike terrain, cliffs and peaks, boulder fields, plunging chasms.

'There's a whole *world*, Ax,' whispered Fiorinda, 'that I've never seen—'

Sage was reading the manual on the dash screen. 'It can climb out of a pit, ten to fifteen metres vertical,' he remarked. 'Tha' sounds like a good trick. Hm, it says here *can be linked to a range of personal digital devices*. Hey, I could slave the AI to my mask!' He had not worn the living skull since the night at Drumbeg, but he kept the button in his eyesocket, for old sakes' sake. 'It's sittin' there, it has stacks of spare capacity—'

'So you could drive by thinking about it?' said Fiorinda. 'Oh no. No, no. You'd forget what you were doing, and tell the car to stand on its head—'

'Would not.'

'I think I'm in love with the modern world,' said Ax. 'You leave my Rugrat alone. I'm gonna get a new implant and commune with it myself. Digital Artists can pay.'

Ax had formerly possessed a brain implant, a primitive and dangerous device that he'd had fitted before the Dissolution, carrying huge amounts of useful information. The kidnappers had taken it out, and sent it back to England as proof of his identity. He'd been told the bastards had probably saved his life, because the thing had been in a state of decay. But his chip had been dear to him, and he missed it.

Sage went *white*, the colour plummeting from under his tan. 'You will not!'

'Huh?'

'You cannot have another implant, Ax. Fuck, I saw your scans. Don't even—'

Ax bristled. 'Is that an order? Listen, Sage, I think it's my business, and what d'you mean, you saw my scans? That's confidential information—'

'Confidential from *me*? Oh, thanks very much. Look, implants are fucking stupid an' always will be, why don't you get an eye-socket—'

'I don't like putting things in my eye.'

'No, you'd rather have dodgy open-brain surgery. Fuck's sake, Ax, you—'

'Could we stop this?' demanded Fiorinda, caught in the middle.

They looked at each other, and how strange, what a rush, to meet the *difficulty* again, something that had not been an issue for so long, the meeting of lovers' glances, so much more complex between three—

Not daring to say a word, Ax put the Rugrat in gear, and they drove on.

Towards sunset they found a campsite in a conifer forest: stone empty. When the culture of plenty withers and fuel prices rocket, only kings and queens, soldiers and gypsies, get to sleep in the woods. Leaving the Rugrat on a flat pitch facing an alpine meadow, they walked into the rustling flowers and sat there for a long time: Sage becoming so still you knew he wasn't there, only cosmic reality was there. 'We could stay here,' said Fiorinda.

'Overnight, anyway,' agreed Ax.

'*Mon auberge était a la Grande Ourse,*' said Sage. 'There will be great stars.'

'It'll be fine,' Sage told Ax quietly as they reviewed the remains of the El Pabellón food while Fiorinda collected kindling. There were frozen steaks and tubs of ice cream in the Rugrat's lockers, but steak and ice cream would make Sage throw up, and anyway, they weren't in the mood. Two peppers, two potatoes, a head of garlic, a couple of wizened carrots, can of tomatoes, can of chickpeas—

'I think Hollywood will be good, not *quiet*, but when people say "quiet" what they mean is no stress . . . Bright lights, fun, admiration, all the stuff she fuckin' deserves an' she's never had. The other business will be our gig, we'll take care of it, she won't have to worry. I like getting the Few over, as well. She's had enough of us. She needs her friends, the ones who came through it with her—'

They had sent Allie a postcard from a call point in El Rosario.

'What d'you think we should tell them about . . . her being in a bad state?'

Sage shook his head. 'I think they know, Ax. They're not stupid, an' they love her. What d'you think we should tell 'em about the Fat Boy?'

'Nothing, until they get here. What is there to say? Let's wait until we know what Fred Eiffrich actually wants from us, which is not very clear as yet. In ways,' he added grimly, 'I now think we should have taken up the movie offer straight off. I didn't realise it was a ticket to California for everyone. The way things are shaping at home, I'll be glad to have my most high-profile friends where I can see them, and out of England—'

'Yeah, but what about telling Allie she's going to be in a *virtual* movie? How do you want this carrot? Slices, chunks, chips, sticks?'

'I don't know, she's a fashionista. Maybe she thinks they're wonderful. I'd like round slices two oh oh five millimetres thick. Just chop it, Sage, fuck's sake.'

'I'm not used to having hands.'

'Bullshit. You were better at the domestic when you had fewer fingers.'

That T-shirt is a disgrace, thought Ax. But he doesn't care. Tees, pants, socks, the raggier they are, the better he's pleased. He's the original absent-minded professor . . . disguised as this slender, graceful, *beautiful* guy with the artist's hands who used to be my big cat. Sage looked up, caught Ax's eye and smiled.

A blue jay landed on a fir branch and squawked at them.

43

'I'll get some water.'

Sage went off to find a standpipe. Soldiers and gypsies use their own supplies only in emergency. Ax sighed, shrugged, and indulged in a secret tryst with the little girl on the label of the Morton's Salt canister as he chopped the veg. In her yellow smock with her big lilac umbrella, striding bravely through the dark . . . *When it rains it pours*. Sometimes his heart was visited, best way to put it, by the spirit of a child who might never be. A gallant little girl, with dark hair and Fiorinda's smile—

Fiorinda had lit the fire using the flint and tinder from the base of her saltbox. There was a big stack of heavier wood, left behind by other campers, plenty for one night. She knelt and watched the new flames. Sage is ten months dead, Ax is almost mummified, the handcuff slack on his dry wrist, strands of dark hair clinging around the dried, open hole in his skull. The walking corpses went about their chores, grotesquely dressed in shabby camping clothes, but in another scene, somehow equally present, they were freshly dead: sliding, tumbling, endlessly, from two body-bags onto a rug, in a room she didn't recognise . . . Get used to it. These flashes will come, just when you are feeling nearly normal, to remind you of the truth. Ignore them, maybe they'll come less.

'Are you okay, little cat?'

'I'm fine.'

'Shall I brush your hair for you?' suggested Ax, casually. 'Sage can handle this.'

'There's nothing wrong with my hair. I just brushed it.'

They decided to sleep out, and spread their sleeping bags on a rug at the edge of the meadow, Fiorinda's newspapers underneath for insulation. It would be chilly, but they'd known worse. The sky was clear: they lay and gazed into the stars that thickly powdered the deep, until up became out and they could feel the world turning.

'What say we take the Rugrat and run?' wondered Ax. 'Mexico's a big place.'

'Harry the repo man would come after us,' sighed Fiorinda. 'I know he would.'

She retired into her cocoon, curled up between these two big male animals, Sage the tiger, Ax the wolf. Usually she didn't like sleeping in the middle, but tonight it was comfort mode. She fell asleep while they were still talking: woke, and slept again. At last she woke and realised she was listening to the sound of heedless movement, somewhere in the trees; and that the tiger and the wolf were sitting up, sharply alert.

'What is it?' she whispered. 'D'you think it's a bear?'

'More likely Harry's back-up,' murmured Ax. 'Discreetly checking on us.'

'I think it's a bear,' said Fiorinda. 'I'm afraid of bears. I've read about them, they come after food, but then they attack people.'

'D'you get bears in Mexico?' wondered Sage. 'I thought they were extinct.'

'There are bear-notices at the *Oficina* here, and the dumpsters have special bear-proof lids that you have to open a trick way.'

'Everything's locked in the Rat,' said Ax, soothingly. 'I read the notices. We're okay, Fee, they're not aggressive. It's just walking around, being a bear.'

They lay down again.

'There's more than one,' remarked Ax, shortly. 'I think there's several.'

'Well, then, Fiorinda can relax,' mumbled Sage, turning his back. 'It's probably range cattle, an' we can go to sleep because bears do not hunt in packs—'

There was a loud crack from much closer at hand, and a rush—

'They do now!' cried Fiorinda.

The bears were in the clearing: a gestalt flip, from noises in the dark to shaggy limber bodies, right there, arm's reach. The men shot to their feet, astonished, very glad they'd been sufficiently on guard not to crawl into their bags. Pale eyes shone with a light from God knows where: one of the beasts rose, tall as a man. It opened its mouth, the teeth and tongue glistening. It seemed to *speak*—

'No!' shouted Fiorinda.

'My God!' yelled Ax. 'Fee, get to the car!' He raced for the woodstack, grabbed a branch and threw another to Sage. Too late, the bears were *everywhere*, eyes blazing lambent white, ten, twenty of them. Sage and Ax, back to back, flailed their branches, Fiorinda crouched in the tumbled bedding at their feet. The beasts backed off and rushed in, again and again, what the fuck is this, what's got into them, is this a nightmare? Ax used his arm to fend off a snarling maw and staggered, the shoulder seam of his leather jacket parting. A bear fell back but immediately there was another one, and what is that light in their eyes, why the fuck are they *attacking* us—?

'FIORINDA!' howled Sage, swinging his futile club, 'DO something, babe!'

45

'I'm trying to think! I'm trying to think!' She scrabbled in her sleeping bag. She never slept without her saltbox, but *where is it, what can I do?* Here's the saltbox . . . *brain won't work*. What can I do? Oh, fuck, someone's *fighting* me!

Oh no you don't, try a taste of this, *wham*.

White crystals flew out, curling through the dark like ribbon. Where they landed they burst into flame, blue and orange flame like a wall, that split to make a corridor. The three of them ran, walls of flame twisting with them, across the clearing to the Rugrat: grabbed the door, and leapt inside—

Fire stood around the car in a seething curtain: then it vanished.

'Don't touch me for a moment,' whispered Fiorinda, huddled against the driver's door.

The bears seemed to have gone. 'What d'you think?' breathed Ax.

'I think she saw them off.'

They took flashlights and went out to investigate. There were solid physical traces of the attack: clawmarks, torn earth, one torn sleeping bag; splintered and tooth-marked remnants of firewood. Sage found the sleeve from Ax's jacket, dramatically sliced as if with knife blades.

'Shit . . . Did that reach you?'

'I don't think so.' When he investigated, Ax discovered four parallel scratches on his upper arm. Not serious damage, but there was a little blood. 'Fuck, I hope I'm not going to be a werebear. What the hell was all that about?'

'No idea.'

Fiorinda had got out of the car. They joined her at the picnic table and switched off the flashlights, which only made them feel exposed in this starlit darkness. Ax had officially given up smoking, but he kept a pack for use in emergencies. He lit one now.

'Well,' he said, since the other two volunteered nothing, 'the world gets stranger.'

One theory says the strange phenomena are some kind of fall-out from the Zen Self, a shift in consensus reality. Others say it's Gaia, finally found out how to express her displeasure . . . Ax believed, with reservations, in Gaia theory: not in the nature deity. Are there *really* more weird things happening, or are people seeing differently but the world's the same as before? He was hoping fusion consciousness science would tell him what to think, when the new model had settled down—

'Ax,' announced Sage, off on his own angle, 'we have to get sorted.

I'm sorry, babe, I know you don't like guns, but it's just not *sensible* to wander around over here unarmed—'

'We'd look a little conspicuous loaded for bear on the streets of Los Angeles.'

'Sage,' said Fiorinda, 'someone was fighting me.'

'What—?' said Sage, snapping to attention.

'The bears,' said Ax. 'Look, I think we should get out of here. I don't know what that was about, maybe we found out why this place is deserted, but we have no quarrel with whatever causes that kind of effect. We should leave, before they come back.'

'Not the *bears*,' said Fiorinda to Sage. 'Someone was fighting me. I wasn't remotely in trouble, just off guard, but *someone was fighting me.*'

'Oh, Fiorinda—!'

'Huh? What's she talking about? What are you two talking about?'

'How many bears were there, Ax?' asked Fiorinda sharply.

'How many? I – I don't know. I'm not sure, it seemed like dozens.'

'There was one. I was fooled myself at first, but *think* about it.'

'She's right,' said Sage, after a moment.

'Yeah,' said Ax, wonderingly, seeing the shadowy beast that had flashed around him, retrieved from his short-term memory. He felt relieved. 'Oh, yeah, I get it. There was one real bear, the rest of them we hallucinated? But not you?'

'Someone set a real bear on us,' cried Fiorinda, her voice shaking, 'and made it seem like a pack of them. *Catch up*, Ax. This means Harry Lopez was right. There is another Rufus. Not as strong as me, not yet, no way, but strong enough. And, oh, shit, whoever it is knows all about us! *Did you get that?* It tracked us, it came and found us!'

'Hey,' said Ax, 'slow down, sweetheart, don't panic, you did good, don't—'

'The bear spoke to me!'

'What did it say?' asked Sage, adding, carefully, 'for me that didn't happen.'

'It said, *kill me*,' breathed Fiorinda, staring wildly, shivering visibly. 'And I know why. It's a monster. It wants to die. I would want to die if that were—'

She broke off, feeling their reaction—

'You think I'm having a paranoid delusion. You think I did the bear thing myself!'

'No!' they both cried, appalled. But they were lying.

Fiorinda's head started to spin. She could not cope with this situation, she was falling into terminal confusion. She clutched at her hair, feeling the wadded thickness, close-packed scenes of horror, collapsing in on her—

'*Sage!* Don't you *realise*, I'm trying to stay in this world, I'm trying to believe it's real, and *the bear makes sense* if this is real! Oh God, don't take this from me!'

Sage jumped up, zoomed around the table, grabbed her and held her on his knees, hugging her tight. 'Sweetheart, listen, listen. I think you could be wrong. Not crazy, wrong. Weird things happen for all kinds of reasons. Don't be scared, darling, this *does not* have to mean there's a Fat Boy.'

A shudder went through her.

'All right,' she whispered, weakly. 'That's doable. I c-can handle "I could be wrong".'

Ax joined them. He took her hand and stroked her hair. 'You could be wrong, but you're not, usually. What do you want to do, angel? We can quit this stupid gig right now. You just say the word.'

'No,' she said, sitting up, her face very white, eyes dark pits in the starlight. 'We can't quit. You don't either of you get it. We have to go to Hollywood and promote the virtual movie. That'll be our cover, while we f-figure out what's going on—'

'Sounds good to me.' Sage rocked her like a baby, looking at Ax over her head. One step forward, two steps back . . . 'Okay, that's what we'll do.'

They all became aware of a strange sound. Ax shone a flashlight on the Rugrat: it was moving, bouncing on its Mars Buggy axles. 'What's going on there? More magic?'

Fiorinda shook her head, mystified. 'I don't think so.'

'I think the car is scared,' decided Sage.

'What?' protested Fiorinda, 'How can it be scared? Everything's switched off.'

'You can't switch off an AI, you'd have to re-install. They're on permanent standby.'

The Rugrat's security package had the capacity to 'recognise threatening behaviour' directed against itself or its personalised owners. It had shields it could raise, heightened responses, and of course, a siren. Ax and Sage had disabled the lot, foreseeing incessant false positives. When they looked for the shaking in the manual, they discovered that the car might 'experience an analogue of disappointment', if it felt it had failed in its duty.

'It saw us attacked and it couldn't do anything,' said Fiorinda. 'Oh *God*.'

'We better let it have its siren back,' sighed Ax. 'I can't stand this.'

The car calmed down. They applied first-aid to Ax's scratches. There was a double bed you could pull out in the back. They shared it: in the same bed together for the first time since Ax had made his grand gesture and walked out on Sage and Fiorinda: which was some kind of epoch. Sage slept like a warm rock. Ax and Fiorinda dozed, woken every ten minutes when the Rugrat was startled by an owl, or alarmed by the malicious creaking of a branch. The bears didn't come back.

In the morning they drove to Tecate, found a hotel and smartened up, making the best of the shopping in a small, dignified pueblo town. Ax visited London via b-loc from their hotel room, talked to Allie and signed off until further notice. They'd be meeting the Few in Hollywood in a couple of weeks. The next day they called Harry and headed for Tijuana. Driving to the border felt like making a video, something brash and raggedy and retro about breaking through a screen: from the real world of deranged, bizarre decay to a dreamland where everything was still fine. It would have been full of irony, this video, finding fear in the heart of plenty, a refuge in the disaster zone. Shame no one had the cameras running.

They hit the approach road singing, *Flew in from Miami Beach BOAC*—

The Mexican guards at Mesa de Otay waved them through. On the US side Ax offered his passport without comment, as he'd been instructed, and they were flagged into a concrete bay. They were dressed like rockstars: Sage and Ax in draped, pastel gangster suits, sharp shirts, string ties; the babe in a slim, vivid yellow dress and slingbacks, with her messy hair forced into a yellow-ribboned braid.

'We should say goodbye now,' said Fiorinda. 'From here on, nothing is real. It's all a performance.' She kissed them sadly, turning from one to the other: the first natural, freely offered kisses she had given them for a long time. 'See you on the other side.'

'I'm coming with you, stupid brat,' said Sage, as they got out of the car. 'So is Ax.'

They waited, alone, in a room like any room of the kind, anywhere in the world: like Newhaven, like Cardiff. It had dusty windows, slick upholstered benches, a vending machine; fluorescent light strips peppered with dead insects. There was a counter, with silent, shadowed regions of officialdom beyond. The aircon was frosty. Sage sat on one of the benches, long legs stretched out, his hands in his pockets from ancient habit, and closed his eyes. Fiorinda and Ax paced, staring at notices. They had plenty of time to remember that Harry had not, in fact, explained how the visa problem had been fixed.

After about twenty minutes Harry arrived, in a nice brown suit and without the hat.

'Hi,' he said, sounding flustered. 'You're here. Um, this is great. There are a few things, a couple of formalities. Er, would you like to talk to Mr Eiffrich?'

'Is he here?' asked Ax, in disbelief.

'No, but, er, I could get him on a phone.'

'Why don't *you* explain the formalities?'

'I – well, I'm afraid you're not going to like this, but it's unavoidable. It's the only way we could get you in. There's a procedure. I don't know if you have it in Europe, DNA imprinting? It's copy-protection, so that gene-thieves won't be able to replicate, uh, anything they steal from you.'

'What are you talking about?'

'It's a harmless chemical masking process. Many US celebrities get this done regularly, even private citizens do. You have an infusion taken, fixed and injected back, it's deep, into bone marrow, but under local anaesthetic, you won't feel a thing. Twenty-four hours, they do a few tests, and you're clear for entry. Celebrity gene theft is a real problem. There'll be unscrupulous people close to you, no matter what. All they need is a hair from a comb, an eyelash, er, body fluids, a few saliva cells from the rim of a glass.'

'You don't have laws against this?'

'Well, yeah, but it's a grey area, difficult to prosecute unless the cells are germ cells, stem cells, or the DNA is patented. If a case comes to court it's usually fraud. Some snake-oil clinic promised the customer a famous nose and it didn't work out. But the risk of sequences being replicated and distributed among the population is real.'

'I'll pass,' said Fiorinda. 'I don't like injections.'

Harry cleared his throat, more flustered by the second. 'You see, uh, Fiorinda – may I call you Fiorinda?' She shrugged. 'You see, it's not optional. That whole area has proved to be the stickiest in negotiating your entry. There's the Rivermead gene-mods. You and Sage have been treated, that's public knowledge; and the American people have a right to refuse. If someone steals cells from you guys and replicates the DNA, it won't be your fault, but those novel sequences may alter our gene pool. If any visitor has, or is suspected of having had, gene modification outside the US, immigration is entitled to insist on imprinting. The procedure we use is approved by the NIH, it's classified as effective for three months, during which time you're not advised to seek to become pregnant—'

Fiorinda stared at him, amazed. 'Mr Loman, you can't be serious. You think we'll *spread*? Do you know how many DNA bases there are, in three hundred million people?'

'It's Lopez. We tried, Fiorinda. I'm with you all the way. This is the best we can do. *Please* agree to the procedure. This is legal. It's a barrier that's been raised, and the best way to deal with it is to respect it. We called you here. But it's your cause, and the future of the world you'll be serving. How much does that mean to you?'

'Well,' said Ax, 'what do you think of all this, Aoxomoxoa?'

Sage still had his eyes closed. 'I think we should do exactly what the man says, Ax.'

'If Sage thinks it's okay, I don't mind either,' said Fiorinda, after a moment.

'Oh that's wonderful. I have the release forms here. If you could just sign.'

'There are three forms?' said Ax, taking them.

'Well, yes? One for each of you?'

'Wait a minute ... *I* have to take this, this racial purity treatment?'

Harry's relief vanished. 'I'm afraid so, Mr Preston. Uh, I thought I'd made that clear.'

'*Me*? Why? There's nothing wrong with *me*! I'm perfectly normal!'

'Mr Preston, it's not—'

'What the fuck are you afraid of? The Boys from Brazil?'

'Brazil?' repeated Harry, bewildered.

Ax discovered that he could not bear to explain the quip, it wasn't funny. 'No, I'm sorry, fuck off. I don't take forcible medical procedures. This is bullshit, I won't do it.'

Fiorinda said, 'Mr Lopez, could you leave us for a moment?'

'Ax, it's an outrage,' said Sage, when they were alone, 'but imprinting is harmless, it doesn't do anything much, and the US Immigration Service is more powerful than God. If they want to give us a hard time, they will do it. I've tangled with them in my stupid rockstar days. It doesn't work.'

'We can tell Harry no,' said Fiorinda, 'and try to negotiate, but I don't think it'll do any good: or we can give up and go away. I won't make you do this. Your call.'

'I don't want to go away.' Ax pulled himself together. 'We've come this far. I've heard of imprinting, I know it's harmless. It just . . . it just unexpectedly threw me—'

'I know,' said Fiorinda, hugging him. 'I know, my baby.'

They kept you chained up. You endured everything, including anal rape, staying calm, staying alive. Then one day they brought along some half-skilled freelance brain surgeon. They held you down, they cut your head open and tore out the implant so they could send it to your friends. But needs must, you accept the forcible medical procedure again, and you feel a strange relief. You realise this may be easier than trying to live with memories that won't let you sleep at night. Better to go forward, though it's into the maelstrom.

The party for the English invasion was held in the Pergola Hotel, an A-list venue, though no longer right at the top. It occupied the penthouse floor: two imperial suites and a ballroom-sized reception area. By ten, most of the people Harry needed had turned up. Janelle Firdous, a Hollywood veteran with her future in the past and the past in her immediate future, forged through the maelstrom, checking the quality of the flowers and the catering staff, checking off faces and looking for Mr Lopez, to congratulate him. Harry was a protégé of hers, a sweet kid, a real talent: she wished his project well.

In one of the bedrooms of the Louis XIV suite she located the radical rockstars, playing their guitars while a gaggle of movie brats in fabulous designer clothes sat on the floor like hippies, gazing upwards. She made her way to the stage; or king-sized bed.

'Hey, d'you guys do Hendrix requests? Can you do me "Midnight Lamp"?'

Ax Preston ignored her. It was the skinny high-yellow girl who answered, in an unbelievable cut-glass voice, like Vivien fucking Leigh, 'Do you mean, "The Burning Of The Midnight Lamp"? I don't know it very well, but I'll try.'

Doom doom ba doom ba doom doom doom—

She listened to the loneliness, and the circus in the wishing well, she got the the sweet pain: but felt short-changed because it was the girl singing, and playing her Fender. Mr Ax guitar-man Preston was sitting it out, with a little strum or two of his semi-acoustic. The next number jarred on her. As did the arrogance of the happy couple, locked into each other, talking in this private language and passing it off as entertainment. She left, and nailed Harry out in the reception area: where futuristic floating screens, gliding over the heads of the crowd, Digital Artists swank, were showing crappy archive footage from the

English Revolution rock festivals. *Without* the soundtrack; wise decision.

'Hey, pumpkin. Be proud, be very proud. It's looking great.'

'Oh, hi, Janelle!' His smile was distracted. 'Are you having a good time?'

'I always have a good time ... The party's very cool, but you should stop them from bringing those guitars everywhere. It makes them look like hired help.'

'You think that? Oh. It was my idea. It makes the point that they were swept up into history, but they're *musicians*. Ax Preston, he gets up in the morning and he plays guitar, he's at a party and he plays guitar. Like Hendrix. It's romantic.'

'Did you remember to invite the expats?'

'Yeah.' Harry shrugged. 'It was the right thing to do.'

'And they remembered not to come,' remarked Janelle, smiling wryly.

The A-list Brit community tended to be United Kingdom loyalists.

Marshall Morgan came along, and Janelle had nothing to say to the CEO of Digital Artists, so she moved on. Far be it from Jan to fuck anything up for her young pal. He shouldn't be fraternising with the damaged on his big night.

'Hi there.' A sweaty hand landed on her arm. 'How's it going, baby? Is the shit kicking you, or are you kicking the shit?'

'I'm kicking.'

'Bully.' Her assailant grinned like a rancid muffin. He was pretty drunk; he clearly did not at this moment remember her name. 'It's a scam, a pure scam. Tell me this, how can we run out of energy? How can that happen? The sun is still shining! But *we* have nothing to worry about. The industry grows in a downturn. The deeper it gets the more we'll grow, we should *cut* prices, I've been saying it for fucking years, that's the way to shift units in a bear market, you shift *more* units—'

Someone else she didn't want to talk to.

'You should tell Harry,' she said, gushing. 'You may think he's just a golden kid producer with a dazzling tech background and top White House contacts, but he *loves* money jokes. You tell Harry the sun is still shining. He'll find that fascinating.'

A step beyond the muffin, and she knew her mouth had run away with her. Oh, fuck. Verbal diarrhoea strikes, you start shitting on everything. Time to touch base.

Where's Puusi?

The reigning queen of post-modern tinsel town, her voluptuous

charms swathed in silver and gold, gauze and veils, was in the Golden
Age suite: propping up a white, cocktail-bar grand and surrounded by
giggling young men. Jan and Puusi had arrived together, but the star
had been in a spiteful mood. Reigning goddesses don't appreciate being
invited to meet hot new faces, however unlikely the competition. A fix
of male admiration had worked its magic: the more camp the better,
Puusi had classic diva tastes. She shrieked in delight – it was screaming
pitch in here. 'My girlfriend! Lover come back! Where have you been!'

They hugged, Puusi snuggly as a kitten, big firm breasts that needed
no support. She slipped her arm into Janelle's and tugged her away,
with a high-voltage, professional goodbye smile for the drones.

'Okay, yaar, now I want to meet this Fiorinda. Have you seen her
yet?'

'She's in a bedroom, playing guitar.'

'My God, was that the noise I heard? Does she really have all that red
hair?'

'Yeah, but it's dirty and messy.'

'Is she *really* thin?'

'Like a stick.'

Puusi's huge eyes gleamed. 'Ha! Then she's a loser. Being beautiful
means never having to be thin. Is she young?'

'She's twenty-three.'

Ominous silence, a little frown between the perfect arcs of Puusi's
brows as she continued sweeping Janelle along, bestowing showers of
luminous glances left and right.

'Hm. That's not very young.'

'Being beautiful means never having to be young.'

There were surely many examples of this truism here tonight.
Beautiful, famous and successful women, sixty and seventy years old,
thickly laced the throng, in the suite which Madonna had called her
favourite gaff, or doss, or some other god-awful Anglicism (the Pergola
wanted a plaque on the wall, but they hadn't been given permission), all
hating each other because to be lovely at seventy-five was no longer rare
... 'Oh, you bitch.' Puusi cracked up, gazing around her insolently.
She's a *lovely* person, Puusi Meera, but she bears a grudge, and some of
these fabulous matrons had made her suffer, when she was the gauche
young Bollywood import.

If you like hanging out with the stars, you learn to service their
simple pleasures.

In the Louis XIV bedroom the set was over. The former Dictator of
England was on his feet, using those blood-soaked hands to light a

cigarette: taller when you see him in the flesh, and looking curiously isolated at his own party, as if he really was just a hired musician, on the point of shouldering his gig bag and walking out. His slick dark hair, hippy-length, was combed straight back into a braid. A fine-boned face, good nose, good cheekbones, very sexy brown eyes ... His girlfriend was beside him.

'I *like* her,' announced Puusi. 'The hair is awful, and don't these English ever wash? Stinky-poo, I can smell her from here. But she's sweet. Introduce me.'

Be afraid, Ms Slater, thought Janelle. Be very afraid.

A waiter drifted up to advise Mr Dictator about that cigarette. He smiled, crushed the lighted end between his fingers and frugally returned it to the pack. Good smile. Very.

Puusi made a small, involuntary sound like *Mm!*

'I can do better than that,' Janelle offered, chicken-hearted. 'I'll take you to Harry first. He'll tell you everything you need to know. Then you can make a knock-out impression on Fiorinda and, er, Mr Preston.'

'I think everyone calls him Ax,' said Puusi. 'Is he bisexual? I heard he was bisexual.'

On Yap Moss, thought Janelle, at the last battle of the Islamic Campaign, the Yorkshire rivers ran with blood. The Deconstruction Tour had smashed through England by then, laying waste to fast food joints and car outlets and pile 'em high planet-destroying supermarts. The Ivan/Lara virus that wrecked the European datasphere came later. Then there was the Danube dambusting, and the Flood Countries Conference. He may not have been personally responsible, but he's *the face* on a revolution. Now he's in Hollywood, all caught up with the strangest threat the human world has ever known. That's *Ax Preston*, you idiot. But hey, let's tackle the important issues. Does he like it both ways?

'I love you, Puusi. You're so real.'

Puusi kissed her cheek. 'You're lovely. Harry? Is that Harry Lopez? I don't know him, he's a geeky techie. Take me to him.' Her gaze returned, swift and sure, to the locus of desire. The way she can *direct* those eyes is stunning. You have to soften the effect in the virtual studio or it would look overdone; cartoon animation. 'Just think,' she breathed, awed, 'Europe has been isolated for seven years! He may even not have heard of me.'

'She.'

'Huh?'

'It's Fiorinda you wanted to meet.'

'Oh, yes. You know, they should have a house on the beach. Near to me.'

She deposited Puusi on the arm of the chair where Harry was sitting and hissed into his ear, *Here's Puusi, and she wants to meet your Fiorinda, who loves you, baby?* The star, who was fully intended to hear this aside, dimpled delightedly. Janelle left them discussing real estate, and went to look for the object of her own fascination. She felt relaxed now, she felt steady. She could deal with the ghost of a young man she had once met, at a hotel party after a rock gig, a long, long time ago.

'Hi, Sage. Remember me?'

Ax and Fiorinda took a break from mingling, and stood looking out through a wall of glass into the night, where bright galaxies streamed away, endless in every direction, phalanxes of towers shooting up like fountains of interstellar gas. It was an astonishingly beautiful sight. 'It's a time warp,' said Fiorinda, 'a Titanic that didn't sink.'

Ax had done his Lennonisms, Fiorinda had done her cut-crystal accent. They'd been graceful with the tactless, modest with the gracious. Anyone actively interested in rock music, and there were one or two of them, presented a challenge: but Harry had briefed them sufficiently to gloss over their blanks. Fiorinda had been nervous, but she needn't have worried. She hadn't forgotten how to do this. You switch on the old routine and let it run.

They turned from the view to admire the crowd.

'That's a whole lot of bears,' murmured Fiorinda.

'Yeah, but we can tame them.'

Proofed against gene theft, expensively dressed, he seemed to have shed ten years since they'd arrived in Hollywood. He was reminding Fiorinda of the Ax Preston she'd known at the beginning: that quiet guitar-man with the reckless gleam in his eye, and the insane notion he was destined to save the world. A fine example of body-modification went by: a twitching spotted tail, slyly emerging from the backside folds of a pair of glittering harem-pants; and then a famous couple, honed to unreal physical perfection, who lit up their famous smiles for the ex-dictator and his girl.

'I urgently need more briefing,' muttered Fiorinda. 'I don't know *anything*.'

'We can get by,' said Ax. 'Smoke and mirrors. Besides, we have Sage.'

Sage was their secret weapon. He'd been in Hollywood before, on the Heads' first and only US tour. He claimed (probably truthfully) to remember little about it, but they weren't relying on Aoxomoxoa's dubious record. Sage had a separate reputation as the inventor of immersion code, which was apparently important to virtual movie makers.

'As long as we don't have to deal with anyone from Maverick.'

Aoxomoxoa and the Heads had parted from their first record company with extreme acrimony, a lengthy break-up after a short and tempestuous relationship.

'Or the Bible Belt,' added Ax. 'D'you know he's still banned in fourteen states?'

Fiorinda was accosted by a sparkly lady with a stunning décolletage, a British expat who wanted to explain that she didn't like the Counterculture, but she loved *Yellow Girl*. Ax moved off, not to get in the way of this, and met a barrel-shaped character, invincibly unmodified, ugly as a toad, who told him the sun was still shining.

'So you're Ax Preston? Say, does BOAC still fly into LAX?'

'We don't have a national airline at the moment,' said Ax.

'Oh, right. One of those. Too bad. Whaddya do these days? Swim?'

'We drove up from Mexico.'

'That's what I'd do myself. Whaddaya drive, Ax?'

'A Toyota Rugrat.'

'Aaah!' said the drunk, fuddled eyes brightening, 'you got a Rat! Way to go. You got companionship, service, and a fuckin' hot set of wheels, all in one package. I love that. I have an AI car myself,' he confided, 'but the Rat's kinda sporty for me. I'm Lou Branco, pleased to meet you—'

Thank you, Fred, thought Ax, shaking the hand of one of the great Hollywood money men. You're a wise and devious fellow; and so now I'm a slaveowner. Ah well, at least we own an A-list member of the new underclass.

'We got to meet,' confided Lou. 'We got to get going on this thing, Harry's movie. Fred's talked to me, he has a high regard for you. How about lunch—?'

Ax agreed, escaped, and rediscovered Fiorinda. They spotted Sage, by the buffet in the reception area, talking to the tall woman with the crisp semi-Afro who'd been in the audience when they were playing guitar. She wore a big white shirt over narrow black trousers: a stylish, fuck-you option among the glitz and the jelly-bean party frocks. Fiorinda, wearing a jelly-bean party frock that she'd let Harry provide, felt inferior.

'I wonder who that is. She looks like a fashion editor.'

'Probably someone he met when he was here before.'

'I must get myself some clothes. We have to make an impression.'

Ax fielded an anxious glance and signalled, I'm onto it, she's good, everything's in hand. We can do this, he thought (while that shot of blue sent a tingle to his bones). Don't know about the pacifist propaganda, but we can promote a movie: piece of piss. It thrilled him to think Fiorinda's soul needed only the balm of party frocks and treats to bring it safe home. He stayed close as they worked the crowd, always watchful, trying not to look like it. When she lets me brush her hair, then I'll know she's going to be okay.

Sage had let Janelle leave him, unsure how he wanted to deal with that old acquaintance: but now he'd lost sight of Ax and Fee. He lurked around the food, pharmacologically starved, ready to go home (that is, back to the other hotel), but too proud to go and find them and whine that he was tired. Shit, how do people *endure* this kind of thing sober? It was an energy crash. Sugar, I need sugar … He dosed himself with party dessert and felt the impact immediately. That's an idea. I can use food as drugs, uppers and downers—

'Hi!'

A young girl popped up, a plump kid with blonde hair, half-dressed in a perky, cherry-red number that barely grazed her tits and didn't reach far below her crotch.

'Hi to you.'

'My name's Billy. I wanted to say, I'm not into techno, but I love your stage act. With the skull mask, and the stunt dives, the fantastic body, and everything.'

Sage was trying to be polite with people who wanted to talk to Aoxomoxoa, but he was finding it a trial. 'Oh really? And which gig did you most enjoy? You must have been about three years old when the Heads were in California.'

'Okay, I love your *videos*. I heard you're fabulous in bed, would you do it with me?'

Of course, a rockstar party should be supplied with high-grade amateur sex workers. Well done, Harry. Sage had a lot of time for party girls, brave little adventurers. There'd been several years of his life when he wouldn't have any other kind of sex. Sure, it's corrupt and awful, but you can live in the belly of the beast, and still have fun. Been there, done that. 'Hahaha. Billy, tell the truth, I look a lot better with my clothes on, these days.'

'You don't have to undress,' she explained, naïvely. 'I have a room in the hotel. I know you don't have a girlfriend with you tonight, I do most things, and I'm a virgin, well, partly a virgin. You won't be sorry.'

'Thanks, but no sale.'

'Okay, later, okay, and you'll wear the mask?'

He went to look for his lovers, but before he found them he was forced to head for the roof-garden, under the imperious command of a bout of nausea, cutting his way with dazzling smiles (an entirely unconscious reflex). What has happened to this town? You'd think you could rely on the sweets at a Hollywood party to be fat-free. The garden was not a refuge. It was low lights and serious conversations, arbours for coupled bodies. The air was not fresh, it was tepid and harsh in his throat. He tumbled down on the steps of a fountain, water hissing over him.

'Hey, uh, Sage? Are you okay?'

It was Billy the party girl.

'Oh, shit, you look awful, you got some bad gear, should I call an ambulance?'

'Just leave me alone, Billy, like a good kid.'

She wouldn't leave, this kindly child. She sat beside him and patted his hand, prattling about her own bad drug experiences, telling him no need to worry, I have my phone, I'll call someone, breathe deep ... Sage could have killed her, *I need to concentrate or I will throw up*, but he was touched, and there was nothing he could do anyway, past the brink, ah, fuck, so much for the suave, sophisticated new Sage.

When he'd finished spewing his guts into the fountain it was Janelle Firdous beside him, with her beautiful, sombre dark eyes, and a crooked little reminiscent grin.

'Hi again, you.' She handed him a tissue and a bottle of water.

'Where's Billy?'

'Your little bunny scooted. Jesus, Sage. Isn't bunny-fucking in public and throwing up over the décor undignified for your present role? Do you want me to fetch Ax and Fiorinda, or should it be Harry?'

'Ah, God ... No, no, don't fetch anyone. I'll be fine.'

'Sure you will. C'mon, baby. You've had enough. Let me see you home.'

Fiorinda had fallen asleep on a lilac leather couch in the master bedroom of their suite. She and Ax had come back here to find Sage collapsed, tended by his fashion editor friend. Janelle had discreetly departed, they'd run a first-aid check, and his LFTs gave no cause for concern. He'd just eaten something stupid ... But fear for him was so ingrained, she'd been too scared to go to her own room. She had been dreaming of fashion editors, huddled in her jelly-bean frock under a quilt: she woke with a shock of panic to the chiming, chiming, intensive care unit alarm. *Sage is dead!* It was the landline phone beside her. She groped for it. A female voice, saying could I speak to Mr Preston? There was a video screen on the handset, but she didn't know how to turn it on.

'Who is this? How did you get this number?'

'I've got it, Fio,' said Ax's voice from the big bed.

He took over while Fiorinda fought with a kaleidoscope of horrors, pouring through the walls of this horribly oversized room. She had better get dressed. Sage is dead, Ax didn't come home, I must get dressed.

When she came back, in sensible clothes, Ax was looking mystified 'That was the FBI. We're requested to visit a crime scene. They're sending a limo.'

Sage stirred and sat up. 'A crime scene? Huh? What the fuck time is this?'

'It's just after seven. Hey, don't look at me, I haven't a clue. I wanted Harry in the conversation, but the woman said no, not appropriate. I'm calling him now.'

Ax called Harry. He apologised profusely, didn't sound surprised, and said he would sort this out. Shortly, he called back. Everything was fine. They should go downstairs and get into the limo, sorry for the inconvenience.

'What's going on, Mr Loman?'

'I, er, I'll talk to you in the car.'

They scalded themselves with a few mouthfuls of coffee and went downstairs. Sage, who had insisted on coming along, wore bruise-coloured pits under his eyes and moved with the careful concentration that meant he felt in danger of falling down. The limo was waiting with its doors open. Harry was in the back.

The doors shut themselves; the car zoomed off.

'Good of you to come and fetch us,' said Ax, icily. 'What crime is this? What does it have to do with us?'

'It's not my gig,' said Harry. 'I'm very, very sorry. It's better if we just get there.'

They'd seen their A&R man in his glory last night. This morning he was a crushed, resentful errand boy: radiating indignation, and fear. They sat in silence. The English waited for Harry to speak to the driver. Then they realised there was nobody behind the opaque screen, and felt as if they'd just arrived from the rainforest. The limo sped for miles, from Hollywood into the city of the plain. Sage leaned back with his eyes closed; Fiorinda stared at the floor. Ax checked off the roadsigns, trying to keep track, trying to remember where they were on the map. He hated not knowing where he was.

At last they left the freeway grid and the limo stopped beside a call-point pillar in a sector of the streaming galaxies which in daylight and close-up resembled a spaced-out, shabby English inner city. There was a children's playground with faded murals, in front of a flat-roofed, municipal-looking building: maybe a community centre. Little kids were running and playing. It might have been Brixton or Birmingham, except there was no city in England where you would look up and see such an expanse of sky. They'd been in the USA four days, cocooned in aircon limos, hotel rooms, private shopping trips. This was the first time they'd stepped onto the surface of the planet.

A fit young white woman, in very clean jeans and a button-down shirt, opened the door before it could open itself. 'Hi!' she said, with the friendly ease of a certain kind of American functionary (which does not mean they are on your side). 'I'm Agent Phillips. Thank you for your co-operation, Mr Preston, sir; Mr Pender, Ms Slater. I hope you had a smooth journey.' She showed them her badge. 'Hi, Harry,' she added, as to a colleague for whom she didn't have a great deal of respect. 'Phil's down there. Sorry we had to drag you out of bed, after the big party and all.'

It was warm outdoors, warmer than was seasonable at this hour even in southern California. LA was having a spring heatwave. Agent Phillips led the way through a gap between the playground and another building (the children gathering to stare), along a path behind some warehouses that were being converted and onto waste ground that stretched to the horizon: invaded by desert scrub, wrecked cars and dumped freezers. In the midst of the waste stood two long white vans, and some other cars that were not wrecks. A small crowd hovered at a police taped perimeter, otherwise the scene was strangely empty. No sign of the police, or any of the peripherals of disaster.

But they knew. Oh, we have been here before—

'You guys are the experts from England, right?' said their guide, conversationally.

Harry glared at her.

'I'm not sure how to answer that,' said Ax.

'How d'you like LA? I love the accent. That's great, the way you can travel again now. It must be tough, living over there in all that civil unrest.'

'England's not too bad,' said Ax, mildly. 'Compared to some places.'

They reached the perimeter. They could see the towers of downtown in the distance, like a spaceport in the haze; like a toy. The crowd surged, a single animal, towards this new event. Agent Phillips lifted a loop of tape from one of the plastic supports and stood aside to let them through. 'It's the tape that attracts them,' she remarked, dryly. 'Do you get that in England? Murder, rape, mugging, drug deals, no one sees a thing. The tape appears and the assholes gather, like sharks to a drop of blood.'

'Yes,' said Fiorinda. 'We get this too.'

She thought she could already smell the blood. Been here, done this, oh yes. What made me think it would ever stop? It never stops. She was afraid she was going to look guilty, because she was NOT going to be able to look surprised. A fat man in a Redsox T-shirt caught her eye. If you have no reason to be here, she thought, then *get the fuck away*. Or may something happen to teach you a lesson, shit for brains . . . She had never cursed anyone before. It felt surprisingly good.

Beside the incident vans (they would have been incident vans in England) a broadly-built, bearded black man dressed in unconvincing leisure clothes was waiting.

'I'm honoured to meet you,' he said, 'Mr Preston, Mr Pender, Ms Slater. Harry, thanks for your promptness. I'm Philemon Roche.' He showed his badge, and surveyed the three with gravitas slightly tempered by the satisfaction of someone meeting celebrities. He had a marked Jamaican accent, which put them off balance.

Ax nodded, dismissing the badge. 'Are you going to tell us why we're here?'

'I don't know what Harry told you—'

'I haven't told them anything,' snapped Harry. 'But I want to say, for the record, I don't like the way this was done, I think this is insupportable.'

'Good, that's good.' said Roche. 'Something happened here last night,' he said to the English experts, 'that you may be able to help us with. The police have taken a break. This is off the record, there will be no publicity, no media, and we won't be interrupted.' He addressed Fiorinda. 'Ms Slater, we're about to view human remains. They died violently. I'd like to leave my partner here, to keep a h'eye on those idle citizens, but would you prefer to have a woman with you?'

'I'll be all right.'

'Very well, please follow me. Keep to the tracking. I know you've had experience, I'm sure I don't have to remind you: touch nothing.'

They followed Roche, Harry trailing behind like a sullen teenager, along a quaking plastic walkway and into a hollow in the wasteland; into the smell of blood. 'The area has a regl'r population,' remarked Agent Roche, the familiar cadence of his speech weirdly at odds with his manner, and with this alien place. 'Winos, junkies, crazies, long-term homeless. Ferals. One of the ladies from the daycare centre at the street was doing a soup run yesterday. She says she walked right past this dell around six p.m. and saw no't'in. The bodies were reported by an anonymous call just about dawn this morning, and I was alerted at once. Be careful of this last section, h'it's unsteady. It's in here.'

They passed between tall white screens and were confronted by a butcher's shop tableau. On a slab of waste concrete two bodies, male and female, had been hung from a frame of metal rods, the woman by her wrists, the man by his heels. Their injuries were extreme. They had been young, and brightly dressed, from the tatters of clothing that remained. Body jewellery still glinted: earrings, a nose stud. A flag of blonde hair, a close-cropped head dyed cobalt blue. Blood was pooled under them: still viscous, looking like melted chocolate ice cream. The rods were copper plumbing pipes. A sheet of canvas had been stretched behind the corpses: there were words scrawled on it. Flies buzzed, on the bodies and the blood.

Agent Roche said, 'Well—?' He looked at them expectantly.

The woman's face and torso had been flayed, the skin peeled back meticulously from around her staring eyeballs. Her liver dangled, deliberately on display.

'You have Aztecs?' said Ax. 'Commiserations. We get loonies too.'

'Hm . . . See that?' Agent Roche, appearing disappointed in them, pointed to a shallow pit in the ground, to the left of the altar, ringed in stones, natural water-worn stones that didn't belong to the waste. The pit contained newly flensed, red and yellowish bones. 'Those aren't human, they are the leg bones of a horse and a hound,' said the FBI man. 'There are other details I t'ink you would recognise, if you look close?'

'So you have Celtic wannabes,' said Fiorinda, cutting the crap. 'I do apologise, on behalf of the four nations, for the bad example, but I still don't get it. Why are we here?'

Agent Roche looked at Harry, Harry looked at the ground. 'Well, ma'am,' said Roche, 'Whatever you have seen on the tv, human sacrifice as a h'act of public worship is not a common pastime in LA. We get ritual murder; we get snuff, faked and genuine. We have folks who are convinced they are vampires, and they behave accordingly. We have all kinds of diversity. We believe the first of *these* happened maybe a year and a half ago. It became a federal investigation after what we now t'ink was number four: this is number eight, by our reckoning. All in LA County. Always in empty places, desert wastes; always the pair, nubile young male and female. No other sexual element, far as can be determined after the way they're killed. Always extreme blood-letting, though the met'od varies, and the bodies left on display, and the animals, horse or hound, in some form.

'But you know what's the thing that keeps me awake at night? We'll question the ferals. Some of them will tell us there was a party here last night. We'll examine the ground. Forensics will tell us between thirty an' forty people were here to watch, and they can promise us DNA profiles, they can give us shoe-sizes.'

Harry gave a sharp, impatient sigh. Roche ignored him, and continued, 'And it will go nowhere. If there are eye-witness statements they will vanish, and the witnesses will never be found again. There will be no forensic evidence worth a shit. If there is any lead to follow, that might identify a single one of the congregation, it will close up, it will fold down, it will be taken from our hands by some mysterious means, and there will be *not'in* we can do.'

He watched their faces. The English experts looked politely blank.

'Well, that's where we are . . . As far as the LAPD is concerned, we cleared the site and called you in because this is a copycat crime, a repetition of things that happened in England, h'in the green nazi occupation. Between ourselves, Harry and I are working for the same boss. I called you this morning because I hoped you might be able to break the spell an' tell me somethin' real while the scene is fresh.'

'This happened *last night*,' said Fiorinda, not a question but a realisation—

Roche nodded. 'On the night of your movie star reception. Don't alarm yourself: the programme for these killin's was fixed a long, long time ago. H'it's Beltane in three days.'

'Beltane . . . ? Oh. They follow the Celtic calendar.'

'Yes, ma'am. We t'ink they repeat the procedure in every respect they can, way a scientist would, not knowing what is essential, an' what is jus' old wives' tales.'

Fiorinda was tallow-pale, but she studied the tableau without flinching. At last she turned from the bodies and considered the FBI man.

'Do you believe in magic, Mr Roche?'

'The LAPD don't. They believe in any kind of crazy nastiness, but they don't believe in supernatural dark forces, actin' directly, even if they are religious believers. Their experience is, evil always turns out to be of livin' human origin. At the Bureau we are divided. Me ... I was never so sure that witchcraft don't exist. You tell me, Ms Slater: is what happened here part of a new science, ugly as gunpowder but essentially no different? Or is it straight from hell?'

'Agent Roche,' said Ax, 'could we continue the discussion further off?'

'You're right.'

They had been standing in the miasma of death as if before a carved altarpiece, a brutal sacred sculpture that required hushed voices, but no revulsion. They followed the plastic walkway back again, and stopped by the white vans. The crowd had moved off, maybe on the orders of Agent Phillips. The silence, the stillness, where there should be busy police: the absence of the ritual that was the opposite of murder, was deeply uncanny.

'Ms Slater,' said Agent Roche, 'a straight question. Were they killed by magic?'

Fiorinda raised her eyebrows. 'They were killed by the people who killed them. If you want to know whether anything physically impossible happened, you'll have to wait for the autopsies. I can't help you ... What was the writing? The stuff about washing in lamb's blood? And a little child shall lead them? That's not Celtic, that I know of.'

'H'it's from the Bible. The Celtic sacrificers leave quotes from other religions, to confuse the investigation. Christian scripture, Aztec rites, Irquois: also Satanist, voudoun. They want us to believe they're some homegrown, neighbourhood crazy blood-cult: and officially, that is what we believe ... You don't know your Bible, Ms Slater?'

'No. I don't like religion.'

Sage, who hadn't said a word so far, glanced at his brat and smiled.

'But you do know the purpose of the ritual that was performed here?'

'Yes.'

Roche sighed. 'Will you tell me?'

'The blood sacrifice increases the occult power of the magician, which increases the material power of the group. Human sacrifice is taboo, but just like in real life, forbidden things are powerful. You do them when you need a big result; if you dare.'

'So every time it's performed, this ceremony would make some leader or sacred person stronger in evil magic?'

Fiorinda shrugged. 'Evil, I think you could safely say. Magic only if there's potential. A million times nothing is nothing.'

'Would the magic priests, or magicians, need to be present?'

'Where's Harry?' asked Fiorinda, looking around. 'Where did he go?'

Harry was no longer with them, and they didn't know when he'd left. Fiorinda's question broke a spell. The man from the FBI suddenly appeared to realise the distress that her cool, tough manner belied. He took out a phone, and turned away to speak—

'Harry's back at the street,' he reported, 'I should let you join him. Mr Preston, Mr Pender, and Ms Slater, I apologise for havin' put you through this. I t'ought it might be our breakthrough. If I did wrong, I'm sorry.'

He held out his hand, thought better of that; and simply nodded.

'You won't see these sacrifices reported much. We're not allowing them any publicity, and I know you'll respect that. I'm glad to have met you. I'll be in touch.'

Agent Phillips walked them to the street, making sunny conversation. Harry was staring through the wire mesh of the fence around the playground: which was empty now. Phillips went over to him and asked, in an undertone. 'Are you okay?'

'I'm okay,' he snapped. 'I'll take over.'

When she'd gone, heading back to the butcher's shop, Harry said, 'Oh, shit—' He crossed the sidewalk and sat on the kerb, head in his hands. The few passers-by looked at him curiously. Sage tried to put his arms around Fiorinda, but she evaded him, shaking her head. He propped himself against the wall of the daycare centre and closed his eyes. Fiorinda tugged at the door of the automatic limo, which was waiting. It wouldn't open.

'Shall we go?' said Ax, 'Mr Loman? We're a little conspicuous here.'

Harry turned on him, wild-eyed. 'How can you believe in the existence of a good God?'

'How can you believe in the American Dream?' enquired Ax. 'Each to their own.' He took out a cigarette and paced up and down, rolling it between his fingers. He had no sympathy. He was furious with Lopez; and with himself, for getting suckered into this.

'Ax,' said Fiorinda, 'I don't think he'd ever seen anything like that before.'

'Oh, really? Welcome to our world, Mr Loman, isn't it romantic?

What's the problem? I'd have thought human sacrifice was just the thing to get bums on seats.'

'It's LOPEZ,' wailed Harry. 'Could you bastards fucking at least give me my right *fucking* name when you insult me—'

Sage opened his eyes. A message passed between the Triumvirate partners. It said, *this is where we turn him* ... Fiorinda settled on the kerb by the A&R man and dug in her bag for her smokes tin; Ax and Sage sat on the other side.

'Did he give you no warning?' asked Fiorinda. 'The bastard.'

'He'd called you first. He said I mustn't say anything. I am so fucking sorry you had to go through that. I am so outraged that you were treated that way. The bastard thinks he outranks me, and I should say *sir* ... Is that cannabis, Fiorinda? Er, I—'

'English Government approved. It really does calm your nerves. They let me bring them in, remember, when they searched us before the injections thing. For personal use.'

She handed him a green-skinned Ananda. Harry accepted it with a shaking hand. 'You – you can get Maryjanes on the grey market. I can do that for you. You don't understand. Those ... the victims. I could have *known* them.'

'Why didn't you tell us, Harry?' asked Sage. 'You didn't say anything about this, when you pitched your pitch. You only mentioned a movie.'

'I *did* tell you!' Harry wailed. 'I told you there was evidence. There's strong rumours of a Fat Boy from inside sources, and there are these sacrifices. I didn't know you were going to be required to view bodies ... I didn't know it would be so soon, so *crude*. I'm a movie producer. I know Kathryn Adams. I believe in the power of the entertainment industry, I wanted to use that power for good. The President asked for me on his team, would I say no? I was a courier.' Harry shuddered, and wiped his eyes. 'I could have known them. The victims of the murders are Hollywood scruffs, the kind of kids who'll follow the bogey-man down any dark alley if he says *I can get you this invite*. Oh, fuck, they knew it wouldn't stop until they were dead. I can't ... I've – I've—'

'What makes your friend Roche so sure there's a connection between a series of unsolved ritual murders and what's happening at Vireo Lake?' asked Ax, taking the Ananda. 'You know, the police fail to solve things all the time in our country.'

'They aren't *sure*. If they were sure, my God, we wouldn't be here, the lab would be closed down ... You heard him. They're blocked. I don't know everything, but I think the level of organisation involved in the cover-up, the kind of thing that happens, tells them it could only be the Pentagon. And the sick truth is, Vireo could have a use for the . . . the dark force of things like this. We know that. You know it.'

'Who is "they" Harry?' wondered Fiorinda. 'Who are these people?'

'The Committee. It's called the Committee. There's Roche and his partner. An FBI chief who is Fred's man. Some high-up guy in the funding establishment, who is scared to death but can't go public. There are others. They answer to Fred Eiffrich, nobody else.' Harry caught up with himself, 'Uh, I can't . . . I shouldn't tell you.'

'The feeling you have now,' Sage told him, passing back the illicit cigarette, 'as if someone just tore a limb from your own body: hang onto that. It's your sanity talking. Let it guide you. Don't start thinking you should shrug and accept.'

'I wanted to make my movie,' whispered Harry. 'I'm sorry I did this to you, I'm sorry about that bastard Roche . . . I just wanted you guys to be here.'

They finished the Ananda. Harry signalled to the limo, which opened its doors like a servant in a fairytale: they got into the frosty interior and drove away.

As sunset blanked the distant windows with an apricot glaze, the Triumvirate sat together on the bed in the master bedroom, at sea in a creamy ocean of designer-linen. Sage had slept all day. Ax and Fiorinda had been out with Harry, discovering a different Los Angeles, a human city of funky streets, organic food stores, antique clothing markets. They'd searched for and found a special edition import of the Heads' pre-Dissolution album *Bleeding Heart*, in a secondhand and rareties music store. Sage loaded it into his board and opened a place between the credited tracks. A shamelessly *pretty* confection of sound and light, edge and hue, grew around them, like frost flowers on a windowpane: a castellated house, with a tiny orchard, a stable inhabited by silver-maned, candy-coloured ponies; and indoors, enchanting furniture, hidden items in all the rooms, candy-coloured monsters to fight.

The hidden track was called 'Fiorinda's House'. Aoxomoxoa had built it when he was pretending he had only big brotherly feelings for his brat. Fiorinda, who'd been a well-hard fifteen-year-old punk diva when *Bleeding Heart* came out, affected to find it mortifying, but loved it dearly. Ax thought (a guilty secret) that if he'd known about 'Fiorinda's House', in those ancient days, he would not have been able to kid himself he wasn't stealing Sage's girl when he made his move. But things happen as they must.

Sage tweaked the immersion so the house jumped in scale for their perception. They sat on the green marble floor, in a room with a fountain full of perfect little goldfish: and they were like software people, hidden in the code.

'We have to get a place of our own,' said Ax.

After what had happened this morning, surveillance in the suite was not in doubt.

'Yeah. This will work, but it's very fucking obvious we're talking secrets. Whoo. This thing unfolds.' Sage chewed the lower joint of his right thumb. 'Are you okay, Fee?'

Fiorinda sat with her arms wrapped round her knees. 'I'm okay. Well? *Now* do you believe me?' She ducked her head and retired behind a matted veil of hair.

'I believe what we saw,' said Ax. 'But this is unreal. Fred Eiffrich knows that a team of scientists financed by his Defense Department are practising *ritual human sacrifice* in the hopes of helping their project along, and he can't pull the plug . . . We should never have come here. I'm very, very sorry, Fiorinda.'

'Don't be.'

'Do we know that much?' wondered Sage. 'What did we see this morning? A couple of badges, some petty rivalry, which could have been staged for our benefit—'

'I thought I was supposed to be the paranoid.'

'I'm just saying we're out of the loop. We don't know anything, Ax. Roche was treating us more like suspects than visiting dignitaries. I started to think I was fucking glad we had an alibi.'

'No, I think Roche is okay. He's in over his head, that's what we were getting—'

'We don't have an alibi,' said Fiorinda. 'No one has an alibi. My father was hundreds of miles away when he was running Fergal. The Fat Boy candidate could be anywhere.'

'The Vireo Lake lab could be a blind? The real stuff could be happening elsewhere?'

'Vireo Lake?' Fiorinda pushed back her hair. 'Forget that. The bear said "kill me", that's our only clue. Except that we're here . . . Did you get that the victims have been Hollywood scruffs? People Harry might have known?'

'Yeah,' said Ax. 'I'm not following this, Fio. Where are you heading?'

She pressed her hands to her temples. 'I'm not sure. Could you stop the immix, Sage? It isn't helping. I can't think in a doll's house. Please stop it.'

'Sorry.'

'Fiorinda's House' vanished like a dream. They sat in silence.

Ax sighed, and got down from the bed.

'Where are you going?'

'To pray. *Facing Saudi*, which is always something I've really enjoyed about my religion. I suppose I better pray that that evil empire endures in health and prosperity.'

Fiorinda did not share her thoughts. The suite oppressed them: they went out in the dark to look for a restaurant and walked on Hollywood Boulevard, where Harry had installed them, for the atmosphere, in a refurbished classic hotel. The night was soft and warm, the asphalt sparkled under the streetlamps. 'It has broken glass in it,' said Fiorinda. 'I read that.' Advertisments postured. A stream of traffic poured by, neverending, roaring, goggle-eyed monsters. They were savages, fresh from the rainforest. She walked ahead, the two men followed: not too closely, giving her space.

'How d'you feel now? Will you be careful, in the restaurant?'

'Knock it off. I didn't gorge on key lime mousse out of reckless debauchery. I had an energy crash, I needed sugar. How was I to know there'd be fat in the goop?'

Dried fruit, thought Ax. I'll get some dried fruit, and have a supply with me. 'I didn't like the way Roche kept asking *her* the questions,' he said.

'I think he was addressing the person who would give him the time of day. I was out of it, and you ... You can be scary when you're angry, Mr Dictator. Did you know that?'

'Ex-Dictator. Sage, they took tissue samples at the border.'

'Allegedly not retained.'

'Yeah, sure. A few cells would do it. What would her DNA tell them?'

'Nothing they don't know. She's Rufus O'Niall's daughter, that's all. I'm sure someone will announce a "magic gene" soon, but there's no genetic profile for what Fiorinda is. Identical twins can have wildly different brains, Ax.'

'I'm afraid for her. I'm appalled at the Neurobomb shit, but they're wrong and they're not going to get anywhere the way they're going. It's Fiorinda I care about. I'm afraid of the effect of all this, but I'm more afraid of trying to take her away.'

They were on the Walk of Fame, treading between the brass plates of a pavement crematorium. She had stopped to peer at some bygone illustrious name. They remembered the moment, in the Mexican forest, when she had almost fallen back into fugue. The light of sanity going out, the agonised ghost that would remain—

'Me too,' admitted Sage. 'Thank God we're in it together.'

The look that passed between them was so close and needy it was like an embrace. It embarrassed them both. They took refuge in joining Fiorinda.

3

Dead From The Waist Down
#1: Bandit Queens

'There are two ways to live—' called Janelle, from her kitchen, 'on the beach, and all other places, don't you agree?' She carried two fat-free bioactive juice cocktails out onto the sunny deck, above the white, untrodden sands of Rosa beach.

The Rosa Peninsula had once been the private property of a President's mistress. It'd had its lapses, but currently it was desirable, expensive, top-range territory once more. Every morning that she woke here she thanked God she'd hung onto the cottage when all else was falling apart. The house was tiny, but the décor indoors was individual without being pretentious (she told herself). And the location was perfect. The sun rises in the east and sets in the west. Shame you can't have it both ways: that was her only complaint.

Sage was sitting up on the rail, in a loose white shirt and grey three-quarter pants. She remembered him at nineteen, explaining to interviewers that three-quarter pants were not his fashion choice. His height was so extraordinary in stunted little England, these were the only trousers he could buy ... She missed the mask. There's something so fucking *naïve*, so young, about a rockstar in a digital mask, a walking piece of music television. In ways she was sorry to know he hadn't been stupid-drunk the other night, when she found him vomiting into the Pergola's swanky fountain. But no, he's recovering from a duel to the death with the world's first actual evil magician. Heigh-ho.

She handed him the glass. 'You're never going to touch booze again?'

'Thanks. Depends who you ask. I reckon I'm working up to my first taste soon. I believe a new liver *needs* a little exercise. But opinions differ.'

'I'll bet they do.' She sat in a long chair, where she could look at him.

'D'you mind if I ask a delicate question?'

'Go ahead.'

'Which of those two are you fucking? Is it Red, or is it the guitar-man?'

'Hahaha. I'm a bodhisattva, me. I don't fuck anyone these days.'

'You know, I heard that. Someone's putting it about that the new Aoxomoxoa couldn't get his rope to rise with a magic flute. I didn't believe it.'

He smiled enigmatically, tested the drink and screwed his beautiful face up. 'People can be so cruel. What is this, Janelle? It tastes like compost.'

'Quinoa, spirogyra algae, ginko, pear and lime. And a stack of life-enhancing bacteria and vitamins. It's good food, drink it up. So, what? You tag along? Travelling around with them like a royal Zen chaplain?'

'They need somebody to lose at Scrabble. What's your interest in the state of my cock, anyway?' He leered at her, a stunning blast of magnetism. 'Is it personal?'

She laughed. 'Just a pure passion for dirty gossip. Okay, forget it, smartass. I'll find out. Well, you want to know how virtual Hollywood works? It works the way Hollywood always did: parties, agents, deals, wheels. We tried, believe me, but movie business without the stars is like the paperless office, it's a basic misconception. They're unionised, they're tough, and they have agents. Geeky-techies make the virtual movies. The stars take the money, oh, and they do the human touch, promotion and lifestyle, mainly on the tv. They're indispensable, it's been legally confirmed.'

'And it all happens here?'

'It happens in Hollywood's silicon valley, just up the freeway. There was no percentage in starting a new capital city, Sage. The movie business belongs here: cheek by jowl with a crawling, sprawling, falling-apart, searing-hot metropolis where monsters roam and water doesn't come out of the taps . . . Maybe it's the light, maybe it's the history, but there's power in this location, and somehow it's still a fabulous place to live.' She grinned. 'Shit, this is where global culture comes from, it's the beating heart of the modern world. Who's going to quit that and move to San Diego?'

'Uhuh . . .' He nodded. 'What d'you think of Harry's movie?'

'I think it's an excellent project,' she answered, briskly. 'You have a terrific human story, boy-next-door becomes king of England: with a free soundtrack and romantic British locations, which the studio will be able to create easily from file. Harry's lucky no one else thought of it first, and he's luckier than hell that the studio is going to let him do it. Do you know how old he is? He's twenty-five. All you have to do is keep it personal, personal, personal. Europe was in turmoil, yeah: but no rhetoric, and no environmental horror stories. Stay off Islam. And remember, Ax didn't want to be king, he only wanted to play guitar. He was forced into it, for the good of the people.'

'Right.'

'This is a conservative community, in case no one ever told you. They fear our feeble native eco-warriors like the plague, they hate the Counterculture and they're twitchy about refugee hordes: we have our own, we call them Mexico. Don't make the internet collapse a big deal; some folk around here already think you are plague carriers. Oh, and having the free soundtrack is good, but not too much about rock music in the narrative, because that's a rival sector of the organisation—'

'Shouldn't you be telling Harry all this?'

'I tell him these things. I'm Harry's little Jiminy Cricket. But you need to keep an eye on the boy wonder, because he's not *arrogant*, he just sometimes doesn't see the pitfalls. You'll have script approval, use it. But the main thing you have to do, to improve the movie's chances, is get yourselves liked. Be fun, be modest, be quirky: but not alien.'

'Okay.'

'And watch out for dirty tricks.'

'Oh yeah?'

'You're going to have enemies. First, there's the producers at Digital Artists who didn't get the money because it went to Harry, and all the people involved in the projects that didn't make it. Then there's the classic-film establishment. They may not be making movies on the backlots but they still live here, they despise us, they can't believe how successful we are, and they'll screw things up for any virtual movie, if they get the chance. Last but not least, there's the liberals. Your secret agenda has been leaking like a sieve, everybody in town knows that the President of the United States wants this vehicle to raise the profile of Ax Preston, the guy he's chosen as the face for his peace and love campaign. That's not going to do you favours with anyone, but your worst enemies will be the mavericks with the radical opinions. You might imagine they'd be on your side, but forget it. They don't rate the President as a force for good, and they'll hate having the British muscle in on their tiny patch.'

'English.'

'And *never* correct anyone when they say something that sounds dumb, or out of touch from your perspective. You're the strangers here. Do like the Romans do.'

'You're absolutely right to call me on that.'

'And you should tell Fiorinda—'

At the sound of her name, he's *on*, she noticed. His whole body

75

quietly snaps to attention: not even sexually, more like a guard dog. She'd seen this at the party. The eccentric English have no discernable bodyguards, but Fiorinda's lover and his lanky white homey are constantly on the alert. At any moment they know where she is, who is near her; and just how fast they could reach her if they had to. It's eerie.

'Her accent is wonderful. She *must* gain weight before she tests for us, and it doesn't matter that she's so smart because nobody understands what she's talking about. But—' (No, don't mention the hair. Enough candid remarks, already.) 'But she must never explain herself. Stick to the kooky sayings, *Breakfast at Tiffany's* touch. Then our capricious emperors will say she's very intelligent and charming, and love her.'

'We have capricious emperors at home.'

'Good, so you understand.'

A pause, Sage unselfconsciously silent. The brilliant light picked out laughter lines around his eyes, around his fabulous mouth, but the effect was good. He has grown into that face, she thought. He can wear it now, he doesn't need the mask.

Ah, it was so long ago ... Such a gulf of years.

When new-born virtual Hollywood heard about *Morpho*, the first immersion album in the world, they'd been on the attack at once. Janelle, then the queen of the geeky-techies, had sent her team of disinformationeers into overdrive, with orders to kill the concept. Virtual movies are magic and fun, immix will rot your brain. It's only a light show; it's creepy mass hypnotism; it's degenerate. Aoxomoxoa and the Heads are a crass, loutish little Brit tribute band, totally out of style ... It was nothing personal, it was just that they feared for their own product.

She'd gone along to the party after the Hollywood gig, curious to see the Great White Hope from across the pond in the flesh. (She hadn't bothered with the gig.) She'd found herself talking to a funny, crazy, gangling nineteen-year-old with *fabulous* chemistry. He didn't give a sign of knowing who the fuck she was, he just wanted to get her into bed. She was in lust, and something worse: instant tenderness. She took him to the young company's hospitality suite, because she didn't know what was under the mask, and she didn't want to wake up with something ugly next to her on the pillow at home. They walked in, they did some heavy necking. Then he backed off, and the mask vanished. She probably stood there with her mouth open, staring at this puckish, depraved young angel. He put a roll of bills on the night stand. 'You better count that first,' he says, in his Disney bumpkin accent. 'See if it's enough. This stupid fuckin' currency all looks the same to me. Hey, and don't forget yer tip.'

Ah, you had no idea, my rockstar beau. You were such an innocent, you had *no idea* how much that would hurt. How often a woman in a man's world can feel like a whore. How often I'd been on my knees in the boardroom, swallowing every drop; fucked where it hurts, and had to say thank you—

Later that night she'd tried to make him take back the roll, but he'd refused. He was drowning in money. She'd counted the bills and found she was thirty thousand up on the deal . . . They'd had ten crazy days, Janelle leaping on planes and chasing the band around, doing the whole rock-chick scene. He'd been travelling with his two-year-old son, and an au pair everyone hated, and one of the guys in the band was called George. She didn't remember much else, except the feeling of being in love.

'D'you remember the night we met, Sage?'

Oh, fuck. What made her say that? Verbal diarrhoea strikes.

He came out of his reverie, the laughter lines deepened. 'Er, yeah.'

Of course he remembers. People always remember the things you most want them to forget. He remembers the stupid, wide-open hurt he saw in her eyes—

'I was so full of shit,' he said, 'when I was nineteen.'

'Heheheh. I was *equally* full of it when I was thirty-nine. We were even, kid.'

She was thinking: how long did we have alone together? Maybe thirty hours, max? A thousand dollars an hour, not bad for an amateur. And I know how little it meant, and that's my last word.

Just come and see me sometimes, while you're in town.

'I'll help you all I can,' she told him, recovering her poise. 'I'm no neuroscience nerd. All I know about "fusion consciousness" is the pap that's been on the science news, plus what scraps Harry thinks he's allowed to pass on. But I'm fucking sure I don't want it used as a weapon of mass destruction.'

'Thank you,' he said, gravely. 'I think you're the best friend we could have.'

She allowed herself to stare, for the first time, at the hands she had known as crippled paws: missing one thumb and half the other; half of the fingers creepy little stumps. Sage noticed her attention, and immediately stuffed them in his pockets. Yeah, that gesture too. Masked or not, he used to hate anyone to look—

The word from Europe was that the Crisis was over. Sure, there are

77

floods and famines; there are hordes of refugees on the move. But the green nazis have been disarmed, and the moderate Celtics are people you can do business with. Fucked-up, twenty-first century normality has been restored. But it can't be true, because the awesome invisible wave that crashed through the British Isles last summer is still building. It's just hit California, and here is the human embodiment—

'I could tell you,' offered Sage. 'About the Zen Self, if you want to know. The technical version is long, and I'd need my board, but I could do that. I'll trade you. You be our native guide, I'll bring you up to speed. How about it?'

'Deal,' she said, instantly. 'We'll make a date ... Is it true you get visions of the future? Or you know your own future? Fuck. I would hate that.'

'Me too. Nah, it's not so bad as that. You must have heard, I didn't go all the way. That prize is still to be claimed.' He grinned. 'And not by me, even if I felt like changing my mind. If I mess with my brain like that again I die, straight off: I've had that impressed on me strongly. I was part of an experiment, Jan, involving smart cognitive scanners, very heavy neurosteroids, and a brilliant Welsh neuroscientist called Olwen: Olwen Devi, the Zen Self guru. Maybe you'll meet her one day, I think you'd like her.'

And this was another older-woman lover, she instantly knew—

'I reached fusion with information space, I came back, and that's the whole story. I have nothing extra, no super-powers, I'm just myself: er, except that I'm alive when I ought to be dead, and I have a ten-month-old liver that currently thinks it is about eight. But it's a modern medicine liver.'

Her chief interest in the top secret science lesson was that it would bring him to her house. Yet she was fascinated, despite herself. 'But you were *there*,' she said, leaning forward, 'you made it, you were beyond the veil. What was it like, Sage?'

He looked very serious. 'You want me to tell you the secret of life?'

He who hesitates is lost. 'Yes. Do it. Tell me.'

'Are you *sure*? Hmm, I dunno. Are you sure you're ready for this?'

She drew a breath, a tingling in her belly and throat. 'I'm ready.'

'Okay, here goes. You want to achieve the Zen Self? Follow these instructions. Chop wood, draw water. Don't cling, don't strive. Look around you, this is all there is.'

'You bastard.'

'Hahaha.'

'You fucker, you really had me going.'

'And I really told you. What did you expect? Stock market tips?'

'Congratulations, Aoxomoxoa. Enlightenment hasn't changed you a scrap, you're still one of God's own assholes.'

'Thank you, thank you.'

They grinned at each other, eyes meeting. 'You look great,' she said, softly. 'You're better without the muscle-man rhino suit. Now you look the way God intended.'

'Huh. I disagree. I *miss* my rhino suit.' He pondered for a moment. 'What happened with you and Digital Arists, Janelle?'

Touché. Never get personal with someone when you can't afford for them to get personal back. 'Ah, yeah: my brilliant career.' She was gallingly sure he knew the story, probably had it from Harry. Okay, so cut it short and don't whine. 'I fell out with Marsh, that's what happened. I wasn't a kid like the others. I'd done my time in games development, I was pushing for significant art. I thought we could do more than goshwow graphics, brain-burning fx, same stupid stories over and over. We stopped having a relationship, then I made the mistake of withdrawing from the endless fucking meetings . . . One day I got a text, telling me I was out.'

'Classic.'

'Yeah. I was proud, to have it happen such a classic way. After that, other things went wrong. Car broke down, dog died, you know . . . I did the downward spiral. But I'm okay now. I have work, I have a rep. I have friends who are a lot younger than I am, like Harry, the kids who are doing the exciting things. I just never found my way back to the money, that's all—'

'Did you ever think of moving on?'

She laughed. 'To Mumbai, maybe? Or Tokyo? Nah, I'm too old, too female, the Afro-American ancestry wouldn't be an asset, and most of all I don't want to. I'm good where I am. I have a life, close to the beating heart. I like it here. What about you? Did you ever regret giving the immersion code away like that? You could have been rich forever.'

After all that disinformation, the dirty tricks had been for nothing. Sage had made the key building blocks of his code open source, and the virtual movies had thrived.

He laughed, full-on sincere amusement. 'Nah! That was a *wise* deed. One of the few in my life. It got me phenomenal cred. Listen, I didn't give anything away. I put the ideas back where I'd found them, in the public domain—' A small frown appeared between his golden brows. 'Hmm.'

'What is it?'

'Oh, nothing.' He looked out, over the sands and the untroubled ocean. 'Doesn't it bother you that you can't walk on the beach?'

The Rosa Peninsula had fallen victim to that toxic bloom, the nerve-poison one that had come up from Florida and was patchily infesting the whole west coast. There was nothing you could see, nothing ugly: but it wasn't safe to step off the deck.

'Not really. The water's too fucking cold for swimming anyway.'

He glanced at his wrist, where he'd had a phone implanted, answering a summons she hadn't heard, and dropped lightly from his perch. 'I'd better go: the car's here. We're house-hunting.'

Harry was shipping over the whole revolutionary tribunal, a move Janelle approved. The English would need a private army for the turf wars in this town. Puusi, true to her word, was helping them find the right castle. She went with him through the cottage. It was their Rugrat waiting outside, Red in the driver's seat: so make this a short goodbye.

'Sage, there's just one thing. Be *careful* of Puusi. I love her dearly, but—'

'Oh yeah?'

'She's a wonderful, sweet generous person. But she's a goddess. Be careful.'

'I'll remember that.'

Fiorinda slid over, leaving him the wheel. 'Hey . . .'

Sage was an *atrocious* driver, and the new hands had made no difference. In traffic, his lapses in concentration were terrifying. Most of his friends, including Ax, were intimidated into letting him play helpless; Fiorinda believed in tough love.

'If you don't try you'll never learn. Pretend it's a video game. How was Janelle?'

'Oooh, waspish. Mean, bitter, not a good word to say for anyone.' He grinned. 'Perfect for us. She's going to be our native guide.'

Fiorinda gave him a cynical look. 'Oh, good.'

'She says we're in great shape as long as Harry's movie doesn't involve, lemme see, Environmental Issues, Refugees, Climate Change, Utopia, Social Welfare, Data Quarantine, anything too English, I mean British, back-pedal on the rock music, and did I say don't raise the subject of Islam?'

'Terrific.'

'No, no . . . Shit, why all these cars? *We* should be the only ones with a car, what happened to the fuckin' fuel crisis? I want to go home, no, forget I said that, ouch . . . ' Lane change, squeak by. 'Don't listen to

80

what they say, go by the tone of voice. Janelle's full of awful warnings, which is good. If she was being *nice*, I'd be worried. She asked me what's the real secret of the Zen Self. D'you think that's suspicious?'

'What did you tell her?'

'The truth, but she didn't believe me.' Another near-miss occupied him for a moment. 'Something she said gave me an idea,' he remarked, when they'd survived it. 'About the Ban the Neurobomb agenda—'

Their relationship with the FBI had blossomed. Roche and Phillips were okay, on an interpersonal level: once you got past their poor regard for the golden boy of virtual movies ... Philemon Roche had brought his casenotes to the hotel (trusting nothing to the datasphere) for a lengthy session. They knew more than they'd ever expected to know about LA County's unsolved cult-related crime, and especially that string of sacrifices. But that was all, so far—

'What kind of idea?'

'Not going to tell you yet, it's too bizarre. You know, maybe I should switch the nannying back on, when Ax isn't ... Oh, fuck, that's our exit—'

'SAGE!'

'Whoops, no, sorry, too late—'

The Rugrat had inadvertently entered a locking zone. At least there was no more driving, he just had to keep one hand on the wheel ... Janelle's sombre dark eyes. He remembered (one of the few things he remembered, apart from the money prank) that she had told him she was old enough to be his mother. He hadn't believed her. He'd thought she was about thirty, which seems ancient enough when you're nineteen. He could see it now.

'Janelle's had a hard time. She's made mistakes, she's been a drunk: downward spiral, ooh, I've been there. But she's come fighting back, she has a lot of respect, and she knows everyone. It'll be good to have her on our side. The only problem is, hm ... I did something, years ago, that I thought was funny and ... it wasn't. One of those tiny things that burns deep. She hasn't forgiven me, and she always pays back.'

Mysterious. But she knew she wouldn't get the details out of him. Sage was annoyingly chivalrous about his one-night-stand career. You never got any unseemly gossip about the *mille e tre*. 'You make this old flame of yours sound a real charmer.'

'No, no. I like her a lot. It only means we better watch out, and we knew that.' He turned and grinned at her.

'Eyes on the road.'

'It's a locking zone ... Are you my girlfriend, Fiorinda?'

'Yes,' she said, with a conviction that went straight to his heart; and his balls.

'Just checking.' He concentrated on the cars again. 'Hollywood is saying the new Aoxomoxoa is permanently off sex. Can't get his rope to rise, what a cruel expression.'

'Is it true?'

'Not anymore.'

Eventually they recovered from the missed exit and reached another beach enclave, five miles or so south, called Sunset Cape. It wasn't as A-list as the Rosa, where Puusi had her mansion and Janelle Firdous her little cottage, but it didn't have toxic algae, you could walk and swim. Harry, Ax and Puusi Meera, accompanied by an awesomely well-preserved real estate matron, were waiting at the house: a cinnamon-washed ranchero in a Mission-style courtyard; street address on Hunter Thompson Drive, but the house was actually down a public access road, right on the beach. It was furnished, with a full staff. Ax, Sage and Fiorinda knew within about a minute (going by the tone of voice) that this was the house they were supposed to take, for some reason they might never learn. They accepted fate; despite the news that the spa in the basement couldn't be used, as there was typhus in the pool water supply. They hadn't come to California to assert themselves. On the upper floor there was a dance studio, facing the ocean. Sage took off his shoes and walked into the light-filled space while the rest of the party stayed at the door.

'Is this okay?' asked Harry, solicitously. 'Is this place really okay for you?'

'It's big enough,' said Fiorinda, seeing no need to grovel. 'That's the main thing.'

She watched Sage as he stalked about, soft-footed and curious. He had bounced right back after the Pergola party incident. He isn't an invalid anymore, she realised. He is well. *This is Sage*: all better, and more fucking gorgeous than ever. She glanced at Ax, and caught the same thought in his eyes. Ax grinned, a little sheepishly.

Oh, what a spark of memory kindled between them ... She looked away, the blood thrumming in her veins, frightened and confused.

The Triumvirate had come in by the back door. The revolutionary tribunal flew from Liverpool to New York on a private charter and crossed the continent by H-train. Their arrival at the studio village was a circus: Stop the Neurobomb protestors; Plague Ship Europe Go Home protestors; Celtic wannabes in full regalia, confused about the

Reich's allegiance, a largesse of mediafolk, and lines of studio police to hold back the excited crowd. The Few had to get out and go walkabout while airborne cams dodged around them and the scene was replicated on big floating screens, with live commentary from a chirpy Digital Artist softbot-couple pasted in there . . .

Here's Allie Marlowe, the rockstar king's admin queen, *sooo* elegant in a silver tunic and black quilted pants, her black curls caught up in a snooty Directoire knot (I want to look like that right now! squealed DeeDee, the girl-half of the promotions software). And that guy in the dhoti, tossing virtual flowers from his fingertips, hey, it's Dilip Krishnachandran, the superstar DJ who brought immix to the mass market! There's Anne-Marie Wing the hot folk-violinist, and her partner 'Smelly' Hugh Raven (wow, *they* brought the whole hairy band along!) . . . There's 'Chip and Verlaine', the kooky Adjuvants (what did *they* do in the Revolution, Bob? No idea, DeeDee, but don't they look cute?). That's Rob Nelson and the Powerbabes in the sassy Prince of Wales chequers, costers' caps with pearl buttons: the Snake Eyes family, from England's favourite big band. Isn't it sexist for a guy to have three laydees, DeeDee? No, Bob, that's *polyamory*, all the kids are doing it, it's kind of the miniskirt of our times—

And these are the people who were caught up into history? Yep, these are the very people. One day they were aspiring rockstars, next moment, they were riding the thunder—

Just the way we do it in California?

You betcha, Bob! Like President Eiffrich says, no way round this, got to go through it, stick together, ride out the storm, and always do the best we can!

Chip and Verlaine had been shopping in New York. They merrily videoed the more mundane reporters with their monocle eyecams, and handed out instant clips—

'Why are you all in black and white?' asked a laughing journalist.

'So we can take on local colour,' explained Chip.

'It's a reference tone,' said Ver, doffing his rebel black beret to reveal a mop of silky brown curls, and bowing extravagently, 'recorded at our operating level.'

'It symbolises our openness to the cosmic rainbow.'

Fiorinda cursed everyone who annoyed her, which kept her busy.

Crowds are cheap in a downturn; the colourful protestors provided themselves. The media storm had gathered because the lords of that great industry intended to punish Fred Eiffrich a little, in the person of his protégé. You have to set them up before you knock them down. Prepare to be flavour of the month, Mr Preston!

The circus outside the gates, the studio execs inside, then it was into the limos again and off to Sunset Cape: change out of the fancy dress and straight to an A-list studded reception, at which they met Puusi Meera, and many other divinities, ancient and modern, with whom they had never expected to press flesh. It was hours before the Few experienced the bliss of seeing the last guests depart. Ears ringing and smiles aching, but stone-cold sober (they had an aversion to getting drunk at public parties) they were alone at last, with their lost leaders.

'Aren't they all fucking wonderful people?' demanded the impossibly tall and slender fashionplate who barely even looked like Sage. 'Ain't you fucking glad we made you change your minds?'

'I keep telling you to watch that mouth,' said Californian Ax, arrogant and unnerving in his pastel gangster suit. 'Harry's had several kindly complaints about your language.'

'That would have to be my *fucking* language, would it not, Sah?'

The Few looked to Fiorinda for guidance. Ax and Sage had both been away a long time. Their rock and roll brat had been with them all through the green nazi occupation. But Californian Fiorinda, her skeletal thinness glamourized by a couture T-shirt and dark red toreador pants with garnets sewn along the seams, was smiling very strangely.

'Let's have some immix,' she said. 'Make it something from *Arbeit*, Sage, that really audits the cost of living. You know my taste.'

'Great idea.'

The hired catering staff could be heard clearing away, carrying stuff to their van ... Sage must have the entertainment system slaved to his mask button, or his phone implant. He didn't touch anything. A deep, disquieting pulse welled up, filling the air—

'Hey—' began Rob, uncertainly, 'if we have a voice in this, I think—'

Too late. The pulse became a harsh, riveting bassline with a hook like barbed-wire, and they were engulfed. You see grey, you feel cold, you see a tall fence, there's a stink, your skin is crawling. You have the shock of realising you are *not in control* of the images the beat conjures up. You may hear (some do, some don't) an urgent, fragmented whispering, in which you might make out the words *please no* if you happen to understand German; or Polish. *Don't make me see.* You have the second shock of realising that the enforced perceptions aren't inside your head, they *surround* you, you are immersed in, you glimpse the bodies first in disbelief and then glimpse them turning, falling, shovelled up and falling, you are immersed in a tumble of slack leathery limbs: the complete, gagging, synasthesia conviction that you are experiencing this fall of bulldozed corpses, and you're never going to be able to stop, never escape, the beat has its hooks so deep—

And that's just the intro. It was 'The Pit', from *Arbeit Macht Frei*, the harshest of all the Heads' albums: a textbook of what could be done with immersion code at the time; maybe not as compassionate or as wise as Aoxomoxoa had once thought—

The Few were stunned by the onslaught. Before they could gather their resistance, they were further outraged to feel hands tugging at them—

'Sorry, sorry,' hissed Fiorinda's voice, 'there's a reason, honest—'

They were led, stumbling and bewildered, through a door, out of the immix and down some stairs: into a calm, blue-painted hall where plaster statues posed and potted palms rose from big planters around an empty swimming pool.

'Sadly,' sighed Fiorinda, 'we can't use any of this. Puusi says there's typhus in the pipes.' Sage and Ax were stripping the plastic dust cover from a smaller empty pool. The floor was littered with books, rugs, wine bottles, ashtrays: all the debris of a squatters' camp. 'You can't get the help,' apologised Sage. 'Well, truth is we had servants, but Ax fired 'em. He's in *imagine no possessions* mode.'

'Whose idea was the black and white?' asked Ax. 'It was very good.'

'Allie, of course,' said Felice Hall, senior Powerbabe. 'What the fuck's going on?'

Allie stumbled down the steps and collapsed on the moulded bench around the side of the kidney-shaped tank, head in her hands. 'It had to be "The Pit". Why the fuck did it have to be "The Pit", Sage, you bastard—?'

Arbeit had this effect on Allie. She wasn't likely to have an epileptic fit, but she was one of those people who cannot take immersions.

'I'm sorry, Allie,' said Fiorinda. 'It wasn't aimed at you, it was aimed at the shits in the unmarked van. We want them to think they're getting brain damage.'

'*What* "unmarked van"?'

'The one that's been sitting in the car park at the end of the beach access road since we moved in. We call it the unmarked van; actually it's posing as a van full of paparazzi. They still have those traditional stakeouts over here. But is it fuck. It's the surveillance.'

Allie looked up, blankly. The rest of the triubunal stood in a bunch and stared, the six hairy hippy musicians of Anne-Marie's folk ensemble a little apart from the rest.

Ax laughed. 'Start again.' He sat at the top of the whirlpool steps. 'Okay, the house is wired. That's why we're down here, under a ton of brain-burning sensitive political comment from the young Aoxomoxoa. No one's going to get anything intelligible out of the place while *Arbeit* is running in the front room. But we can't keep doing that, and we can't keep sneaking off to lurk down here. We have to behave as if nothing's wrong—'

'We think we've nailed most of the cameras,' said Fiorinda, 'and we haven't found any emissions in the spa, or in the bedrooms or bathrooms, except there's one old camera in our bathroom . . . We hang things in front of it. But of course we can't be sure—'

'The house is *wired*?' cried Rob, catching up. 'What? Wait a minute, the house is *wired*? Shit! Who by? What are we going to do? Have you told the studio—?'

'Cameras in the *bathrooms*—' exclaimed Dora, the middle Babe, round-eyed.

'I don't think so,' Ax reassured her. 'That would be hostile, and illegal without a warrant. This is grey area. We think it's purely business, nothing worse, probably a friend of ours; and we know how to deal with it. We were just waiting for you to arrive.'

'Some friends you have!' snapped Rob, amazed—

The hairy hippy musicians looked at each other. One of them, with a self-conscious grin, took hold of his moustache and peeled it off, removed a pair of bushy eyebrows, excavated the gel pads that had given him lugubrious jowls and was revealed as Doug Hutton, long-time chief of the Few's personal security.

'Hi Doug,' said Ax. 'Sorry about the pissing around. It's good to have you with us.'

'It's good to be with you again, Ax,' said Doug, with feeling. 'And Fiorinda . . . You too, Sage.' The rest of the 'hippy musicians' voiced emotional agreement.

The studio had insisted on domestic bodyguards: Ax had insisted on having his own people. The 'hippy musicians' ploy had made entry easier, but Doug and his crew were not contraband. They would be recognised as private police by LA County law enforcement, and they would have conditional immunity, should they be obliged to use lethal force.

'What about this van, then?' asked Doug, 'you want us to see to it?'

'Nah,' said Sage. 'Much as the idea appeals. There's a better way. Sit down, everyone: security ought to hear this too.'

They sat around the bench in the whirlpool, Sage and Ax on either side of Fiorinda. 'We're not going to tell the studio,' said Ax. 'Nor are we going to call the anti-bugging firm, with whom we have a contract that came with the lease.'

'They probably installed the cameras,' put in Fiorinda darkly.

'I wouldn't be surprised ... It's like this, Rob. We were warned to expect dirty tricks. If we complain, we lose face. We deal with it, without saying a word, we show that we can look after ourselves, and they might kindly leave us alone ... We're going to do like the Romans do: play games. Sage, your movie.'

Sage rifled the litter on the pool floor and produced a new toy, a digital editing projector, US style. He pasted a white screen on the blue wall of the spa hall; they shifted until they all had a view ... and the Few saw themselves, in crystal-sharp resolution, chatting and laughing (no sound), in a sunny room walled in angled glass, with 'Aztec sculptures', a defunct water feature; cacti planted in great stone bowls—

'They want home videos,' said Ax, vindictively. 'We'll give 'em home videos.'

'That's this house,' said Allie, bemused. 'But ... How did you do that?'

'I used the Bridge House Tapes,' explained Sage, turning to face them, leaving the rough cut to run. 'I had a copy in my board's archive. I cut us out of there, reformatted us an' pasted us into the estate agent's distinctly fictional video of the ranchero—'

The year after Ax became Dictator, the Few had spent several weeks at Bridge House in Taunton, headquarters of Ax's family band, the original Chosen Few – which was still the home of Jordan Preston, Milly Kettle the drummer, and Shane Preston the bassist. The house had been wired: they'd been on live tv, with many illustrious visitors, making music, having fun, discussing Utopia, living the life. The multimedia collaboration that had come out of their stay was regarded at home as a masterwork, but it was not well known outside Gulag Europe.

'This is the idea,' Sage went on. 'I hack their system, intercept the output pipe and replace it with this chimera. It's all wireless, no pulling up floorboards or making holes in the walls, an' I've figured most of the snags. What d'you think?'

The Few watched the remix: it was curiously compelling; intensely nostalgic.

'We're wearing the wrong clothes,' said Dora, at last.

'Well spotted, Dor. Plus, one of us is half the size he was then, and never wears a skull mask. And some of us,' Sage shook his head at Chip, who had elected to have his nappy hair ferociously straightened for this trip, and combed shiny-flat from a centre parting, 'are surely wearing the wrong hair. Everything's fixable. All I need is an update for the final mix, a little clip of each of you; a little work on the dialogue, and it's ready.'

'How long did it take you to learn to use that thing?' asked Dilip, intrigued.

'No time at all. NME had a primitive early model when we were doing *Bridge House*. I picked it up then. It's easy, anyway. Dead intuitive.'

'Think of this, brothers and sisters,' said Ax, grinning, 'next time he tries to convince you he can't remember what he was doing an hour ago—'

'Totally different kind of memory, Sah.'

Everyone laughed, with real relief now: touched beyond measure to have Sage back on form; *viscerally* reassured to have things back the way they ought to be, the tiger and the wolf teasing each other; the Triumvirate in charge.

'But why don't you just jam the signal?' wondered Anne-Marie. 'I dunno anything about it, but isn't that what people do, normally? You can get a kind of a gadget—'

'That's what *I* said,' said Fiorinda. 'You tell 'em, Ammy. They ignore me.'

'No, no,' said Sage. 'This is better. This is *funny*.'

'There'll be continuity flaws,' remarked Verlaine, who liked to think he knew about vision-mixing. He and Chip had moved up, irresistibly drawn to the editing projector; and were eyeing it with longing. They were in love with the modern world.

'Shitloads,' agreed Sage, cheerfully. 'We'll make a feature of it. We don't expect to fool anyone for long. Just give them, er, a non-violent riposte.'

There was a pause. So much to be said, where to start? The Triumvirate sat there smiling, united; but silent, and the pause grew a little too long.

'D'you want us to do the updates now?' asked Allie, at last.

'The sooner the better,' admitted Fiorinda. 'I'm not in the mood for being reality tv.'

The security crew remained impassive, sure they weren't involved (they were mistaken: Sage wasn't going to leave them out). Smelly Hugh cleared his throat, diffidently. 'Uh, is this it then? We're makin' a video? What about the Hollywood movie deal? Did that fall through?'

'No, Hugh,' said Ax, 'the movie's still happening; but there's further developments. There are a lot to talk about. Can we do this first?'

The empty spa had a desolate air, an echoing emptiness.

They were live wires, this gang; and they *loved* each other's company. When they came home from a hard day's night of promotion socialising (Harry Lopez was working them like dogs), they didn't go their separate ways. They ditched their wraps and gathered in the kitchen, or the gallery upstairs, but mostly in the desert biosphere they called the Cactus Room, and laughed and talked and fooled around until the early hours.

Felice, the big, tall caramel-complexioned beauty who plays the trumpet, wants a round of *Name That Classic Video!* Her fellow Powerbabes, elfin little Cherry Dawkins, and the quiet one, Dora Devine, with that terrific dimpled smile, vocally concur. Their boyfriend Rob, the speak-out political brother, wants a discussion of Utopian politics. Mr Preston just wants to pick out a little something on his guitar, quietly in a corner ... Rob gets shouted down, in a verbal duel that makes political rap worth listening to: and baby-faced Chip Desmond grabs the kaleidoscope spinning top they used as a choosing-die.

Sage is on, and up he leaps, but immediately they're yelling *Billie Jean* and hey, no, maybe it's *Thriller* ... and jeering at him for being a big sad Jacko fan—

'It's a shame,' grumbled one of the watchers in the van. 'Why don't they let him make his moves? Same reason they don't let Ax play guitar. Because he's fucking brilliant, that's why. Professional jealousy, it's a terrible thing.'

The heterosexual males wished for cameras in the bedrooms, they wanted to see Cherry Dawkins naked. Respect human dignity, yeah, but that curvy little bod had gained whole-hearted admiration. Access to intimate relations would also solve the question of Sage and Ax, trailed incessantly on the Digital Artists' promo channel. Sexual affection was never seen downstairs. It's frustrating how reserved these English are—

Now the cat appears, a white stray that'd moved into the house: the others call it Ax's cat. Fiorinda says Ax has decided to call it Tommy ... The cat steps on a house computer remote on the floor, causing the

audio ambience to flip from gentle ska to rancid hardcore punk. 'Hey—'
says Mr Preston, his head popping up from behind one of the big stone
bowls (the great dictator having sneaked off to pick his strings out of
sight). 'If that's how we're choosing the sounds, I want *Arbeit Macht
Frei* off there.'

'Oh! God!' cries elegant Allie, horrified. 'He's right! Off, off, off!'

'And *Stonefish*!' yells Dora.

'What's wrong with *Stonefish*?' demands the aggrieved immix
maestro.

'Some bits of *Stonefish* are okay,' concedes Dora. 'I like the start of
"Kythera". But then, hohum, we have to have the blackened corpses
swaying in the breeze—'

'You watch your mouth, that's my *Baudelaire* quote—'

The cat steps on the remote again, the music becomes unbelievably
loud and strange. 'Why d'you call the cat Tommy?' shouts DK the DJ,
'is that an ironic Tommy?'

'No. It's because it's—'

'*WHAT*?'

'Deaf!' bawls Fiorinda ... but now the cat has vanished.

'The cat's disappeared again!' reported one of the duty shift in front
of the monitors, leaning over to make a check on the postit Strange Cat
Incidents log.

'That cat is weird!' shouted one of the armed guards from the cab.

'What's the music?'

'The soundtrack of *Stonefish*, I think—'

They were on hostile reality tv for two days, before the chimera was up.
It was a spooky feeling to be plunged into, straight from the H-train,
but they weathered it. Late on the third night they came in from a
swanky restaurant party (promotion gig) and went down to their
basement bunker. Technically they'd have been safe upstairs, but no
one felt comfortable in those haunted rooms. Chip and Ver immediately set up the projector, to find out what the unmarked van was
viewing. The chimera had the house-video spa on it: scuzzed-up, and
with the water edited out of the pools, but it would be alarming if that's
what the spies were looking at now. No, hey hey, it was Cactus Room
cabaret.

'Escape from the Panopticon,' crowed Chip, 'heeheehee! I love it.'

'Like shooting fish in a barrel!' gloated Verlaine.

'Could you turn that thing off?' said Ax.

They were alone; the security crew had moved into the gatehouse.

They settled in the dry jacuzzi, which had become – instantly – their analogue for the circle of old schoolroom tables where they used to meet in the Office at the Insanitude. Fiorinda sat on the steps: Sage on her left and Ax on her right.

Ax remembered a meeting long ago, held in the vandalised breakfast courtyard of a Park Lane hotel, when everyone here had just survived a bloody coup disguised as a terrorist massacre. He saw the marks of time and stress, the way you do when you've been away from friends, and then you meet them again: and wondered, resignedly, what they saw written on his own face. There's Rob, *paterfamilias*, thicker in the middle, soft around the jaw. Felice and Dora are mothers, and it shows; Cherry's all grown-up. Ah, rebel music days. They used to be *such babes*, those three, dooling round Lambeth in their old pink cadillac. There were shifts and gaps in the ranks. Roxane Smith, veteran music critic and flamboyant post-gendered person had decided hir health wasn't up to the California trip. Ax hoped this only meant Rox had better things to do; he would have to get the truth out of someone. Anne-Marie Wing and Smelly Hugh had been on the bad guys' team, on the grim morning when the Reich was born . . .

He had a sad task on his agenda: he must convince them it was finally time to quit: no more clinging to the wreckage back in London. But not tonight. That'll wait.

'Okay,' he said. 'We're as secure as we can be, bar going out and sitting on the beach, which might not be secure at all, given the futuristic devices of the modern world.'

Faces around the dry pool: braced for the bad news, confident Ax would know what to do. I'm not that person, he thought. Don't look at me like that.

'How much trouble are we in?' asked Rob. 'What's this all about?'

'More trouble than we thought,' said Sage, 'when we sent you the postcard.'

Ax sighed. 'Well, it's like this—'

He explained, with Sage's additions, the situation they'd walked into. The President's letter, Harry's Fat Boy pitch. The mysterious werebears incident; the butcher's shop in the waste. Philemon Roche's casenotes; the secret Committee.

Fiorinda said very little.

Out in the Anza-Borrego desert, a hundred miles east of San Diego, volunteer military neuronauts were having their brains rewired by something like the same method that had taken Sage to the Zen Self . . . but different in closely guarded technical detail. In another age, the very existence of this project might have been highly confidential information. In post-modern America, Vireo Lake had its media coverage, its camp followers, its faithful protestors: but the public relations firewall was magnificent. This kind of 'fusion' was pure science and technology, it had nothing to do with the occult. Even President Eiffrich, expressing his distaste at the development of 'human weapons', did not break ranks on that. Some of the protestors were less circumspect, but they were cranks.

Chip Desmond, Kevin Verlaine and Dilip had been Zen Self labrats along with Sage – until he'd left them far behind. The others weren't weird science nuts, but you could say they had a grasp of the issues, after the nightmare of 'Fergal Kearney's' régime.

Verlaine broke the silence first. 'But that's . . . I mean, apart from the incredible scandal if they got busted, the Vireo Lake people must know that blood sacrifices won't work! Okay, the distance from the lab is immaterial, magic is non-local, but you can't boost a normal brain to the Zen Self state by exposing it to horrors, no matter what. Even if you were flaying people alive in the same room—'

'Thanks for the charming image,' said Ax.

Verlaine glanced at Fiorinda. 'Sorry.'

'Don't worry,' said the rock and roll brat, haggard but bright-eyed in her dinner party finery. 'Horrors have no effect on me, either. I'm over-conditioned.'

'I think the Committee is ahead of you, Ver,' said Ax. 'The implication of everything we've been told, and shown, is that they believe the Vireo Lake team has given up on rewiring normal brains. They're trying to weaponise natural magic.'

'But why this pussyfoot investigation?' Dilip shook his head. 'I don't understand. Why can't your Committee get access to the labs on some pretext? Why can't they question the staff, interrogate the experimental data?'

'It could be they've found out that Vireo Lake is a blind,' said Ax. 'The team there knows nothing about the black magic, and the real business is going on elsewhere. All Roche will say is there are reasons, and Fred Eiffrich will explain it to me. But maybe we're better off finding our own answers. Put it this way, we're not absolutely sure that we have the same agenda as the Committee on this thing.'

Ax's urgent meeting with the President had to wait until later in the month, when Mr Eiffrich's normal schedule brought him to California.

'But . . .' Rob rubbed his forehead. 'This, er, Fat Boy? That's what you get if you weaponise someone like Rufus O'Niall . . . okay. What were they *supposed* to be doing at Vireo Lake? Wasn't that what they were trying to do, make a magic weapon?'

'Wash your mouth,' said Sage. 'Fat Boy is not what anybody wants. Officially, they're supposed to be building a stable fusion consciousness, switched on all the time – which could, say, be directed to vaporise a few Islamic missile silos, thousands of miles away, with no loss of life. Or something on those lines. It's the clean, green future of warfare.'

'*Really*? So, it wouldn't be too terrible if they were to succeed? I mean, with the official programme.'

'No, not really, because in my opinion, in many opinions, it's impossible. If you reach the Zen Self, what they call fusion over here, Rob, then you either stay there, and you ... you are in no state to be nuking missile silos. Or you come back, and you very rapidly lose your ability to win an argument with Rufus O'Niall.'

'So that's why they gave up and started on the Fat Boy?' said Dora.

'And if you have a Fat Boy, then you're in the "It's a *Good* Life" scenario,' explained Chip, helpfully. 'Meltdown, hell dimension. Rufus could think meanly about you, and you'd drop dead. The Fat Boy decides Saudi Arabia is a bad place: make it gone. Gone.'

Dora struggled with this. 'Could that *happen*?'

Sage shrugged. 'Anything could happen, Dor. The moon could turn to green cheese. The Fat Boy could decide to abolish electricity, and then we'd be in trouble. It's the doomsday scenario ... Mr Eiffrich's rogue weaponmongers cannot possibly be aiming to create the Fat Boy. They *could* be trying to create a natural magic weapon out of some crew-cut soldier who can guess Zener cards better than chance, or make a pencil wiggle without touching it. If that's what's happening, we're in no danger, no matter how many blood sacrifice raves they sponsor—'

'If they have a candidate who can touch Fiorinda,' said Dilip, 'that would be different. And maybe they would not know, until too late—'

Rob shook his head. 'Fuck. We're a long way from building Utopia, Ax.'

'Tell me.'

The hollow shell of the spa echoed around them. Dilip leaned back and stared at the ceiling: imagining phantom ripples of light on water, shimmering up there. What games were played in this temple of pleasure before the microbes of disillusion crept in? And what astonished ghosts are here, he wondered, listening to this surreal discussion? There is no way back, and no place to hide, even in the heart of empire ... But I knew this.

'I'm confused,' said Allie, at last. 'I thought Rufus was like nothing on earth, the only monster that there's ever been, and there could never be another—'

'Well, there's me, Allie,' Fiorinda reminded her.

'Oh . . . But you're not a monster! Nothing could make you into a monster!'

'Perhaps not,' said Fiorinda, with a wry little smile. 'But here I sit, proving that monsters exist. I thought the way you did, Allie. I've been trying and trying to convince myself it was over, but I'm still here, so that was a problem. Now there's someone else. But it isn't any kind of military volunteer. I knew that the moment they told me Harry's story. If there's a Fat Boy candidate, it has to be somebody like Rufus O'Niall. Someone *exactly* like my father: a freakishly talented natural magician who is also the idol of millions. I'm right, aren't I, Sage?'

'Hm . . . well . . .'

Fiorinda tugged at a lock of her ragged mass of hair, frowning. 'Magicians get their power from other peoples' arousal,' she went on. 'It's how conjurers work on stage, it's what ritual magic assumes; and it's what happens, if you have the wiring to go with the . . . the instinct about magic that everyone has. I don't know the information-space equations for it, or the neurology, but I know that because I know . . . Natural magic is not a strong force. However talented you are, you need access to a huge number of people before you achieve anything spectacular. My father was the perfect storm, a very rare strange brain; just like me. But he'd have stayed a suburban monster, wrecking a few lives in weird ways, except that he became a rock god, with hordes of fans, and he was up there for decades. That's when he achieved fusion, and he never came back.'

She swallowed, as if trying to get rid of a foul taste. 'At Rivermead, the winter of the occupation, I used to listen to the green nazis saying they must get more blood sacrifices going, because this would make Rufus stronger. I'm sure he appreciated the rocket fuel. Fear and disgust and horror pump up arousal: the occult tradition has always known that, the world over. There's sex too, but fear and horror and disgust are much more reliable. But I don't think he needed it. He was already weaponised. All the Celtics did was to tell him what he was capable of—'

'I've always had the gift,' volunteered Anne-Marie, uneasily. 'It needs the right light, but I see the colours around people, and it tells me things about them. When I'm making medicines, if I'm meant to heal that person, I feel something pass from me, I mean, through me, into the spirits of the herbs. It's not *all* wicked—'

Fiorinda gave her a pitying glance. 'Not all of it, Ammy. Just the sort that works.'

'One idea in fusion theory says all the weird phenomena are big number artefacts,' murmured Verlaine. 'We reached a critical mass point, with the billions of people, and the globalisation of everything, and that's what flipped us into another state of the fifteen dimensions. The Zen Self route was opened by tech advancement, which is closely related to population size. The magic route was opened by the explosion of the global audience, which made Rufus O'Niall possible—'

'Techno-utopia, the Dark Ages,' said Chip, balancing these imaginary choices on his palms. 'Or, hey, a *third way*! Previously impossible hell-dimension. We could give it a name. We could call it Fiorinda's Hollywood Conjecture!'

Sage gave Chip a hard stare.

'Sorry.'

'So, this is what you're going to tell the President?' said Rob, trying to sound businesslike. 'You're going to tell him his rogue weapon-mongers have recruited a global megastar with a strange, nasty reputation—?'

'I'm sure there are one or two of those around here,' muttered Felice.

'I'm not going to tell the President anything,' said Fiorinda. 'I don't talk to Presidents. I'm probably not going to tell anyone outside this circle. I think this is ours: or at least mine. I didn't come here for the stupid movie, I came to find the Fat Boy candidate. If you want to help me, that would be good.'

'Fiorinda,' said Dilip, sitting up, 'whatever you say: but what do you want us to do? How can we investigate the Hollywood A-list, if that's what you're suggesting? We're minor players here, we have no contacts, we have no clues.'

'I know. I know how it sounds. But we're not completely helpless, DK, and we do have a clue. The bear said *kill me*. I don't know if it was a challenge or a cry for help, but it tells me *we were summoned here*, to Hollywood, and not by Harry Lopez. I think it'll be someone we know, someone we meet, someone who gets involved with us—'

'Would you recognise this . . . person?' asked Dora. 'Are there signs?'

'Like I recognised my own father?' asked Fiorinda. 'When he turned up wearing Fergal Kearney's body?'

'Auras can be disguised,' put in Anne-Marie, wisely.

'There are no signs,' said Fiorinda. 'It doesn't have to be a man, it doesn't have to be someone with an evil reputation, and the Committee can forget about evidence connecting this person to the blood sacrifices.

95

Or with any military neuro-lab ... My father passed for normal right until the endgame. It just has to be someone with access to the big feeding trough, major magic talent and some reason why they would be prepared to do this.'

'But what if we nail him for you?' asked Allie. 'What then?'

'I'm hoping it will be obvious what to do when the time comes, but meantime you've all got to be very careful. As of now, you don't have to worry about the candidate getting past me, that's not going to happen. But this person is getting stronger, and also bound to be bonkers. One thing we know for sure is that committing effective magic makes you clinically insane, and the more you do it, the crazier you get.'

'I'm still hoping Fiorinda's wrong,' said Ax, into a lengthening silence.

Sage nodded. 'Yeah, me too. Everything she's said makes sense, but there could be other explanations – equally screwy, but not so drastic.'

'Well,' said Ax. 'That's it. You won't see the Celtic murders getting media coverage, and we've been told to keep our mouths shut, so whatever we do in the way of investigating, it has to be discreet. Meanwhile, weird as it might seem, we're supposed to be promoting a movie. Frankly, I think the idea of a cartoon biopic of the Reich as pacifist propaganda is ridiculous. But this is our alibi, so I suggest we make it work, and I suggest we can also make it work for us. I can't tell you how shit I feel that you wasted those years, and came out of the blood sweat and tears with nothing—'

This roused them, startled and indignant.

'*What?*'

'*Ax*, how can you say that?'

'*Nobody* thinks like that!'

Shit, thought Ax. This is not the moment ... He shrugged. 'Okay, but I never intended to leave you lumbered when I quit the dictatorship. There comes a time to move on, folks, and I think you should make the most of this chance.'

Dilip said, 'No!': lay back and looked for his ghost-ripples again.

'All we got to do is stick together,' said Smelly Hugh.

Allie sighed. 'I'm exhausted, it's nearly three a.m. Shall we go to bed?'

In the bright morning, another grueling promotion day ahead, Felice stood by the windows of the master bedroom in the Snake Eyes suite, staring out. Rob sat on the end of the bed, his close-razored head bowed, hands clasped between his strong thighs. The sunlight glinted on his rings.

'Sweetheart,' said Felice, 'my man. Before Dissolution, *you* were the guy next to the fire, and Ax Preston was the country boy, friend of ours. There were choices Ax made, that you would not make. I loved you for it then, I love you for it now. You are a rare and righteous soul. But we got to get away from the Lambeth collective . . . We have *kids*.'

'I don't want to talk about this. I don't want to talk about it now.'

'Then, fuck, *when*? When the fuck else? We at home, you always with the fuckin' brothers, never ARE with me. My house is full of guns! Full of fucking yardies an' white desperanto gang boys, and still there'll come that knock on the door, one dark night—'

Keep your head down, he thought. One person loses it, you have a fight. When two people lose it at the same time, it's carnage . . . That strange expression, *Fat Boy*, jarred on his mind, and he knew Fiorinda's bleak conviction was working on F'lice too. Sometimes with a shock you remember the world that was, and you know you can't stand any more of this unbelievable shit; but you have to. Close your eyes and pray.

Dora and Cherry had been with the babies: Felice's daughter Ferdelice, and Mamba, Dora's little boy. They envied and despised Anne-Marie, who had left six kids behind, ranging from adult to infant, without a qualm. They'd thought they could stand it, with bi-location. But to hold a child in your arms, b-loc, is like holding a dream.

Dora wiped her eyes. 'I swore I'd never do this. I'm a fucking rockstar mum.'

'We can get them over.'

They couldn't hear the fight, but they knew it was happening: trouble in heaven. They didn't need to hear the lines; they knew them all backwards.

'Chez, are you really thinking we should stay? Would they let us stay?'

'Why not? We have marketable skills.'

'Are you kidding? The USA has a shortage of black musicians?'

Cherry got down on the rug beside sister Babe and hugged her. 'Listen, Dor. I would never, never quit the Reich, but *Ax is not coming back*, and we can't survive in London without him. We *have* to believe we have a future. We have to believe that.'

They had given Dilip the watchtower, a square turret above the upper floor. DK always liked to be high. He sat in the lotus, which was as easy to him as breathing, and watched the morning analysis of his blood. He had been sero-positive for seventeen years, no, it must be longer. So many returns to life, so many respites, but oooh, this time I'm going down. The figures were not so bad, he had seen far worse: but he knew. For the sword outwears its sheath, and the soul outwears the breast.

Ram ram, ram ram. I am dying.

Allie Marlowe paced her room. I am thirty-four years old. What am I doing with my life? She had to talk to someone, but she was too proud to knock on DK's door. That's over, we were just fuck-buddies for a while. She stared into the open closet: comforting herself with good decisions. The silver tunic, I thought that wouldn't work, but it does. My antique red leather Gucci jacket, which I love more than my life.

Am I shallow?

Fuck it.

She knew she would find Sage in the dance studio. Ax was there with him. She stood at the door, watching the leaders of the pack. Sage was teaching Ax a routine that was doable, but challenging for the non-dancer. They hadn't noticed her, wrapped in each other, and in the music she couldn't hear. *Name that classic video*, she thought, with a pang for Bridge House days. Oh, we were in all kinds of shit, but we were happy ... She slipped off her shoes. Sage would kill her if she walked into his temple with shoes on.

'Hi.'

'Got to go,' said Ax, 'things to do. Later, Allie.' He left, with a brief smile. Sage gave her one of those too, and went on dancing: a beautiful, irritating sight—

'Sage, can you please switch that off and talk to me?'

He dropped out of it, came and sat crosslegged beside her on the sleek blond floor; and then she didn't know what to say.

'Sage, why didn't you want the Heads over? I know you told them not to come.'

'Mm. Well, they have lives, families. An' it can be annoyin' trying to be with Ax and Fee, and with my band, at the same time. Didn't feel like it.'

Allie did not like Sage Pender. She loved him, by now, closer than a brother, but she would never *like* him. He was too big, too clownish, too good at everything, too childish: too alpha-male, basically. But in ways – and ironically it was while he was supposed to be the casualty, the invalid – he'd become the only one of the three she could talk to.

'How is he?'

'Ax is good. You'll see little glitches, and he still doesn't want to play electric guitar, he thinks he's lost his edge. But it's psychological now, he'll get past it. For someone who had a mouldy hardware sliver yanked out of his head with rusty pliers, he's fantastic.'

'I didn't mean that. I meant . . . He's not coming back to us, is he? Maybe not even coming back to England.'

Sage looked at her compassionately. 'I don't know. Maybe not.'

She thought of him carrying that dog-eared Cornish postcard around with him.

'What about Fiorinda?'

'She's fine.'

'Sage, don't bother. I know she is not fine. Last night, when she was talking about the Fat Boy, I had the most horrible feeling she was talking about herself. I knew she was not "fine" before you went down to Tyller Pystri, I think we all did. Her eyes had that look . . . a creepy strange blank look, that I remember from the Fergal time. Did something happen? Did something go . . . wrong with her?'

He picked up the ends of the towel around his neck and wiped his face.

'D'you think she's better, or worse, than when you saw her last?'

She felt a shock, and realised she'd been hoping he'd deny everything. Fiorinda isn't going nuts, you're imagining things . . . 'You and Ax don't think there *is* a Fat Boy, do you? I spotted that. Oh, God. Why did you bring her here? She can't take something like this, why did you drag her into it, you heartless *bastards*? Are you out of your minds?'

'You didn't answer my question.'

She stared at him. 'Better,' she said at last, seeing that he was dead serious. 'She's better. She's here with us, she's herself. But *Sage*, that doesn't mean she should be in a situation where *insane magic psychopaths* are a constant topic—'

'I don't think there's a Fat Boy candidate,' said Sage. 'I think the Vireo Lake researchers are dabbling in black magic for no reason except they're idiots. They'll get themselves shut down; an' the werebears were some other kind of thing. But Fiorinda is convinced there's a monster, and she has to be here, facing it. I'm not going to take her away from that; Ax feels the same . . . And she could still be right. Have you thought about that? What if she's right?'

99

Allie nodded, unable to meet his eyes. 'Are you scared?' she whispered.

'No,' said the bodhisattva. 'I don't get scared, I'm a bodhisattva, me ... I could be *terrified*, Allie, and what would be the use? But if she's right, at least she's here. We have Fiorinda on our side, with her magic. Now, can I get back to my work-out?'

'Don't overdo it.'

He grinned. 'I won't.'

Between Allie and Sage, this last was an exchange of warm affection.

She met Fiorinda on the stairs, Fio with the haunted eyes and matted dreadlock hair. They looked at each other, and moved into a long, wordless hug.

They settled in. They remembered how to live with the fear of the incalcuable and still turn in a great public performance. One afternoon Chip spotted something odd, behind the coffee table books on a bookcase in the upstairs gallery. He fetched Fiorinda, who was also at home, lurking down in the spa. She came at once, and tugged out a soft bundle that smelled of sour lavender and rot. The wrapping was red silk, scrawled with brownish hieroglyphs, folded and knotted around something that bulged and made a dark stain. Without a word, she headed for the nearest bathroom, the one Chip shared with Verlaine. He followed, and watched as she tore the packet into fragments and flushed it.

'Is that all you have to do with them? Does that fix it?'

'Yeah,' she said, preoccupied, rubbing her arms and staring down the toilet bowl. Then she turned on him, eyes blazing. 'No! That is what *I* do, Chip. If you find anything remotely suspicious, you don't touch it, you don't even *think* about it more than you can help. You fetch me, or Anne-Marie if I'm not here—'

'Okay, okay, Hey, I didn't touch it. I'm not stupid. When d'you think it got planted?'

'At the reception, most likely. It was harmless, hippy-dippy nonsense. Anything in this house will be harmless, I think I can promise you. But *never* take a chance.'

'What if it's not recognisable? A charm doesn't have to look like something out of a folk museum. It could be haunted hair wax , a hexed face flannel, anything at all—'

Fiorinda set her teeth. 'Just be careful. Watch for things that look out of place.'

Magic had been her private problem, with only her father to

challenge her. Now she could feel the horror leaking out of containment, not only in the big terrible way, but in so many stupid little ways; fucking stupid *bastards*!

She hurried to the Triumvirate suite and locked herself in the bathroom. Her hands were shaking so much she had trouble stripping her clothes off. I bet it was Billy the Whizz, trying to improve her chances. Why doesn't Sage just fuck her? Why doesn't Ax do Puusi Meera? She keeps coming onto him and I know she's his type. Big tits, dark eyes, plenty flesh ... The Few had doubtless spotted within minutes that the Triumvirate weren't fucking, you can't hide anything from them. *I hate my life*. She turned on the shower full blast, wilfully greedy and antisocial: climbed into the tub and crouched under the scalding torrent, arms around her knees, boiling water pounding her head. Foul memories, thick and fast. She began to cry, in loud fury, and once she'd started she couldn't stop. She screamed and howled, flailing at the tub with her fists: until she was hoarse and her hands were hurting. When she stopped, the roar of the water was enormous. She turned it off and listened in trepidation. No one came running, thank God. She sat there naked as a baby, getting chilled.

I must accept what happened to me, and move on.

The thought came into her head, dead straight, no craziness, no jabber of conflicting realities. The bathroom was a bathroom in California, it was all there, right into the corners, and she was someone who had been foully treated, shamed and violated, but it happens to a lot of people, and you have to move on ... She looked up at the old cam-eye in the ceiling. And *you*, she thought. You can have all the harm that's good for you, you spying bastard, whoever you are.

Then she was horrified, because she was risking her new-found sanity.

But it felt surprisingly good.

Harry told Ax he'd let the mysterious Committee (that they couldn't meet) know how displeased Ax had been at being dragged to that crime scene. Oh, terrific, now the FBI will never speak to us again ... But maybe they had to find their own answers. Allie set up an office for herself and took over the diaries. They must turn down approaches from the Counterculture or anything eco-activist, otherwise yes to everything, well at least that's straightforward. Between phonecalls she set up a database of 'involved' megastars, mostly Aoxomoxoa's back history, and the expats; and ran a comparison with Rufus O'Niall's résumé: the public facts. Chilled by the secret history she saw between the lines, she backed off from the screen and wondered, was she looking for a monster or was she trying to save her friend's sanity? She didn't know.

Fiorinda went to visit Puusi Meera.

Minions rushed to take the Rugrat as she pulled up on the immaculate gravel sweep. The wheel rim shivered. Be a good Rat, she murmured. Someone had told them all AI cars have individual personalities, that can't be altered and can't be got rid of. This one was a timorous beastie. Someone else had said they take on the personality of the current driver. Whoops. And they pick up your emotional state. Ouch.

The world was paper, and she was convinced her father's carrion tool was fucking her, in another dimension, this very moment as she walked up the movie star's plushy stairs, following a white-robed middle-aged minion-lady. I have times when everything seems real now, for which I am grateful, but this isn't one of them ... She was delivered to a stiff, fussy living room: full of polished wood, embroidered runners, gold fringes, tassels with everything. There was a scent of rose incense and brass polish. She looked around, and saw what she knew she would see: a little shrine to Ganesh by the door. Oh, what? she thought, I could be in Neasden! Tears rose, absurdly: what's this? Can I be *homesick*?

A lady in rustling silk bustled towards her. She thought it was the next-door neighbour who had once been kind to a friendless little girl. But no, this is not Mrs Mohanjanee, this is Puusi Meera, idol of billions, one of the genuine post-modern megastars.

'Ah! How lovely you look, Fiorinda! You should smile more often!'

'I brought you a present.'

Puusi nodded briskly, and stripped off the wrapping.

'Oooh! Huntley-Palmers! The Pet Rabbit! Oh, that's clever of you.'

Thank you, Allie.

Puusi had a huge collection of British Empire memorabilia. You could view some of it on her *Puusi At Home* website. She was specially keen on art-pictorial biscuit tins.

'It's from Reading Museum. It's very rare. I asked the curator did they have anything that might interest you, and he sent this. I made the Shrewsbury biscuits myself, but the recipe's authentic.'

'Ah yes, Reading, location of the original Huntley-Palmers factory.' Puusi opened the tin, and frowned. 'You enjoy coooking? I wish I had time to be a housewife. Never mind.' The present and wrappings were handed to the white-robed attendant with a rapid fire of instructions, which seemed to be about tin-fumigation.

'You understand Hindi?' Puusi asked, suspiciously.

'Not . . . er, not at all.'

'Good. I'm going to put your movie on my show, did you hear? As a favour for Harry, he's such a nice boy. The Puusi Meera show, which is just me, you know, going about my daily life, with an audience of more millions than you could believe. I fantasise that I visit England. I see all the changes, and meet Ax. I ask him why did he leave the path of his talent for politics, I welcome him back to the sacred craft, and we sing together . . . something devotional but funky. I *think* that's how it goes; they never tell me all the details. My dream sequences are very influential. Come, sit by me.'

One wall of the homely room held ranks of screens. Puusi hopped onto a couch facing this array, tucked up her feet and arranged her silks. She patted the cushions beside her. She didn't glance at the fly-eye: of course she knew her mark. Fiorinda sneaked a look and spotted (among the movie news channels and CCTV from the house and estate) a skinny, yellow-faced girl in green shalwar-kameez, a silver veil over her hair: a meagre little stick beside the opulent, exquisite movie star.

'My staff are family to me,' said Puusi. 'It breaks my heart that I can't have my husband and children with me. But I visit as often as I can, though travel is so difficult—'

This must refer to the first husband, back in India. There'd been others.

'Now, tell me all about yourself. You were the singer who became queen of England, and then when Ax was taken hostage and the Rock Reich was toppled by the green nazis, you were raped and tortured, thrown in jail, tried as a witch and put on the fire. How does it feel to have survived such things?'

The promotion onslaught was not getting Fiorinda down, because she'd found out how to deal with it . . . but she wasn't going to risk cursing a goddess. However, Puusi, though I am a klutz at not getting raped, someone should have told you, *professionally*, I can take care of myself.

'It feels like living in a house with bloodstains on the walls,' she said, with grave simplicity. 'And bits of bone, and smears of tissue . . . You scrub it all off, but the stains come back. You do that again and again, until you realise that the stains will always come back. You can't leave, because the haunted house is your own body. You have to become the kind of person who lives with bloodstains, and stays human, and isn't damaged by it; and it's hard. But I'm learning.'

'Ah! That's very moving!'

For a second, Puusi wondered, had she met her supplanter? There was box-office in this girl's presence: her large grey eyes and her sorrowful clear voice. But happily, Fiorinda couldn't be in the movies. She's *not* the queen, because not married, but she *is* the consort of a Muslim prince: she has no freedom. Also, Puusi had discerned instantly, at the Pergola party, something in Fiorinda that would repel the virtual avatar process. Something icebound and sealed up forever, in that house with the bloodstained walls.

'But before you were queen, you were the daughter of Rufus O'Niall, the rockstar, who seduced you when you were barely in your teens and left you pregnant with his baby; and who died last year. Do you still hate him?'

'I feel I understand him better all the time.'

'Good! Now tell me about Ax. What is it like to be the king of England's girlfriend? He is such an interesting person, and such a great talent—'

She had been prepared for anything, including *Puusi Has Strange Lesbian Encounter*. There are things that Puusi Meera can't do, but girl-on-girl romps were easily within her divine range. She might have known she'd end up talking about Ax. But it was okay. It was fine, after the slight gaffe with the biscuits. They had chemistry. Their chat lasted about ten minutes. Not live, so there's no guarantee, but she thought she was on.

'It's been delightful,' said Puusi. 'I love intelligent conversation. I knew we would be friends! Now I'm going to give *you* a present. Wait there!'

She returned bearing in her own hands a tikkal-work casket. 'You should wear diamonds,' she remarked, rifling the glittering contents. 'Diamonds for your birthsign; you see I know everything: and for your colouring. Red hair, diamonds. Isn't it extraordinary, how little jewels cost? Look at these, a few thousand dollars, one wants them to be worth a king's ransom. You don't have pierced ears? I will arrange it for you, it doesn't hurt the way they do it now. We will do lunch.' She dimpled. 'Do you know why the women in this town *do lunch*? It's because everything you eat after four o' clock in the afternoon will *make you fat*. That is infallible, it's the only true diet trick.'

'Oh,' said Fiorinda.

'Oh!' repeated Puusi, with a wise little smile, and touched her finger to the tip of Fiorinda's nose. 'Isn't that interesting? Eating after midnight, of course, will make you *pregnant*. But these, with the rubies, have clips. There, let me look. Yes, that's pretty.'

The fly-eye wall showed Fiorinda that gaunt, yellow girl, her appearance not greatly improved by two wonderful falls of icy white; mingled as if with tiny drops of blood. She'd had diamonds of her own once. Sage had bought them for her. They'd gone, with everything else, during the green- nazi occupation.

She remembered telling Chip, be careful of anything that looks out of place.

She removed the earrings carefully, and kissed them. 'Bless you, Puusi. They're lovely. You keep them for me, just for now.'

They did tv, they did interviews, they did chatrooms, they did parties, they did premières. Harry announced he'd booked them for a supergroup live gig, for which Sage must create one of his Rivermead masques ... The virtual avatar tests were supposed to be happening any day; and the paparazzi stake-out stayed on the bluff, unphased by a ghost cat; or the running joke about Mr Preston not being allowed to play guitar; or the endless specious pretexts for song and dance routines; or even, on one occasion, a curiously youthful Mr Preston wandering around in his underwear playing 'Staying Together For The Kids', very loud, and singing very badly ... Fascinated, they'd do a burst of *real* reality tv, planting jokes and disinformation, to see where they surfaced. But Hollywood must be some kind of quantum computer, because things that could only have come from the compromised surveillance turned up everywhere at once.

A set of freak storms rolled in, wildly hyped by the weather media. The Sunset Cape neighbours packed up and fled. Puusi and Janelle moved off the Rosa and into a hotel, and pestered the English to do the same. The English (who had never met the neighbours anyway) dismissed the idea with scorn. We come from the Flood Countries, we're not scared of a bit of wind and water. The night the big one hit, Mr Preston scraped plates and stacked the dishwasher after dinner, grumbling bitterly, 'I swear, Emilia, if she was *starvinginaconcentrationcamp* she'd spend an hour mushing her potato-peelings around her plate, and leave half of them hidden under her fork.'

'Si, Señor Ax,' said the cook, swaying her bulk across the room with a tray of glasses. They'd hired Emilia from a local bulletin board, and let her organise the cleaners. The staff Ax'd fired had obviously been spies, and maybe Emilia herself was selling domestic secrets: but nyah, you can't stop all the holes, it gets ridiculous.

He decided he'd better walk her to her car. The Mission-style courtyard was roaring. The crimson bougainvillaea that half-covered one wall struggled and leapt like a wild animal; the ten-foot palms in their pots had been cast down and were rolling about madly; débris from the shore whirled overhead, the sky was black.

'It is the wrath of God, Senõr Ax!' cried the cook, hugging Ax's arm, anchoring him; and perversely, he felt his spirits leap. To be alive in this wildness, to be battling with the storm that breaks nations—

'It's magnificent!' shouted Emilia, and he knew his face was equally transfigured.

Yeah, the wrath of God. We're in for it. It's magnificent.

'Come back indoors!' he yelled. 'Phone your family before the masts go down. You can't drive in this. You'll have to stay the night!'

Fiorinda stepped out of her shower (a responsible three minutes, and no screaming); rubbed her hair and let the towel fall. Puusi has a point. I have no breasts, I have no bum. I am not anorexic! I like food. It's just ... I take a couple of bites, and then it seems such a chore. Why did I bless her? Did she make me do it? Close up, you knew Puusi Meera was *considerably* older than she looked, but she bore none of the delicate stigmata of surgical work, and she didn't strike Fiorinda as the GM type. Maybe she just has great genes. But she's a goddess, she certainly feeds on human flesh; is she the one?

She tugged at her damp hair, wanting to tame it into a braid. The coconut-fibre mass ripped like tearing cloth, which gave her a queasy feeling. She wrapped her old gold and brown shawl over her nightdress and went out onto the gallery.

Ax was there, carrying a tub of ice cream and a spoon.

'What are you doing with that?'

'I'm not doing anything with it. You're going to eat some.'

Sage came up from the Cactus Room, where the rest of the company had gathered, and found them sitting on a ruby-red Monroe sofa, passing the ice-cream spoon between them while the tempest raged. 'It *used* to be a disaster movie,' Fiorinda was saying, 'now it's a bogeyman thriller. Many of us will have to die horribly.'

'Harry,' suggested Ax. 'That would be a result. He has shreddie written all over him. I think it's my turn with that spoon, Ms Slater.'

'In a minute. This is very good ice cream.'

'Full fat, real sugar. Emilia knows where to find these almost vanished traditional delicacies. Sorry, big cat, you can't have any. What's going on down there?'

'Nothen' much. Doom surfing on the cable tv. I don't want any. Gaggh.'

'He's too sophisticated to like chocolate ice cream,' said Fiorinda, licking her sweet moustache. 'It's been a limitation on his erotic career.'

Ax put the ice cream aside. 'Fiorinda, there's something I want to say. It's about that night at Tyller Pystri—'

'*Don't!*' she whispered, in mortal dread. But she stayed where she was. Sage sat down beside her, his blue eyes calmly telling Ax, yes, go on, go ahead, both of them ready to back off *instantly*—

'No, let me tell you. I want to say I'm sorry, little cat. I don't think I ever said I was sorry, and it's been bothering me. I knew you weren't really up for it. I wanted to prove I was a man again, that's the fucking stupid, embarrassing truth.'

'I shouldn't have said yes. Ax, I ... I ... could have killed you.'

'I could kill you, Fiorinda. With my bare hands, probably, if you didn't use your magic. And I *have* killed people, unlike you, protector of the poor. You've trusted yourself to my arms time and again. Why wouldn't I trust you the same?'

The storm raged, a few inches away, wild and tremendous. Ax stroked her hair, dear to him even in ruins, put his arms around her and drew her close—

A flying palm branch *crashed* against the glass. Fiorinda gasped and pushed him away, blank terror and panic in her eyes. 'Augh!' she cried. 'The fish in the barrel! The paparazzi van! I think they're still out there!'

She jumped up and ran, her shawl flying behind her. Ax and Sage were left stranded, in hope and dread, fully aware of the appalling danger they were in, stone-cold sure there was no other way. No way to win this but by risking everything.

The paparazzi van had been picked up by the wind and thrown across the soft slope that led down to the ocean. The surveillance team and their armed support had managed to get out of the wreck. When the Rugrat arrived they were on the bluff, gathered round an injured teammate. The night was full of whipped sand and water and flying gouts of spume. The noise of wind and waves was incredible, like a battlefield.

Doug Hutton got out. The Rugrat only moved for its personal owners, but it was possible for them to assign another driver. Fiorinda, for some reason very anxious about this worthless shower, had come to the gatehouse in her nightdress and a waterproof, ordered them out here, and assigned Doug. 'Come on,' he shouted. 'Let's have yer. Not even peeping Toms deserve to be out in this. Git yer arses in the car.'

4

Dead From The Waist Down
#2: Equally Cursed And Blessed

Ax approached his long-awaited lunchdate with Lou Branco in a fairly confident frame of mind ... only slightly irritated by the automatic limo that was sent to fetch him (hate those things). Who's Lou Branco? He's the most powerful agent in town. He handles everything: foreign distribution, home-use retail, tv, internet, download warehouses, music television, books, comics, games, toiletries, fast food, sporting goods, you name it. Without Lou Branco, or someone like him, a project does not exist. Ax had been briefed, and he'd done his own research. He was ready for off-the-wall opinions and strange questions: he thought he could handle one more capricious emperor, after all these years.

The limo took him to a brazen tower in searing, gridlocked Downtown LA; a young woman in a suit showed him to a hushed reception area. He was provided with glossy magazines on an e-reader and a tray of snacks, and left to wait. Here I am, he thought, dealing with the entertainment industry, the parasite that ate the world, on a level the most mega-successful, rich-as-fuck rock gods barely reach. The ghost of a very long buried Ax Preston stirred, and he laughed. The receptionist, if that was the appropriate term, smiled at him uneasily.

Wonder if she's real.

Mr Branco finally appeared, dressed for a game of golf (US suitish leisurewear): the barrel-bodied toad Ax remembered from the Pergola party, but sober. He spoke warmly to his doll-perfect receptionist, and gave Ax a shifty, flat-eyed look.

'I hope you didn't mind me sending the car?'

Oh, so the limo can be a put-down, in Hollywood syntax. Always grateful for local information. 'Not at all.'

They went around the corner, walking in the astonishing heat and glare and eye-stinging fumes of downtown, to an intimate little Vietnamese kitchen. The restaurants Mr Branco had mentioned at the Pergola had been show-off venues: this was not one of those. Hm.

Something going on. Maybe he likes me so much he's promoted me to best-buddy secret lunch counter status. Or maybe not.

'Is this place okay?' asked Mr Branco, airily, as they sat down. 'D'you like Vietnamese food? I'm expecting a call. I thought, I should choose somewhere you wouldn't be embarrassed if I have to run and leave you with the cheque.'

'This is fine,' said Ax, wondering what the hell was up. 'Whatever suits you.'

They ordered noodles. Hollywood's most powerful agent looked thwarted when Ax proved able to handle a pair of chopsticks. 'Now, about Harry's movie. I have to tell you, Ax, there's things that worry me.'

'Oh yes?'

'This is a story about rockstars. But your, uh, band, the Chosen Few, never had a record deal. You never had a US tour either, am I right?'

'Yeah.'

'You were burning your albums in de back bedroom in de projects, Mom and Pop helping out, and selling them over the internet. Until the net in Europe collapsed.'

'We did everything ourselves, that's right. With the gigs, we made a good living.'

'That's very cute, I love it, and the little British pay-download site. But e-commerce with Europe is something US citizens still don't want to mess with, and over here you have nothing, except in the used and obsolete-format stores, am I right? So we have Sage, whose records are banned in seventeen states, which doesn't work for me at all. And that's it. You're a complete unknown, and so is your, uh, nice little girlfriend. Look, Ax, I don't know. A movie about rockstars is a long shot. What is there that comes to mind? There's *Spinal Tap*. But when that came out the general public had heard of Spinal Tap, even if they were only funny, stupid English has-beens. The average American has never heard of you guys.'

'I see.'

'Your little amateur videos may be very amusing, but who's seen them on MTV? It's not enough, I'm sorry. I don't know what we can do with this.'

Amateur videos. A light dawns. Oooh, *fuck*.

Ax concentrated on his noodles. 'This is very good food,' he said, after a moment, looking up with a flashing smile. 'Thanks for bringing me here. You know, I can see why people love LA—'

*

Sage had taken his board to Janelle's cottage, to trade information. They sat in the tiny studio where she worked from home and talked about the virtual movies. Emotional triggers, *qualia* triggers. How to write code that will step up for the controlled-space which is the ideal venue, but step down smoothly for home use or a conventional theatre, when the movie is being delivered to several hundred, maybe a thousand, different sets of optic nerves and wiring—

'The people still want to go out and sit in the dark,' said Janelle, 'even if they're paying hellish prices for the gas to drive there: and we like that, it's hugely valuable for the associated retail, including our cut of the gas money. It's a constraint. We have more and more custom-built venues, which means more and more people finding out what virtual movies can really do. But we're legally obliged to keep the immix, what we call dcd, direct cortical delivery, to a minimum, and we don't push that limit, or we'd scare them. You can tell them to take the risk, Mr Rockstar Genius. We can't. We have to obey the mass market.'

'Right.' It was news to Sage that he was an effete pure artist. But you accept the jibes, because you know why—

'But we have our dirty tricks.'

'Janelle, it's all dirty tricks. Everything that goes on in the brain is cut and paste, make-do, recycling and gaffer tape, it's amazing we can even get around—'

'Heheheh. No one's as dirty as me. Try this.'

The screen image, notebook-flat, showed a tall young woman with buck teeth, in period costume, sitting alone in a darkening arbour. It had the slightly *off* finish that is inherent to digitised graphics. 'Now with the qualia triggers.' The scene instantly looked as if it had been recorded outdoors, twenty-four frames a second, on silver-nitrate coated celluloid. 'That's Eleanor Roosevelt,' said Janelle's voice. 'She's just discovered her young husband, the rising FDR, in his first major infidelity. She's deciding to live with it, because the marriage is the best deal she can hope to get. You notice the way I make it feel like film? That's a trick in itself, and it pisses the classic movie people off, but they can't stop us. Unmediated code-built perceptions, the kind you give them at your gigs, don't sell. The mass market can't handle more than three per cent reality. Are you ready for the emotional triggers?'

The arbour implicit, the synasthesia of this darkening grove with grief and shame and desolation, bitter fury you must suppress forever—

'Whaddya think?'

'I think I'd rather be poked in the eye with a sharp stick. I'm impressed.'

(the awful pain reminded him of Fiorinda—)

'Is this the writer of *Arbeit* talking? Well, there she is. The greatest American that ever lived, and I made her. I made her, the way she feels inside.'

For a moment they were stilled by Eleanor, the artist and her student both—

'She founded the UN or something, didn't she? Hmm.'

'Nyah, you English are such fucking cynics. Okay, that's what immix code has done for the virtual movie business, for which we thank you kindly. We don't have to sweat our guts out pixel by pixel, creating emotion out of light and shadow. We can lie about the quality of the illusion, direct to those frisky, trusting little neurons.'

Sage was trying out the wireless contacts that virtual reality designers in the US used now, in place of eyewrap technology. They process photonic code, and they have a working memory . . . You have to blink, in a controlled manner, to get the virtual movie to reveal its secrets: then you can read the structure of the extra information that your eyes are receiving, riding on the visible light—

'The Eleanor movie. Does that make you one of the people whose project didn't get the money because the studio gave it to Harry?'

'I wish I could say yes, but nah, I'm not even at the end of that line. Don't feel bad: I couldn't stand to make Eleanor as a washed-out three per cent studio release. One day, when I'm old and rich, I'll do her the way I want her. I can live on the dream.'

He blinked and looked around: Janelle's face an iridescent blur through the veil. She was grinning. 'How does it feel, seeing the world through my eyes?'

'Excellent. Can I open a clear window, so I can see out while I'm working?'

'No, but it's not a problem. You keep a pair of fx-blocking eyeglasses by you. If you like 'em, coding lenses you shall have. They cost, but Digital Artists can afford a few freebies. When did he take over, Sage?'

'Who?'

'Ax Preston. You were *Aoxomoxoa*. You were god, you were the one with the screaming hordes of fans. I was just wondering: how come *you* didn't end up king?'

'He didn't take over.' Sage gazed into the code, his hands moving over the toggles on his board, finding out what she did: getting the feel of this. 'We gave him the job. Janelle, we were a bunch of stupid arrogant music-biz kids, who thought it was cool to be up close to the momentous events of our times . . . So young, unbelievably young, it seems now. One night at a government reception, the guns started blazing and we didn't have a clue. I'd seen friends and strangers mown down in front of me. I'd been beaten up, I'd had to do whatever the revolutionary goons wanted me to do. Then this guitarist guy, who had saved our lives . . . I'd known him for years, and thought he was a jerk, but also,' a private grin, 'mm, somehow an attractive person. Well, he had a plan. He said *follow me*, so I did.'

'And on this rock Ax Preston will build his church?'

'Nah, nothing like that. If you're looking for a new religion, Ax is not your man. I thought you were Jewish, anyway?'

'Halfbreed, by ethnicity only. Allie Marlowe's Jewish, isn't she? Your fashion princess office manager. Tell me, how does she like *Arbeit Macht Frei*?'

'Not a lot. Are they still running Hollywood?'

'You bet. Where do you stand on all that, by the way? Islam versus the West?'

'Ooh, a plague on both their houses, what else? That whole thing is a distraction from the main event, it's a waste of time. Okay, now I show you mine. What do you want to know about the Zen Self?'

'Anything a humble movie-techie can understand. Hey, you better take out the lenses, that's enough for a first trial.'

She took the contacts from him, warm and sticky from his body, and dunked them into the miniature autoclave that stood on the desk beside her. 'One day we'll have *disposable* super-computers you can wear on your eyeballs, my God, but so far, you get a good pair of these you fucking treasure them like you treasure your eyes . . . I keep two pairs, more I could not afford. You know, there's one thing I can't figure. European fusion consciousness experts don't believe the Pentagon project can produce a weapon?'

'We think they're heading up a blind alley.'

'It's impossible, but you want the research stopped anyway. Right.' She gave him a sidelong glance. 'But if the brain lab process can't make a human superweapon, how did you beat Rufus? Can you tell me that? Or is it top secret?'

'By convincing him to try arm-wrestling with me, basically.'

'Huh?'

'If he hadn't accepted the challenge, I couldn't have touched him. It had to be of his own free will. I'm going to need to install some stuff, temporary buffer, it'll vanish in a few hours. Is that okay?'

'Sure. Fuck, is that the deal? Fusion consciousness gives you superpowers, but no first strike capability? You can't use them, like, for profit, or in anger?'

'No, Janelle. The science is neutral, as always, and the barriers the Pentagon effort faces are technical. That's what happened to me.'

Their eyes met, and she felt a shiver of awe: *he truly knows, he has truly been beyond* ... Then he smiled, a grim little smile that changed his beautiful, wide open face. 'But I knew he would fight, Jan; and I knew I would win. That wasn't a duel, that was premeditated murder. He didn't have a chance.'

'You're a strange kind of bodhisattva.'

'I know. Let's start with some basics. I do this with hippy kindergarten classes in England, you should be able to keep up.'

They worked for an hour or two, talking Zen Self science and dissecting, bit by bit, the tricks that Jan and her code-monkeys used, to make the best of their minimum immix. It was Janelle who called a halt to the concentration, which pleased Sage mightily. A break for compost juice, out on the deck.

'Sage, are you in personal danger on this, this peace mission?'

'In *danger*? How would I be? Nah, I don't b'lieve so.'

'I don't know. I get the feeling of wheels within wheels. Well, I'm glad,' she said, seriously. 'You're important to me, Aoxomoxoa.'

'You're important to me, too,' He hadn't the slightest memory of the sex, but he had rediscovered a kindred spirit, an equal, and that doesn't happen often—

'I'll fix up a fitting for your lenses,' she promised, as he was leaving. 'And they'll be the best. You know, you guys ought to try harder at the unreasonable demands. I told Lou – you know, Lou Branco? I told him he should be glad you have this craze for taking care of things yourselves. But he's an agent. He expects his clients to come to him if they have a problem. You should remember that.'

He noted the malicious twinkle and wondered what traps she had laid now. He was convinced Janelle had been behind the industrial espionage, though he didn't expect to be able to prove it. But that's Jan. She plays this game hard, because nobody was ever easy on her. And fair enough. We need to hone our survival skills.

'We'll bear it in mind. Thanks.'

Fiorinda, as an authority on the European drop-out hordes, was speaking at a LA County Homeless Persons day-conference. Rob and the Babes were with her. Sage checked with them to make sure she was okay ... not including Fiorinda in the conversation, because she mustn't feel watched. Thank God for the Few; and yet in a way he resented the dilution. Ax and I should just be *with her all the time*. That's what life should be like ... At Sunset Cape the house was quiet. He walked into one of the big, bland, reception rooms and was surprised to find Ax alone, watching himself on tv. The superstar-anchor-person was asking about Yap Moss. Five hundred people dead in an afternoon, Mr Preston, in a bloody, brutal mediaeval battle in the Yorkshire countryside. Is that your idea of non-violence ... ? The mediafolk were *fascinated* by Yap Moss, to Mr Preston's disgust. It's the rockstar-warlord image, turns 'em all on.

Sage sat on a different couch. 'Why are you watching this?'

'Reality check.'

On the tv, Mr Preston gave a decent, moderate answer to the violence question. Looking good, guitar-man. Ever thought of going into politics?

'How was lunch?'

'Diabolical.' Click. The English, in a body, all smiles and kooky cameraderie, swanning into a music gig. 'Mr Branco has discovered that I never headlined on *Top of the Pops*, so he can't work for the movie.'

'Huh?'

'You know that surveillance we had such fun subverting?'

The shipwrecked paparazzi had spent two days at Sunset Cape. They'd departed when it was possible, with their ruined van on a recovery truck, thrilled and eternally grateful. They had been asked no questions. The Few had decided it would be cooler just to see what happened. They'd been watching the Hollywood quantum computer for information, but nothing clear-cut had surfaced.

'Yeah?'

'It wasn't your friend Janelle. Or if she set it up, she did it for Mr Branco. He's been watching our old videos, and never suspected a thing. Now he knows we made a fool of him, and he does not see the funny side at all.'

'Oooh. Tha's unfortunate. How bad is it?'

'Dead in the water.'

'Grovelling apology?'

'Red rag to a bull. He didn't confess. You could say I'm just guessing. But if I'm right, and I'm sure I am, an apology would be worse than useless. We'd just be telling him to his face we know we made an idiot of him.'

Ax continued his dour ego-search and turned up a shopping channel that was auctioning antique Insanitude T-shirts. Sky-hook prices.

'You did headline on *Top of the Pops*,' said Sage, at last. 'October of Dissolution year, 'Dark Skinned They Were And Golden Eyed', Ax Preston *and the* Chosen Few, as I recall: and Jordan went mental.'

'Oh yeah, you're right, I'd forgotten. But that was after I went into politics.' He switched off and tossed the remote aside. 'You know ... those stinking fights we used to have, it wasn't always entirely Jor's fault. I was ... Hm.'

'You had your eyes on the prize, my dear.'

'God, I was such a wanker. Why did anyone put up with me?'

'Carn' imagine.'

Ax leaned back and stared at the pastel ceiling. 'How was your session?'

'Ooh, barbed, interesting. Dropping things in the quantum computer. Janelle is no pussycat, but ... Oh.' He had remembered that malicious twinkle. 'You're right. She knows about Branco. Shit. We are idiots. Why couldn't we just block the signal, like Fee an' Ammy said?'

'Because we're idiots.'

The bastard won't even sit down next to me, thought Ax, because he knows how I'm feeling. Thank God they no longer had to share a bed: it would have been awful, impossible. Every time Sage was near he kept flashing on unbelievable memories, kissing the guy passionately; how it felt to hold this man's naked body in his arms—

He laughed, Sage laughed. They didn't explain why they were laughing.

'Oh well,' said Ax. 'There goes world peace. I better tell Harry.'

Harry already knew. Harry is clearly one of those people (make a note of this) who just *won't* deliver bad news. He'll leave you to find out for yourself, at the worst moment, like that forcible medical procedure at the border. Mr Branco had been so impressed with his stolen footage of the Few's home life he'd decided to package it as a bootleg and sneak it onto the grey market, anonymously: a ploy within normal limits for Hollywood, if a little cavalier about his clients' privacy. A routine international copyright search had turned up the resemblance to a legitimately published work, and if the thing had ended there there'd have been no harm done. Alas, the story of how Mr Big got dusted, by a mere ex-dictator from a minor European state, had leaked, and was being whispered (in the secret worlds foreign visitors couldn't penetrate) all over tinsel town. Branco was *furious*. And it gets worse. Much as many people hate him, it's going to be tough finding an agent who'll take on the movie Lou dumped.

The A&R man was shattered, and he couldn't hide it.

In England a piece of legislation was passed on bonded labour: not unexpected, but a shock to global opinion. The Internet Commissioners, who had passed on vital information to their prisoners all through the data quarantine, took it upon themselves to special-deliver the news to Ax, which pissed him off. So what? Let the rich take the poor into private ownership, hey, it's the post-modern alternative to the welfare state. He was grateful to the Commissioners later, when bonded labour joined Yap Moss as most favoured hostile question. The Commissioners didn't tell him about Jordan, in negotiation for the Presidency, agreeing to accept the fancy country house that the government offered him. He had to find out that in the middle of an interview. *Fucking hell*, Jor. Couldn't you have waited a week or two, did you have do it right next to the Bonded Labour Bill? But maybe Jordan saw no connection.

Ax had no intention of trying to find out.

The President of the United States came to Bellevue, his beloved retreat in the San Gabriel Mountains, and the former rulers of the Rock and Roll Reich were invited to his Memorial Weekend barbecue. They drove from LA in the Rugrat, with a second car full of minders (studio minders, they weren't allowed to take their own security): they ran the gauntlet of big fences and heavily armed soldiers in a crawling motorcade, waited in line and passed through the cattle-gates where the great and the good were scanned for bio-weaponry and suicide bombs; and made their bows with the throng, to the leader of the free world.

Fiorinda was dressed as Fiorinda, in the kind of small-waisted full-skirted frock that had been her signature when she was a teenage punk diva: blue satin, with a random pattern of gold scribbles in oblique ref to the flag of Europe – but this dress didn't come from a charity shop. She hadn't paid for it at all, which felt like a demotion. In England *Fiorinda* had never taken freebies, she wasn't a designer's dummy ... The President shook her hand, able to do so because she'd been scanned by something fearsomely invasive, and said, 'I'm proud to meet you, Ms Slater. I'm Kathryn's Uncle Fred, you know. She talks about you so much. You're a very brave lady, and I thank God you came through.'

Kathryn Adams, Ax's pal from the Floods Conference, had made contact with Fiorinda by a secret data link when the green nazis were in power and everyone thought Ax was dead. Her messages had been the *only lifeline*—

But Fiorinda couldn't form a sentence for Uncle Fred. She was having trouble with this VIP crowd, so oblivious when such appalling things were happening to the world. If she didn't get away quickly, she would be cursing the fucking lot of them ... She smiled, and scooted; crossed the Japanese-landscaped terrace where the barbecue was being served, and hid behind a screen of trees.

Forested ridges stretched away forever. The heat was leaden, the light strangely layered through a gleaming overcast—

'Fiorinda?'

Sage had followed her. Damn, he's always watching ... 'I'm good,' she said. 'It was the crush at the entrance: everything went a bit unreal. I'll come and mingle.'

She turned around, reached up to straighten his black tie, which did not need straightening, and laid her hands lightly on his shoulders. 'You two look *fantastic* in formals. I'm okay. It's just, that nice middle-aged bloke sh-shakes my hand, and I feel queasy, déjà fucking vu, you know? Government receptions are difficult.'

'My brat. I know you're okay.'

'Hey, not the nose. Don't kiss my nose. Not in public!'

'Nyah, we're behind a tree. Listen, Ax has been told that the unofficial meeting won't be 'til late. You an' I don't have to stay. We can leave now.'

'*No.* Please don't baby me. I can work a crowd, thanks.'

They went into the house, a seasoned, mellow log cabin on the grand scale. In the hunting-lodge front hall they were accosted by a whey-faced young woman with tiny eyes and lank, colourless hair, wearing a purple trouser suit that did nothing for her shapeless bulk. 'Hi,' she said, shyly, 'Fiorinda? I'm Kathryn. I missed you at the meeting, greeting. Oh, it's so cool that you're here—'

Kathryn had been a trisomy, a Downs Syndrome baby. Her parents had had the cognitive and internal deficits fixed, but no cosmetic treatment, because they were extreme Christians of some kind. Grown up, she'd decided to stick with the deal.

They had never met in person before. Fiorinda held out her hands, with her old starry smile—

'Text pal! Oh, this is great! It's very cool to *be* here!'

Sage stayed long enough to be sure that Fee was really happy, not faking it, and went to join Ax. They walked around together, noting the exits, the distribution of concealed weapons, the layout. They couldn't stop themselves doing this when Fiorinda was in the question. They were popular: plenty government and industry luminaries wanted to say 'hi'. It would be a different story, alas, when the news got out that their movie was on the rocks. People are so shallow. After a while, the ex-dictator got into a conversation and Sage struck out on his own. He had made an appointment – and Mr Eiffrich hadn't forgotten. A female suit in very sober formal wear came up, murmured that the President was waiting, and led him away.

Mr Eiffrich was in his study. He was by the bookshelves when Sage was shown in, somewhat stagily examining a volume of poetry. He peered over the top of his reading glasses, like a schoolmaster. 'Do you know Houseman, Mr Pender? Or should I say Aoxomoxoa? *"What God abandoned, these defended, and saved the sum of things for pay . . ."*'

'Sage, please.'

'Okay.' He didn't say, *call me Fred.* He brought the book with him to the rustic fireplace, where a pair of armchairs presided over a summer firebasket of decorative logs and cones. 'Come on in, sit down with me.'

'To save the sum of things for pay—' he repeated, when they were sitting opposite each other. 'That's what it means to be a soldier: *soldari, solidus*, a man who has sold himself, sold his will and his bodily strength to be freely spent, hopefully in a cause he can believe in . . . I remember my niece Kathryn, and her friends, smart young kids, going *wild* over Aoxomoxoa, years ago. It was a mystery to me, I have to admit.'

'No problem.'

'But you gave it all up. You didn't run out, you stayed to serve your country in time of need. I admired that very much.' He looked hard at Sage, as if trying to locate the admirable bit and failing. 'You won't be joining us at the meeting later?'

'No, I'll be taking Fiorinda home.'

'I see! Well, er, Sage, this is your gig. What did you want to discuss?'

Sage had met some strange reactions on this trip. He hadn't expected downright hostility from Kathryn's Uncle Fred, but there you go. Blame it on Aoxomoxoa.

'I don't want to discuss anything. I'd like to give you this.' Sage reached in his pocket (and saw the President react despite himself, a quickening in the eyes, the fight/flight twitch, hey, *compadre*). He brought out a tiny glassine envelope, containing a pinch of white crystals.

'What is it?'

'It's cocaine, Mr President. Organic cocaine, from Drumbeg Castle, Rufus's place. I got hold of it from the Gardia, that's the Irish police, some months ago.'

'Hmmph. I know who the Gardia are. I'm sorry, I don't—?'

'When Ax was rescued, last year, organic cocaine was found in the kidnap house. I want to know if Rufus's supply came from the same source. The Mexican authorities don't have that evidence any more, but if it still exists, I bet you could have access.'

Mr Eiffrich took the envelope. 'I believe the possibility of a connection between Rufus O'Niall and the hostage-taking was investigated. It's an obvious issue.'

'Yeah, but humour me. Ax was taken hostage, supposedly by a bunch of amateurs, coincidentally leaving England open to attack. The ringleader, the Brazilian João, is still at large, and you may have a problem with magic. I don't know, but maybe it's suggestive. I thought your private network in the enforcement agencies might check this out, if it's still possible.'

'Ax wants me to pursue this?'

I killed the bastard who tortured my Fiorinda, thought Sage. I'd like a few minutes alone with the bastard who did the same to my beautiful guitar-man ... No, no, no, perish the thought (also I'd probably get stuffed). This is not revenge.

'Ax doesn't know. Ax thinks the kidnapping was his own stupid fault, and that he's to blame for what happened in England when he didn't come home. I'd like to be able to tell him he didn't fall, he was pushed.'

Mr Eiffrich gave Sage a hard, wondering look. He stood up, went to an antique library desk and locked the envelope away. 'Leave it with me.' He came back to the fire and announced, sternly, 'We're completely private in here.'

'If you say so, Mr President.'

'On the other hand,' the President cleared his throat, and passed a hand through his rusty, thinning hair. He continued at speed, 'The Bellevue estate is fully surveilled, and I'm informed at once of anomalies.' He touched the earpiece of his glasses. 'By an AI. So that's fine, that's okay. No human agency. But I can't *guarantee* no one will walk around the trees. I consider Ax Preston a personal friend of mine. I'm not saying anything against a very brave young lady, but I thought your affair with your friend's wife was a thing of the past.'

Sage put his hands in his pockets.

'I know this is not my business,' exclaimed Mr Eiffrich. 'European mores are different, the heart has its reasons, but it is *vital* that you, and Ax, and Fiorinda, present a united front. Call it hypocrisy, naïveté, but that's what the American people will expect. I'm not passing a moral judgement, I'm not threatening to tell tales. But could you, for God's sake, be more discreet?'

'Thank you, Mr Eiffrich. I'll take that as a friendly warning.'

'Good. That's good.' Mr Eiffrich took his seat and ran a hand through his hair again, only succeeding in tousling it further. 'Sage, I'm sorry I had to ... We really should talk. We have a lot to say to each other, and I'm glad—'

'No worries. Thanks fer your time. Got to go now.'

The younger crowd had gathered in the billiards room, drinking champagne and chattering, around a closely contested game. Fiorinda sat on the edge of the group, knocking back champagne (which helped her temper) and listening carefully to these inner circle juveniles. They knew the buzzwords on Crisis Europe, and on the fusion consciousness revolution, but they would, wouldn't they? She couldn't spot anything out of place ... Kathryn had found a place to sit by Harry, where she could laugh at his jokes: Fiorinda had caught her gazing secretly, whenever the dandy young producer was looking the other way.

Oh dear, poor Lurch. I hope that's not too deep, because it looks painful.

Lurch was the name that Kathryn used online ... Fiorinda was wondering, irresistibly, if there was any way she could safely tweak things for her friend, when the gilded youths close to her fell silent and she saw Sage come stalking up, graceful and intimidating. She'd seen them walking around together earlier, and wondered if she should tell them they were scaring people: but it would only have made them worse. 'Hi, Sage—' piped up one bold gilded youthette.

'Hi,' said Sage, destroying the girl with a glance; and sat by Fiorinda.

'How are you?' she asked, cautiously.

'Pharmacologically starved. You had enough of this?'

'Yes. Let's find Ax and tell him we're leaving'

'Ax is fine, let's just go.'

On their way out they crossed paths with Lou Branco, who pretended not to see them, and said to the woman with him, 'Fred ought to get himself a better party organiser. Someone who knows you don't have to invite the whole town.'

They waited to get the Rugrat out of bond, in a stark bus shelter where they were probably getting scanned again, and militarised flunkies stood presenting arms. Sage drove without being asked; they swept down from the hills in a dazzling twilight. Neither of them said a word until they hit the LA grid, and the unacceptable face of car culture reasserted itself.

'What d'you want to do?' asked Sage, restlessly, as they crawled, nose to tail, nose to tail, nose to tail as far as the eye could fucking see. 'Go back to the house?'

'No.'

'Shall we look for an immix theatre an' do some research?'

'I don't want to *think* about movies.'

'Okay, got an idea. Let's find the Steel Door and see how Chip and Ver make out with the local heroes. But first *I want a drink.*'

The Steel Door was a hot club where Chip and Ver, in their techno-duo identity as the Adjuvants, were guesting tonight.

'Fine,' said Fiorinda, recognising a lost cause. 'Beer, not vodka.'

'Deal.'

'Three per cent?'

Mysteriously, this was a terrible thing to say. It earned her a truly *savage* look, like the living skull of old breaking through the veil of flesh.

'*Fuck* that.'

God, how nostalgic. She hadn't realised how much she missed the mask ... 'Just don't blame me if you throw up. Let's see if we can get the Rugrat to find us a nice bar.' The Rugrat adamantly refused to find them a bar unless they answered a multiple-choice question sheet, designed to prove you were sober now and wouldn't dream of driving after taking liquor; not even on automatic. Ax and Sage had omitted to disable this wrinkle back in Mexico (they hadn't been thinking about alcohol). Once they'd started trying to answer the stupid questions they could not switch it off ... In the end they parked on the street, vaguely in the region of the Steel Door. Unlike Ax, they weren't trying to grasp the geography. The City of the Plain was just *there*, in varying states, when you got off the freeways. They found a bar that was quiet, froze out the friendly waitress, and drank Sam Adams.

'Are they supposed to be doing the Steel Door gig, or is it samizdat?'

'Dunno. I've lost track.'

Harry's radical rockstars weren't supposed to take gigs without his approval, but they did: which panicked the golden boy. Sage stared gloomily, Fiorinda chugged her frosty beer, and it was good.

'Cheer up,' she said. 'It could be worse. We could *really* be trying to get into the movies, like the stupid, futile post-career rockstars that we are, and fucking it up.'

'Hahaha.' He stopped glowering and grinned at her: a tingling warmth ran through her: what, is this life returning? 'I love you, Fiorinda, because you are so wise.'

'What happened at the party? Did something bad happen?'

'Nah, something and nothing ... I had a couple of things I wanted to say to President Eiffrich—'

'The cocaine?'

'Yeah, and something else, which I didn't get round to, but I—' He lifted his glass, and she saw that his left hand was bare, a pale band where the braided gold should be.

'Sage, what happened to your ring?'

'Oh. Er ... it's in my pocket.'

Fiorinda trembled. 'You took it off. W-why did you take it off? What's wrong? Is it something to do with me?'

'No, of course not! Hey, hey, stupid brat, come back. Look, here it is.' Sage produced the ring and put it back on. 'See. Ring is on finger ... I took it off because—' He twisted the braid around, his beautiful mouth downturned. 'I was chatting with the President, an' he told me that his cameras had spotted me kissing the boss's girl. He said he didn't want to moralise but could I for God's sake be more discreet.'

'But why did you *take off your ring*? Why didn't you explain?'

'Didn't feel like it. If he's the only person in California who hasn't heard about the intriguing fucking ménage à trois by now—'

The waitress came over with refills. 'I took it off because someone accused me of cheating on Ax,' said Sage, when she'd gone again. 'An' it's true, I did cheat on him.'

'Yeah, so did I. Get over it Sage. What do you want? A medal for being sorry that we screwed around?'

'Vicious brat. You're always so good to me when I'm in trouble.'

'Hey, Sage ... You're *not* in trouble. Well, not with Ax ... Only with a huge Hollywood money man, and oh, the leader of the free world, and the golden boy, and of course the monster that's stalking—'

He shook his head, sank half the refill, and signalled for another. 'I can't talk to him,' he said miserably, twisting the ring, eyes down. 'There's something wrong. He ... he doesn't want me. He thinks I'm not human any more, that I'm not really his big cat. Shit, I shouldn't be talking to you like this. Forget it.'

'Hohoho,' said Fiorinda, 'Aoxomoxoa, you know what? I think you're in love.'

He screwed up his face, colour burning across his cheekbones, which looked *enchanting*. 'Fuck off.'

*

The Steel Door was in a neighbourhood where there were barricades, broken roadways and not much street lighting apart from oil-drum fires. Nevertheless there was a crowd of swanky autos, getting taken away by flunkies in private police uniforms, and a line of people in designer evening dress at the plate-metal doors. They handed over the Rat, joined the line, and all went well until they hit the door police—

'Excuse me, mizz, would you mind telling me how old you are?'

'I'm twenty-three.'

'Can you prove that?'

'What—?'

'Do you have hard-copied photo-ID?'

She did not. Photo-ID had not been required at Camp Bellevue. 'Oh, come on. I do not look under eighteen! I wish I did.'

'I'm sorry, mizz. No can do.'

'I can't believe this. I'm twenty-three. Look, I have my driving – I mean, driver's – licence, here on my phone, see—'

Sage was staying out of it. He didn't care if they got in or not, and he was very sure *step aside little lady, I'll handle this* was not the way forward.

Door police grinned all over his fat face. 'Yeah, well that's not good enough. You have to be twenty-one to get in here, and if I question your age, you have the correct photo-ID, hard copy, in your hand, or I can't let you by. Sorry Fiorinda. Sorry big blond dude, we hate to spoil your evening. Please move to one side.'

Ah, fuck it. Leave gracefully. She was moving to one side, when she realised what the bloke had said. 'Wait a minute. You called me Fiorinda. You *know who I am*, and you're carding me? How the fuck does that work?'

'I'm sorry, but it works in America. Don't matter who you are. No photo-ID, no get in.'

She should have let it go, or at least said nothing out loud.

'Okay, *fine*,' snarled Fiorinda. 'I wish you all the harm that's good for you, sunshine, and *I hope it is plenty*—'

She heard a sharp intake of breath and knew she was busted, but Sage didn't say a word. They waited on the corner for the Rugrat, paid the car-minder flunky with a credit card (tipping heavily, in spite of his bastard colleague), and left the scene. Sage let the Rugrat take them, quickest route off the surface and back to the freeways.

'What a wanker.'

'Mm.'

'Why are people such jerks? We should have said we were with the band.'

Sage offered no comment.

'You'd better stop.'

He pulled off onto the shoulder; luckily there wasn't much traffic in his way. She tumbled out, fell on her hands and knees and threw up.

Sage took a water bottle, got down and waited until she was finished. He handed her the bottle. 'How long have you been doing that?'

Fiorinda crawled away from her vomit and huddled under an Adopt A Highway sign in the scrub and rubbish at the foot of the steep verge. 'Drinking too much? Quite a while, I'm afraid. Since I was about twelve.'

'Cursing people.'

'I didn't do him any harm!' she wailed.

'Yeah.' He sat beside her, took out a pack of grey-market Maryjanes and lit one. 'I heard the ingenious form of words ... How long?'

'I don't know. A while. Since we came to Hollywood.'

'Oh, Fiorinda—'

'Please don't *oh Fiorinda* me. Look, I am not committing magic. I will never. Never ... Nothing happens that couldn't happen. No one gets hurt, only, tweaked. It just ... It makes me feel better. It's my medicine. *I need this.*'

'Hm. There's a word for what you're doing, Fiorinda.' He sighed; watched the Maryjane smoke rise. 'The word is methadone ... Don't bother, sweetheart. I know about that stuff. It just prolongs the agony.'

Fiorinda stared at him in the cold, roadside light and saw that he knew, *of course* he knew she was hungry for the drug she swore she hated, and that she must never, never touch. 'You always have to have been there, done that, don't you, know it all. Why are you so fucking *mean* to me, whenever I'm in trouble?'

'So you won't have to visit the same abysmally stupid places ... Did you curse the surveillance team?'

'Yes,' she whispered, hanging her head.

'Ah. I should have known. And whoever had set them up?'

'I ... I may have done. Oh, Sage.' She pressed the heels of her hands to her eyes. 'Oh, shit, okay, you're right. I have to stop, I'll try, I will try—'

'C'me here.'

'Smelling of sick?'

'Tuh. You've seen me face down in it often enough.'

He hugged her close, and the warmth of her skinny, resistant, reckless little body flooded him with painful joy, because he loved the grown-up Fiorinda, protector of the poor (sometimes known as Ax's Fiorinda), but this was his own girl, his wild child, soul mate, that he'd never hoped to hold again. '*Stupid brat*,' he whispered, rocking her, '*stupid brat, it will be all right*'. But oh fuck, oh fuck ... Fiorinda tugged his dinner jacket around her shoulders and burrowed against his side—

'Now you're horribly angry with me.'

'Don't see how I can be. It was Ax an' me insisted on pissing around. If we'd jammed the signal, the way you said, there'd have been no problem.'

'But we'll never find another agent.'

'Fiorinda, get a grip. We don't *want* to be in a cartoon. Fuck the movie.'

'Are you going to tell Ax? Let me have a hit of that.'

Sage tucked the Maryjane into her mouth, and smiled down at her worried, guilty face. Long ago, he had discovered that Fiorinda had unusual talents, and she'd forced him to keep her secret, even from Ax. Things happen as they must, but this had turned out very badly.

'Not me,' he said, firmly. 'This time, princess, *you* are going to tell him.'

The warm transparent darkness smelt of petrol (gas), and dust; and fugitive desert scents, along with the taint of vomit. Cars like tanks and long shiny trucks thundered by, within yards of their dusty verge; strange great lighted shapes of concrete and steel loomed around, but they were as if invisible, hidden in the cavernous belly of this alien world.

'You know, I'm sure there's a touch of nicotine in these things—'

'Shock, horror,' said Fiorinda. 'I feel as if we've stowed away on a huge spaceship. The spaceship doesn't care about us, we don't know where it's going, and we had to leave everything we possessed behind. But I don't mind. It's so incredible just to be alive and together, I could be happy anywhere.'

'I get that too.'

'If only magic (how I hate the word) didn't exist. If we could wipe the filthy stuff off the board, the way we thought we had, that night at Drumbeg. Things would still be falling apart, but they'd be falling apart in normal ways, and we could spend our lives helping Ax try to save the world, hopefully not by being the henchpersons of a benign dictator ... But you'd have to be dead and I'd have to not exist, so I can't make that world real, and trust me, I have tried.'

'Mm . . . There could be a reason, you know, why *this* world is the easiest to maintain and, er, believe in. Once you have the trick of it.'

'Yeah,' she said, sweetly. 'Because this is the real world, of course. Don't be silly.'

Oh, my Fiorinda, he thought. You are still far from home. He was in awe at the courage of his girl, fighting her lonely battle, and the terrible thought came to him that maybe this was what life would be like: Fiorinda smiling and happy, acting like herself: but robbed of the most vital of her senses, secretly believing herself alone in hell, and refusing to let it get her down. But don't think like that. She is *better*, she's our darling, and it's a feedback loop. The more she acts like herself, the more those pathways will be strengthened—

'Hey, shall we call him? It's late. He must be finished with the President.'

'You want me to tell him what I did *now*?'

Possibly Sage was blushing again. 'Er . . . No, I just want to hear his voice.'

They called Ax. He wasn't answering, and they couldn't locate him. They tried Sunset Cape: he wasn't there. He'd called to say he was on his way back, but he had not turned up. Oh, shit. Where is he? Oh, *shit*. This is how it happened before.

Ax had expected a whispered summons from an aide. In fact, Fred Eiffrich came looking for him as the party was thinning out: a touch of consoling attention for the ex-dictator, who can't come in by the front door. They went along to Fred's private sanctum. There was a silver tray, bourbon, ice and glasses, on a table by the fireplace.

'Will you take a drink with me, Ax? This is great sippin' whiskey.'

'No, thank you.'

The President poured himself a small drink, no ice.

'I guess you got my letter.'

'Yes, Mr Eiffrich,' said Ax, giving nothing back to the warmth in the President's manner. 'Harry delivered the letter, and gave me the rest of the pitch. We came to Hollywood, and we were taken to view a reasonably unpleasant murder scene by your Committee's FBI contingent. That was a little unexpected.'

'I wish you'd call me Fred,' said the President. He sat down, indicating the other armchair. 'I'm sorry I had to do that. It seemed as if sending Harry to track you down on vacation was the only card I had left. I'm sorry about the murder scene, too. But on the whole I think Phil was in the right, it could have been a breakthrough. You would have known more ... I would have told you more if I'd been able to make contact.'

Ax had refused to touch his official mail since the day he'd resigned.

'Your redoubtable secretary – is that her title? – Ms Marlowe, wouldn't give me the time of day; the phone numbers I had didn't work. I tried to reach you personally by digital means.' Mr Eiffrich frowned, and lifted his chin. 'Well, they say I'm a technophobe. Maybe I don't understand my own email program, but I wrote you about a dozen times, last winter, and every one of them bounced.'

'I was reading them,' said Ax. 'I had resigned the Dictatorship, and I meant it. If anything that looked like state business turned up in my personal email, I would check the contents and either forward it to Westminster, or have Sage seal it up again and return it failed delivery. My boyfriend's part geek, you know ... You didn't say anything about Celtic blood sacrifices, or a Fat Boy, Mr Eiffrich. You raised your concerns about orthodox 'fusion consciousness' research, an issue I didn't feel was—'

'How could I tell you,' demanded the President, 'until I knew we were in secure contact? Uh, did you say *boyfriend*?'

'Yeah?' said Ax, raising an eyebrow. 'Sage.' He shouldn't have confessed about the email, that was a wrong step. He felt this interview was going to be full of them.

'Sage Pender is *your boyfriend*?' The President looked extremely taken aback. His ruddy complexion had darkened alarmingly. Oh please, thought Ax.

'Yes, Mr Eiffrich. Sage is my boyfriend, Fiorinda is our girlfriend. It's a bisexual ménage à trois; it's a little uncommon, I suppose. I'm sorry, I didn't mean to shock you: it's public knowledge, not a secret.'

'No no. That's okay. I just, er, I just hadn't picked up on that.'

The President sipped his whiskey, and looked into the cold fireplace.

'Well, now you know,' he said, having recovered his poise. 'Phil tells me you guys have been very helpful, but so far you can only confirm what we suspected ... I've done a lot of reading about fusion consciousness, Ax. I considered it my business. I've talked to our guys, I've talked to the guys who say that the Vireo project is impossible, and I guess I can follow the arguments, I have a postgrad in chemistry, far back in the mists of time. But the occult tradition, Jeez, that's a nightmare. Spirit journeys, Kabbalistic rituals, voudoun, psychic aura – is that *aura*, or *aurae*, in the plural? Clairvoyance, card tricks, blood and entrails.' He shook his head in disgust. 'It's a mess. Not only distasteful:

unintelligible. No structure, mutually unintelligible competing structures. There's no way to make head or tail of it. I badly need someone who comes from there, and has been involved in the . . . the business in Europe, who can *tell* me.'

Over my dead body is that someone going to be Fiorinda, thought Ax.

'It's *aurae*,' he said, 'but you hear both. Mr Eiffrich, I don't think I understand the situation. If you have convincing reason to believe that your fusion scientists, financed by your Defense Department, are attempting to weaponise natural magic, surely that's enough? Surely you can close them down – to say the least.'

'It's a delicate matter to investigate.'

'Do you know if the Vireo Lake neuronauts are being selected for, er, psi talent? I'd say that would be a smoking gun.'

Mr Eiffrich looked at Ax severely, and did not answer this question. 'I have one undisputed fact that I consider significant. Did you know the guys at Vireo got hold of Rufus O'Niall's *head*, from your Celtics?'

'I knew it had gone missing,' Ax shrugged. 'It was to be expected.'

The President stared. '*Expected*,' he repeated. 'That's a turn of phrase. We can *expect* the heads of our enemies to become objects of exchange value?'

'It's not unreasonable that they'd want to look at Rufus O'Niall's brain, you know. Did they find anything of interest?'

Mr Eiffrich shook his head. 'Soup, or so I'm reliably informed. It was flash-frozen, but they didn't manage to defrost the soft tissue successfully.'

'Ah, well, too bad.'

'Ax, you make my blood run cold. Okay, then, in that case, I have no evidence of anything improper going on at the Vireo Lake labs, and if there's another lab, so far I can't find it.' He paused, considering his words. 'The situation, Ax, is that I have information, apart from those sacrifices, which strongly suggests that this is going on, and . . . playing with fire will always attract some fools.'

'Does the Fat Boy candidate feature in this information?'

'Hm. We had word-of-mouth testimony, from sources inside the Pentagon if you must know, to the effect there's a Fat Boy in the making. We lost the witness, and all record of the statement. I'm afraid the details are sensitive . . . Could it happen, Ax? I'm at a loss, with the wilder shores of fusion consciousness. I can't tell what they mean when they say this is a genuine possibility—'

'I wouldn't lose sleep,' said Ax. 'Every big theory has its lunatic fringe.'

'Mm . . .' Mr Eiffrich leaned forward, elbows on his knees, nursing his glass. 'Ah, well . . . If I started to tell you the rest of my current problems, we'd be here all night. Things fall apart, Ax.'

'Yeah.'

'Since I took office, I've been a thorn in the side of the people and the vested interests in this country who just *will not read* the writing on the wall, though it's in letters a mile high. But what scares me is the social collapse, inherent with the other problems . . . We didn't reckon for that: now we see what happened in Europe, and we understand it's inevitable. It's hellish. How can we use the tools of civilisation to repair the damage to our ecosystems if civilised society itself is vanishing?'

He took a sip of whiskey. 'You know the most appalling thing? When I was told the fusion consciousness project could be tainted by black magic, *I was relieved.* I thought: way to go, now I can stop them. And I believe I can. When I track down this rogue project, fusion weapon research will be killed stone-dead, never to rise again.'

'But you have no evidence.'

'We'll get there. We're looking at the terrorist group option also, of course, but I'm convinced it has to be our own people. Oh, don't worry. I'm going to stop this. But it will have to be done *sub rosa*. The public mustn't know that this has happened. That's one reason why I called on you, and your partners. My victory will be secret, but the people also have to be convinced. We have to show them another way—'

'As of now, your public seems generally convinced that fusion consciousness power is a good thing. They even like the weapon.'

'Yeah. That's what the polls are telling my advisers, in spades. I don't care how clean and green it is. I am not "against" fusion consciousness science, as some of my detractors claim. But to use *the information*, the pure power of *being* as a weapon of destruction, oh no, no . . . that is utterly forbidden. Do you truly believe in God, Ax?'

'Yes.'

'Then work with me. Help me.'

Whatever happens will happen, thought Ax, and finally, mercifully, it isn't in our hands . . . He decided against trying to convince Mr Eiffrich that he could take refuge with the Lord of the Daybreak, and simply nodded.

'Does Sage believe? I mean, in the conventional sense?'

'You'd have to ask him.'

'Uhuh.' Mr Eiffrich poured himself a little more bourbon and sat back. He smiled. 'My God . . . The last time I saw you, Ax, you'd just been hauled out of a year's brutal imprisonment and you were setting off to invade your own country in a state of barely contained mental and physical collapse. It was the most gallant, bloody-minded stubbornness I ever saw. I hardly thought I'd see you alive again. But you came through . . . It was a fine thing. But recovery from the kind of trauma you had has to be slow. You can play guitar again?'

'Yeah,' said Ax. He stretched out his right hand and flexed it. 'It's better all the time.' Probably his fine motor control would never be *completely* what it had been; but he wasn't going to whine about details.

The President was looking at him with great kindness.

Ax wondered if he should confess that he had no memory of the meeting Mr Eiffrich had described. He had gaps in his record: the days just after the rescue were blank (and most of the invasion too, tell the truth) . . . He had been *frightened* of this meeting. He'd been sure he'd be forced to talk about England; asked to explain what was happening there. He ought to have known better. Kathryn's Uncle Fred can be hasty, he can be intemperate, he's been known to bluster. But he's not a bully, and he's definitely no fool.

'D'you feel like answering me a couple of questions, Ax?'

Ah, shit. Here we go, after all. 'What kind of questions?'

'Secret history, of course . . . *Was* it you and Alain de Corlay behind the operation that wrecked the Channel tunnels beyond repair?'

Alain de Corlay was Ax's counterpart, *enfant terrible* intellectual and sometime front man of the Eurotrash outfit Movie Sucre: currently one of Europe's most formidable techno-green leaders.

'No, that was a group run by one of the French governments, I forget the name . . . one of the four-day efforts, the spring of the year after Dissolution. Alain and I merely collaborated in letting them do it.'

'Ah. But why did he agree to that? I can see *your* reasons.'

'If you want to reduce traffic,' said Ax, 'close some roads. The tunnels were a siphon, drawing a mass of refugees through France to the northern coast and England. When they were gone, that problem dissipated.'

'So, you were to some extent responsible for the Boat People armada that took the eastern route up the Rhine and Rhone and ended up crossing the North Sea?'

'The situation was already there. But yeah, you could say that was one of mine.'

'What can we do about the refugee situation, Ax? It's one of the most intractable problems Europe faces, or it seems so from our perspective. Do you have any ideas?'

'Are you kidding?'

'No I am not *kidding*. I'm not in the mood for kidding.'

'Marshall Plan, Mr President. Rebuild the countries that the refugee hordes are fleeing. I don't even know if it's possible. The environmental devastation is beyond belief, in some places: I've seen it. But you could try.'

'Good words. But for Marshall Aid, the precedent says first there has to be a war.'

'We have wars. Wait for the big one, if you like. You may not have to wait long.'

The President nodded slowly. Both of them looked at the fireplace for a while, in silence. 'My wife gave me this house,' Fred Eiffrich remarked, 'when we married. She died young, you know: Hodgkin's. That's her, on the wall above the fire. It's a good portrait. Our daughter Sally fell to an armed opposition assassin's bullet in Colombia, nearly ten years ago now. She was working with a human rights group. She was twenty-four: hungering and thirsting after justice; I hadn't seen her for eighteen months. I miss them still. I always will.'

Fred Eiffrich had never remarried. He had girlfriends: he was a serial monogamist of discreet Washington matrons, quietly acknowledged, never in the public eye.

A smiling woman in the clothes of thirty years ago looked down on the quiet room. On the mantelshelf her daughter, in a yellow slicker, laughed and leaned over the side of a sailing boat, dark hair whipped in tendrils over her rosy cheeks.

'You're sure I can't tempt you to a little bourbon?'

'Not tonight, thanks. Another time.'

'It's good that you drink. That you're an Islamic prince who takes alcohol, in moderation. An eco-warrior who loves a good car ... in moderation. I want you on my side, Ax. I want you to help me to stop the weapon research: but I want you on my side regardless. The movie's going to be good. It'll raise your profile like nothing else. I want what you did in England presented as an ideal. The rockstar king who rode out the storm, and kept the lights burning. With his queen, the heroine of the resistance; and the very perfect knight who hath achieved the Grail.'

'But first we have to create those fictional characters,' said Ax, dryly. 'Mr Eiffrich, how serious is the problem we have with Lou Branco?'

He thought he could rely on the President having heard the bad news.

'Oh,' Fred Eiffrich glowered. 'Don't worry about Lou. I'll talk to Lou ... And you talk to the people, Ax. Do what you do, be who you are. We have eighteen months.'

'That's when the Vireo Lake project is due to reach critical mass?'

'That's how long I can rely on staying President.'

If you've been talking to the Pres, and your ride went home without you, you get a helicopter with a real human being flying it. Ax sat in the back, in hushed luxury, irritated that he wasn't beside the pilot, and evaluated. Fred Eiffrich has crucial information he's not going to share with us; they're investigating the possibility of a terrorist group (but the high level cover-up suggests otherwise): but not a hint that the President was considering Fiorinda's hypothesis, which Ax thought had to be good news. He believed that Fred Eiffrich's horror of the weapon research was genuine, too genuine for his own good, maybe. Don't protest too hard, or they might take your God game away from you ... But no, Fred was too wise to be caught like that. Hence the imported ex-dictator, who will take the flak, if the propaganda campaign proves unpopular ... No problem. Thinking like Ax Preston for a moment, it's not when you're 'in power': it's when the powerful have a use for you, that you get a chance to pursue the agenda—

He had called Sage, *my boyfriend*. Oops. I should have cleared that with Harry! But the claim warmed his heart, futile as it might be. The City of the Plain lay beneath him: a great shimmering raft of stars, setting sail into the dark ocean. He called the house at Sunset and learned that Fiorinda and Sage had not come back. He wasn't concerned. One *good* thing about loving those two is that you really don't have to worry about them being waylaid by the bad guys. Pity the bad guys.

He felt he shouldn't pursue them, but he didn't want to go home alone—

A gleam in his eye, he tapped the button on his armrest.

'Hey, pilot?'

'Yes, Mr Preston? It's Lieutenant Joe Kevah here, it's a pleasure to be your sky-driver, sir. What can I do for you?'

'Change of plan, lieutenant. I want you to take me to a different address.'

'Is that the native English, that left-tenant? Not Sunset Cape, sir?'

'Yeah, that's native English. D'you know a gated place called Copperhead Glen?'

'I know it. Out along 101, near the state park. If you mean the Copperhead where Mr Branco lives?'

'That's right. You don't have to wait.'

'I'm supposed to see you safe home, sir.'

'I can get my people to come and fetch me. If I need you, I'll call Bellevue.'

'Sure thing.'

The machine touched down, with a minimum of fuss, on the pad outside the enclave gatehouse. Ax let it lift and soar away, Joe Kevah waving cheerily, then he strolled up to the gates, through the razor-sharp shadows of the floodlighting. He parleyed with the intercom, feeling guns trained on him, and thinking, what a way to live. But they had armed guards at Sunset Cape too, it's the world we live in. The guards called the Branco house. A delay followed, during which the men came out of their dug-out and talked to Mr Preston through the bars. They were hard rock fans. They said he didn't look like Axl Rose. They wanted to know, what did something like Yap Moss do to the Chosen's music? Did that make you feel like, you were *real*?

Sigh.

The message came back. Mr Branco will be home shortly; would Mr Preston please come to the house.

Lou Branco's house was behind more massive walls. The front gates opened for Ax and he strolled up between shaven lawns. Sprinklers hissed; there was a beautiful scent of jasmine. The great money man lives alone. He has ex-wives and grown-up children, but they don't visit. He has a father in a nursing home, far gone in decrepitude. He's heterosexual, but has no regular girlfriend (apparently he prefers to be a paying customer). No one calls him a friend. A lot of movie people, virtual and otherwise, hate his guts, because his crude and poor taste *dominates* the kind of work they can do; and because he's as unpleasant to deal with as a spoilt toddler. But everyone does his bidding, because he has a stunning instinct for making money.

Sounds like a lonely kind of life.

The door of the main house was open. A barefoot teenage boy stood there, dressed in soccer shorts and a faded Brazil T-shirt. Everyone was in bed, because Mr Branco had not been expected home. The boy was the housekeeper's nephew, he had been watching the tv in Mr Branco's kitchen, he was allowed to do that, it was a better tv than his tía had in her cottage. The guards had reached Mr Branco on his cell, and Mr

Branco had called here to say he would be back very soon ... Ax followed his garrulous guide through to the kitchen, which he felt was a better option than sitting alone in the lounge.

The kid's name was Daniel Ortega Morales, and he was far too young and full of himself to give a shit for the warlord of Yap Moss. He was not a servant, he was living here because there had been trouble at home about his school results. He had left, and his father, who had left the family years ago, had refused to take him in, so he was living with his tía. She kept wanting him to behave like a houseboy, so he could get a job: but he didn't know how, and he didn't want to learn. What he really wanted to do was act. Or maybe play guitar.

The housekeeper, who did not consider it was her role to get up in the middle of the night, had called from the cottage and ordered Daniel to lay out snacks for the visitor. Mr Branco would be expecting this. Daniel didn't have a fuck of a clue. He opened the doors of cupboards as he talked, with an air of aggrieved helplessness. Okay, said Ax, I'll show you something. When I was starting out, I worked as a short order cook. You'll hate me for saying this, but it's good to have a fall-back.

Lou Branco arrived some thirty minutes later to find Ax Preston, still in evening dress but having shed his black jacket, in possession of the kitchen, supervising the preparation of a perfect Spanish tortilla (it takes a good frying pan, good oil; a blender, parboil the potatoes before you put them near the fry, and do everything really slowly). Mr Branco had changed his clothes somewhere since the Bellevue barbecue. He stood in the doorway, very confused by this scene.

'Hey,' said Ax, 'there you are, Lou. I dropped round, on the chance you might have time to talk. I've been thinking: about the bootleg remix video ... Great idea. I've been looking at Harry's demographic maps. Where are you planning to sneak it out?'

There's an interesting moment, when you wait to see how the dice will fall—

'Well, hi, Ax,' said Mr Branco, and turned furiously on the boy, 'Daniel, what's the matter with you. Where are your shoes? Did you offer Mr Preston a drink? You think I'm paying you to stand around staring at my guests?'

Daniel at least had the wits not to protest that he wasn't on the payroll.

'I'm very sorry, Mr Branco.'

'He's been fixing me some supper,' said Ax, 'maybe you'd care to join me?'

'You're a night owl, eh, Ax? Like me. Okay, lemme get my shit together, let's discuss. Prepare to learn. The US of A is a much bigger cabbage patch. Fuck, *California* is a much bigger cabbage patch than you have back in England.'

Mr Branco went to fetch some hard copy. He sat at the breakfast bar, took out his palmtop, and raised a spreadsheet on the excellent screen of the kitchen tv. It was a transformation. Social niceties were a closed book to this man, but with his tools in his hands he was unstoppable, amoral, stunningly acute, genuinely fascinating: and thankfully, Ax had done enough of this sort of thing in his misspent career to be able to appear to keep up.

'Ax,' said Lou, 'I have to tell you, as a rockstar, you'd make a good analyst.'

'Yeah, well, you have to learn a little about marketing when you're running something like the Reich. The tortilla's getting cool, Lou.'

Daniel, aggrieved at losing Ax's attention, had brought over the frying pan and plonked it down, with the bowl of salad. 'You should bring plates,' Ax prompted him softly. 'Silverware. Water, glasses. No, straight glasses—'

They ate, they talked. Lou looked up, and exclaimed with satisfaction, 'Hey, I've got the king of England, having a midnight feast with me!' Struck by the presence of Daniel Ortega (the kid didn't know he should leave, he was sitting sulking in the background), he cried, 'Daniel, pull up a stool. Take a plate, have a slice of tortilla . . . This is what I love about the story,' he said to Ax. 'How you put the drop-outs back to work. Got them doing what they could do, paid them in beer and fried potatoes. Give them dignity, that's what we need over here, my opinion. I wanna have Harry work that into the movie, but he'll say it isn't art, it isn't *romantic*. Daniel's like family to me.'

'Right.'

'Nothing funny, though.'

'Of course not.'

'Not that I've anything against gays. Now, let's do the figures on—'

It was very late when Ax walked out of Copperhead Glen. Sage and Fiorinda were coming to pick him up, but he'd told them he'd be outside. He didn't trust those two not to give his newly turned money man the *you are a non person* treatment. At which they so excel. Besides, he liked being out in the heat of the night. He walked up to the turning circle at the end of the access road, under the misted stars: thinking about his father. In ways, Ax's entire career had been based on being different from his dad: Dan Preston, pub-culture layabout, shameless grifter, dead two years now. But you get older and you understand that you can't get away from those tumbling dice. Dan would have understood this episode; and so many others. You get that *white light* feeling, and you know the cards are with you.

The toad's in a hole. He can't possibly want to be in this hole, pissing off the President, all Hollywood sniggering behind his back. He's not stupid. Offer him an easy way out, it's better than even money he will take it. All you need is the DNA, or whatever it takes, for seeing chance as opportunity—

And what kind of world will it be when the real revolution takes hold? When we live in a palimpsest of minds, competing and co-operating to form consensus reality: and no final barrier between thought and 'material' things? The answer's obvious, it will be this world. The same place we were living in before, seen in a new light—

Someone's watching me. He felt the presence with a soldier's instincts, and moved so he could look behind him without seeming to. There was someone standing under a tree by the helipad. Starlight glinted on a stubby rifle, cradled against the figure's chest. A raw-boned, rough-headed outline, naggingly familiar. Hm. I *know* that guy. But what's he doing here? The shadow turned and looked his way, steady gleam in hollow eyes.

And vanished, as the Rugrat zoomed up.

They leapt out and grabbed him.

'Don't *do* that!' gasped Sage. 'Don't do that to me! Please!'

'What's the matter? I came here by presidential helicopter, and I'm standing under a gun emplacement. What could happen?'

'No, you're not,' said Fiorinda, 'the gun emplacement is over there ... You can't frighten us like that, Ax, you can't vanish off the screen, *please* don't do it again—'

They parted from the three-person embrace, not knowing where it could go; a little shy. Ax decided that he wouldn't tell them, especially not Fiorinda, about the other presence. Nothing had happened, and it would cause needless panic.

'How did you get on with Branco?' asked Sage.

'Fixed, I hope. I've been discussing where we put out that white-label video.'

'You, beyond belief. What about President Eiffrich?'

'Not bad. But no news, just confirmation of Harry and Roche's story.'

Rule One for dealing with the quantum computer: don't raise the subject of Celtic sacrifice unless someone else raises it first; don't mention Fiorinda's magic, and play down what happened to Sage. This is to avoid confusion in the populace: the Fat Boy candidate doubtless has the lowdown on our bodhisattva and our lady. Rule Two, Chairman Ax says there are no rules. Say what you like, do what occurs to you. Assume everything's on the record, and be yourselves. But remember, it knows we are here, it *wants* us here. Watch out for secret messages, watch for things that look out of place.

Chip Desmond and Kevin Verlaine, aka The Adjuvants, had no trouble with Fiorinda's version of what was going on. It seemed to them both plausible and interesting. They weren't scared. Allowing that Ax might be phased by supernatural conflict (though Ax is *powerful*, and that goes for all the dimensions), what, pray, is going to get through Sage and Fiorinda?

They played their set at the Steel Door, unaware that two of their leaders were having trouble outside, and, as usual, more or less oblivious to the presence of the audience. The applause from the whackily garbed mosh surprised them, and they were moved to hang around for the main event. The Rectal Vixens turned out to be bog-standard grunge. But their look was okay.

The Adjuvants' crew, hired hands under the supervision of one of Doug Hutton's men, packed up and departed. The Adjuvants joined a dressing room scene involving the Vixens and their entourage. Pills and poppers were freely dispensed, tequila flowed. The English rolled up contraband Bristol skunk to pay their way.

'What was that last thing you did?' asked Jody, the Vixen's singer. 'Fuck.'

'Autocondimentation?' suggested Verlaine. 'I think.'

'Whatever. That was fucking esoteric. I thought it would never end.'

'That's how you're supposed to feel,' explained Chip. '"Autocon" is designed to cause desperation. It's an expression of the feeling you get when you try to open a plastic sachet of ketchup in a half-derelict Welcome Break motorway services where everything tastes of salad cream, in the early hours on a cold, rainy night. Few people appreciate us, on a global scale, but we know we're right.'

'Our art is slavery,' said Verlaine. 'Our life is art.'

'Hey, I don't need no fanbase!' said Chip. 'I have driven a Number 17 bus!'

'I have swabbed cholera patients,' boasted Ver. 'They struggled in vain.'

'We have stacked the sandbags of solidarity, in the shop doorways of hope.'

'Fuck. Have you guys ever thought of selling a few records?'

'We're not old enough to earn our living,' explained Chip, taking offence.

'*Has* Sage turned gay?' asked someone else, growing impatient with this banter.

'Nah,' said Chip, accepting another popper and applying it to his throat.

'He's a miserable sod,' said Verlaine. 'It's all lies.'

'What about the hedgehog farming?'

'Oh, now, *that*'s true,' Chip confirmed, with an air of relief. 'The boss wouldn't lie about hedgehogs. That game is huge in England. Urban gardeners were crying out for them after Dissolution, when the use of slug pellets became a capital crime. It snowballed. There's a hedgehog fancy now. Shows, breeds—'

'Siamese hedgehogs,' chipped in Verlaine, necking tequila freely. 'Differently abled symbiote fleas you can get for them; it's a whole industry.'

'What about the group marriage?'

The Adjuvants said solemnly, in unison, 'We can't talk about that.'

The Vixens were tall and huskily built. They wore a band uniform of loose dark T-shirts, gold-trimmed, and baggy shorts of unequal length, also gold-trimmed. Jody and Rex wore their hair combed back and clubbed in the nape of the neck. Lex was slapheaded, naturally. All three had light voices, smooth faces and serious boobs, but they did not seem to be dykes; they seemed more like minor-league Sumo wrestlers. Rex, the drummer, astride a chair turned backwards, brawny arms folded, stared back at the English youths, assessing their anatomy with equal frankness—

'You two still have the meat and potatoes, don't you?'

'Er, what?'

'We can tell. Don't have to check your shorts, it's written all over you.'

'You've all had the surgery, then?'

Laughter went round the room. 'Nah. We've had the *treatment*,' said Lex.

'Nobody has the surgery, now. Only perverts have the surgery.'

'Nah,' said Verlaine. 'We don't need to change. We like being boys.'

'We're just never going to become *blokes*,' said Chip. 'We're into neoteny.'

'You should do it,' said Jody. 'It's the most fucking liberating thing, to watch your dick melting away. It's self-sculpture. It's what you've been looking for without having the concept. You're unfulfilled, you're halfway uncertains, I know you are.' He, or s/he, grinned warmly. 'Hell, I'd like to convert you both, *right now*—'

Hm. This begins to sound like Jehovah's Witness territory ... Chip grinned warmly back, and gave Ver a swift *make our excuses and leave*? Verlaine concurred. But in one of those puzzling shifts that happen when you're drunk and spaced, especially in a place you don't know, instead of leaving, they found themselves in a corridor they didn't recognise, walking up and down with the fourth Vixen, the one they hadn't noticed. S/he told them to come to the party, and gave them an address.

Next thing they knew they were on the sidewalk, alone in the dark, in a different derelict neighbourhood in the vast city of the angels. No sign of the Steel Door, or the Rectal Vixens, or any rich kid punters; a dim knowledge that they had come here in a cab, but the cab was now gone. All they had was a scrap of matchbook, on which the fourth Vixen had written the address of the party.

'At least it's not raining,' said Chip.

'It never rains in southern California. We must be here.'

Chip agreed with this deduction. 'Otherwise we wouldn't have got out of the cab.'

They saw a lighted building. It was tall and smart, though not a skyscraper; it looked recently renovated. The name on the plate outside the lobby matched the address on the matchbook, so they went in. There was no sign of life. The renovations were very recent; the builders didn't seem to have moved out yet.

'Top floor,' said Verlaine. 'I hope the lifts work.'

'Elevators ... Ver, I think there were only three Vixens.'

'What d'you mean? So, it was one of the other dudes. Guest list.'

The lifts were not working, so they climbed the stairs: talking cheerfully to avoid the silence, which can become threatening when you're a little dazed and confused.

'He hasn't changed, has he? He's still totally our Aoxomoxoa.'

'Hence the expression, Zen *Self*, dork—'

They fell silent. It couldn't have been more than four floors, but the climb took forever. Chip's mood plunged into one of those my-life-means-nothing chasms. He was a futile hanger-on, an overgrown pageboy at the court of King Ax (who has abdicated) ... Verlaine started thinking about Rox. Roxane Smith had been his lover, parent, mentor, patron at the time of Dissolution. When Ver and Chip had become an item, s/he had bowed out with *incredible* grace. Our court philosopher, the elder of the tribe. *Rox is getting old.* Food stains, confusion. Oh God, how long before I'm visiting the nursing home ... The mainstay of his life was giving way.

They reached the top floor and faced each other. Telepathy artefacts. They were both veterans of the Zen Self experiments: Chip had dropped out, Verlaine might yet travel further along the path that Sage had taken. They recognised the penumbra of something psycho-physically untoward here.

'It's a very quiet party. What d'you think? Are we onto something?'

'It's a hedgehog party. Uncertain weirdness fills the air.'

'Would physical contact be in order, young Merry?'

They approached the double doors to the loft arm in arm and pushed them open.

They were facing a wall of windows, mainly dark, with patches of twinkling light. The room that held this darkness was big as a barn and almost bare of furniture. There were naked flambeaux hanging, on long chains, from the exposed timbers of the cathedral roof. Heavy-scented smoke wreathed in the air and coiled across the floor, which was covered in a white layer of plaster dust. In the middle of the floor stood a framework of builders' ladders and planks. A young woman and a young man were hanging there, he by the wrists, she by the heels, eviscerated, their entrails lying heaped on the floor, their arms and legs split open like anatomy drawings. The dust on the floor was darkly trodden ... insolently, deliberately ... by many footprints, as if a crowd of dancers had just vanished.

'Two out of how many?' whispered Chip. 'Poor kids, God help them.'

It was important not to be awed. Don't get horrified. You must not get horrified.

'Look at the woman, Chip,' said Verlaine. 'Look at her. It's Billy the Whizz.' Billy the sweet-natured party girl, her sugar-blonde hair dripping blood from its sticky strands. She'll never score with Aoxomoxoa now.

'What's the emergency number?'

'You're going to call the police?' breathed Verlaine. 'What, and wait here for them? Chip, *the blood is still running.*'

'I meant the, the Committee number, the one we're supposed to use if anything happens. But you're right. We should call nine one one.'

'I don't trust that fucking Committee; who knows if they're the good guys.'

They stared at each other. 'I don't think we should stay here a moment longer than we have to,' said Chip. 'I don't think we should meet the LA police. But there's one thing we could do, to screw the bastards.'

Fiorinda wouldn't have liked it, Sage would have been noncommittal, but we all have our own cultural ways of obeying instinct, when it comes to opposing malign magic. They got down on their knees, the way they knew Rox would have done, and prayed for the dead. Then they left. They called the police when they had managed to find a lighted street and flag down a yellow cab. They then decided they'd better maintain radio silence, but made a thorough search for the scrap of matchbook that the fourth Vixen had given them. They couldn't find it.

5

November Rain

Chip and Verlaine did not have to go downtown. They were interviewed at Sunset Cape, by Philemon Roche and his partner, then next day by the LAPD, with Harry Lopez and a pair of Digital Artists lawyers in close attendance. The police interview was minimal, and conducted with a veiled resentment which was wounding: in the Reich, the police and Ax's friends had been on the same team. The Adjuvants played innocent in both the sessions – not much of an act; there were no awkward questions.

The night after the police came Fiorinda dozed, trying to carry water in her cupped hands, the drops escaping as tiny wriggling babies, and woke from this task knowing she was alone in the suite. Ax? Sage? No, they're dead, of course. She got up and wandered, the weight of her hair heavy and sticky on her shoulders, laying her palm on each bedroom door, to keep her friends safe. At the bottom of the stairs she sat and thought about poor Billy. Oh, shit, I didn't protect Billy. Did I kill her? Maybe I killed her? She felt guilty, but confused. What am I doing here, what is this place? Why are we here and not in London? There were voices, coming from Allie's office at the back of the front hall. She drifted over there and listened. 'East Hollywood Reformed Mosque. It's a big modern Islamic centre, they'd like you to speak after the Friday prayers. The studio wants you to do this one, it's nonsectarian.'

'What does reformed mean? *Salat*-in-English? I won't do it if I have to make up new-agey prayers, can't stand that. Oh, and I won't dance either ... I've nothing against Sufis, but—'

'No, no, it's kosher—'

Soft laughter.

'Forget I said that,' said Allie's voice. 'Reformed only means the men and women pray together. They asked me how you'd feel, because they know you're rather strict with Fiorinda—'

'Shit. Ouch. Where did that come from?'

'The fact that she never leaves the house without a male family member, or an AI car as equivalent guardian. The fact that she never appears in public as your first lady; and they see her dressing very modestly—'

Fiorinda opened the door. 'Hi Allie.'

Ax gave Allie a glance she understood. She closed her laptop. 'Well, just about finished,' she announced, with false cheer, and quickly left the room

'What's wrong with her?' Fiorinda sat down, trying to think how to recover her position. But Ax knew she had not seen him when she walked in here. She struggled with the inchoate fragments that poured by, jostling for attention. Ax is dead, no he's sitting there, Chip and Verlaine found some bodies, where are we?

'Oh, nothing,' said Ax, calmly. 'How are you, Fio?'

'Yes.' She dug her fingers into her hair, puzzled at the resistance, what is wrong with this hair? It feels horrible . . . 'Ax, d'you think Sage is having a fling with Janelle Firdous? I don't mind. I just need to know what everybody is doing—'

'I'm sure he isn't.'

'He spends a lot of time with her. Billy spent time with Sage, and she's dead.'

'He isn't having a fling with anyone. He's upstairs asleep. Let's go to bed.'

'I thought he wasn't there. Ax, I'm better, really. I'll be better in the morning.'

'I know you will, my little cat. C'mon, upstairs.'

The Rugrat was at Fiorinda's disposal; they hadn't taken Harry up on his promise of more and nicer cars. Sage arrived at the splendid estate of an old friend in a studio limo. His host came to the gatehouse to meet him: a tall, black man, extremely goodlooking, in fabulous physical shape and dressed in perfect casuals. They strolled through the grounds together. This was a beach *and* canyon pad: a rocky valley running straight down to the Pacific, full of specimen trees and majestic groups of beautiful, alien boulders. A small river ran through it, with rainbow-spinning falls spanned by a crystal bridge (the water must cost a fortune).

'Fuckin' shit, Sage! How long you been in town? Why didn't you look me up before? How long's it been, shit, ten – twelve years? Where's the mask?'

'I don't do that anymore. Yeah, too long, Laz.'

'You're looking good, bro,' said Lazarus, politely. 'Time has been kind.'

'You too.'

His name was Lazarus Catskill, just *Laz* to the fans. He and Sage had been newly famous bad boys when they met on the Heads' notorious US tour. For a few years they'd crossed paths, the way you do . . . Then Sage had vanished into Crisis Europe and his revolutionary adventure, and Lazarus had taken the industrial route. He'd made the transition into movies and tv, become unbelievably successful and was now more or less a god.

Laz wanted to show off his Peter Pan features so they did a tour, reminiscing about the outrageous days as they had fun with the treetop rollercoaster, the vintage animatronic gunfighters, the secret passages, the holodek and immix room in the caverns behind the waterfall. On the sweep outside the house there was a gold panning alley: a stepped, wooden trough knocked together with rusty metal; a diverted offshoot of the river running into it from above, along a crooked little aqueduct on stilts. Ancient pans, lanterns, picks and shovels were on display—

'Is this a real fake ancient Californian diorama? Or just a replica?'

'This is authentic man, there *was* gold in my valley. You got to try this. This is the greatest game. You have to pick up that rock and dump it in the chute.'

'And then what happens?'

'Something cool. It's the best feature of my whole theme park.'

Sage looked at the boulder, the boulder looked at Sage. Fucking hope there isn't a lot of gold in that mountain. Ah well, do what god says. He picked up the rock, made it look easy, dumped it in the trough, and *wham*, a section of the aqueduct opened and drenched him in icy water. Laz ran indoors, cackling in glee. Sage ran after him, cursing and swearing vengeance. A maid was waiting with an armful of fluffy white towels and a merry smirk: this must be one of those jokes that never stales.

Laz tossed the towels to Sage. 'Bring us some coffee, Maria. And cookies—'

He led the way into a baronial hall, panelled in carven oak, with tiers of lambent stained-glass lancets, and lit a fire in the great hearth with a snap of his fingers. Sage saw that he was going to have to take his shirt off, which he did not want to do.

'*Jeeezus*! Fuckin' mother of shit! What did that? Shark attack?'

'You could say so. Hey, I did not lose. You shoulda seen the shark.'

Lazarus gaped in awe at the ropes of purplish scar. I'm getting rid of them, thought Sage, towelling his head. Call me childish, but if I ever have any loose money—

'Well, my God, Sage. Thank the Lord you're still with us . . . Here's a dry tee. You want to change your pants? I guess only your shirt got wet, you jumped so fast.'

It was a Laz Catskill T-shirt. Childishly, he decided not to bother. 'I won't catch cold.'

The coffee and the cookies came, the maid took away the towels and Sage's wet shirt. The heat from the gas flames fought with the frost of the air-conditioning, and the former bad boys sat quietly sipping coffee. 'You like the stain-glass? You like the oak? All from Europe: shipped over when the fucking place collapsed. You wouldn't believe the stuff I picked up. I had to tussle with my conscience over some of it, no way it was the legitimate owners selling: but shit, it's safer over here, right?'

'Absolutely.'

'Kaya will be pissed that she missed meeting you.' Kaya was the god's wife, A-list R&B diva: she had changed him mightily, it was said. They had a stable relationship, one child a couple of years old.

Sage nodded. 'Sorry I missed her, too.' He imagined Kaya probably spent her life trying to keep Laz away from his former associates and his evil past.

'And you got your hands fixed,' said Laz. 'Nice job. I heard you went to Japan. What made you do that? You always swore you never would.'

'Everybody changes,' said Sage, trying to fit together the raucous brother he remembered with this family-values perfect specimen. I went where all the colours blend into one, Laz, he thought. And I came back with these hands . . . But no. I don't know you, and if I wanted to confide, something tells me this is not the setting.

'So that's where the loot went, huh? I heard you were broke—'

'Flat busted. The yachts, the drugs, the hospital bills. It adds up.'

Laz nodded, but he was staring, gravely fascinated, unable to take his eyes off Sage's hands. 'Hey!' He touched the braided ring. 'Whoa, you *married*?'

'Betrothed.' Fiorinda and Ax would say plain no to that question, but he liked *betrothed*. Nothing to do with a vision of Fiorinda in a cloud of white tulle, no no.

'Well who's the laydee? Uh, I guess that's not Mary—?'

Mary Williams had been Sage's girlfriend when he was a teenage junkie; she was the mother of his son. They'd broken up before Marlon was born, but he had carried the festering corpse of that relationship around with him for years, a sick obsession. The worst things he'd done in his life he'd done to Mary ... 'No,' he said, jolted by the question. 'Not Mary.' This gig was turning out to be a series of pokes in the eye for the former Aoxomoxoa. Is that suspicious?

Or merely inevitable.

'I heard you were in a threesome with the revolutionary king of England.'

'Something like that,' said Sage, bracing himself for further pratfalls.

Lazarus had very dark skin that glowed, like his whole presence, with Hollywood perfection. His eyes were light hazel shading to green: an arresting effect. For a long moment, he considered Sage, 'Who the fuck knows the truth about anyone?' he said at last, without a smile. 'Like you said, we all go through changes.'

They finished their coffee and toured the house, checking out the wired rooms where *Lazi and Kaya* conducted the obligatory reality show. Lazarus recommended the life of a post-modern movie star highly. 'All I have to do is be me,' he said, with unaffected charm. 'No script, no acting talent required! Refresh my avatar when they tell me: and maybe twice a year I put out a single, which goes platinum to the nth.'

'You don't tour?'

'Shit, no. Those days are gone, man. The security got unbelievable.'

'Well, it sounds thrilling. What d'you think about the movie, anyway?'

'Harry Lopez, isn't it? He's the golden boy: it'll be a big fat success.'

The shirt reappeared, freshly washed and crisply ironed. Sage's humble auto was summoned to the carriage sweep; Lazarus came out to see him off.

'You could make a new start,' he said. 'It'd be cool to have you around. You know, we might have more in common than you think.'

'Oh, really?'

Lazarus nodded, with a big perfect white smile and sober eyes. 'Yeah, really. Hey, promotion takes it out of you; do you guys feel like unwinding? I have a cabin you could borrow. It's pretty, peaceful and commuting distance, we go up there when we can't get away, like *away*, you know. Great little coffee shop in the village too, you should check out their live music ... How about it?'

'We might take you up on that,' said Sage. 'Thanks.'

Sage sat by the dry fountain-pool in the courtyard at Sunset Cape, thinking about that meeting with his old acquaintance, and the memories it had invoked: the several hells he had escaped from. Ah, but those Peter Pan features! Nice cage you got, Laz ... Dilip came by. They sat together, on the rim of amber stone, and DK broke the news that he was dying. He said he didn't mind. He didn't want to leave the party, but he felt that it was time. He had been HIV-positive for eighteen years, nearly a third of his life, and he'd been very well for most of that, but he was *tired*.

'I want you to do something for me,' he said. 'When we get back to England, I want you to talk to Olwen Devi—'

'Okay,' said Sage, with a good idea of what was coming. 'What am I to say?'

'That I want to die trying. I want to be in the Zen Self lab, at the end. I want her to give me a massive dose of snap, put me under the scanner and watch it happen.'

Snapshot was the nickname of the formidable drug cocktail the Zen Selfers used to facilitate their path to fusion consciousness.

Sage managed to laugh. 'Oh, I get it. You're going after the unclaimed prize.'

'You betcha,' said DK, grinning. 'Will you do that for me, my lord?'

'Olwen won't like it. She's going to call it assisted suicide. But I'll try.'

They hugged: Dilip was like dry leaves. 'You're sure we'll get back to England?'

The mixmaster shrugged, already indifferent. 'I'm sure some of us will. If the doomsday scenario gets us first, you are absolved.' He lay back and gazed into the pearlised evening sky. The day had been hot and calm, nothing to shift the smog. 'I'm glad to be in California again. I've had good times on this crazy, corrupt and golden shore. Ah, long ago.'

'Have you told the others?'

'Not yet. I plan to do it by degrees. Everyone knows I'm in a low energy phase, and that's enough for a while.' He sighed. 'It will be hard to tell Allie. I'm an old man, and now I feel it, but she doesn't see it.'

'This could still *be* a low energy phase. An' there must be new and easier drugs, fuck, this is California—'

Not for Dilip. He'd never had any luck with the newer treatments; he'd been seropositive too long. But you can't help hoping.

'Tree-hugging conservative,' said DK, affectionately. 'You never want anything to change, oh master of change. But the sword outwears the sheath. These times! Whoo, it has been punishing, riding the death of Babylon, but I would not have missed our glory days. I've never been so high as with Ax.' He reached over his head and gripped Sage's hand. 'I'll go indoors now.'

Sage stayed where he was, crosslegged on the rim of the pool, gazing at the tumult of colour where the crimson bougainvillaea spilled over the wall. He tried to think about Dilip Krishnachandran's beautiful life: artist of friendship, lover of the world, a true adept of the *dao* of fun. All he could feel was loss. The gatehouse floodlights came on, because the evening was growing dim, and suddenly he was plunged into utter blackness. There was a shift of orientation: not facing the same way, and I'm indoors, not outdoors. Fiorinda's voice said, softly, '*Hello*?' He felt his own surprise; and an inexplicable dread. 'Hi, baby, what are you doing here?' He heard her step. She was in his arms like thistledown, and he knew she'd come to say goodbye (where was she going? That wasn't included) but all he could see was blackness—

Gone. He was back in the pastel courtyard in California; and *that* was a snapshot flashback. He'd taken so much of the fucking stuff, in the last phase of the Zen Self, he supposed he'd be getting flashes all his life. Was that a glimpse of the future, something from the past, something that will never happen—?

He realised that there was someone behind him.

He did not look round. He saw, with the hyperreal clarity of internal vision, the man who was standing there: raw-boned, middle-aged bruiser in battered jeans and a fringed Celtic mantle, with a broadsword at his back and an assault rifle in his arms. It was Fergal Kearney – the Irish musician whose dead body Rufus O'Niall had used as a disguise. He was haggard as a corpse, and his breath was carrion.

'Is that you, Fergal?' But no, that's not Fergal. '*Rufus*? Is that you?'

'Aye ... ' The crunch of a heavy footfall, shifting on gravel. 'Fergal Kearney has no more use fer this stinking carcase. Since I took it from him, I must wear it now.'

'Would you mind telling me what the fuck you are doing here?'

He had the impression that the ghost took proud offence. 'I'm here to guard and protect my daughter, Aoxomoxoa. And I'll thank you not to get in my way.'

'Ooh, I'm *not to get in your way*? Rufus, I think we've had that conversation—'

The vision was gone.

Very strange.

What do they mean, these phantoms of the mind? Fiorinda had not mentioned Fergal Kearney's ghost since Baja. If he'd understood her, she'd seen the visitation as benign ... but he wouldn't tell her about this. She'd come back from the shock of Billy's death; he wasn't going to risk sending her into fugue again. So what was that? A warning of some kind: he felt warned. He was starting to feel he would *really* like to get out of California, if only they could persuade Fiorinda to leave . . .

But what does it mean, if I have this mindless urge to run for my life? He dropped to the ground and went into the house.

The avatar tests came around, delays and difficulties vanishing now that Lou Branco was back on board. Harry had impressed on them that this day was a *very big deal* in the virtual movies, the schematic equivalent of weeks or months of action in front of the cameras. Custom-scanned characters signalled an important project, and this was the live performance. It was traditional, technically irrelevant, but actually a movie-breaker: you knew where you were on the status tree by looking at who turned up. You'll be performing for the stars and money-mavins and the hot mediafolk, he said, as much as for the lasers: and they know their stuff, they're very sharp, even the ones you'd least suspect—

Then he was afraid he'd scared them, and back-pedalled madly.

It's nothing. It doesn't matter. Just be yourselves—

Limos were sent for them at a viciously early hour and they were on the Golden State Freeway soon after dawn. At the entrance to the studio village they had to wait for someone to open up, and had time to appreciate the Abe Stevens quote, worked in metal in the arch over the gates: Digital Artists' mission statement:

> *A rock is a rock, a tree is a tree,*
> *Shoot it in Griffith Park.*

Griffith Park itself, the green oasis somewhat smaller than it had been before Silicon Hollywood arrived, made a peaceful backdrop to the concrete plains of parking, the dorms with their leisure facilities and mall; the stark inventory hangars; the industrial units where code-monkeys slaved. The theatre allotted to them was reached through Inventory C, the biggest building in the village: where custom objects were being scanned into code. Every virtual movie needs a few new properties.

Harry was nowhere to be seen. His assistant, a charming, ditzy young woman named Julia, apologised for him profusely: a more efficient girl handed out name tags. The radical rockstars nibbled pastries from the breakfast trolley and wandered. They'd done a studio tour, but they hadn't been back here since. The inventory had everything, from full-size trees to torn and bleeding human body parts. Rob and the Powerbabes stopped beside a shabby old armchair standing in state on a circular flatbed, ready for the lasers. There was something familiar—

'Hey,' said Dora, 'mister? Is this chair for our movie?'

'Yes, Ms ... Devine,' said the techie, checking her tag. 'Custom scanned, from-real. This is the armchair for the basement in the Snake Eyes house on the Lambeth Road in London, England, where Ax laid his plans for the Reich.'

'Is that what he was doing?' said Rob. 'I thought he was putting his moves on a certain red-headed babe. But, er, this is not the real, actual chair—?'

He had visions of that lunatic Harry Lopez scouring South London for Few memorabilia and shipping the stuff over by the containerload—

'We threw out a chair like that,' mused Cherry. 'I *think*. Years ago—'

'Well, yeah. This one we bought from a thrift store, and worked on it to make it like the original. I have to say, we really bless you guys for all the news footage, and those natural-environment videos in your homes.'

'We did it just for you,' said Felice.

'Uhuh. Frequently we have to reverse-engineer, from the code patch to the story content, because it's impossible to get the object to scan: and if you do too much of that the quality goes. We use a piece of code that was a suppurating sore from a horror-medical; the firing values say it makes a sunset effect, but something's *off*—'

'Gross.'

'No, ma'am. Just a little *off*: cartoony. It's kinda mysterious, nobody really understands it except the qualia coders, they're the ones who kick up hell when that happens. The dcd code, direct cortical delivery, will give this the qualia of a real object, and then the emotional track will make it deliver what the scene requires. You see, what it says on the gates, that's not really true: a rock is never just a rock. A chair is not a chair, it's an experience. It might be *the chair that nobody noticed*, or *the chair that was filled with horror*, or *the chair where I sat when I first said "I love you" to my baby* ... But direct cortical, what you guys call *immix* in Europe, we don't do that here. The people who do it are mostly freelance, hotshots like Janelle Firdous, too good to be tied to the studio.'

He made some adjustments to the rows of toggles on his long desk, watching waveforms on the monitors above.

'Yeah, mm. Janelle is pretty much god. I've met her. She's a nice lady.'

They watched the chair as it waited humbly to be zapped with fellow feeling: cameraderie for a copy of something once part of their lives; waiting to be copied itself, into the brain of the machine. 'Hey,' said Cherry, 'if it gets good notices, will it be a virtual sofa next time? With a hot love scene happening on it?'

This technician wasn't strong on humour. Maybe the tone of voice didn't translate. 'Uh, probably this exact scan is a one-off. But pieces of it might turn up again—'

'Like pus in the sky,' murmured Dora. 'But you don't do that to our avatars?'

'Not my department, but you guys have a contract, don't you?'

'No substantial reuse,' said Felice.

'Right ... I'm warming up now. You can stay, but please use your eyeshields.'

They moved on, exchanging glances: there's nothing here for us. We don't want to get mulched down to pixels. We'll stick with the music biz.

The scanning theatre was *uncannily* like a *Star Trek* transporter room, except for the raked seats that surrounded the flatbed. It filled up while the techies were doing their final checks: Digital Artists hotshots and Hollywood liberal luminaries elbowing for the best seats. Harry seemed to be doing well. Puusi Meera and Janelle Firdous chose their spot with care, face-on to the laser engineers in their box up above. Kathryn Adams arrived with media friends (in working life she was a journalist). Her uncle had returned to Washington after Memorial Day Weekend: she was staying in Los Angeles. She'd convinced her news syndicate they needed the 'Ax Preston comes to Hollywood' story; in depth.

'The whole operation is *so fucking perverse*,' muttered Chip, who was suffering badly from audition nerves.

'We are to be punished for our art,' Verlaine told him, in hollow tones. 'The lasers rip us up and suck us into the machines: but only simulacra come back, that's what they don't tell you. This is it. Farewell, Merry my lad.'

'Fuck off.'

'Okay!' cried Harry, '*please*, ladies and gentlemen, I don't have to tell you this but I will anyway, *use your eyeshields*. If you are seated by an exit, and you aren't fit for those duties, speak to one of the cabin staff. Strap yourselves in. We have lift-off.'

No make-up, no script, no music. Just be yourself. You read from an autocue (something personal, that you had provided). You move around as you like, and the feed in your ear tells you if you should do something else. You get a 'rehearsal', then you do it over again for the lasers. On the flatbed you don't need an eyeshield; the only danger is of stray beams escaping into the audience. There's an element of performance, but it's the technicians who decide if your soul is stealable. If it is, you come back another day to get sunk in a tank of electrolytic goo and the avatar is made. If you can't be mugged, that's the end of your career.

Harry had spent the morning dealing with terrible crises, such as Puusi's favourite brand of spring water failing to turn up. He was a wreck. He sat with Ax and Sage and Fiorinda in the character-test holding area down the front, trembling. 'We can afford a couple of failures,' he muttered, 'it happens, about one in ten. There are big stars who never made it across the divide. We can paste the faces and gaits from file, onto crash-dummies . . .' Crash-dummies were the virtual studio's equivalent of central casting. 'You know we had to audition live human actors at the start? Did you hear that story? Screen Actors Guild insisted, but we're *still using the same thirty scans*, half male, half female. You never need something you can't find the code for. Thirty people is all we'll ever need, for all human variety: isn't that amazing?'

'Amazing.'

The process sounded simple but was *interminable*, worse than the weariest recording session; however, all went well until Harry's running order (which had a rationale known only to Harry) hit Allie Marlowe. Allie couldn't do it. Five takes, worse results. In their raked seats the demi-gods and emperors murmured, holding up their eyeshields like opera glasses, comparing notes and turning down their thumbs. Allie was mortified, on the brink of tears. 'Fuck this,' muttered Ax to Sage. 'C'mon. Let's tell her she doesn't have to do it.' They advanced on Allie and took her out of the theatre. Fiorinda had a better idea. She got next to Harry, who had gone off to be alone on the steps up to the flatbed and was sitting there looking tragic.

'Bully her.'

'Oh, no, Fiorinda,' said Harry woefully. 'It's not like that. The test is objective. It's a psychophysical and somatic scan that picks up the actor's specific, individual expressive presence, that we can genuinely translate into code, or . . . Or we just can't. It won't make any difference how she's feeling, any emotional state will do—'

'Yeah, I'm sure. But get a grip, Allie never got to the lasers yet. She wants to do this, but she has stage fright, and she doesn't understand that you ignore that feeling. Just tell her she's on. Make your wishes clear. That's all she needs, for it not to be her decision. Pretend you're in charge, why don't you?'

So Harry bit Allie's head off. Allie tried again, and she was good.

Rob did well. Sage caused consternation until they got him to take the mask button out of his eyesocket: they had to work around his phone implant. Virtual movie stars can't have permanent personal digital devices. Ax caused a stir of a different order, because the live audience regarded him as the star of the show. Fortunately, the lasers also liked him. Then it was Fiorinda's turn. She seemed good. To her friends she seemed really herself, no trace of the after-effects of Billy the Whizz getting eviscerated: very skinny but not *skeletal*, moving with energy, giving them the old calm little Fiorinda grin. But the demi-gods were silent; and they were right. She tried again, the engineers still said no. Harry consulted with them, and went and had a confab with Marshall Morgan, the Digital Artists' CEO.

'No problem,' he announced. 'We'll test Fiorinda another time.'

Smelly Hugh and Anne-Marie and DK took another couple of hours. They passed.

Afterwards there was the traditional party, on the beach at Harry's place in Malibu. Stars and execs, techies, mediafolk and support staff cheered Harry's thank-you speech. There was a buffet and a bar, waitrons in incongruous black-and-white; there was a Mariachi band on the prowl, and people trying to dance on the sand.

'Now!' said Puusi Meera, leading Ax to a heap of cushions under a spangled awning and settling her curves beside him. 'You must tell me everything; I can help. First things first, is she getting enough sex? You yourself did a wonderful test. I knew you would. So sexy and such charisma, so strong in your delivery, so responsive. You are truly one of us—'

Fiorinda wandered on her own, letting the party carry her. She'd never failed an audition before: of course it didn't bother her, but she felt self-conscious. The nice old bloke who often talked to her at these things came up with two frosty bottles of beer, so she went and sat with him near the bonfire. 'It's bullshit,' he said. 'You'll go back another day, without the fucking sharks circling, and you'll be good. I know you will. You're a performer, aren't you?'

'I used to be a singer with a little punk band,' said Fiorinda, gloomily. 'That's all.' She smiled at him. 'I'm sorry, but who are you? I can't just go on calling you, that nice o— er, bloke with the blue eyes who is kind to me.'

'It's Bob. Redford.'

The young Englishwoman nodded hopefully, waiting for more help. 'Robert Redford.'

'Auggh! Oh wow! You're the Sundance Kid!'

'Hahaha. Yeah, I'm afraid that's how old I am—'

The Few had circled their wagons, graciously allowing a few movie-world Bohemian folk to join them, particularly the ones who had real drugs. They spoke of the Celtic murders, a subject which was utterly forbidden. It's the Invisible People, said someone, and refused to elaborate. The bastards have police protection, said someone else; this opinion was general. Friends in high places, why else were these spectacular murders buried on inside pages, and *nothing made of them?* They hadn't known a victim personally until now, Bohemian LA having many tribes: so Billy was a notch up, the breath of the beast on their necks. 'Poor kid,' sighed Julia. 'She's gone like into water, the surface closes over. You think you hear her voice, you look around and it's another girl just like her.'

'*Did* she do Aoxomoxoa?' asked one of the girls, sadly. 'It was her main ambition. It would've been nice, before she died—'

Harry was wearing his straw hat for sentimental reasons. He tipped it on the back of his head and explained to Kathryn's media friends, at the bar, that this was the hat that Sage had told him to eat, as a Zen koan: which he had yet to understand. 'Give me enlightenment but not right now,' commented some wag: which got a laugh because the mood was upbeat, the problem with Harry's leading lady set aside.

'I'm surprised Laz didn't make it, Sage,' remarked Harry.

'Laz—?'

'Lazarus Catskill? He loves you guys, he's a big sad Reich fan – no offence. He was rooting for me to do the movie all along.' The A&R man peered around, divinely discontented, 'Huh. Maybe his studio told him to stay away. Pixelity, you know, that's not exactly Liberal Hollywood—'

'I'm gonna rescue Ax. D'you want to come along?'

The rescue was easy: Puusi had an aversion to Aoxomoxoa; she took herself off. Harry called to Marshall Morgan, the Digital Artists' CEO, who was passing with Lou Branco. 'Hey, Marsh! Lou! Come over here and talk to my stars!'

'Where's Fiorinda?' asked Ax, quietly. 'I thought she was with you.'

'Fiorinda is getting cosy with Robert Redford. You want me to break it up, Sah? Is this code for: leave me in peace with my ripe and voluptuous movie queen?'

'Lay off. That woman scares me.'

Marshall and Lou were in a relaxed frame of mind. Lou had taken off his sandals: he wiggled his toes in the sand. Harry adjusted his hat and glowed (it's not so bad, losing just one, shame it was Fio though—).

'You know,' said Marsh, 'there's something I'm dying to ask, but it's rude.'

'Go ahead,' said Ax.

'It's about the money. Okay, I know you weren't in it for the money, and I applaud that. And I know this was Crisis Europe, but you were selling like the Beatles: don't tell me there wasn't any mazoola. How the fuck did you guys end up so broke?'

Harry frowned. Lou Branco looked taken aback, his new religion cast into doubt.

'You know those stupid deals bands used to sign, back in the nineteen sixties?' asked Ax.

'Yeah?'

'Where the mansions and the champagne and the private jets would turn out to belong to the management, and the rockstars would be left with pocket-money?'

'Uhuh.'

'We did that the other way round,' explained Sage. 'Apparently.'

'The Reich belongs to us,' said Ax. 'We used to make ends meet, hustling money out of various donors, scrounging, selling our products, as well as putting in a share of our personal income. The Second Chamber government took over the books when Fergal Kearney was in charge, and the ends have never seen each other since. We're trying to get ourselves out of it, but they have a lien on our global earnings, and at the moment it doesn't look good. Some of our associates have escaped, and we might rescue the Few and Fiorinda, but Sage and I are fucked. Probably ruined for life.'

Fiorinda watched them from the other side of the bonfire. What's so fall-about funny? she wondered. The bigshots seemed equally puzzled ... There is an inside life and an outside life, she thought. We're all on reality tv. We spend our days putting on an act, for people we love and people we fear, and people we don't even know. The thought of the years ahead of her daunted her heart. *Sometimes I will be in hell, with the dead man fucking me, and either that means I'm nuts or one day I will wake up in the bad place; and then I'll know, because it will seem real, which this world never will because I have committed magic and there's no cure for what I am ... I will unpick those little tweaks I made, I will keep off the juice: if necessary I will fight another boss fight with a monster, and all the time, I will be faking it. But no one will know.* She smiled at her lovers across the firelight, the shadows and the party flares. *Goodbye,* she thought. *Fiorinda's going underground.*

I can do this. I'm going to live. I can even be happy.

The cabin was two hours from Hollywood, reliable in most traffic conditions, and there was a helipad. The Triumvirate moved up there a few days after the tests. The Catskills' simple retreat was an L-shaped, substantial, architect vision, surrounded by mature pine forest, with an indoor and outdoor pool, parking for a tank division, and a formidable perimeter fence, with watchtowers and a platoon of armed guards, who came as a fixture; but you couldn't see the fence from the house. The nearest neighbours were in Silverlode, a tiny touristville two miles of switchbacks away, down a roughly graded private road.

They waited to see what would happen: nothing happened. If Laz Catskill had wanted to talk somewhere other than his playpen, he seemed to have changed his mind. They moved up on a Monday. On Thursday afternoon Ax had to get back to do some live tv. A helicopter picked him up; he'd be spending the night at Sunset Cape, touching base. When he'd gone Fiorinda and Sage stayed by the pool, listening to birdsong and silence, until the shadows of the conifered peaks closed over the water. Then they retired indoors, because there were mosquitoes here with no respect.

Fiorinda walked around the house looking at photographs, of which there were plenty. There seemed to be a contest between Kaya and Laz: who could display more flashy *auteur* photoshoots, interactive video collages of star-being-democratic-with-backing-band; broody studio portraits. Kaya, Laz ... Laz and Kaya, Kaya and baby. Laz and baby; Kaya, Laz, baby.

Baby, baby, baby, baby, baby ...

She looked hard at the images of Lazarus Catskill. All she could see was a beautiful man, with the whorish eyes of someone who has faced far too many cameras, but he still enjoys it ... She went back to the kitchen and signed off with the perimeter guards over the house computer. They had to do this, night and morning, to prove they hadn't been killed by sneaky celebrity-stalker commando attack. Sage was looking at food possibilities. They'd declined the loan of the domestic staff: don't like having servants around, especially not other people's servants.

'I feel like a tethered goat.'

'Nothing's going to happen,' said Sage. 'I misread the signals, that's all,' . . . but then, almost immediately, 'Fee, I want to sleep with you tonight.'

Ax and Sage were sharing a room (twin beds). Fiorinda had a study/bedroom on the ground floor, on the long stroke of the L.

'You want to have sex?'

'No,' he said, cut to the heart by her cheerful, obliging tone. 'Thanks for the generous offer, but not without Ax, babe.'

'I want to,' said Fiorinda. 'Soon. But not without Ax.' She mugged apology, and walked into his arms, 'I didn't mean it to sound like that, poor Sage, I'm sorry, I take it back. I'm *spooked*. This place is spooky; Ax didn't feel it, but I know you do.'

'I dunno.' He rubbed his cheek against her hair, a rusty thicket smelling of pool chemicals. 'Maybe. Let's sleep in the same room, that's all. Now, what about a nice omelette?' He was hideously obliged to make Fiorinda eat: one could get tired of your mania for regular meals, Mr Preston.

They slept in the same bed. Lying beside her, chastely clothed in boxers and a T-shirt, he had the sad thought that he missed the innocence of El Pabellón, when sex had been out of the question. This is the difficult time, when she knows we're hungry and she will do her best to please us. I can't take her on those terms, Ax. I just can't. He listened to the silence, feeling the penumbra of something strange, wondering if it was his imagination. Wonder if Fergal's on guard tonight . . .

In the night they turned to each other, easily and sweetly, as if nothing had ever gone wrong. 'My baby,' she mumbled, hugging his head against her breast, wrapping her legs around him, 'whassermatter, little Sage, had a bad dream?'

'No, nothen bad now, jus' woke up, oh yes, more of that,' he whispered, kissing through her nightdress, 'tell me I'm your baby—'

There was someone talking, in the next room. No, several people: the words indistinguishable, an urgent muttering—

Ah, shit. They moved so they were face to face, lips almost touching.

'Did you hear something?' she breathed.

'What happened to women's lib? Why do you say, *did you hear something*, when you mean, *Sage, get out of bed and take a look—*?'

'Because I *don't* mean that, idiot. I mean, Sage, don't move an inch without me.'

'I'm not going to argue with you. C'mon.' He took an automatic pistol from under the pillow – which Fiorinda had not known was there.

'That's going to be a lot of use against werewolves, unless you have silver bullets.'

'It makes me feel better.'

There was nothing going on in the room next door. The cold, tasteful furnishings stared back at them, surprised by the sudden light. The kitchen computer said no sign of intruders, but they went through the cabin, careful to do nothing that would trip the alarms and bring the platoon down on them. They found only the immanent silence that had been plaguing them all week. The living room beside Fiorinda's study/bedroom faced the pool. There was a wall of sliding glass doors, hidden by heavy, woven curtains in a vaguely Aztec pattern. Sage prowled, checking the locks and the view of the night. Fiorinda sat in a wide leather armchair, looking around.

'This is weird. Shit. I thought you told Ax that coming to California would stop me going loopy. Now here I am staring at invisible people—'

Sage crossed the room to get another view, making a detour to bend over her chair. 'You were *not* meant to hear that.'

'Tuh. I didn't have to hear it. I always know what you two are saying.'

'There's nothing moving out there. I think it was our imagination.'

'Sage, have you ever considered the reason why nobody except me believes in the Fat Boy candidate might be because *there is* a Fat Boy candidate?'

'I *do* believe you. I'm not at my best at this hour. Give me a break.'

She sighed. 'Okay, okay. False alarm. Let's go back to bed.'

The next day Fiorinda had an interview with Kathryn for the news syndicate story. Sage was riding into LA with her; she was going to drop him off so he could meet Ax after his gig at the East Hollywood Mosque. They called Ax when they were on the way down. Fiorinda's bodyguards both thought they should come and join her after her interview; Fiorinda thought not. She said she didn't know how long she would be.

'You two can drive back in a studio limo, and I'll see you at the cabin.'

'It makes far more sense if we meet up,' reasoned Ax. 'Then we can come back together.'

'Please. I *can* do things by myself occasionally.'

'Let her alone, Ax. She wants to say terrible things about us. We'd be spare.'

This was code for: don't be overprotective.

Ax went along to his gig. The crowd at the Mosque (all ages, all dress codes, by no means all of them Reformed Islamics) was big enough to be slightly alarming: he was glad he'd said no to the press conference. He escaped, met Sage, and they drove away. The limo, which had a driver because it was taking them out of the LA freeway grid, went a few blocks and stopped at a run-down supermarket and fuel station.

'Okay, Mr Pender?' said the driver.

'Yeah,' said Sage. 'C'mon Ax, we get out here.'

The limo departed. Sage went over to a motorbike that was standing on the forecourt, a classic black and silver beast, the make not immediately apparent to Ax, who was not a fan of this means of transport.

'D'you like it?'

'I tolerate your bikes,' said Ax. 'What does this one have to do with you?'

'I just bought it. I mean, Digital Artists bought it. I went for expensive, I find that's usually best with an impulse buy ... I thought it'd be preferable to the limo.'

'Are you joking?'

'I'm an idle freeloading post-career rockstar. Why shouldn't I buy a motorbike?'

'No reason, no reason at all.'

They looked each other over: Sage, slender and whipcord without the freight of muscle, in black jeans and a breathable neoprene biker jacket, Ax in his new best suit, which was dark red with a nehru collar like his last best suit (he's such a fogey); but cut for fashion, in a modern silk twill that gleamed with gold and violet highlights.

'Here, catch—'

Ax caught the helmet. 'Did you discuss this purchase with Fiorinda?'

'No, because her phone's switched off.'

'You're sure she's all right?'

'I didn't leave her 'til I saw her safe with Kathryn.'

'Sage . . . Did something happen at the cabin last night?'

'Could be,' he admitted. 'Lemme get something to eat, and I'll tell you.' They ate hotdogs, and Ben and Jerry's fat-free, sugar-free, Madagascar Vanilla (an ice cream Sage had decided he liked) leaning against the bike, where the weeds grew through the margin of the stained pad of concrete. Sage described the night visitors.

'D'you think there was anything in it?'

'I'm not sure . . . D'you want to change that pretty suit?'

'Nah, can't be fucked. Let's just ride.'

Sage was better on a bike than behind the wheel. He negotiated the superheated concrete maze of the freeways without giving Ax much cause for alarm and pulled off above San Fernando at a shack cafeteria that advertised *Antojitos y comida corrida*. They bought soft drinks and sat watching the Friday afternoon traffic as it swooped and looped through the Sepuldeva pass: quite a show to the refugees from Crisis Europe. The dry heat was intense, the light a searing haze.

Sage told Ax about the ghost of Fergal Kearney, or rather, Rufus O'Niall. 'I didn't tell you on the Baja because, I don't know, it got lost. She was quite clear what she was doing. She'd elected Rufus as her guardian angel, to comfort herself.'

'Sage, that is very sick.'

'Is it? I thought it was smart of her. She doesn't deserve to have a total bastard for a father, why shouldn't she imagine him repentant? But I'm wondering what it means that I've seen him too—'

'So have I,' said Ax.

'*What?*'

'That night you came to fetch me from Lou Branco's. He was standing there, under a tree, while I was waiting for you. I mean, I saw a figure, it looked like Fergal . . . I didn't tell you because, well, it got lost. Sage, what are we talking about here? Could that really be *Rufus?* . . . Shit!'

Sage chewed his thumb. 'Hm. Fiorinda's guardian angel has appeared to both of us. Makes sense: she wants to protect us. What worries me is this seems like more of her magic, seeping out of containment under stress, and *that* is a scary thought.'

Ax had been told about the cursing. He nodded, ruefully. 'Yeah. Bad news . . . You rule out the idea of a ghost as somehow the actual dead person?'

'Rather than something projected from a pattern of fire, in the virtual space contained in Fiorinda's head? At fusion, of course, there'd be no difference—'

'Sorry, bodhisattva. You've lost me.'

'Ah, well.'

They were silent, thinking of the great gamble they were taking.

'We should move back to Sunset,' said Ax. 'You were wrong about Laz; we revert to plan A, which says Fred Eiffrich has a problem, but there's no megastar Fat Boy candidate, and Fiorinda will accept this soon, because she's getting better.'

'Setting aside the mindbending fear that there really is a monster.'

'I'm full of mindbending fears. It's my natural state.'

All the earth is a mosque, thought Ax. He remembered certain seasons, times of night and evening, when the motorway landscape in England had taken on beauty: flying down the sweeping curves of the M4, M5, riding the rivers of light, the red brakelights one way, silver the other, the vistas of the West opening before you—

'I wonder how long a city like Los Angeles can keep going with no functional public services, no cheap fuel, and the domestic water system fucked.'

'They're not doing badly,' said Sage. 'I think the lack of a centre helps.'

'If they had a Tour they'd be in trouble.'

The green revolution in England had been initiated by a Blitzkreig of righteous destruction, universally known as the Deconstruction Tour: bad news in a natural desert, inhabited by some of the spoiltest brats in the known universe, and several millions of their disaffected poor, all with free access to lethal weapons—

'Mm . . . D'you remember the crash, Ax? We were in a VIP lounge at Gatwick, on our way to . . . was it Africa Live or Hard Fun, can't recall just now. The markets were in freefall, realtime on NASDAQ tv. We were cheering. We thought it was hilarious.'

Yeah, thought Ax, without rancour. My mega-commercial friend, you never thought it could touch *you*. 'I don't remember where I was, but I expect I was cheering too. We had no idea, did we?'

They watched the rivers of light, with the nostalgia that hurts like mourning.

'Sage? What d'you want out of life?'

'Since we can't ever get back there?'

'Since we can't get back there.'

The haze had thickened, folding the city in a cloud of ochre shadow. 'I want to live,' said Sage. 'Just to *live*, with you and Fiorinda, chop wood and draw water. I'd like children, if possible. And a garden, oh, and a pool with fish. I like fish.'

'The only thing that worries me is the fish,' said Ax, after a pause for thought. 'I think I can provide the rest, though I can't promise you her children. But I've a feeling I'm not going to have a settled life. I don't know what I'm going to do next, but I can't leave this struggle: I'm in too deep.'

'Hahaha. I figured that out, babe, a long while ago … Shit, are you pissed off with me because of the bike? Private transport hypocrisy?'

Ax laughed. 'No!'

They disposed of their soda cans thoughtfully, and rode on.

Fiorinda had brunch with Kathryn Adams, in the Bullocks Wilshire Department Store, a splendid 1920s landmark building in the nearest you get to a historical centre of LA. Harry Lopez arrived to join them, after Sage had left. He wanted to talk to Fiorinda about additional dialogue: things that people had said off the record, authentic treatment of native English, if she could help him, he'd be immensely—

That bad, huh? thought Fiorinda. She knew there wasn't going to be another test. The lasers had spoken and she was out, no matter what Robert Redford thought. Not that she cared, but it was annoying having Harry be kind to her. 'I'm a member of a collective, you know. I'll be censored. Rockstars are so vain.'

Harry's face fell. 'Oh.'

'But I think I can get clearance for some of the memorable lines.' She sucked the dregs of her mango smoothie. 'You ought to make more of my frocks. I'll help you with that. My party frocks were vital cultural icons—'

Kathryn caught her eye, and they both started to giggle.

'What?' said Harry. 'Why do girls *giggle*? Teeheehee. It's like kindergarten.'

'It's meant to scare you,' explained Fiorinda. 'Does it work?'

'I'm leaving now. I'll fax you the latest marked-up script, Fio.'

'Oh, no! Don't fax me the whole—!' But the golden boy was gone.

'Do you like him?' asked Fiorinda, when they'd stopped laughing.

'Harry's had things very easy,' (she explained this as if it were a disability). 'But he's not just out for himself. He cares. That's important to me.'

'Yeah, mm.'

'I like him,' said Kathryn. She shrugged, her little eyes wry with self-knowledge. 'But I hear you: and don't worry about me, Fio. I'm not stupid.'

Fiorinda left shortly after Harry. At her final destination she parked the Rugrat on the street, as she didn't want to be videoed entering the secluded parking lot, and disabled the security. The car knew what she was doing; it shivered in protest. 'Sssh. If I don't do this, someone will look at you funny and you'll start yelling, you know you will. If my plan works, fine. If not, *no one must ever, ever know*. I'll be back soon.' Her mouth was dry, her hands were shaking ... She was wearing her sunshine-yellow dress, with her hair tied up in yellow ribbons, and her best make-up. She knew she looked good, better still, she looked like *Fiorinda*, foreign celebrity, with an album high in the charts; and featuring in Harry Lopez's new movie ... She could not tell if the physical session went well or badly, but she did not panic, not even when it was painful and invasive. Then the terrifying interview. The consulting-doctor, a slim and elegant middle-aged woman, started by complimenting her warmly on *Yellow Girl*—

'There's something you should know,' said Fiorinda, when she'd been given hope, and warned against disappointment. 'I can't pay you for this, except by endorsement and publicity. I'll do as much of that as you like, if we can come to an agreement.'

'Would that be conditional on successful treatment?' said the doctor, at once.

'Up to you. I suppose it depends how confident you are.'

They talked it over. The doctor was businesslike and kind; she made it very smooth. In the end she said, 'Now all you need is a second appointment. But before I see you again, I want you to gain fifteen pounds.'

Fiorinda stared in horror. '*What?*'

'Fiorinda, er, Ms Slater, that's not at all excessive, for your height and build. We talked about the problem of re-establishing your menstrual cycle—'

'Look, I know I should weigh more than I do just now, and I'm working on it, but I'm naturally thin. I have birdbones. I *cannot* put on fifteen pounds. I just can't.'

'Call in and make the appointment when you've gained weight.'

'Ten.'

The doctor shook her head. 'I'm sorry. It's not a bargaining situation.'

Fiorinda went back to the Rugrat, shut herself in and cried. Well, *fuck you*, smug doctor-lady. There are other clinics. Now I know my beautiful plan works, I can find someone who isn't so *fucking* snotty and unreasonable . . . She dried her eyes. It got through to her that the snotty and unreasonable doctor-lady had given her hope.

I could have a baby.

She stared through the windscreen, overwhelmed, her blood thrumming, her head spinning: impossibly balanced between joy and consuming horror.

Sage and Ax parlayed a little with the guards at the cabin gates, and rode the bike up to the house. They showered, changed their clothes and discovered that Fiorinda had left a message for Ax, saying she was on her way. She'd left it on his message board rather than calling him. When they tried to call her, her phone was switched off. Well, no worries, that's our babe, she hates telecoms. This little solo expedition scared them, naturally, but they had their overprotectiveness under control.

They took a couple of beers (Ax had accepted the *fait accompli* on mild alcohol) to the living room that faced the pool terrace, switched off the aircon and opened the glass doors. Pine-scented air flowed into the room like hot, clear syrup; it was five in the afternoon but it must be over forty degrees out there. But the heat pleased them. It made them feel rich. Ax put *Yellow Girl* on the audio ambience, Sage lay stretched out on a leather and hessian couch, Ax sitting on the floor beside him, and they talked, about this California experience, what was going on with the Few (what about that Chez Dawkins, isn't she the eye-candy), about what a prat Jordan was being (but Sage refused to be drawn on this subject); Digital Artists—

'How d'you feel about her not being in the movie?' asked Sage.

'I'm not heartbroken,' confessed Ax. 'As long as she's okay about it.'

It was pure superstition, considering the kind of thing alleged images and versions of their babe got up to on websites of the free world: and possibly overprotective. But neither of them liked the idea of Digital Artists having a virtual Fiorinda on file.

'Ax?'

Ax tipped his head back, and looked up with a smile. 'Yeah?'

'I'm in love with you,' said Sage, looking at the ceiling. 'I wanted to tell you that, in case you don't know . . . In case you'd like to know. And no oxy,' he added.

They'd done far too much of the intimacy drug oxytocin in those days when the three-way love affair was on the rocks: sinking their differences in a ruthless, jacked-up hit of tender devotion hormones. Fiorinda had *hated* that—

'I'm in love with you, too,' said Ax. 'And no sex. I love you anyway, my big cat.'

Sage considered, still gazing at the ceiling. 'No sex . . . ? Dunno about that, my dear. How's yours?'

Ax set down his empty beer bottle. He got up on the couch: they lay facing each other, breathing slow. Ah, there's grey in your hair, my guitar-man. You've lived hard, in ways harder than any of us, you lunatic . . . Ax traced the outline of Sage's beautiful mouth with a callused fingertip.

'Is it *true* you'd never done anything sexual with another bloke before me?'

'Ooh, I remember this conversation, Mr Chameleon. Why does it matter, Ax? You've done other blokes. Fiorinda has been fairly omniverous—'

'It's not *important*. I'm just curious. D'you say you slept with her last night?'

'Shared her bed. No fucking, give me credit, I would not—'

'Hey, don't be like that. I'm disgustingly jealous, but . . . was it good?'

'Mixed. Awkward when we lay down, but in the night, when she woke up and hugged me, really, arms and legs, God, that was sweet—'

They began to kiss, a shocking joy after so long.

'Kiss not fuck—'

'Yeah, understood—' but immediately they plunged deeper, soul-kissing, Sage folding Ax so close, hard on hard, making them both laugh and gasp; the weight of those arms gone, the same big cat embrace, fucking *wonderful*—

They pulled out of it. 'Being realistic,' Ax said, 'we better stop, or we won't. Can we just lie here?'

'I could cope with that.'

They fell asleep in each other's arms. The shadows closed over the pool. Sage woke from deep, soft oblivion to hear Fiorinda's voice.

'Hello?'

She was sitting in one of the blowsy, glossy armchairs facing them. He knew she'd come to say goodbye—

'Hi sweetheart,' said Ax, sleepily, sitting up.

She's smiling, but something's very wrong.

'I came to tell you I'm going away for a few days,' announced the Yellow Girl, poised in her slim, yellow dress, wearing the kind of make-up Fiorinda never wore in private life. 'Allie knows, I've called her. I've nothing scheduled, I've got my credit cards, and I'll take the Rat, if you don't mind.'

'Going away?' repeated Ax, dumbfounded.

'What, right now?' said Sage. 'Why? Where's this coming from—?'

'Do you realise how long it is since I did anything on my own? Like today, Sage made sure he saw me to the restaurant, Kathryn made sure she saw me to my car. It's been *years* since I did anything by myself. I need to regroup, and this just seems to be the time. I'm not in a bad state anymore, and we've done the promotion.'

'All right,' said Sage. 'Let's talk about it. We need to know where you're going.'

'That's what I mean,' said Fiorinda, reasonably. 'I need you not to know.'

She was calm, she was adamant. She packed her bags. They followed her out to the Rugrat, in the dying heat of the day. She kissed them both. They watched her drive away, and turned to each other in utter consternation.

'We shouldn't have touched each other,' said Ax, savagely. 'This is because she came in and found us, like—' He headed back into the cabin.

Sage hurried after him. 'Ax, that's crazy, I'm sure it's not that. We should have seen this coming. We should have known we couldn't keep her on a leash. She's working something out, and I trust her. I wouldn't have let her go if I didn't think—'

'How were you going to stop her?' Ax looked for his phone. He replayed her message. *I'll be with you soon. I love you very much, Ax, and I don't want you to worry about me anymore.* 'I'm going to call Allie.'

Wow. That was a *tour de force*.

Now she was in the Silver Mule, the red and white coffeeshop in Silverlode, in front of her a large and complicated ice cream in a blue glass dish, which she was determined to eat, though the task looked impossible. What would she do with her new-found freedom? She tried to recall the girl she had invoked at the cabin, teenage runaway, no-fixed-abode Fiorinda, coming up from the streets: the effort of memory did nothing to staunch the confusion bubbling up inside. Faces and voices from the past rushed on her, and all of them were Fiorinda – in the Escher perspective where the thing that perceives lines up and becomes one with what it is perceiving, but *oh boy*, never like this.

Why, she thought, *why* did I do the baby thing? A bridge too far, total madness, people trying to pass for normal always overdo it by a mile. Do I fuck want to be free. I want my darlings. I know what I'll do. I'll spend a night in a hotel, for pride's sake, and go straight back to them—

She was sorely tempted to call them now and confess the little act had been bullshit and she was *drowning* ... But she couldn't do that: because this is mine. Ah, shit. Not only drowning, gulping down the water into my lungs with fearful hunger.

Chin on her hand she smiled at nothing while the avalanche thundered, and every vestige of shelter was torn from her. What's happening to me? I am not conscious any more. I don't know what you call this state I'm in.

The shop was quiet, but not empty. Middle-aged tourist couples, a woman with a baby (well, hello, young lovers ...), and the evening crowd starting to gather at the tables near the tiny stage. The Silver Mule was something of a hang-out, far enough from LA to be frequented by the free-thinking natives of the forested hills. Never call them Counterculturals (perish the thought), but these are Californians who don't like foreign wars (or taxes or gun control, let it be said). They like renewable energy and sustainable farming, and prefer the civil flag to the normal stars and stripes. The Silver Mule had a civil flag, red stripes vertical instead of horizontal, and blue stars in a white field, at its door ... It's not illegal. One could imagine Fred Eiffrich approving the sentiments, though of course he was stuck with Old Glory.

One of the younger funky men was staring intently. Point that somewhere else, she thought, I'm on my break, and anyway, I'm not supposed to talk to you lot. She looked again ... and wondered, good God, maybe we were supposed to come down here to make contact, not wait at the cabin. Well, how were we supposed to know?

Magical people don't think like that. They think like, fate, which is maybe related to the concept of entanglement. Things can't help falling into phase.

'I'll be back,' she said to the ice cream, and went over, smiling, to the other table.

'Hi, I'm Fiorinda Slater. Mind if I join you?'

The Silver Mule became its evening self: a singer-guitarist with the dork's job of providing token organic entertainment; low lights, a roar of conversation. She stayed with her new friends, listening to the tone of voice, pretty sure that she was making contact, though not at all sure which of all the many things she perceived was actually happening. Her hand and forearm on the table were burned black, charcoal sticks, with

168

white, calcined lines around the wrist and knuckle joints: she was playing with fire. And Fergal Kearney, whose presence she had summoned for protection, was presiding in the background with a smile of lordly malevolence that made her flesh creep. But it was okay. She was sober, she had more sense than to drink when so spaced; and in no more danger than she would have been in England, where she used to do this sort of thing, walkabout, like you fear nothing, all the time—
until they tried to burn me . . .

The contact people wanted her to come somewhere else. She agreed, though she didn't like it when three of them travelled in the Rugrat, inside her *purdah*. The drive was long, full of strange intimations, ebbs and flows in her internal adventure. When she finally parked she could hear the sea, and wondered if she was back in the Baja. Then she realised she was with enemies, and snapped into focus: in the time it took her passengers to get out of the car she had restored the Rat's security (I won't leave it helpless). She touched the dashpad, last thing, and said conceal, immobilise. Be a good Rat, she thought. I'll come back. Where the fuck am I? Walking, in dark streets lined with palms. A blue-painted wooden bungalow in a garden of rose trellis and geraniums. She thought it looked like something in a fantasy game.

Inside the blue bungalow she crossed a boundary. The Silverlode people were handing her along the underground railway, and this was as far up the line as they *ever* fucking wanted to go: if not farther. They left quite soon. Fiorinda stayed up late, listening to the tone of voice, getting a picture that would have made her hair stand on end, except that it was ultimately disappointing. She woke in a strange room, in her underwear, under a strange quilt that smelled of rose-oil and cat's piss. She'd left her bags in the Rugrat; she had to put her yellow dress on again before she could go looking for a bathroom (there was a robe she could have borrowed, but she didn't fancy it). Her little purse was by the bed, no shoes. She vaguely remembered leaving them in the car. It didn't matter, her feet were hard as nails. She found a funky bathroom (toilet didn't flush) and returned to her bedroom, noting all the hippy-dippy magic stuff and remembering her disappointment. She'd thought she was being so clever, but she wasn't going to find her Fat Boy candidate here. This wasn't the right kind of venue at all.

Downstairs, she learned that she was going somewhere else. Apparently she'd agreed to this, in her quest to get closer to the fire. She thought of Ax and Sage, but she wasn't sure those people existed; her world at the moment was very small, access all areas far beyond her. Someone asked for her keys, so they could fetch her bags. She didn't trust them. They looked like the kind of people who might kill the Rugrat if they found it. An AI car doesn't have keys, but she just said no. 'I don't want my bags. Fuck 'em. I'll come as I stand.'

This seemed within their idiom. Then they produced the shackles, twisted bracelets of iron, strung with bones and feathers: hippy-dippy handcuffs. She told them they had the wrong idea, and it wasn't necessary, but they begged to differ. The shackles were a dealbreaker, so she accepted them. Then she realised a strange thing: she didn't have her saltbox with her. It was in her shoulder bag, in the Rugrat. It had often been farther away; she didn't have to hold her talisman in her hand. But this was different, schematic, it was out of reach . . . She looked at the cuffs, understanding at last what the saltbox did, and why it had been given to her, long ago. It limited her. It was a channel into which she flowed, like current down a wire. Now there was nothing to contain her.

She remembered an ice cream in a blue glass dish, but too bad: she must go along with the idiots who thought they'd taken her captive; and with her father, who was grinning in triumph there, though no one else could see him.

The Rugrat had moved to another spot in the parking and was deploying its *conceal* feature, mirroring the surfaces around it so it was functionally invisible. It knew that the hostiles were standing a few metres away, saying things. If a hare crouched in a furrow *hopes* not to be seen by the hounds, then it did the same. The two young men, slacker-clad surfie types, had a radiophone. The senior of them (in the invisible ranks) reported that they'd found the AI car. It was camouflaged, they'd detected it by its e/m. They described the location. Don't try to get into it, said the voice at the other end. Leave it alone, that suits us fine. The Rugrat watched them go, experiencing an analogue of proud relief; and an analogue of trust. I'll wait here. She'll come back for me. The scouring, sandy wind blew and the cool nights passed. But she didn't come.

Ax and Sage returned to Sunset Cape the next day. Fiorinda did not call. She'd taken a wad of cash out of their joint credit account, which chilled them: our babe doesn't mean to be traced . . . On Thursday, when she started missing diary dates and she still hadn't contacted anyone, Allie told the studio. Digital Artists' damage limitation went into gear. There'd been no accidents involving a brown Toyota Rugrat, no one answering Fiorinda's description had been admitted to a public hospital or private clinic in LA County, no dubious transactions on her DA credit cards (no transactions at all, actually), no young red-headed female dead bodies either. Further levels of pursuit weren't deemed appropriate: stars involved in this sort of escapade could get extremely pissed off and litigious over invasion of privacy. The studio concluded that Fiorinda was adult and had gone AWOL for her own reasons. Her friends should relax, and keep it quiet.

Ms Slater's been advised to rest, and is taking a break out of town.

Her friends could not relax. They were as murderously anxious as the leaders of the pack: imagining Fiorinda in some strange hotel, suffering total amnesia, or worse, out on the streets, joining the homeless people as she had done once before in her life. The studio had *no idea* . . . Ditzy Julia said, don't panic, it's the artistic temperament, hey, maybe she's gone to look up her father's family in Chicago, have you thought of that? Unlikely. The orphanage where Rufus O'Niall had spent the first years of his life no longer existed. If there'd been records of his natural parentage, they were gone too. The magician had been persistent, and thorough, when he bore a grudge. It had taken years and cost him his life, but maybe he'd finally succeeded in destroying his daughter.

After a week Kathryn Adams came to Sunset Cape, and wanted to talk to Ax and Sage about Fiorinda's disappearence. They took her to Allie's office.

'She hasn't disappeared,' said Ax, firmly. 'She's taking a break.'

'There's something you should know,' said Kathryn, intimidated by these two beautiful, powerful men, and their hostility, but determined to speak. 'That day, when she came into town to do the interview with me, that was Fiorinda's idea.'

Ax shook his head. 'I'm sorry, I don't get it.'

'She set it up. I was to tell anyone who asked, including you two, that we'd arranged it ages ago, but it wasn't true. I think she had another appointment that she didn't want to tell you about. You'd fixed up to go to Laz's cabin, so she had to have an excuse to come back to LA that day. Wherever she went it can't have been far from Wilshire—'

'Did she *tell* you she had another appointment?' asked Sage.

'No.' Kathryn's whey face turned scarlet. 'She didn't tell me anything. I knew I was covering for her, so I didn't ask. But that's not it. I – I have to tell you this. She was frightened. She didn't show it much, but I know her, and I knew. Whatever she was going to do, when she left me, it frightened her . . . Listen, I know something about why you're here, besides the movie. I think maybe she was following a lead—'

They stared at her, stone-faced.

'Don't worry,' said Ax, finally. 'It can't have been anything significant. She was fine when she got up to Silverlode a few hours later.'

'But then she took off, you don't know where and you don't know why!'

'No offence, but this is personal. It's not really your business.'

'Journalists,' said Ax, when Kathryn had gone. 'I hadn't the heart to tell her. Fiorinda's been known to cut short a boring interview before this.'

They were sitting at Allie's desk. The litter of the life they'd tried to leave behind – Allie's document files, boxes of clippings, promotional freebies, a diary planner screen taped on the wall – lay like a mask over the alien character of the room they had looked into, one day long ago, with Fiorinda beside them . . . 'We should talk to the Committee again,' said Ax. 'I mean, to Roche. I won't talk to Harry Lopez.'

'They know as much as we do.'

'No, they don't, Sage. They don't know that the woman who has disappeared was mentally unstable, or that she is – has – the qualities a rogue military project would look for if they were trying to weaponise natural magic.'

'She is not mentally unstable.'

'Oh, yeah. She has untreated schizophrenia, that's different.'

'It doesn't mean you're incapable. It's an altered state. It's possible to live with it.'

'As you would know, oh bodhisattva.'

Sage stared at him, hollow-eyed. They weren't sleeping. There was no question of sharing a bed: they could hardly bear to be in the same room . . . 'As I would know, yes. She has not disappeared, not the way you mean, Ax. Listen, try to follow this. I have blindsight. I went to where everything is known, and it's outside time and causality, so to say I came back doesn't really cover it. I can tell you, *non-consciously I can't prove it*, that she left us of her own free will, she's not in trouble, and wherever she is, it's by her own choice.'

'So why did she go?'

'Because we were smothering her. Because we were always there.'

They had taken a terrible risk; they had played and lost. Now everything they'd done since the A&R man turned up at El Pabellón seemed like criminal insanity. They hated the sight of each other, and tore at each other with words, only stopping short of physical violence: past caring whether they kept the rending and tearing out of their friends' sight.

When Fiorinda had been missing for two weeks, the English had a meeting about the gig Harry had set up at the Hollywood Bowl. It was held in Allie's office; they did not have the heart to use the spa. The discussion, burdened by bitter, unspoken things about whose fault this disaster was, quickly degenerated into acrimony. The Few declared, unanimously, that they didn't like the way the Hollywood Bowl thing was shaping. They felt they were being treated as Brit nostalgia, as cute curiosities. They hated the 'hippy DJ' number: it had to go. They didn't want a hired orchestra, they didn't want to do a variety show. They weren't old enough to retire from street credibility, thank you . . . The whole thing was beneath their dignity.

This was news to Ax. The Crisis Management Gigs had never had any pretensions.

'We're not in this to look cool. When were we ever? You do whatever's necessary, to please the crowd and keep them sweet—'

'I hate that part,' said Verlaine. 'I always did. I'd rather swab pus.'

'But *why* are we doing this?' demanded Felice. 'We've promoted the movie. We haven't done the dipped-in-goo thing yet, but that's Digital Artists' problem—'

'You told us we should look out for ourselves, Ax,' Chip pointed out. 'This isn't going to sell any Adjuvant records. It's the wrong message'

'I think we should wait for Fiorinda's opinion,' said Anne-Marie, primly.

Silence followed this, and lasted too long. They were clinging to the pretence that whatever had happened, Fiorinda must be okay. She couldn't have come to any harm. Who could get through Fiorinda? But they were very, very scared.

'Fiorinda wouldn't have an opinion,' said Sage. 'She wasn't going to do the gig anyway. She wasn't going to do any more stage gigs, ever.'

'I think that's for Fio to decide.' Smelly forgot all respect. 'Not you, Sage.'

'All right,' snapped Ax, white-lipped. 'This is senseless. Allie, call Mr Lopez, tell him the Hollywood Bowl is off.'

The meeting broke up. They went their separate ways, unthinkably divided from their leaders. Later that day there was a call from the

LAPD. The Rugrat had been found, undamaged, at a small resort called Carlsbad, about fifty miles south of LA.

Sage and Ax went down there. They identified the car, and unlocked it. Fiorinda's bags were inside, and her phone, and her yellow shoes. Nothing seemed to be missing. There were no signs of violence; there was no note. The car had been immobilised, and its conceal feature had been switched on before it had been left here. Even an AI car has its limits, and the conceal had finally failed; that's how it had been discovered. The local police believed the car could have been there for a while, it could well have been there for a fortnight. This was an unsurveilled area, extra parking for the beach, and this season it hadn't been been much used. The forensics team moved in. Before long, they were pretty sure no one had been in the car with her.

They stayed in the little town. The studio had booked them a hotel suite, and it was better than going back to Sunset Cape. The day after they saw the Rugrat, the long heatwave broke in a tremendous downpour that went on through the evening. Ax sat in the hotel room window, watching the palm trees standing stoically upright under the grey rain that fell thick and steady over the Pacific.

'Prayer is like lassoing the sun,' he said. 'It isn't about belief, it isn't about hope. It isn't really about begging God for mercy. It's something you build out of the void, a projection of the mind, out of this hell, into an unreal orbit. It's mathematical. Hey, Sage. How's the Buddha-like calm?'

He'd reached a dead level, where his pain was so great it felt like nothing at all, and Sage was like a buzzing fly, a presence he could not shake off, not a person, just a scab to be picked. Sage was sitting on the floor, arms wrapped around his knees, like a gangling sick spider. He leaned his head against the wall, eyes fixed on nothing.

'Leave me alone.'

'She knew what kind of life lay ahead of her, the horror buried inside, never going to go away, buried in her like the dead man's cock. She knew as well as we did, and if we'd been true lovers we wouldn't have *humoured* her. We'd have talked to her about the craziness. She was smiling when she left us because she was already in fugue. But she was sane when she said goodbye to me. Hey, Sage, wake up. Tell me again she's in Canada, starting a new life.'

'She's not dead.'

'I thought you said you didn't know. Could you explain? I'm confused.'

'I can feel that she's okay, emotional truth. It's non-conscious, I can't know it.'

Ax curled his lip. 'Nah ... Sorry. I don't get it, oh sainted one.'

'Fuck you. I don't know where she is, I don't know what she's doing, I know she went of her own free will. She walked out on us. People do that, when they've had enough.' He blinked away tears and wiped his nose with the back of his hand.

'You're not making sense, Sage.'

'We were suffocating her. I knew I was doing it, I couldn't stop myself. I never had a girlfriend except Mary. I didn't know how to ... how not to fuck up. I wanted to *hold her*, all the time, she was sick of it, so she ran away.'

'You think she hated us enough to vanish, knowing we'd be terrified, and leaving us helpless to deal with the Fat Boy menace, which she absolutely believed in?'

'You think she hated us enough to kill herself?'

'Maybe the Pentagon did it,' said Ax. 'How would I know?'

He got down from the window. Without a word, without any change in the bleak, savage misery in his face, he knelt and took the sick spider in his arms. Sage resisted, and then gave way like a falling wall.

The rain continued. It washed the beaches and drowned the summer gardens of the little resort towns that stretch in an unbroken chain, prim as Devon, from LA to San Diego. It sluiced the débris of high tides out of the storm drains, it drenched the police as they searched, sad description, for the girl in the yellow dress. Fiorinda's lovers stayed at the hotel, alone by their own choice, having nothing to do with the search, through another day and another night. Early the second morning they got the call. She had been found, dredged up from a sports-fishing boat inlet, a couple of miles north of where the Rugrat had been parked.

The Rugrat was in custody; they had a car supplied by the studio. Sage drove up Highway 5 and stopped at a cafeteria, choosing a truckstop place that looked Mexican. Prosperity had skipped a beat here. Everything spoke of poverty, or of the military, because of the Pendleton base. A Mexican girl with sad and gentle eyes served them two cups of hot water, a plate of flyblown donuts and a jar of Néscafé. 'Are you okay?' said Sage, very softly, touching Ax's hand. 'Can you do this?'

'I can do it.'

Harry Lopez was waiting outside the single-storey white building. It stood in a garden, with a tall metal fence around it; there were flat gravestones in rows in the green lot outside. They went into the building, shoulder to shoulder, and met the police and the morgue functionaries. They were shown into a room that smelled of disinfectant, with a taint of marine decay. This is it. There she lies, on cold metal, one hand slipped from under the grey sheet, discoloured and abraded, her body hidden. 'Her face is not recognisable,' said the medical examiner, gently. 'You're not asked to make a formal identification. The body's in good shape, but the water's cold, and the way she was wedged there, she could have been there for a week, or longer.'

'Turn back the sheet.'

The examiner hesitated. 'The injuries are all post-mortem,' she assured them—

There she is, her frail breast and slender throat rising from the neckline of the stained and battered yellow dress. Not recognisable: no. No one spoke. Ax studied the mutilated face, the pallid and sodden flesh, stripped of skin except for one shard over the right cheek. Some impact which had torn a groove through the soft remains of the nose had also broken the upper teeth. The blueish lobe of one ear emerged from the seaweed masses of her hair, like a clinging globule of marine life. He could see an open slit, like a tiny keyhole. He looked up. He and Sage exchanged one glance.

'I'll take this,' said Ax. He lifted the dead woman's left hand and removed the ring: no one tried to stop him. He looked at Sage again. 'We should go now.'

Harry followed their car and found them on the shore, sitting on a flight of shallow steps that led from a parking lot to the beach. He sat beside them. Mr Preston's fine profile was impassive, dry-eyed.

'I am so ... very sorry.'

Sage nodded. Ax went on gazing in front of him, at the sunlit ocean.

Harry rubbed the back of his hand over his face, wiping a dew of tears out of his felt-tip moustache. 'She was great. She was truly a *great* person. Why would she take off her shoes? Why did she leave them in the car?'

'Fiorinda couldn't walk in high heels,' said Sage, absently. 'They were just for dandy. If she was walking on the beach for the last time, she'd want to be barefoot.'

'I feel so bad about this. She was talented and wise, and beautiful, and, and funny, and I suppose she'd just ... just been through too much. I hope to God you don't think it was failing the avatar test that finally—'

'Go away, Harry.'

'I'm sorry, I'm being crass, you want to be alone. Uh, later.'

Ax turned and looked after the A&R man, making sure he went back to his car and left the parking. 'Can you believe that bloke?'

'No.'

They had washed Fiorinda's ring in the sea. They clasped hands over it. Ax reached for Sage, blindly, and the big cat rocked him, hugging tight.

'Sssh, ssh, baby, baby—'

'Sage. The Fiorinda I knew didn't have pierced ears.'

'No. No piercings at all, she didn't like the idea.' Sage drew a shaking breath. 'T-that was a fucking stupid oversight on someone's part—'

'She could have had it done after she left us, for some reason we can't guess. Oh, I don't know. Maybe we're kidding ourselves. Maybe that was Fiorinda.'

'It wasn't her, Ax. It *wasn't*, and we both knew it. Cling to that.'

The official agenda had been clear from the start. Fiorinda's flipped, she's wandered off, suffering from post-traumatic stress, what a shame. Nothing to do with a horrific series of murders, or a terrifying rogue Pentagon project. When Ax had talked to Philemon Roche, the response had been *sympathy*, and then no further interest. Unbelievable. The Few had been railroaded into accepting this bizarre response at first, but they'd recovered their senses, if Ax and Sage had not. They believed in their rock and roll brat, hard as nails and totally courageous. *Something had happened* to Fiorinda that afternoon, in the window between twelve-thirty, when she'd left Kathryn Adams, and five-thirty, which was approximately when she'd arrived at the cabin in the hills. Somewhere in those few hours they would find the key to her disappearence.

Anne-Marie had performed ritual magic, hampered by the fact that Fiorinda's lovers refused to take part, and reviled her attempts. She didn't like doing this without her mistress's consent, but it was an emergency. (Dilip called Sage *my lord* sometimes, and got away with it. Ammy knew she better not call Fiorinda *lady*, or *mistress*, to her face. But she often did so in her mind.) She asked the incense fire, in which one of Fiorinda's yellow ribbons burned, to give her a word, a message: guidance. Where did Fiorinda go? Did she check into a hotel for an hour with a Latin lover? Did she sing for the lunchtime trade in a piano bar, in the hope of founding a new career? Did she meet one of our movie-star acquaintances and recognise the monster within? Or was there something we can't imagine? A door that opened onto an abyss? Kathryn Adams says she was afraid.

What's Fiorinda afraid of?

Doctors.

This was the word that Ammy had been given.

Draw a circle round the Bullocks Wilshire, make it half an hour's LA driving in radius. Remember she had the Rugrat, ace negotiator of the freeway maze; remember she could equally have stuck to the surface streets, or reached her appointment on foot. They did not know why the word *Doctors* had been given to them, it was just the clue. They had downloaded lists of medical practices, hospitals, clinics, medical suppliers, from the public net. Ammy had cut up the lists, played with them and slept with them, and reduced the horrendous number. Now they worked with shoeleather and persistence. They were covering the territory in pairs: the women doing the gynaecology, paediatricians, female cosmetic surgery and related, Chip and Ver heading out into the suburbs with a hired car; Dilip and Rob on general medicine. You locate one of the places Ammy rates as a possible: you call her. It's important, apparently that you be physically *there*. If she says yes, one partner stays outside. The other walks into reception, shows the picture, asks the question. See what happens after that.

Ammy rarely said yes.

The Rugrat had been found, with all Fiorinda's possessions inside. Her lovers were at Carlsbad, waiting for the worst bad news. Fiorinda's friends were doggedly pursuing their mystery. Dilip and Rob, who were buddies because Anne-Marie had vetoed mixed couples, preferred to travel by bus and taxi. They took the MTA into downtown and proceeded to the neighbourhood where they had left off the evening before. It matters, even if she's dead. The rain had vanished, the sky was grey but the temperature was back in the mid thirties. They worked for a couple of hours, and stopped to eat corner-store sandwiches in a little park with the inevitable palm trees, which no longer gave them that eyekick that says *you're not in London anymore*.

'The house where they filmed *Thriller* is around here somewhere,' said Dilip.

'We'll have to bring Sage.'

They forgave Ax. Any fool knew that Ax had been fighting demons of his own all through this trip: no wonder he'd cracked up when she disappeared. They had to forgive Sage, because ... well, the Zen Self champion, towering genius of the Reich, is wet Kleenex in an emotional crisis. The guy can't help it.

Rob sighed. 'I wish he was with us on this. I hate to have to say it, because I truly love him, but Aoxomoxoa can be a *flake*, betimes.'

'I hate to have to agree with you,' said Dilip. 'But you're right.'

'Back to the foot slog? Maybe we'll snag another false positive.' The false-positives had acquired irrational value, because they were such a relief from the endless negative. Chip and Verlaine, indeed, would go into places when Ammy had said no, and do their private detective thing. The others frowned on this practice, but the kids maintained it couldn't do any harm. Fiorinda's disappearance was public knowledge now. Rob glanced up at the dull sky, will it piss with rain again? Trust us to come to Southern California the year they have a shit summer.

'DK? How much, er, *talent* do you think Ammy has?'

'A nano-teaspoon in the Pacific ocean,' murmured Dilip, leaning back on the bench with his eyes closed, 'into which by some complex chance a fish may swim.'

'You're bushed, man,' said Rob. He was trying to give DK plenty of rest-stops, without letting the guy know how poorly he looked. 'There's five on foot here, I'll do them and we'll quit.'

'No,' said Dilip, 'I will perform the ritual with you. It's all we have. Ah, *Fiorinda*, who would have thought I would follow you down to the river?'

They walked together: the South London band-leader, righteous political brother; and the tranced-out Midlands intellectual, dance-culture veteran ... alone in this alien city, bound together by a lost Utopia, and their devotion to a certain wilful red-headed babe. The next address was upscale, with a parking lot shaded by real, leafy trees.

'This should be on the women's list,' said Rob.

Sometimes Rob's trade-union points of order can be exhausting.

'Let's do it anyway.'

They called Ammy, who was back at Sunset Cape, sky-clad, breathing the smoke of lavender and rosemary to sharpen her inner senses, with Smelly Hugh in solemn attendance. They sent her a picture. She said yes.

'False positive,' said Rob. 'Fuck. Have you seen this girl? No, I'm not the police, I don't have a licence; and then the bum's rush. Do people really do this for a living?'

'Shall we both go in?'

'No,' said Rob. 'You stay out here.'

For a moment Rob paused to consider that this might be the door with monsters on the other side. He was scared for himself, and scared of fucking up. He was not good with personal danger, and he knew it. Wish Ax was here: wish Sage was here. He squared up to it and went in. Dilip walked down the street and waited: with the option that he would *get out of here*, and report back, should Rob fail to reappear.

Rob talked to the receptionist, who said, whoa, that's Fiorinda!

'Did she have an appointment here? About two weeks ago?'

'Oh, you're one of those English radical rockstars. I recognise you! You'd better talk to Dr Trigos.'

Ten minutes later Dilip saw Rob coming along the hot, grey street, in his parrot-blue suit: shoulders hunched, head bowed. 'What happened? False-positive?'

Rob shook his head and thrust into Dilip's hands a page copied from an electronic appointments book. He turned away, trying to control his emotion.

'Oh, God,' breathed Dilip. 'She went to see a doctor—'

'The doctor-lady says it was a positive consultation.'

'What shall we do?'

'Call them.'

Rob called Ax. 'Hi. What's happening with you?'

Silence, and then—

'We've seen a body with no face, a suicide we are told. We're on our way back.'

Well, fuck that. Rob swallowed. 'I don't think Fiorinda killed herself,' he said, so choked he could hardly speak. 'Whatever the bastards want us to believe. We've just found out what she was doing that afternoon. She went to a fertility clinic, and the doctor-lady told her she could have a baby.'

6

The Scientist

'Did you know, this freaky rain is supposed to mean the big one is finally on its way? It's all over the doom news.'

'Really.'

Janelle brought two juice cocktails out onto the deck. Today it wasn't raining. The poisoned beauty of the Rosa was a dazzling symphony of blue and white. Come and see me sometimes: well, she had her wish. Here he was, with his back to her weatherboard, arms around his knees like an Aztec mummy: the sun glinting on his cropped head, eyes hidden behind heavy shades.

'Or would you prefer something stronger?' she asked gently.

'No thanks.'

'Yep, this is earthquake weather. Atmospheric disturbance ... But they say that every year, and any kind of unusual weather will do. It's great, Aoxomoxoa.' She sat in her long chair, and sipped the cocktail. 'That Snake Eyes number—'

'"Up Down Street"?'

'Uhuh. Hard times anthems, I love 'em. The feeling you got on that reminded me of John Huston's boxing movie, *Fat City* ... Did I ever make you watch that? One of the definitive California movies, maybe the greatest. The valour people find, when they know their defeat is everlasting—'

'Mm, right.' The shades still fixed on the ocean.

'I thought you were coasting on the special effects in your work after *Arbeit*, but now you're playing with the full deck. Isn't that how it feels?'

They had been getting into the immersions for *Unmasked*, over which Sage had struggled for so long. She could have been resentful if she'd felt like it, because Aoxomoxoa had moved into her territory. But she was safe: he'd never be interested in natural realism for its own sake; he was hooked on spectacle and fireworks—

'The actual *whole deck* would be powers beyond what I've done so far,' he said. 'The wildest thing is that it might be possible.'

'Tuh. You'll be there in a year or two, I know you. Hey, you should take the contacts out. Be careful, you don't want to overdo it.'

He stirred, 'Oh, I suppose—', took off his fx blockers and slipped the coding lenses out of his eyes. His beautiful hands stumbled over the task of getting them back into their case. Shit, he's going to tear them.

'Let me do that.' She felt like his mother, the original older woman, and this was painful, but it was true. His grief made him a child again, available to her the way the adult male stranger had not been ... She wanted to say something about his loss, but it's hard to guess what will comfort the bereaved.

The English could be proud. The death of their rock and roll brat was a hit with the public. The traditional fanshrine – at the gates of the studio village – had become an instant tourist attraction crawling with media hounds; a hazard to traffic. No flowers, that was the strange thing. Candles, soft toys, embroidery, messages: no bouquets. Apparently the little diva hadn't liked cut flowers. Digital Artists planned to hold a beautiful memorial service once the body had been formally identified. The funeral would be private, though. There's nothing romantic about a coffin going into the ground, or through the curtain into the furnace.

'You don't know that she killed herself. You only know she went away to study her soul, and took a walk on the beach. It could have been an accident.'

She wouldn't insult him by suggesting the body wasn't Fiorinda. They both knew the 'formal ID' thing was a bureaucratic idiocy.

'Does the ... the bodhisattva thing help?'

'I'm living in the same world as you are, Jan. In which everyone I love is going to die, including me. If not now, then some day, if not one cruel way then another cruel way; it can't be avoided. Yeah, maybe it helps. But only in a way that's available to anyone ... though it's not as easy as it sounds.'

'Is this the chop wood, draw water thing?'

'You're having a nightmare. A ravening beast is rushing towards you. You run the other way, and there's another monster. You realise there are monsters rushing at you from all directions, and you're defenceless. How do you escape?'

Janelle shook her head. 'Forget it. I can never get those fucking logic things. Drink your juice, it's getting warm.'

Obedient as a child he picked up the glass. 'You wake up,' he said;

and smiled at her, the full voltage, from a core of happiness so untouchable it was chilling.

The body stayed in Carlsbad awaiting a formal DNA match, and Fiorinda's dental records from London. The autopsy report, some of which Ax and Sage saw (clearly it had been decreed their wishes were to be respected, in every possible way) confirmed the assumptions that had been made. There were no signs of violence or sexual interference. The face had been destroyed by accidental post-mortem damage, the lungs had been full of seawater; the body could have been in the water for two weeks. She'd been in her early twenties, underweight but healthy. She had borne one child. The photographs of the faceless face showed more soft tissue damage than they'd seen in the morgue. There was no telling whether this drowned woman had ever had pierced ears.

Sage visited Janelle Firdous; Allie talked to Kathryn Adams. Ax accepted the condolences of the FBI, on behalf of the President's Special Committee, and took a personal phonecall from Fred Eiffrich – he was prostrate with grief, however, when the English PM called. They waited for a hint of mercy: for something to happen or *someone* to break ranks. There was not a sign, not a crack in the wall. Sage and Ax called a meeting in the derelict spa.

Their friends arrived to find them sitting on the floor of the whirlpool, talking quietly, Sage with Ax's arms around him, the ex-dictator's chin resting on his former Minister's shorn yellow curls. They did not spring apart. It made a pleasant change from the way the leaders of the pack had been treating each other.

'Hey,' said Cherry, junior powerbabe; tactful and brave. 'What happened to the rockstar ambivalence, you guys?'

'Ambivalence is not the message,' said Ax, keeping a firm hold on his big cat.

'Don't think we'll do ambivalence again,' said Sage. 'I don't like the afterburn—' and for a moment the tiger and the wolf were lost in each other's eyes, a silent, public declaration. Then they took their usual places and spent the rest of the meeting separated by an empty space. Anne-Marie arranged incense and myrtle twigs in a small stone bowl borrowed from the Cactus Room. They had *Arbeit* running upstairs too, and an off-the-shelf signal jammer on the side of the pool. It was all ritual, the tech the same as the magic; it probably didn't achieve a thing, just made them feel a little better. No one spoke while Ammy murmured words of warding, partly traditional and partly of her own invention. The incense smouldered: she stayed for a moment with her head bowed, then went to sit by Smelly.

'First off,' said Ax, 'We lost it, it was horrible, and we're sorry.'

'Goes for me too,' added Sage.

There was a murmur of forbearance and relief.

'Just glad to have you back on board,' said Rob.

'But no cuddling in session,' said Allie, with a noble attempt at levity. 'Or we'll make you sit on opposite sides of the classroom.'

Everyone laughed, as best they could.

Ax felt that these people should fire him, but no, they could do worse, and they were doing it: he was going to have to lead the meeting.

'We're in bad trouble. I'm responsible, and Sage is responsible; and we know it. We were told there was an illicit Neurobomb project, trying to weaponise natural magic. We brought Fiorinda here, knowing that she was just the person the bastards involved in something like that would be looking for. We had our reasons, but now is not the time to make excuses—'

'And now they've got her,' said Chip. 'Whoever they are.'

'Whoever the fuck *they* are,' agreed Sage, giving Chip a glance of bleak acknowledgement. 'Our best guess is the same as yours. She found out something. If it didn't happen that afternoon in LA, it must have happened after she left us. She went off on her own to think about the personal news: she found out something, and decided she had to handle it herself. But she got caught. We believe she's still alive and we believe she's . . . not likely to be harmed. But for whatever reason, she can't contact us and she can't get away. The body on the slab tells us she's in trouble—'

'She's trapped because she won't commit magic,' said Rob. 'She won't do what they want. We know she'd rather die.'

Something passed between the leaders, a dark thought they weren't going to share. 'Yeah,' said Ax. 'So it's up to us. We have to find her, but we have to do it without challenging the official story. She's dead, suicide, very sad . . . We have to co-operate, behave as if that's the truth. What about your doctor-lady, Rob? We ought to keep her clinic appointment to ourselves.'

'I covered it when I was there. The doctor said her staff don't tell tales, and for a baby farmer (Rob had been through the fertility clinic mill, he was cynical) she talked like someone with ethics. Maybe one of the women should go back, make the point we don't want a media fest over the tragic irony?'

'Better not. Let it be.'

If you want something kept quiet, never say so twice: it's asking for trouble.

'Why the fuck *not* challenge the official version?' demanded Felice, burning with indignation. She could remember Fiorinda at sixteen, the proud little wild soul, before ever that red-headed girl became unofficial Queen of England. She'd been enduring the bereavement circus in growing fury. 'It's shaky as all shit. What about that money she took out? Where is it? Where's her purse? What was she doing in that Carlsbad place? Why *can't* we say these things? Ax, listen to yourself. That's like, someone's trying to rape you, and he says, *don't scream—*'

'No,' said Ax. 'This is like, someone's trying to rape you, and he has you handcuffed to the wall with his pals holding you down and a gun at your head. If you don't scream, you might stay alive . . . The purse was probably found on the beach and stolen; either that or it's still in the ocean. Why was she in Carlsbad? Why not? I'm sorry, it won't work. The clothes were hers, the ring is hers, there was no face to identify, and I'm sure that if it comes to it, the DNA and the dental records will confirm that that's Fiorinda. The moment we saw that body and knew it wasn't hers, we knew we had to keep our mouths tight shut. These people aren't pissing around, and this isn't England, F'lice. We have no way to get past them.'

'We're up against the US government,' said Sage, 'on an issue of national security. There is *nothing we can do*. They can simply deport us if we cause them any aggravation, and be sure they will. That's not going to help Fee.'

'Okay, I see that,' muttered Felice, subsiding. 'I just, God, *hate* this—'

'So do we all.'

'Why d'you think they kept her phone?' wondered Verlaine, helplessly.

Fiorinda's possessions had been returned. The saltbox was among them, with the other contents of her shoulder bag, tagged *wooden ornament*. Nothing was missing except her purse, and the phone, which had been kept by the police for 'further analysis'. The Rugrat had been released and delivered to Sunset Cape, valeted to perfection inside and out. It was in good shape, except that the working record of its last journey and the Carlsbad car park stay had been wiped.

'They probably broke it,' decided Chip. Fiorinda had been using a freebie from a breakfast cereal called Whale Song Blue Corn as a personal communications device: it was hard to believe the police had found anything to analyse. 'We'll get it back, eventually, sewn up and made respectable for the funeral.'

'Thanks, dipstick. I really needed that thought.'

Dora crouched forward and crushed the smouldering myrtle twigs. The smoke had been rising, threatening to trigger the sprinklers. 'Ax . . . d'you think, could President Eiffrich have . . . *lured* you here, and it was all a plot, to get hold of Fio?'

Ax shook his head. 'I don't know. God help me, I can't believe that of him. But who the fuck knows, Dor? Heads of State can get forced into a blind alley, and do terrible things, when there's no choice but bad or worse—'

'I will *never, never* believe she killed herself,' whispered Allie. This was Allie's mantra, repeated incessantly. Everybody hated it, but she obviously couldn't stop herself. Front desk hell was getting her down, but she refused to share the job.

Dilip took her hand. 'Sssh, it's okay,' he murmured, without meaning—

Ax combed his hair back with his fingers. 'Allie, I have a wild, crazy idea even the President of the United States doesn't expect us to *believe* it but—'

He had the smell of disinfectant in his throat.

—seaweed mass of hair, the flowerstem line of a girl's throat, undisfigured—

When President Eiffrich had called to express his shock and sympathy, Ax had thought he could hint at some doubt about the drowned woman. He had received a kindly, final rebuff . . . 'I can't give you the hope you're asking for,' says Kathryn's Uncle Fred, after a tiny pause. 'The facts seem clear. It's a terrible tragedy, words cannot express my sympathy, I just wish I'd known how vulnerable she was, before I called you guys here. I know the bureaucracy of it is hard to take. When that's done with, and they're able to release her body, it will be easier to accept—' Ah, God, when he had heard that . . . The little halt in Fred Eiffrich's warm, homely, patrician voice, of a country-bred aristocrat. When he had heard that, and known his babe was alive, but he had nowhere to turn, no appeal—

The body was still in limbo. The residual fingerprints recovered from the drowned woman were inconclusive; there was a bureaucratic hitch over the DNA matching, something inadequate about the dental records sent over from London. Fiorinda's friends took faint comfort in the mysterious delay. Somebody (maybe Fred Eiffrich himself?) was holding off from final commitment to the cover-up, until . . . Until what? Ax swallowed bile and looked down at his clasped hands. The Triumvirate ring gleamed; on his right hand he wore the ring she'd given him long ago, with the carnelian bevel inscribed in Arabic, *this too will pass* . . .

He hadn't finished his sentence, and they were all waiting.

Sage stared at the incense bowl. 'I just wish to God we'd never brought her here.'

Emilia's cleaners weren't allowed down here. No one had tidied away Fiorinda's stray belongings. A book of hers lay on the tiles by the swimming pool, a silver scarf was hanging on the hooks by the defunct sauna; a pair of scuffed beach sandals, traps for her friends' glances. Poor Fiorinda, she's gone like into water, the surface closes over. You hear her step, you look around and no one's there.

Smelly Hugh said, 'But you didn't bring her, did you? It was the lady brought you guys. Don't beat yerselves up too badly, mates, it was her gig. I remember that.'

Sage smiled wanly. 'Thanks, Hugh.'

'Well, what I think is, if it was Fio's idea, it was probably, like, a good one.' Smelly sat back: proud of his contribution. Nobody looked at him, not even his helpmate, but he didn't mind. He felt he was getting the hang of this round table palaver at long last. When to put your hand up, when to keep your head down—

'We can ask questions, Ax,' said Chez Dawkins, with determination. 'We can go back over the ground, making it like: we know she's gone, but we need to hear all the details for ourselves, so we can mourn and move on. I think of the studio—'

'Her phonecalls, can we get the records from the company?'

'I think of Silverlode,' said Dora. 'It's the last place we know.'

The Digital Artists troubleshooters had established that Fiorinda, in her yellow dress, had stopped off at the touristville coffee shop, in the early evening of the fatal day, eaten an ice cream and gone on her way. This had later been confirmed on the CCTV tape: at least, there was a clear shot of her, smiling, walking into the place—

'No,' said Ax (and wondered why the fuck they should take his orders). 'Don't start asking questions yet. Not before we've talked to Laz Catskill. He's agreed to see us; we're going to meet him up at the cabin.'

Laz and Kaya had been out of town. They'd sent messages of shock and sympathy, naturally. They were back in LA now. The Few looked at each other: strange glances. Laz Catskill was a genuine megastar, one of those people who hardly seemed real, and he was someone known to Sage, someone who had been 'rooting' for the English to come to Hollywood. He fit the profile.

'Sage,' said Dilip, slowly, 'do you think Laz Catskill might be the candidate?'

'No, I don't,' said Sage, dismissive. 'Nah, that's not what I'm thinking. We talked, and I felt he had something more to say. He invited us to that cabin, then Fiorinda disappeared, and the more I think about it, the more I want to talk to him, tha's all. Could be there's nothing in it.'

The Few weren't fooled. 'Sage,' asked Anne-Marie, uneasily, 'when you went to see him, at his house, did he give you anything, from his hands to yours?'

'Nah. Fucking poor planning on my part. I could have screwed a private jet or so out of him, I didn't think of asking. Why?'

'Maybe food or drink?'

'Hm. A maid brought coffee. I poured my own.'

'Did he touch you?'

Aoxomoxoa and Laz might have hugged, or slapped hands, but they'd never been touchie-feelie, so maybe not. Nowadays it was A-list manners (daft, when there were so many more risky occasions) to avoid skin contact. 'No,' said Sage ... 'Oh, wait, shit. He *did* touch me. He touched my ring—'

'Ah.'

'You think Lazarus Catskill did a hex, on *Sage*?' exclaimed Chip. 'Whoa!'

'I don't know,' said Anne-Marie. 'I'm just thinking.'

'What are you thinking?' asked Sage, who had become very attentive.

'I'm thinking that's the way magic is. I couldn't harm anyone. I haven't the power, and I wouldn't if I could. It's wicked *and it comes back on you.* But that's the sign of a hex. It's not what people think, it's subtle. It twists the world so ruin falls on someone, like, horrible coincidences, evil bad luck. That's what used to happen with people who crossed Rufus. Check it out.'

'I don't need to, Ammy, I know.'

'Barely distinguishable from background noise,' murmured Dilip, looking up at his ghost-ripples. 'Invisible and odourless—'

'But Fiorinda disappeared,' protested Rob. 'Nothing happened to Sage.'

Sage gave him a look of disbelief, worthy of the living skull.

'Sorry.'

'I'm not saying you shouldn't go,' said Anne-Marie, her black Chinese eyes lowered, embarrassed at giving advice to the mighty. 'Just be careful. I know what you are, Sage, but this is another kind of power and it could hurt you.'

'Don't worry, Ammy,' said Ax, 'We'll be careful.'

'Ideally, ask him to take the hex off.'

'I'll try to find an opportunity,' said Sage.

Lazarus had agreed to the meeting without any difficulty, which had surprised them. They were expected; the guards let them pass without a hands-on search. They parked, alone in the tank-division parking, and – concealed by the Rat's one-way coated windows – opened the safe box in the floor of the cab (the stash for illicits, that they'd failed to find in Mexico). It was proof against most scanning systems. They'd borrowed side-arms from Doug Hutton's armoury.

'Are we sure about the guns?'

'I'm not sure about anything,' said Sage. 'Your decision, Sah. But we don't know what we're walking into.'

They knew that the Rat was bugged, and they knew they'd better leave the fucking thing alone if they ever wanted to see her again. Listen all you like, you bastards: we're rockstars, we have no private lives. If you don't like what you hear, if you don't like what we get up to, then *do something*. Connect with us. Break the silence ... They took the guns, back of the waistband, under the jacket. Their right to carry concealed weapons was something to argue about should the occasion arise. When they looked back, the AI car seemed to be watching them, alert and anxious on its Mars Buggy axles, pleading for them to listen to the story it could not tell.

Laz was on his way. The guards had unlocked the cabin's front doors from the gate. They walked in and prowled around, opening doors, peering into closets: the freezer room beside the kitchen stocked like the Overlook Hotel for the winter to end all winters; the sumptuous master suite, the racks of shoes that Laz and Kaya kept in this second-best holiday home; the sedimentary deposits of perfect casuals in the walk-in closets. Nothing had changed since they were last here.

'All this could have been ours,' said Ax. 'Well, yours, Aoxomoxoa. You were on the golden road, do you realise? Before your career was rudely interrupted.'

'I prefer things the way they turned out.'

Ax grinned. 'Even with the revolutionary tribunal?'

'We're lucky we still have our heads, citizen—'

'We lost her. They'd have been justified in any reprisals.'

Ax saw himself in the walls of photographs, as someone who had never made it as far as those pictures, never more than a beggar at the shrine of corporate whoredom. Sage remembered the very bad years, his taste for domestic violence, the hateful underside of his fame and fortune. He opened Laz's bathroom cabinet, and recognised most of what was in there by the long, complicated names in the small print, although the labels were brighter on this continent. Heavy glow. Strange how some people can only get off on prescription drugs . . . They found nothing like an office, nothing but the house computer in the kitchen, with which they were already familiar, and if it had hidden depths, they were very well hidden.

They met on the open-plan redwood stairs.

'What d'you think?' said Sage.

'Nothing out of the ordinary.'

'The oldest profession,' said Sage. 'Oh, I have been here.'

They were very angry. This place was mocking them, telling them that yes, it had taken Fiorinda, and they would never find out how or why—

Downstairs. They went to the living room on the long stroke of the L with the glass doors to the poolside. The chill of the air-conditioning fought with the blaze of the sun – which at this hour filled the glass with a diffuse, fluorescent glare, so the pool appeared and vanished, depending how you turned your head.

'Just out of interest, if it turns out this is the candidate, do you have a plan for dealing with that?'

'No,' said Sage. 'But don't worry, it'll be okay.'

'Non-conscious,' Ax recalled. 'I am getting to dislike that term.'

A door opened and shut.

They let Lazarus come to find them. He was looking good, toned and graceful. He walked in, smiling with unaffected feeling and natural uneasiness. Sage noticed that the star was not wearing make-up; except for the surgical enhancements. At his LA house Laz had been painstakingly blushed and glossed, sponged and lip-brushed: one of the things that had warned Sage that no matter what it looked like, they were never going to be off camera.

'Hey. Hi, Sage. You must be Mr Preston. Sorry we have to meet this way.'

'It was good of you to let us come back here.' Ax sat in an armchair.

'You might have thought it was a fuckin' imposition,' said Sage, likewise.

'No problem,' the star assured them, facing them on the leather and hessian couch. 'I'm glad I was able to make it. No words can express how sorry I am about the girlfriend. What is it I can do for you? I get that she was with you for the last time right here. If you want to be alone a while, that's cool, I can leave.'

'Oh well,' said Sage, turning the ring on his left hand, his blue eyes wide and insolent. 'Chicks, bitches. One more or less. Who can figure 'em? There's always more. It's you we're interested in, Laz.'

'We were wondering if we could negotiate you into joining our club.'

'You seem to have the credentials. We just need to know a little more.'

'About your résumé,' explained Sage. 'With which chapters are you already affiliated? The initials will do: so long as we know who's riding.'

Ax was afraid they had fucked up. They had not attempted to script this encounter; the hostility had just broken free, irresistible. But fuck it, we are rockstars, our girlfriend died, we don't have to be nice and polite . . . At Sage's last words, the megastar's look of surprise collapsed into intense, angry shame.

'No one rides me!' he cried.

Ax's heart jumped. Paydirt.

'Oh, really? We think otherwise.'

He was swept by rage. When the fucking callous lying breaks down, when the bastards let you glimpse the truth, that's what betrays you. He could barely restrain himself from leaping across the room and throttling the shite—

Who are you working for? What have you done with her?

Sage gave him a glance, and Ax held it back. But pursue this!

'Are we on camera now?' asked Sage, cheerfully. 'Nah, you don't have to answer. I'll take my chance if I'm being recorded for the fans, or for your keepers, big boy. You see, we need the details of how she died, so we can grieve and move on. We want to know *who* was riding you. Who told you to invite us, Laz? Who told you to invite us up here, so they could take our girl, kill her and dump her—'

'Okay, listen,' said Lazarus, his hands on his thighs, his long fingers stretching and clenching. 'Listen. We're not on camera, we can talk, but it has to be short. I am . . . Lemme try an' explain. Someone can be on a mission. I knew someone, white, I didn't care, someone I used to call Aoxomoxoa . . . We used to talk about things like where the world was at, and how someone ought to put a hand to the wheel an' *do something*; among a whole lot other piss-up-the-wall nonsense. But I don't know him anymore, he's a stranger to me. A person like me can get involved in something. It might be big, and important, and *necessary*. One of you is Ax Preston. I'm not sure I ever met the other guy before the other day. But I'll talk. I came here to talk.'

They looked at each other, amazed.

'It's like a religion,' said Lazarus, unstoppable, 'but stronger than that. It's love of my country, born in the USA. You know what I mean? It also happens to be secret, but you come from Europe so you know what I'm saying, even tho' Sage talked to me as if I was a moron that day when he came to my house—'

'Did they tell you to *touch* me?' demanded Sage.

'They ask me to do things.' Lazarus plucked at the sleeve of his shirt, a loose, white sleeve, in some glimmering modern textile that moved like fine cotton. 'Mostly they want money, and I'm glad to provide, but sometimes they ask me to do things. They asked me to invite you up here. Okay, yeah, they also asked me to touch the ring, or the world won't continue turning right for me. I touched the ring. I had no reason to think any harm. I thought it was a *ritual*.'

'Bullshit. You knew what you were fucking doing. How *was* I supposed to talk that day, Laz? Who the fuck was I talking to?'

'Hey,' said Ax, 'let the man tell us, Sage—'

Laz was still plucking at the white sleeve. 'I'm here to explain, and then you'll know I did you no wrong. You may think I ran out; it wasn't like that. I had to go away, it was a working vacation. When I heard she was found dead, I knew I had to tell you guys the truth, soon as I could. As much of the truth as I know. I have to get this off . . . I'm still on the mission, but nobody *rides* me. There's gonna be a discussion of terms. I didn't know what was going to happen until it was happening, I swear to God, Sage, and even then I didn't know what it meant—'

His task was giving him strange difficulty, as if he was very smashed, or trying to do something in a dream. They watched, fascinated as he managed to fumble and nudge the fabric out of his way, revealing a dark bracelet of plaited cord, almost the same shade as his skin. 'I need to get this off, first. Then I'll tell you—'

Sage said, in a changed tone, 'Laz, I don't think you should do that—'

'Fuck you.' Lazarus gave the cord a sharp jerk and it parted. He looked up. His light-coloured eyes were shining, as if with tears. He gave them a wide, vivid smile, like someone who's burned his boats: and then turned his head, listening.

'Ah, shit,' he said. 'We are about to be interrupted. Be cool, it won't—'

He listened again to the voice in his ear and his expression shifted into deep disgust. The sound of an approaching vehicle: it drew into the cabin parking space. All three men listened, Lazarus silent and disgusted, but seeming neither afraid nor surprised.

'Are you guys armed?' he asked, casually.

'Yes,' said Sage.

'Huh. Thought you might be. Half-assed terrorists. Don't show, even if you are provoked, or you'll catch hell, and me too. I can handle this. C'mon.'

They left the chill room and its paradoxical flood of baking light and repaired to the cathedral-roofed entrance hall, where they met a party of estate guards: five uniformed men. Their uniforms and peaked caps bore the Pixelity Studio logo, the little heap of rainbow-cubes. They were armed, but apart from the officer's pistol in a buttoned holster, the weapons were non-lethal; the mood wasn't hostile. The guards were black, naturally enough, like their nominal master. The officer was Asian.

'Hey, you goons. The servants' entrance is around the side—'

'I'm sorry for the intrusion, Mr Catskill.'

'It's Roy, isn't it? What the fuck is it, Roy? What's wrong with the phone? What kind of an emergency brings you to my withdrawing room door?'

'No emergency, it's kind of a mistake. We discovered these guys aren't on the visitors' list any more, access to Mr Catskill's family denied. They're coming up suspected capable of lethal violence, and we have to escort them from the estate. Mr Preston, Mr Pender, this is embarrassing, but it can be okay. It's nothing personal, I know you're not dangerous and what happened in England was not terrorism on your part. It's the studio, I only work for them.'

'They let you in when they're not supposed to,' said Lazarus to Ax and Sage, shrugging, but extremely pissed off. 'I get this all the time.'

'We'll leave,' said Ax. 'No problem. We'll be in touch.'

Lazarus looked from one to the other, with the warmth of someone who has discovered a pair of treasured friends. 'Yeah. Soon, my brothers. An' we'll discuss that other thing. We'll discuss it fully, I swear.'

He turned, with a wry grimace, to retire into the house. Two of the men were in his way, having moved over to make sure the unauthorised guests didn't escape back to the inner rooms. They didn't get out of the way quickly enough. Lazarus might have been jostled as he tried to pass them: or maybe his annoyance at the situation just got the better of him.

'Don't touch me!' he shouted, and lashed out. One of the guards went down, floored by an unrestrained, power-hammer swing.

It couldn't have been the first time. Laz Catskill was a family-values star now, and his violence didn't get into the media, but he'd been as volatile as Aoxomoxoa in his time; most likely he hadn't reformed. But this was that rare unlucky occasion. The two men who'd stayed by the outer doors, confused by the presence of Mr Preston and Mr Pender, grabbed for their weapons. One of them fired a non-lethal stun gun, the other let fly a projectile that burst into a wide sticky net of webbing. The plastic bullet hit Lazarus full in the chest at about five metres: he gasped and fell. For a moment this was masked by confusion. The guard who'd been punched staggered to his feet, his companion struggling and panicking in the web, the other pair rushed to their assistance—

The two Englishmen, caught between, watched this unfold—

'My eyes! My eyes!'

'Keep still, hey, you makin' it worse, stupid fuck, I can't—'

'Fuckin' shit! Laz is down!'

'Oh, fuck, the bastard's not breathing—'

'Get the paddles! His fuckin' heart has stopped—'

Ax and Sage joined the consternated group round the fallen body. Lazarus looked up at them, his eyes half open, gleaming sickle moons. 'I can't do the mouth to mouth!' complained the guard who'd embarked on this. 'The nigger's fuckin' mouth is full of blood! Shit, it was only a plastic—' One of the others came running, with a first-aid case and a defibrillation kit.

'No!' snapped Ax, who had seen the colour of the blood on Laz's mouth. 'Are you crazy? He's got a broken rib, must be sticking in a lung—' Roy, the officer, turned back the embroidered vest Laz wore over his shirt. There was no stain, but a strange depression in the snowy white—

'Fuckin' shit!'

'Do you have a medical imager?' said Ax. 'Fetch it. And get a helicopter ready, fast as you can—'

The imager was brought, and placed over Lazarus's chest. Roy muttered his disbelief, in a language from far away. They didn't need to be experts, it was obvious that the heart was twice the size it should be. It looked like a crumpled blot of rubble, like an asteroid in false colour. 'Forget the machine,' said Sage. 'Get the medics up here, tell them to bring heart and lung bypass, and get him into the freezer room. Chill him. You're not going to start that pump again.'

'Shit,' whispered one man, in a shaking voice. 'We should *move* this guy?'

'I th-think that's kind of an academic question,' said another. The guard who'd fired was sitting on a designer sofa, his head in his hands.

'You better leave,' said Roy, to Ax and Sage. 'Better you were never here.'

The cathedral-roofed hall was full of invisible bodies. There was a murmurous congregation, just out of the reach of sight and hearing, hovering all around.

Ax found a place to pull off, a glade for parking at the start of a hiking trail. He cut the aircon and put the windows down. The spicy, bramble scents of the sun-soaked forest reminded him of the time they'd spent at the cabin, lying by Laz Catskill's pool. So strange, when he'd seen that girl on the slab and known it was not his baby, his next thought, after the wild relief, had been that it didn't matter if it was Fiorinda or not. She's gone, her life cut short, despoiled of her chances and raped of her identity, and it makes no difference who she was, we are so close to each other— He thought of Lazarus Catskill's face in the photos, the soul stolen by fame: but Kaya has still lost her husband, and that little toddler has still lost her daddy.

'D'you think he'll live?'

'No.'

'D'you think that was magic we just saw?'

'Yeah, very possibly.'

'That was magic, Rufus O'Niall style. I wouldn't have called it subtle.'

Sage shrugged. 'Whoever it is is just starting out.'

'Lazarus had been recruited, he was just a go-between. What d'you think? Was he was working for a rogue, occult division of the CIA?'

'I don't know. An' we're not going to find out now.'

They were silent; ideas they had not shared with the Few unspoken. Ax thought of his girl, facing the dreaded whitecoats all alone to find out if she could have her baby. But she'd been convinced she was a monster, forbidden to have a child. What if the good news had sent her over the edge, into total fugue? Where might her broken mind have taken her?

'Some models of the theory say we all have potential for effective magic,' remarked Sage. 'The cost to *la grande illusion*, I mean normal consciousness, is so heavy that our brains evolved full of blocks and checks to prevent fusion from developing. But they could be shifted, maybe in many cases.'

'Great. Armies of magicians, competing to twist reality.'

'Yeah. That's more or less the fusion consciousness theory of everything—'

'We don't understand this situation,' said Ax, leaving the fusion consciousness theory of everything to ruminate with the superstrings, the Higgs boson and whatever other esoteric proposals. 'We can't make a move without screwing up.'

'We aren't doing too well, are we?'

'We should never have left El Pabellón. That was our big mistake.'

The damp fishing-camp cabin, cinnamon buns in the misty morning, seashells and cactus mice; Fiorinda in such a bad state, and Sage so weak and ill. Only pain and sorrow ahead of them, a life spent nursing their darling through her sojourns in hell. Ax remembered it all with passionate longing. And from what grim coign, he wondered, will I look back on this sunlit clearing as some kind of heaven?

Why did I let her go off alone? Why did I make myself dictator? *Why*, having broken up with the Chosen, did I immediately commit myself to *another* family band, totally essential to me, totally intolerable? *No cuddling in session.* I'll have your head on a spike for that, Ms Marlowe. On Tower Bridge, yeah. But she was only trying to be cheerful ... You give all your strength, steadfastly believing you will never need it again, and then you have nothing, when your need is greater than ever. Since Fiorinda vanished he had been trying in vain to kickstart himself, to find the Ax Preston who had decided *I am going to save this situation. Not because I can, but because I must.* There's nothing left, nothing but a blundering endurance—

He thought that Sage had gone off into one of his abstractions. When they'd been soldiers in Yorkshire, in the Islamic Campaign, this used to happen – long before the Zen Self. Sage could go blank, pondering on some bit of code he was writing in his head, while waiting in ambush for a bridge to blow; you could find yourself crouched in peril next to a living statue. He looked around and found Sage watching him like a child; it was Ax who had gone wandering.

'Hey.' He held out his arms. Sage moved over, into the embrace.

'The nearest I can come to a sexual fantasy at the moment,' said Ax (and fuck the listeners); 'We are galley slaves, chained to the bench together, hauling on the same oar, blisters rubbed to raw flesh, and we have to keep going, boom, crash, boom, crash—'

'Mm.'

'Getting whipped sometimes, and it's always dark.'

'Sounds good.'

'Rare occasions, we're allowed to sleep under our bench—'

Sage heaved a sigh. 'Wonderful,' he mumbled; and they were quiet for a while.

'Ax,' said Sage, 'we won't come back here, will we?'

'To Silverlode? I doubt it, not after this.'

'This is the last place we saw her. Let's take a walk in the woods.'

They left the Rat and walked, until the AI car was hidden by a rise of the land and a turn of the trail, then they went into the trees and found a boulder to sit on.

'Shit,' remarked Sage. 'I forgot to ask him to take the hex off.'

And the man's dead, in all likelihood. 'Is it going to be a problem?'

'It'll be okay.'

'Is that what you wanted to tell me?'

'No ... Ax, Fiorinda is not a monster. Not even if she's out of her mind.'

'I *know* that.'

'That's the first thing. The second is, there's something I can try. I can try to locate her, maybe even pull her out. It's a short cut to the information.' Sage looked up into the vivid blue sky crisscrossed by conifer branches. 'The good thing is, we wouldn't need to know who is holding her, or why, an' we could stop trying to figure out whether we're dealing with the CIA or the FBI, or the KuKluxKlan. It wouldn't matter if she was in, fuck, Japan. Venezuela. Or the Anza-Borrego desert—'

'You've been thinking about this for a while?'

'Yeah,' admitted Sage. He chewed on the lower joint of his right thumb, a habit that dated from when his right thumb had been a crippled stump. 'We'd have to revive plans for the live show. It involves information-space science, but not fusion—'

Ax felt the white light. He searched his pockets, found the battered pack of cigarettes he carried around for emergencies, lit one and drew on it.

'And you had to be desperate ... Okay. Explain it to me.'

Some people affected to be shocked that the English were going ahead with their Hollywood Bowl concert, with Fiorinda's body lying in the morgue. But sentiment covered commerce with the usual veil: it's a celebration of her life, of course. Harry hadn't got round to cancelling the booking, so there was no problem in reinstating the gig. They went to inspect the historic venue with Harry and an entourage: studio folk, Bowl staff, security. The amphitheatre was almost deserted in the mid-afternoon, apart from a few stray sightseers, its great white shell like something tossed against the green cliffs and abandoned there by an ancient tsunami. Chip and Verlaine took the elevator to the top of the cheap seats and found a view that held them, respectful, astonished, in the eucalyptus-scented heat and silence.

'This is notably beautiful,' declared Verlaine. 'I didn't know they did natural beauty in Los Angeles. It hardly seems right.'

'How great to see a fabulous ruin in the making. It's as good as anything in Greece, oh, this will be one with Nineveh and Tyre, mark my words ... It reminds me of Epidavros,' decided Chip. 'You know, the big theatre place?'

'Yeah ... But nobody comes here for the healing dreams.'

'Not until now, my dear Pippin. Aoxomoxoa's going to change all that.'

The Adjuvants understood what Sage was going to attempt, and they knew it was right out on the edge of possible, but they had faith. They'd never known the king of weird to fail, if he wanted to take a crowd by the throat and *rule*—

Sage walked out on the hallowed boards, dressed down in worn jeans and a *Hello Kitty* T-shirt, accompanied by Harry Lopez in a pink linen suit. Sage was shaking his head and looking mean. He wanted to do immix, and had been hustling to get the gig moved indoors. But Harry was in love with his Hollywood Bowl plan: either that, or he was determined not to let Sage do any brain-burning. Sage had tried – as Harry had discovered – going behind his back and working on Julia, but no dice. Julia knows who she works for. She's not as ditzy as she makes out.

'Faces east, well, that's essentially *wrong*,' said Sage, frowning mysteriously. He stared up at the ranks of bleachers. 'What's the capacity again? Eighteen k?'

'Seventeen and a half. Or a little over.'

'I fucking hope you can sell those tickets, Mr Loman, to a tired, oversized suburban venue with no public transport, in short order. I would hate to look out there and see empty seats, on Fiorinda's night. That would piss me off.'

'Sage, there's transport, and we'll limo the VIPs: it's *done*. We could sell out over and over. I'm already looking at a repeat performance—'

'Oh really?'

'I thought it would be cool to do the twenty-third of August, the actual date the Beatles played here—'

He was skewered by a vicious stare. 'Don't do it, or you're gonna annoy me.'

'Okay, right, sorry, I forgot. I will not mention the Beatles. Sage, why have you taken to wearing the mask? Not that I object, the mask is very cool, but—'

'It's because I'm fucking miserable, me,' said the living skull, its weirdly expressive empty sockets swallowing the sunlight. 'She is dead, and that's most of what I think about, and if you could see my naked face, I would feel naked, do you see? I don't even know why I'm doing this gig, it just seems I must. I think I'm building a funeral pyre. But hey, I know how much is riding on this, golden boy, with one of your stars a suicide an' all. It'll be a great show.'

'You don't know how sorry I am. Totally sorry about everything.'

Harry genuinely seemed to be suffering. His manner was distracted these days. There were hollows in his soft cheeks, he winced at sudden noises and flinched if you spoke sharply. Some *complicated* remorse that must be!

'Do you have a virtual version of this shite bandstand on file at the studio?'

'I'd have to look that up.'

'I want it. I want a high-rez copy I can use on my board, by this evening.'

'Okay,' said Harry, hope dawning. 'I can get you that. You can do the show somewhere intimate another time: invitation only, I'll sort out some venues. I'm sure you're doing the right thing. It's what she would have wanted.'

'As you would know.'

'Sorry.'

Chip and Verlaine came bounding up from the orchestra. 'Hey, Sage, isn't this place *fabulous*? You have to come with us to the top!'

'You can see the Hollywood sign!' Verlaine informed him joyously.

'Someone put Julius Caesar on here,' Chip added, 'with Roman armies encamped around the canyon, fake aqueducts, fires in the night . . . fantastic, like an overlay from another world. You have to come and see, it's far out—' He noticed that Harry was looking startled, and drew himself up with dignity

'Grief takes us this way, Harry. We can be upbeat; it's how we keep going.'

'Okay, okay,' said Sage, resignedly. 'Take me to see the Hollywood sign; I suppose I need to know what the stage looks like from out there—'

'You're going to do it?' gasped Harry. 'Oh, thank God. *Thank you*. You'll have the file copy in an hour. And you'll let me sit in on a rehearsal soon?'

Sage turned, poised to leap from the stage: the skull's preternaturally white teeth gleaming, tiny flickers of muscle movement skipping over virtual bone; between mockery and derision. 'Real soon now. You trust me, don't you?'

Harry darkly suspected that there *was* no show.

Rob and Ax sat with Dora in the highest box seats, accompanied by Doug and a couple of the lads. The Few didn't go anywhere without their own security now: a token, shutting the stable door too late, but it comforted Doug Hutton. They watched Sage and Harry on the stage. 'The Beatles played in 1964,' said Dora, reading from a souvenir leaflet. 'Wow, I didn't realise it was so long ago. Oh, they once had Captain Jean-Luc Picard from *Star Trek* as King Arthur in a firework finalé—'

'*Don't mention the Beatles*,' said the others automatically. Stupid catchphrase jokes take hold easily in dire situations—

'1964, huh?' muttered Rob. 'Has it been painted since?' He poked at the wood of the seat, which was soft punk, shrivelled by many orthodox Californian summers, swollen by this year's storms of rain. 'I think there's a health and safety issue.'

Ax shook his head. 'Not required, Rob: it's time to stop baiting Harry. Sage has come round to the idea.' They had earbeads: they could eavesdrop on anyone in their party; of course, it was a safe bet they were also eavesdropped upon.

'You think the masque is going to be ready, Ax?' asked Doug.

'I'd be happier if George Merrick was here to kick him up the arse, but he can work fast when he's desperate.' Ax flexed his hands. 'I'm more worried about my contribution on guitar, tell you the truth.'

They fell silent, listening to Julia. She was trying, with the nervous insistence of one who feels her head is on the block, to coax Allie into fixing their avatar lab appointments. 'I'm still prostrate with grief,' remarked Ax, in a pause.

'Yeah,' said Dora. 'I couldn't give anything real to being dunked, not yet.'

They were wondering how long they could stretch this. The polls had declared that Fiorinda's death itself was cool, the punters found it romantic. But the surviving radical rockstars were tainted, and they could hear the sound of their credit running out. Word was, while he was talking to them about reprise dates at the Bowl, their great friend Harry Lopez was telling the studio bosses that he could do without the avatars, and he'd be happy to let the English go.

Some of the preparations for the funerary rites involved the UCLA neurology faculty at the West LA VA, where one of the virtual movie camp followers, Hollywood scruffs, was a postdoc. She'd been able to sneak Sage access to the cyclotron/PET scanner, where he'd conducted Positron Emission Tomography on the Few, in batches, at dead of night. No one had challenged them. They had the advantage that several members of the party were able to look perfectly at home in a neurology lab; should anyone have wandered in. Lissa the postdoc did the raw processing for him. On the fourth trip he went back alone with Doug, in an anonymous secondhand motor, also at dead of night, to pick up the plates.

'Fuck,' said Doug Hutton, sour because he was spooked. 'I've had some peculiar drug requests from you an' Ax in my time, but securing a supply of radioactive carbon dioxide fuckin' tops it. What was all that about?'

'The word radioactive worries people,' explained Sage. 'You have to sign things. If Lissa had nicked what we needed from UCLA, we'd have been spotted. You nick it from some other hospital, we're in the clear. What's wrong with you?'

'I don't know that it was nicked. I just bought it. What's it for, eh?'

'It's a marker. I have the folks inhale the gas, it gets into their blood. Then I can track the increase of CBF, cerebral blood flow, and glucose take-up, across the brain. From there, with a good image, I can extrap – get down – on an immix processor, to fractional firing, single neurons. Not totally accurate, but what I can use. PET tech is ancient, but it is very slick these days, an' it's commonplace. If I'd gone after cognitive realtime scanning, well, I would have had a shitload more trouble getting near. As it is, I have the raw material for an immersion of Fiorinda, enough aspects of her to engineer an entanglement, without—'

'I don't know what you're talking about, and I don't want to know.'

'Then why d'you ask? Just drive around the block while I go in and pretend to be a visiting research doc again. Hey, Doug. I could have worked here, what d'you think? In a real white coat, an' all.'

'I think you're nuts. Take the mask off, at least.'

'Right.'

Lissa was waiting for him: the brainy tinsel-town wannabe, with her pretty body-mods and a topknot of coloured braids. She handed over the stack of slim black boxes that held his darling, and he traded a fistful of backstage passes for the gig, plus a few rounds of her cutting-edge drug of choice. She'd have liked a different deal, but not one he could offer. 'I get that you're monogamous, Sage,' she said as she let him out of the silent basement, her cat-whiskers twitching. 'I mean, binogamous. But no one thinks party-sex is being unfaithful, and it would be good for me, socially, if I could say we did it. Wouldn't it be good for you? I mean, I'm hip and young—'

I am not so hard up, he thought, that I have to *pretend* I jumped your skinny underage little bones. Not that this kitten-faced morsel was underage; Lissa was older than Aoxomoxoa had been when he delivered a line like that to Fiorinda. Her fair-dealing attitude touched him.

He thought of Billy the Whizz.

'No, it would not be good. Don't tell anyone you did anything with me, Lissa. It could bring you bad luck. Don't let anyone know who gave you the passes, either.'

She stared at him. 'Am I in danger? Is this something to do with the murders?'

'You're not in danger, but be discreet. G'bye, and thanks again.'

He sat with the plates in a plastic bag on his knee, watching the swathes of security light on lawns and trees as Doug negotiated the dark campus. The car paused, obeying a stop sign. Who's that, heading back the way we came, crossing the gracious bole of a midnight tulip tree? It's the shadow of a raw-boned middle-aged fellow with a woollen shawl around his shoulders, a rifle in his arms and a whacking great sword at his back. Lissa is under my protection, thanks, he thought. Give me credit. But he believed he knew what seeing the ghost meant, and it comforted him.

You see all sorts of things, in this town at night.

A week before the date they gave Harry a preview, in a theatre at the village, in the faux space of the studio's virtual mock-up of the Bowl. They didn't show him Sage's immix effects, just the supergroup performance, but his relief was pitiful. It was a shame to let the bastard off the hook, but it was safer. The A&R man was looking more and more stressed-out, and was supposed to be on the point of dumping them. If they'd stalled him any longer, he might have decided to cancel.

Three days before the concert, Ax and Sage were summoned to a meeting. It happened in an anonymous conference room in the depths of the Los Angeles Civic Centre. Doug Hutton and Allie came along, but they weren't allowed in. Harry was there, and Philemon Roche and his partner Karen Phillips. So was Lou Branco, and Marshall Morgan from Digital Artists. The other faces around the conference table were new: a big, sixtyish, man in a suit, with a long, heavy-jowled face; two middle-aged power-dressed women, one of whom would surely have been more comfortable in uniform; more male suits; a couple of people who looked like rumpled academics. The big man they recognised at once, and the women were also easy to name.

They could have been visiting their own past. Everything was different; these were not hapless, hijacked young musicians, but the atmosphere of shell-shocked disbelief was the same. It hit them when they walked into the room, and filled them with terror. The big man introduced himself as Joseph Raine, and said he was Philemon's boss. Ax said politely that yes, he knew Mr Raine's position.

No other names were offered; there were no dogtags or place cards on display.

Lou and Marsh looked scared and confused. The white power-lady stared hard at Sage, but he wasn't asked to remove the mask.

Mr Raine told them, in case they hadn't worked it out, that this was the Committee brought together by President Eiffrich to investigate the problem on which Mr Preston, Mr Pender and the late Ms Slater had been consulted. He expressed his shock and sympathy. They nodded.

The news was that the body from the boat dock had at last been formally identified. Matching dental records and DNA profiles had been accepted in evidence by the coroner, plus a faxed affidavit from Fiorinda Slater's legal next-of-kin, her grandmother; who had viewed the less distressing evidence by video link. The body could be released. The expense of the cold air freight for her last journey, back to England, would be covered by the US government, with all honours for a brave lady who had suffered so greatly in her country's service. Mr Raine once more expressed his deep regret. He spoke for the whole Committee; and for Mr Eiffrich.

Fiorinda's gran had been the willing accomplice of Rufus O'Niall in the rape and torture of his daughter. She was over eighty, completely crazy, and lived in a comfortable high security nursing home, under close supervision. The ex-dictator and his former chief Minister made no comment on Gran Slater's mental competence: they did not ask to see the affidavit. Ax thanked the Committee for their sympathy.

'That's all the business,' said Mr Raine, quietly. 'We felt you should hear it from us, in full session. We felt we owed you that. We know the uncertainty has been a cruel addition to your loss, and in a sense we're glad to be able to end it. Now there's a document which we'd like you to sign, drawing the line under your involvement with the investigation.'

One of the minor suits came round and proffered a folder to Ax, a second folder to Sage. They glanced through the printed pages. The clause that jumped out said that they agreed not to raise the issue of suspicious or unexplained circumstances around Fiorinda's death: either with media representatives, or any other public or private agency, in the world, ever.

What would happen if they didn't sign, it didn't say.

'The thing I remember,' remarked Sage, 'is when we came to Hollywood, we were taken to a crime scene. We were asked for an opinion on the significance of Celtic human sacrifice, with your weapons developers maybe messing around with natural magic, an' all. You know, I don't really follow what happened about all that?'

Philemon Roche looked at the tabletop; Karen smiled uneasily. Harry Lopez rubbed a hand across his felt-tip moustache. Lou Branco looked like a toad plunged in boiling water, paralysed by fear and astonishment.

'With the greatest respect, Mr Pender, and Mr Preston, sir,' said Joseph Raine, 'Fiorinda's death is a tragedy for your nation, and a cause of great personal grief to many. I wish to God this hadn't happened, but I believe we have a right to disengage ourselves from any reflection on the highly secret work of this Committee.'

'You've given us a lot to think about,' said Ax, evenly. 'Probably we ought to take legal advice on this, could it be arranged?'

Marshall Morgan said, in an undertone, 'The studio can provide lawyers.'

Murmurs round the table; Digital Artists' lawyers would be acceptable.

'Thank you,' said Ax. 'We'd appreciate that.'

The copies of the document were retrieved. It was agreed there would be a second meeting, straight after the Bowl concert, with the studio lawyers present. Ax and Sage were respectfully escorted from the room.

'They took it quietly,' said Mr Raine.

'They do that,' said Harry. 'Stone-face, it's a double act. They won't throw you a bone. They go away and think about it.'

'Mr Preston is a guerrilla fighter,' remarked the black power-lady dryly. Her accent betrayed that she came from the east, probably from New England, indeed. 'He doesn't engage superior forces in the field.'

'Do you think they know they're under surveillance?'

'Yes,' said Harry, miserably. Of course they fucking know, he thought. Do they look like morons, those beautiful *galley slaves*? They're scripting everything you hear them say. He could not believe how badly this situation was being handled. But he could do nothing; the situation was far, far beyond his reach.

'Is there *no* way we can talk to Sage Pender?' asked one of the rumpled people, a scientist from Vireo Lake: oblivious of the atmosphere. 'An exchange of views, with the Zen Self champion. It would be very, very valuable.'

'We're past there, Joey,' sighed the white power-lady, whose accent marked her as a Texan. She ran a well-manicured hand through her spikey blonde hair. 'We're in the worst case scenario, remember? Can't you keep that in your head?'

'I think I want those two out of the country,' said the other woman. 'With their friends, as soon as possible.' She looked sternly at the movie-men. 'The publicised concert must go ahead, but straight after that—'

Joseph Raine said, 'That's a point, Miriam, but there are considerations—'

Lou and Marsh were like new boys in the playground. They didn't look at anyone, least of all each other. They feared they might not get out of here alive.

Ax and Sage were taken across the hall to join Doug Hutton and Allie, and asked to wait. Maybe it was hoped they'd start babbling wildly. They waited, exchanging banal remarks of mourning, and were released (given clearance to leave the Centre) after an hour. In the lunchtime bustle of the lobby they spotted Harry, talking to the unmistakable Kathryn Adams. Harry didn't see them, but Kathryn spotted them over his shoulder. One guarded, hopeless look, and she turned away. They were not surprised. They already knew Kathryn was no longer on their side.

'This body,' muttered Allie, 'what shall we do with it?'

'Send it home,' said Ax. 'They wanted to burn her. Let the fuckers bury her.'

Back at Sunset Cape they escaped to the Triumvirate suite. Sage's board lay on the rug, facing a row of high-rez screens, and an immix sketchpad flatbed. He was working on his code for twenty hours out of the twenty-four, rooted in front of this array, surrounded by the slim, leaf-shaped 'plates' that were the descendants of the big, old immersion-mastering Black Boxes he used to haul around in the days of Dissolution. He barely ate, he chugged glucose, he didn't sleep. The big gig? First time we've been on stage together in years, and it has to go with a swing? Have to wing it.

Sage folded down at once and reached for his eyewrap. He wasn't using his new contacts. They weren't familiar enough, and besides . . . tainted. We don't know our enemies, we know there's no one we can trust at Digital Artists. Ax picked up his cherry-red Les Paul from beside the bed and sat with it, softly picking. He knew this didn't disturb the maestro.

'Did they really think we'd sign that thing?' he wondered.

'Fuck knows. Do they have to be rational? Was it rational to kidnap her? I have no idea what's going on in their heads.'

They were routinely using signal jammers in the house. They spoke freely in here; if there was some bug they hadn't found, well, God's will be done.

'We don't know who kidnapped her,' said Ax. 'We don't know anything.'

Sage had used the UCLA basement connection because he did not want anyone to spot what he was trying to do. Sheer paranoia, few people in the world could have guessed, and with anybody else but Fiorinda on the other end of this, the task would have been hopeless. He was trying to set up a *cut and paste*, lifting (a known map) Fiorinda, from anywhere in local information space (local being a relative term here) and fusing it with (an entangled facet of the same known map) his immersion at the Hollywood Bowl. In four dimensions, bit by fucking bit—

'How's it going?' asked Ax, a question he rationed with himself.

'Too slow. Shit, my eyes are going to be *fried*. Stay? I like having you there.'

'I'm not going anywhere. Sage, if you can use a b-loc phone to facet someone from England to the Pacific coast, why can't you use b-loc to work with your band or Olwen on this? It would be as secure as you're going to get.'

'Totally different kind of . . . oh, well, maybe. Where is the b-loc?'

'I'll find it. Are twelve brainstate maps going to be enough?'

What he was doing, ironically, was something like reverse-engineering a virtual movie avatar. He had nobody to dunk in a tank, no living presence to scan with the lasers: instead, he was trying to map from percept brainstates – the effect that Fiorinda had on the brains of people who knew her very well – through a digital entertainment artefact, to the real woman, wherever she was. The masque needed to be a show-stopper, so there would be spectacle, but in the centre of it he would be trying to *conjure* her, something far trickier than fooling the punters' brains into believing in the ravening werevoles, the bulldozed corpses, tidal waves, sharks chomping them. Dimly he was aware that if this were possible for Fiorinda, then at some point, whoa, it's going to be *possible*, the non-local, realtime reading of the full deck, that we've fantasised about for—

He'd been very annoyed when he'd come to California and found that Janelle Firdous was already doing the lesser trick that had been such a tussle for him, natural realism. Now he was profoundly grateful for their trading sessions, and the ideas he could use for this further leap, right off the scale. Thank you Jan, an' it's a crying shame they won't let you use your immix in the movies.

We build her like a hologram, the way a scene recalled from memory is built in the non-existent space inside the brain, by Fourier analysis of orientation, spatial frequencies, troughs and peaks of luminance. We do this for emotions, cognition, everything. Right down among the fractional firings, take 'em map by map, there's no problem, it's as clear as print . . . but so fucking impossibly interwoven, *so many connections*. He didn't have the heart to explain to Ax that a secure mega-bandwidth phonecall was not the answer, because he was on his own. There was only one person he knew of who could have followed the game (well, maybe there's pure scientists, but I don't know them and I doubt it) and no, can't ask Jan, if there were time. Trust no one means *no* one.

The guitar sang on the edge of his concentration—

'What did you say? It's thirteen, with Doug. Yeah, I think it works. Hundreds, thousands of different brain-state maps wouldn't be a significant degree nearer to the full picture. This will be enough, sample . . . She is there, she exists, she's a term in the code for now, if you like: and unlike most people, unlike anybody else alive maybe, she's got a big open pipe to information space. She may not be using it, but she can't switch it off. Is that mixed metaphors? Sorry. And we'll have the crowd, many with their own strong percept of Fiorinda. I can take what they give me in feedback to the spectacle, and use it as amplification—'

'Sage—'

'Mm?'

'If she is dead, will this stunt of yours call up her ghost?'

'No. This is the wilder shores of information technology, not necromancy. Put it like this: I can reach her, if I can reach her, because what makes *Fiorinda* there for us, everything that makes the neurons fire about her, is part of this material present. If she's dead, *Fiorinda* isn't there to be found, and to reach her I would have to go beyond fusion, to the state I visited once. But I would not find her, she isn't there. I would be lost myself, in non-being.'

He felt Ax's silent, shuddering recoil.

Ah, talking on automatic pilot while working, never a good idea—

He peeled off the eyewrap. 'Ax looks into the abyss . . . I'm tired. I shouldn't have said that. I won't try to convince you that the abyss is a good thing.'

'Not right at this moment, Sage. Nirvana is just not my drug.'

'Nor me. That's why I'm here, remember. Having such a great time.'

They laughed, helplessly: and for a moment she was with them, in their illusory minds, in the illusory locus of this Californian bedroom suite. A trembling of the air, a fleeting touch: then she was gone. 'Ah, God.' Sage took a slim dark box, identical to the others as far as Ax could see, and bowed over it, hugging it tight in his arms. 'Ax, I don't like the future, it's worse than Yorkshire. Why can't we go home?'

In a corner of the room there was an outfit they were collecting, and trying to compact into two military backpacks. It was vital the stuff should be ready.

The evening of the concert the skies over Hollywood were thick with haze, but there was the promise of a clear night. Around eighteen thousand people (capacity and a little more) streamed from the limos to the VIP areas; from the parking lots and the park and ride buses into the picnic grounds. The atmosphere was of excitement and tension, not of mourning. Along with the curious, the sentimental and the Digital Artists' hired seat-fillers, there were thousands who felt that being here was a statement. Having the rockstar king of England to stay had thrilled many Los Angelenos. He'd given them a sense of the bigger picture on this global crisis, a feeling for the romance of common effort in dire adversity: something that they felt was none too far from their own lives right now.

There will be wars and rumours of wars, there will be signs and wonders—

The warm-up and the opening act were A-grade filler. There were carnival costumed dancers, there was a full orchestra, there were 'DJs' dressed as tranced-out hippies 'largeing' behind a row of decks. None of this was anything to do with the Few, who were backstage, surrounded whichever way they looked by 'discreet' men (and a few women) with guns under their coats – accepting the most brash and callous remarks about their loss, along with the kindest expressions of sympathy or praise for her, with the same total absence of mind: feeling as if they were sharing a profound hallucinogenic experience, that involved famous faces looming out of a fog. Was a lady of immortal years, wearing a long silver fox coat for pure swank in the July temperature, cool as ice, really seen addressing the former Aoxomoxoa, saying to him, break a leg? Or who can tell what . . . ? Nah, that can't have been real.

Ax was numb, dead level, while the rest of them were getting high. He spent some time counting up the extra minders, presumably provided by the Committee, and trailing Allie and Dilip, hoping to catch them getting physical so he could say *no cuddling in session*. He wouldn't have had the heart: DK was looking so fragile . . . But don't think about that. He remembered he'd become an expert at compart-mentalising the fears when he was dictator; and it's not a bad trick. At sunset he found the Muslims and went off with them to pray. By the time he came back the Few were on stage, Rob and Sage at the mics, Felice's trumpet soaring, Dora and Cherry leaping about while they blew their horns. The rhythm section was provided by The Sidemen, jazz musicians with whom Rob and the Babes had formed a relationship over the last weeks, joined by Smelly Hugh on guitar. Ammy's fiddle wandered around merrily; Dilip and the Adjuvants jived on sound and vision. It was a long time since they'd played a make-do for a big crowd. When he was sure it was good, and that the crowd were enjoying themselves, he went to join the legendary Stu Meredith, who was presiding over the onstage sound.

Stu, an ancient monument with a long grey pigtail, ropy arms laden with turquoise and silver, who'd worked with all the gods you could name, greeted Ax like an old friend, though as far as Ax could recall they'd never met before. The alt.big band numbers had gone by. Sage was duetting with Rob, singing Bob Marley, two great voices and the best songs, a surefire combination.

'You know,' remarked the grizzled engineer, shaking his head, 'I sure never figured Aoxomoxoa for one of the survivors.'

'Sage?' said Ax, absently, 'yeah, he should be dead many times over—'

'I'm not surprised he came out the other side of the smack and the booze. Whatever you rockstars have, the docs oughter bottle it and vaccinate kids at birth. You're all fuckin' survivors, you can count the casualties on one hand. Jim Morrison, Janis, Jimi Hendrix, Kurt, I s'pose you could add Elvis, and Garcia. I meant, survived as a human being. When he was here last that was not on the cards. Sweet-natured, yeah, I guess, but he was bouncing off the walls. The band fuckin' worshipped him, but nobody else, even if we knew he was a genius. Even the ladies, and they loved what he did with his dick, couldn't take much; aside from Janelle. He was a spoilt fuckin' disaster, heading for bedbug superstar crazyland.' Stu handed a spliff, with a fatherly smile of approbation. 'Someone must've turned him right around.'

It wasn't me, thought Ax. I think it was a certain red-headed babe.

But something rose in him, something he badly needed tonight. He had always wondered why Sage loved him. He was sitting a few metres from the stage, back to the action, listening to his earbead and watching a screen, and it crossed his mind that they could be thousands of miles away from the actual musicians. The sound at a gig like this had been digitised, managed, subjected to fractional distillation, culverted like a river in a pipe, rebuilt, and delivered back to the performers brand-new, for decades ... This made him think of what Sage was going to try and do, and he felt a distant thrill, a distant memory of the time when he had been excited by futuristic tech – when he'd thought it worth any sacrifice to ensure that the marvels continued, and the modern world didn't go down into the dark.

And the future is what happens while your life gets in the way.

'D'you ever worry that we'll be out of a job, Stu? The way the technology is heading, who's going to need an old-fashioned guitarist or a sound engineer?'

Then he was afraid he'd been tactless, talking to a veteran like that.

'I've worried about many things, over the last eight, ten years,' said Stu, accepting the good grass again. 'You hear about what happened to Europe, you see it starting here. You see your kids get used to doing without things you took for granted. Fuck, you know, my kids don't even *notice* there's no such thing as just taking a plane to another city anymore. They have no sense of loss. And there's worse things ... It wakes you up in the middle of the night.'

He took a couple of steady draws, mashed the roach between his fingers and replaced it in his smokes tin.

'But someone turned me around. I believe we can beat this crisis, and come out with something different but better. No, I don't worry I'll be out of a job. I'll work for the love of it, the way I always did ... I was at the Islamic Centre in East LA,' he added; 'I heard you speak there. I'd never been in a mosque before.' He held out his large, gnarled hand, laden with rings. 'It's been an honour to meet you, Mr Preston, and a privilege to talk with you. It's meant a great deal to me.'

Ax shook Stu Meredith's hand, wondering what he had said at the Islamic Centre: just now he couldn't remember a word. There had been a time when he had worked, constantly, hustling to elicit this response in every person he met; and he had come to hate that in himself. But perhaps it isn't what you do. Perhaps it's what you are, and you just walk along behind it, like a man with a sandwich board.

Now Sage was down the front, singing 'The Ballad Of The Big Tattoo', a humorous number he'd done live for many years, with different idiotic verses every time, finally released on *Headonastick*. He'd shed his suit jacket: he was wearing a white singlet and white trousers, his shoulders and arms gleaming in the stage lights, blue eyes sparkling. He tossed his radio mic, which vanished, because of course it was only virtual, and went into some fuck-you gymnastic clowning, to the delight of the mosh (or posh Hollywood Bowl equivalent). Ax had such memories, his eyes dazzled.

Fiorinda, Aoxomoxoa's back, but where are you?

'I think you're on, son—'

He joined the matrix of light and darkness, into the hands of a competent stage crew: took the Les Paul, and looked out. Strange to see them piling up in big, raked rows, in the out-of-doors. But it could be anywhere . . . Oh shit, *Sage forgot to get Laz to take off the hex*. He had a premonition of doom, but now he must play.

Thoughts of her, rising through the music.

The day I bought her those red cowboy boots. It was September, the leaves were turning on the horse chestnut trees. I had known her for two months, we had slept together four or five times. Oh, remember the quality of those early days. We were walking along the Kings Road together, and stopped to look into a shop window, I saw her drooling, little ragamuffin punk diva, for the red cowboy boots. I took her in there and I bought them. So then she bought me the beaded belt, instantly: no idea how to do it gracefully, matching my price to the cent, because she had to restore the balance. I knew she had no money, and I felt terrible.

But the boots had worked out. Fiorinda had loved those boots to death, and Ax had watched them becoming treasured with a feeling of profound relief; years later he had still looked at them and thought *whew, that was a close one ...* when that edgy little babe had become the woman I knew I would love forever—

just to do it all again—

Harry Lopez was in the Garden seats with the studio execs party Marsh had brought along. He was a member of his boss's entourage, as the Few would have put it, and he felt wronged by the accusation. If things had been different, if Fiorinda had been up on that stage, he'd have been with Kathryn and her pals: but she had decided she didn't want to be here, and he could understand why. He didn't know why he was here himself, or maybe he did. Some deep primordial stupidity in him was still impressed he'd been able to do this, to reach out and make a dream come true, what awesome power is that? 'That guy was one of the greatest living guitarists,' intoned one of his colleagues, a direct competitor, if Harry had any rivals. 'It's a fucking crime he got mixed up in politics, and ended up selling out, doing this kind of variety show.'

'I have all his records,' Harry replied, riveted by the tiger and the wolf in their electric *pas de deux*. He knew for a fact this colleague had never heard of Ax Preston before Harry's project started the movement. The night air was cool, and he wished he was at El Pabellón, and nothing had gone wrong. 'I bought the T-shirt.'

He was in awe of their professionalism, knowing the furious reality of their mood. He did not understand why they were doing this gig, but he was in awe. Did they know the truth? Whenever Harry let himself think about the truth, fear and dread threatened to overwhelm him. He kept on going through the motions, but at any moment he thought he might start start screaming and never stop—

Two and a half hours. It was eleven-thirty when they took a break before the finale. Sage's immersion effects had been lo-key, blending with the Bowl's stage lights, no different from a lightshow: except that these fx would leave no trace on photographic film; or any conventional recording medium. In the break, the amphitheatre became a nest of coloured lightnings. Sage in his white suit had stayed out there alone, doodling on the videographics desks – that the English called visionboards – setting something up, bantering with the front rows. Apparitions flickered over the hillsides and played through the crowd: you might feel a hand touch you, or find an impish face looking over your shoulder, hear the brush of wings, see animals running: all of it really happening only in your brain . . . whatever that meant. Anticipation climbed high, some of it mediated by those little immix tweaks. The brain gets very alert, in response to out of context perceptions, thinking to itself (so to speak) *what the fuck's going on?* There was also the thrill of the cutting edge. The people knew they were getting a show based on information-space science, devised by the first person to use direct cortical stimuli for entertainment. They'd read it in their programme notes.

Cherry and Dora, Chip and Verlaine, gripped hands at the back of the stage. 'You realise we're her occult group?' whispered Chip. 'Don't *say* that—' hissed Cherry, furiously. 'This isn't magic, it's science.' 'There isn't any difference any more, Chez. Honestly, no fucking lie, there isn't!'

'Fuck off, shut up and c'mon, we're on.'

There will be no encores, announced Sage. This is it. And I wonder what it can be? A Beatles medley? Laughter. Opening chords, and a *wave* of laughter. Oh, he has them in his hands, like always. But don't touch him, he's a real live wire—

Relax!

On *Unmasked*, their collection of golden oldies, the Heads had covered the notorious Frankie Goes To Hollywood track, and perversely elected to treat it like a nursery rhyme. This was what the Few enacted, to the joyous childish beat: a kids' version, a Disneyland version, a little child on tiptoe, dazzle-smiled at a wonder show (can you imagine sex like that?). It segued into the immix finalé, which took possession of the Hollywood Bowl: something wicked and innocent, a puckish spirit, doing sneakily impossible things, so that the audience saw the dancers on the stage start dancing into the air, and they went marching around up there, candy-coloured costumes repeating in mirror cascades, bright-eyed faces springing into focus and flying away again: bands of dancers, arm in arm, high-kicking; treading hamster wheel circuits on the darkness, spinning into spirals, a Busby Berkeley phantasmagoria, a mocking, teasing, thrilling compliment to tinsel town.

The Los Angelenos loved it. They were on their feet, en masse, clapping and prancing, chanting the lyrics, grinning in delight. When the wheels ran down and the children all came home, and there was no one left on the stage but the maestro, they stayed on their feet yelling and stomping, until he'd put away the last of the coloured toys, to the fading notes of a nursery rhyme, on solo guitar.

Ax came out of the shadows. 'This is for Fiorinda,' he said quietly, leaning to the old-fashioned upright mic that had been set beside the desks, under cover of the immix. None of her music had been played all night. Silence fell.

Ax played, and the two men sang, leaning close together. No fireworks, no sexy electric *frisson* between the guitar-man and the crowd-teaser this time.

> *Put your sweet lips a little closer to the phone*
> *Pretend that we're together, and alone—*

The sound of their voices, Ax's lighter tone blending with Sage's soft and deep, died away. The stage was perfectly dark now, except for their single spot. Every light in the canyon was quenched, and Fiorinda's voice came from very far away, but quickly growing clear and strong.

> *Love is like water,*
> *it runs downhill*
> *It takes the line*
> *of least resistance—*

The Angelenos held their breath, anticipation ramped up til their ears rang. Sage stepped back behind the desks and donned an eyewrap. 'That means he's going to do this live,' whispered an immix vet, wisely, to her neighbour in the cheaper seats. 'He'll be reading what's happening to the code and feeding the results back into it. I didn't know you could do that in an open space.'

'Right!' muttered the neighbour—

Ax moved into the solo that he'd done for 'Love Is Like Water' on *Yellow Girl*. He was aware of the Few behind him in the shadows, and Sage beside him, incandescent with nervous energy. He was so afraid he was going to lose both of them, he wanted to yell STOP THIS, but the words fell and broke on the boards of the stage; all he could do was play, fear like the taste of metal in his mouth, she was my country, I lived in her, *I'm going to lose both of them*, right here and now, because Sage can't possibly do this, he's trying to cut and paste the world as if reality can be chopped about like graphics code, but there's only one way he can do that, and he'll never come back this time—

But he must play, and feel the others with him—

Something was taking shape in the sky above the canyon. It seemed like a leaf-shaped split in the sky, then it was a flame, a shooting star, flying towards them from high up in the darkness, and spinning as it flew. 'Ah!' breathed Dilip, falling to his knees, 'ah, Shiva Natraj!' Allie Marlowe pressed the heels of her hands into her eyes, but she could not control what she saw, nothing would blot out the letters, Yod-Hé-Vau-Hé, *damn you Sage, don't you do this to me!* She realised in horror that she was resisting the immix that would bring Fiorinda home, and let the name of God fill her mind, so be it, יתוה whatever image works—

> *Love is like fire,*
> *it needs fuel to burn*
> *There's no love*
> *without a lover*

I can do this, thought Sage, amazed, not well (while the code flowed into his eyes and out of his fingers, the hand/eye physicality an essential adjuvant): nothing like as slick as in nature, but I can see, wow, have to be fast, what needs to be done and get there, by any means necessary, but my God! He genuinely had not understood, barely thought about what he would have to be doing, to get her back: only seen the result he needed and ways to reach there, oh, fuck! You and I, Janelle Firdous, movie-maker, because you led me to what I'm doing now, are the first two people to start deciphering information space. Jan, where are you, you should be here!

Look!

Look! What we can see!

And nothing more, because at this point Sage lost it, completely. He couldn't think, he had become a white-hot conduit for what was happening. The clouds parted and down she came, flying, wearing the image that Sage's code had clothed her in, a summoning from an antique fantasy game, and landed tiptoe, in front of Ax, a slender opalescent goddess, power gleaming in the swell of her naked breasts, grey eyes astonished. Sage left the desk, they fell at her feet, they held her hands, warm and living, for a moment *she was there*, not a goddess, not a ghost, Fiorinda standing on the stage clutching their hands, opening her lips to speak, the penumbra of another place around her, and something stands out, what the fuck is that . . . ? Sage cried, ah, shit, no, no, no, please—

She was gone.

Ax came out of a monstrous, wracking, dry orgasm to find himself on his knees, on the stage at the Hollywood Bowl, clutching Sage's hands, in the blank of his mind something saying, *I did not fail, in England. I did well—*

'There was something in the way,' whispered Sage, his face taking shape as if from primordial nothingness, white and black shadowed, drained and haggard as if he'd just run a marathon (where have I been? wondered Ax: where was I just now?).

'I nearly had her, Ax, but there was something in the way.'

He wiped his eyes.

'But I know. I *know*.'

7

Desperadoes

At eight a.m. the morning after the concert, the Few gathered in the dry whirlpool. Doug and the security crew were with them: Sage and Ax had been out in the courtyard to watch the morning sky, and had brought the guards indoors. They could afford to leave the gatehouse empty, the English surely had plenty of other minders, out there in the dunes. The smouldering herbs in the Aztec bowl were a different mix today: a sharp, arousing, acrid scent, not that they needed anything to wake them up. They were still in the penumbra, the aftershock of last night. The spa was intensely blue, the echoes supernatural; every friend's face charged with meaning.

If the Few were glowing, the leaders of the pack were incandescent. They sat with the empty place between them, poised on the edge of flight, radiating the insane degree of energy and will that had once *ruled* the English nation: only more so. Ax had his timber wolf look, steely power; smiling alertness. Sage was like a beautiful gargoyle, a grin he couldn't control, wide-open eyes on fire.

'Now we have to go to this meeting, and ideally we won't be coming back ... Ah, sorry, I didn't mean that the way it came out.'

They were to meet the secret Committee at ten, at the Digital Artists village this time. They meant to go after Fiorinda straight from there, because they felt time was running out fast. They did not know where she was *yet*, but they knew where to get the information. They were frightening their friends—

'We won't be coming back because we will be leaving LA directly,' Ax clarified. 'So this is the last briefing—'

'What if the fuckers pin you down and throw you in stir?' asked Rob.

'Why should they?' reasoned Ax.

'They won't,' said Sage, with really alarming assurance.

Because they'll realise you're off your heads, thought Rob: but it wouldn't help, so he didn't say it. Truth was, he didn't want to hold them back, if he had known a way to try. They were convincing him, just like long ago.

'Oh shit,' said Dora. '*Don't* go in there and shoot your way out, Sage.'

Sage heard Fiorinda's voice, just her sweet, womanly and exasperated tone.

'I won't, Dor. I may not sound like it, but I'm in control. Truly. But we're leaving you, so before I go I want to teach you all to die.'

The Few accepted without question that they weren't coming on the rescue expedition. Doug and his men were not so happy, but they were staying behind too.

'To die?' Doug bristled. 'No one's gonna die, Sage. This place is very defensible. If a situation develops, we'll handle it an' scream for the cops.'

Ax said, 'We know you'll handle any conventional trouble Doug—'

'It's something I can do,' Sage explained, carefully. 'I've thought of it before, because we get into these bad situations, but then it's gone out of my mind, and this seems like the moment ... I can't make you invulnerable, some of you refuse to pick up a weapon. I'd feel happier if I knew you had a way to leave this mortal coil and be okay about the experience, no matter what.'

They knew that he was talking about the doomsday scenario. Nobody cared to ask what Sage *knew*: if he had found out, last night, when he touched Fiorinda, that she'd been right all along and that the Fat Boy was coming—

'I'll take it,' said Cherry, at once. 'That sounds worth knowing.'

'Good. What about the rest of you?'

Dilip, Chip and Verlaine, the Zen Self neuronauts, glanced at each other. But whatever was going on with Chez, it would have to wait for another time.

'Will this be a religious thing?' asked Allie. She had not forgiven Sage for pasting the Tetragrammaton on the inside of her skull, where it lingered, slowly degrading. 'Because if it is, I don't want it.'

'No, it will be a brain chemistry thing, involving neurosteroids and a trick mental exercise. An' I didn't do that to you, Allie. I push the buttons, I can't help what comes up on your screen.'

The rest made their feelings known; nobody left the basement. Sage tested them for contras, dosed them, and taught them how to use the altered state which would now be triggered in extreme conditions. The delivery took about an hour and a half. And then goodbye, no big farewells. You're on your own, folks.

218

They raced up the stairs to the Triumvirate suite, doomed to be rockstar late for the meeting: but Allie would get onto that. Their packs were in the Rugrat. Ransacking the rooms for last-minute items took only a few minutes. They still had to shower and change their clothes, but when the ransacking was done they crashed for a moment. Needless to say, they had not slept.

'We ought to eat.'

'How about alcohol?' suggested Sage. 'Plenty of calories in alcohol.'

'Okay, go for it. Me too.'

The tequila was cool but not frosty, and it calmed them. They sat opposite each other, across a stylish coffee table, and it's strange how memory works. Sage remembered a conversation that had not crossed his mind maybe for years: a night at the end of the Islamic Campaign when they'd sat together like this, in a hotel room in Leeds, and he'd done something like declared his love for this man; or so it had seemed in retrospect. But nothing homosexual, mind you. Good God, no.

'The furnishings are classier,' he said.

'Mm,' said Ax. They shared a smile: telepathy artefacts. 'Still buzzing?'

'You betcha. Swarms and *swarms* of bees.'

'But you'll be all right for this meeting?'

'Fuck off. Will *you* be all right? I will not fall over anything.'

The air-conditioning cut out. Sunset Cape's electrical company was doing unscheduled supply dips as a planet-saving measure. They waited, as if listening, as a tincture of mild warmth entered the air: something coughed and the chill returned.

'We go in there, we do and say whatever, we leave unmolested. That's the objective, no use trying to script it, we'll work it out as we go along.'

'Yeah. Be fluid.' Sage glanced speculatively at an open closet, filled with such Hollywood clothes as it had amused him to acquire, at Digital Artists' expense. 'What shall I wear to meet the Director of the FBI? Hahaha. Maybe I should wear a dress.'

'I'll wear the dress, fuckwit. I'm the one with the long hair. Wear a suit.'

To have been so close and lost her again filled them with dread; everything was omened now. But win or lose, this was unstoppable.

The Committee had borrowed a corporate-gracious salon in Marshall Morgan's office suite. Sage and Ax arrived an hour and a half late, wearing their Mexican suits, for old times' sake. Mr Joseph Raine made the rounds politely this time: introducing Special Agent Andreas Kohl, Counterterrorism; Special Agents Philemon Roche and Karen Phillips, Cultists and Insurrectionists; whom you know. Jan Brudik, Civil Operations Adviser, for the LAPD and the State of California. Marshall Morgan, and Harry Lopez, you know of course. The spikey blonde with the Texan accent was officially revealed as Steph Warchez of I-Systems, world-class Artificial Intelligence scientist-turned-businesswoman. You could take her as representing the secret rulers and the science base. The coloured lady from New England was Miriam Beaufort, Colonel of the National Guard, US Pacific Command: she kept a low profile, not much in the media, but she was a very significant person, these restless days.

Miriam Beaufort and Stephanie Warchez they'd recognised last time. Kohl and Brudik were presumably on the same level. The studio lawyers were called Grizel Watt-Andersen and David Ng, for whatever that was worth. The name check was the first intimation that the charade was over and their hackles rose, they were glad they hadn't scripted anything. They looked again at the faces and saw, falling into phase, that everything was rewritten.

'There have been some changes since we last met,' said Joseph Raine, when it was done. 'I have to offer you an apology, Mr Pender, Mr Preston. We have recently discovered that Ms Slater is still alive.'

'Oh yes?' said Ax, without a flicker of surprise. 'So where is she?'

The FBI chief pondered this response, and nodded slowly. 'Let me start at the beginning. Last winter, two General Electric Gauss 0003/zyg series Cr/t imaging scanners went missing. Yes, I said missing, not stolen. The paper trail indicated that they had vanished within the establishment, by which I mean the Pentagon. The President was informed, because this seemed to be a move in a dark game. We knew that certain of our country's military thinkers, people in positions of great power, had been covertly investigating the "quick and dirty" route to the new super-weaponry. When the Celtic murders in LA emerged, along with rumours of a "Fat Boy", the Committee was brought together. We believed we were investigating an internal scandal. We were wrong. We have discovered, very recently, where the scanners are located, and who is using them.' Mr Raine paused, his long, solemn face growing sombre indeed. 'It's not good news. They're in the hands of a group of Republic of California Countercultural extremists, sometimes calling themselves the Invisible People. They are also holding Ms Slater.'

He proceeded to tell them what had really happened. Fiorinda's disappearence had been treated as serious from the outset. An investigation that the English had known nothing about had been set in train. Before the Toyota had been found in Carlsbad, or the body in the boat dock, the FBI had known that she'd been taken and passed from cell to cell, through an underground network of secret activists.

'We were provided with a body, obviously so that the case of Fiorinda's disappearence would be closed. We made the best use of this, and continued to follow our trail. But the body itself, when examined, gave us alarming information. It was a chimera ... We found we had proof, beyond reasonable doubt, that the Invisible People have access to effective magic. That was the place we were, or thereabouts, when we last met you. We now think we understand why the "Celtic" sacrifices had such immunity; and we are beginning to trace links between the eco-terrorists, the Invisible People, and those murders.'

'A fatal error, or they don't give a damn anymore,' said Jan Brudik. 'We believe it's the latter. The death of Lazarus Catskill is another red light.'

'He was about to talk,' Sage pointed out. 'I suppose that was the problem.'

'One doesn't punish a major bankroller by killing him. Not unless money is no longer an issue. It doesn't encourage the others,' added Raine dryly.

'I thought the US didn't have an aggressive Counterculture,' said Ax. 'You never caught the European disease. Or so we've been told.'

'We have eco-warriors,' Miriam Beaufort smiled, without much humour. 'We don't allow them the oxygen of publicity. Would you, after what happened in Europe? They haven't been considered dangerous. Controllable protests, a steady few arrests across the country; though there are hotspots. We—' She glanced at Raine, a shared agreement to come clean (these two make the decisions). 'We did not know that this Californian network existed. Now we know that they exist, and they are trying to build human weapons, the cognitive feedback scanners prove that. We also know, we've had this explained to us by the experts, that effective magic is the big step. Once you have that, you have someone who can certainly be boosted to fusion.'

'I've been told,' said Raine, 'that fusion in this context could open the door to the "It's A *Good* Life" scenario, the state O'Niall had not reached. Is that the correct term for you? It's the term I've been instructed to use in my briefing.'

Sage and Ax looked at each other, straight-faced.

'What do you intend to do?' asked Ax.

'We must take them out, Mr Preston, to use the vernacular. We were not expecting this, but we will soon have the authority to act, and the firepower is ready to go, because these are troubled times. We have a plan, but your consultancy would be very welcome indeed.'

Sage frowned. 'Why didn't you tell us what was going on? Why did we have to believe she was dead? You know, I think we might deserve an explanation of that.'

'We're telling you now,' answered Mr Raine, with finality. 'You were to be told the full story at an appropriate point; this is deemed to be that point.'

'I'll say one thing,' broke in Steph Warchez, 'about this raid, now our English friends are here ... If you don't destroy the Fat Boy you've achieved zippo, and nothing says he or she has to be near the nest.'

'I think everyone's aware of that line of reasoning, Steph,' said Mr Raine. 'I admit that we do not know where their Fat Boy candidate is, but we know where Fiorinda Slater is, and she is Rufus O'Niall's daughter. Our contact insists that no coercion has been used, Mr Preston,' he added, soberly. 'Not as yet. It would seem she's holding out, but they must have made demands. We don't know the extent of her potential, talent, whatever you call it. We do know she's in an extremely dangerous position, and not only for herself, but for all of us.'

'Would your girlfriend break under torture?' said Special Agent Kohl, a white guy in his forties with receding hair and a neat dark beard. He had dog-eyes, heavily shadowed: nobody here looked as if they'd been sleeping much. 'Excuse me for cutting the crap, but that might be what we're talking about.'

'No,' said Ax, 'I would say not.'

The Committee members glanced at each other.

'There's something I want you guys to know,' announced Miriam Beaufort. 'I'm in favour of low casualties and clean strikes, and I was unsure about the President's line on Vireo Lake, the official project. I'm now with Mr Eiffrich without reserve. I have seen where it's heading and we'd be insane to go down that road.'

There was a murmur of assent, and relief at this ray of light. Marshall Morgan, cowed in the midst of his own splendour, kept quiet. Harry Lopez studied the carpet. He hadn't raised his eyes since Sage and Ax walked in.

'Well, we must get her out,' announced Mr Raine, placing his hams of hands palm down, with emphasis. 'That's what we're talking about, that's what we're going to do. We're going in there in force, overkill, taking no chances. We're staying on the ground, all the way, Mr Preston, with the minimum possible reliance on electronics—'

'We understand that's advisable—?' asked Jan Brudik.

Ax shrugged. 'It's the received wisdom when you're dealing with this. I'd stick with it. When is the raid coming off? You realise we'll want to be attached?'

'Where is this *nest*?' asked Sage. 'It's in California?'

Mr Raine answered Ax, ignoring Sage's question. 'That's something to discuss. There are considerations, not least the safety of two significant public figures. At all events we intend to keep you fully informed every step of the way. This leads me to the waiver, which you have seen before. We need you to sign before we bring you any further in. It's red tape, but it's essential red tape. Let's do it.'

Ah, the document again. Ax accepted his copy. He didn't understand the value of a signature (given under coercion!) on a piece of paper, but he understood that these people had the kind of power he had seen arise in Europe, over the Crisis: pragmatic, secret, absolute. The kind of power he had possessed himself. It was ironic that they thought they'd win Ax's trust by renouncing fusion consciousness, when he was ready to regard the new force as neutral, another kind of technology, neither good nor evil. But now he must sign, or this was a dead end. Horrible, but meaningless and it must be done. He took out his fountain pen – and noticed it was beautiful, an old friend, good to feel in his hand: he was planning how he'd take charge, do an Ax Preston on them. But Harry was looking at the floor.

The room was filled with fear; it bloomed in the air like a black, transparent rose, with misty tentacles of unlimited dread. The black rose was in all those pairs of high-powered eyes, trained on him so intently. Ah. They don't intend for her to survive. Of course they don't intend for her to survive. They're going to kill her.

He did not even glance at Sage, whose presence was so strong beside him.

'Mr Raine,' he said, laying down the pen. 'There's something I'd like you to do for me. I'd like you to call off your secret service; excuse me if that's the wrong term. I want you to leave us without minders, for, oh, twenty-four hours? Do you have that time? You're all over us, and you're very visible. We led you to Lazarus Catskill. I think we could get hold of some extremely valuable information here in LA: but not unless you leave us alone. No reservations, these people are professionals, completely alone.'

'Hm.' Glances around the table.

223

Please, thought Ax, nobody point out that Laz was immediately killed. But he knew there was no danger. He could feel the effect he was having—

'We could do that,' said someone. Brudik. Miriam Beaufort nodded. 'You've got it,' said Joseph Raine.

Sage was turning pages, muttering to himself, marking places. He leaned over, and asked Ax, in an indignant undertone, 'Did you see 37b (iii)?'

'I saw it,' said Ax, with reserve. 'I suppose it must have some relevance.'

'I don't see why.' Sage held up the document. 'Mr Raine, we're happy to look at a waiver to protect the US government from our grievance suits, but I wouldn't sign this thing if my mother's life depended on it. It has to be reframed. We have careers, you know, we can't live without the media. Excuse us, we need to talk to our lawyers.' He bounced to his feet and crossed to the side table where Watt-Andersen and Ng were sitting; Ax got up and went with him. 'Okay, We want you to move fast, you may well believe, but see what you can do about this . . . and this . . . oh, and *this*—'

The lawyers looked to Raine, who gave them the nod. They took instruction, nodding and smiling, looking as if as if they weren't sure they weren't hallucinating all this. 'You can get information the studio doesn't have from Allie Marlowe, at Sunset Cape,' said Ax. 'We'll expect to hear from you with a draft. In a few hours? Sage, shall we be on our way?'

'Don't forget 37b (iii),' said Sage. 'I want you to *lose* that one.'

They walked out, in a swirl of gangster-pastels.

'Well, whaddya know,' said Marsh, with a gleam of *Schadenfreude*. He grinned at the scary ensemble. 'Maybe they really are rockstars.'

They took the Rugrat out of Digital Artists and into the park next door.

'This is a *very dangerous drug*,' said Ax, gripping the Rat's wheel so hard it began to tremble in sympathy. 'What have we just done?'

'I know. I *know* it's dangerous. Fee w-would kill me if she knew I had you—'

They'd been nowhere near to the Zen Self state, last night on the Hollywood Bowl stage, but they had been close enough that they were tanked to the eyeballs on simultaneity. They were manic. Time's arrow was spinning head over heels, every impulse was *right*, every move they made was fabulously, inevitably falling into phase. They knew that this feeling told them nothing about the outcome. You can be gloriously at one with a tragic and terrible fate—

Ax lit a cigarette and drew on it fiercely. 'Sssh, Rat, it's okay ... Oh God, Sage, what if we fucked up our only chance?'

'Nah. We know where to get the only information we need.'

Ax didn't like the tone of his big cat's voice. 'Sage, you are not invulnerable. I saw you last time you'd been out to play with fusion in you.'

'Not invulnerable,' Sage repeated, drilling himself in the left temple and cackling. 'Not invulnerable!' He was using one of the fingers he'd had all along: a bad sign. 'Hey, don't worry. The fusion will drop us, we'll crash and burn long before we get to the sharp end of this.'

They laughed immoderately. Ax gave Sage his cigarette, which Sage took gratefully, although he never smoked tobacco. The black thoughts descended for a moment. They remembered that their babe had been the darling of millions for years, in the hothouse enclosure of Ax's England; that her strange brain had been primed with fear and loathing and disgust for seven months of eternity; that she had carved her name on the hearts of a core group of friends who would willingly die for her—

'They lost the scanners,' Sage shook his head in disbelief. 'Fucking hell.'

'D'you think they have someone on the inside?' wondered Ax. 'Who only just managed to get a signal out? Does that figure?'

'Maybe. And I wonder what his orders are, for when the shit starts flying ...' Sage turned to him, passionately in earnest. 'I don't know what happens. I don't care, as long as this time we don't piss around. We stick together.'

'I was an utter bastard to you, after she left us.'

'I've given you hell, in my time. I know you never stopped loving me.'

They grinned at each other, no effusive embraces: and into the mêlée.

Harry didn't know what to do with himself. He wandered the streets of Westwood Village, afraid to go home, afraid to be alone: staring at racks of funky dead-media music, in the microstores where he'd brought Ax and Fiorinda when they'd first arrived. He loved Westwood. Kathryn's friends lived here, and the whole ambience reminded him of her company. But she was not his pal anymore. The relationship which had been the most solid, lasting thing in his life was over; there was nothing left for him behind Lurch's smart little eyes ...

Sage's effects had given him an immersion hangover, full blown paranoia. He'd been convinced all day, even while sitting in that fucking horrible meeting, that something was about to pounce. He wandered, fighting the brain-chemistry: over-tuned, pumped up, waiting for something to happen that would reveal the grotesque, virtual nature of his environment. Outside the Supernova, a juice-bar haunt of movie wannabe society, he was hailed by Lissa Cunningham, the kitten-faced neurology postdoc who wants to direct (not having the wit to realise directing is a menial task in the modern industry). He sat down with her and she started talking doom news, which he really didn't need.

'You *know*, don't you, Harry?' she said, reaching to touch his arm with the razor-graze of her retractable claws. 'You know something really bad.'

'You should be an agent, not a director, with this clairvoyant gift you have. Money would drip from you, Liss.'

'I dream about the earthquake a lot. Some kind of hellish earthquake, bigger that you could imagine, is that it? Is *that* what's going to happen when—?'

'When what?'

Liss rolled her eyes. 'You know. When the Neurobomb comes on line.'

'Anything could happen. Absolutely anything. Look, I have to—'

He had seen the brown Toyota Rugrat with the scarlet trim and silver wheels. He got up and walked, fast. When he saw the Rat swinging in to the kerb he was outside the Empyrean Flea Market, where he could have lost them in the maze of stalls: but he expected them to leap out of the car. Instead, he was grabbed by someone coming up behind, someone very tall and uncannily strong. Pinioned, moved across the sidewalk like a toy, he was thrust through the opened door of the Toyota.

'Why did you do that to me?' he gasped.

Sage was not wearing the mask. His eyes seemed extraordinarily bright, his height and the long arms and legs intimidating, almost monstrous, in the closed space of the moving vehicle. 'Do what, Harry? I didn't hurt you, did I?'

Mr Preston was driving. He glanced around. 'Better get his phone, Sage.'

'He has an eyesocket button, but he hasn't called anyone and he can't now.'

'Get it anyway.'

Sage held out his hand, grinning with unnerving sweetness. 'Give me the button. In case you're wondering, you won't get an outside line. There's a temp'ry fault on telecoms in an' out of our motor.'

Harry dug for the button and handed it over, bruising his eyeball in the process. He remembered that the minders had been called off, oh fuck and *this was why*. He knew they were probably, almost certainly, armed. He was not.

'Are you abducting me? I can't believe you're abducting me—'

'Nah, nah, nah. It's not like that.'

Sage sat back and seemed to forget Harry's existence: he gazed at the passing scene with shining, smiling attention, as Ax treated the traffic like a death-dicing video game at which he excelled. At length they left the Santa Monica Freeway, on Overland Avenue. The Rugrat pulled up, after a bumpy ride, in a dirt lot surrounded by broken-down industrial units. Some fragment of late-night urban adventure flashed into Harry's mind, as if he'd seen this place before. It was a locale for Bohemian factory parties, for Hollywood scruffs; for human sacrifice. But he recognised nothing. Ax sprang from the front of the car. Sage picked up a rigid white briefcase. They led him to a shipping container, a trailer-sized metal box lying on the ground. Inside, the walls were flooded with aerosol colour and aggressive black calligraphy. Cables snaked around, strings of fairy-lights festooned the roof, the floor was littered with louche detritus. There was a faded smell of body fluids and cheap wine. Ax switched on the lights, hauled a metal panel down behind them with a cheerful clangour, and locked it by means of a padlock on the floor. 'Make yourself at home,' he said. Sage was crosslegged on the floor with his white box open in front of him. 'It's a little pied-à-terre we found, basically a shooting gallery; we found our own level, yeah, but a good place not to be disturbed.'

The white box looked highly ominous, immanent with dread. 'Why have you brought me here? What's going on?'

'He's frightened,' reproved Sage. 'Now you've *frightened* him.'

Ax looked into Harry's face, his pretty brown eyes vividly intent. 'Oh yeah. He's frightened. Harry, here's the key to the padlock. Now, you hold that, in your hand, and you'll know you can get up and leave, any time you like.'

Get up and leave. My God. He'd seen the tiger and the wolf in many moods, often inexplicable, never as dangerous as this. Oh, fuck, I knew we were handling them totally wrong, I knew it. He nodded earnestly, took the key and sat down, the fear mounting on him like a thirty-foot wave.

'Let's do this,' said Sage. 'Harry, you were at the Bowl last night.'

'Of course I was—'

'But you didn't come near us,' said Ax, smiling hard.

'I didn't want to intrude. It was your gig, your c-ceremony.'

'Now he's frightened again. Ax, you're scaring him.'

'No I'm not. You are scaring him, I *am not* scaring him, I'm just telling him, because it's time to cut the crap. Harry, you showed tact. It would have been dumb to fake the dressing room scene. *It's okay.* We understand how you're placed.'

'First you told us you were a talent scout,' said Sage, getting into the spirit of this levelling. 'Then you said you were a hot young movie producer with friends in the White House. Then you turned into a gopher, fixing hateful things for a committee of strange suits. You're a confusing person, we've been confused: but it's all right now. We *know* what you are, Mr Loman! You're someone like us!'

'It's *Lopez*,' whispered Harry. He balled his hands into fists to hide their trembling. Titration effect, he had such a high level of background panic, the awesome wattage of their attention nearly had him fainting.

'Yeah,' said Ax, 'yeah, yeah, of course, Lopez. Stop calling him Loman.'

'It slipped out.'

'Well it upsets him, and it's not funny anymore. Harry, we do not blame you for anything; we know how these things happen. These are *just* the things that happened to us. The President of the United States says: come along Harry, get your life ripped apart, it's in a good cause. What could you do? The Prime Minister of England did not say that to me, but there was the night the guns started blazing, blam blam blam, people falling down all around with big red holes in them. Nothing was the same after that.' Ax paused in this rapid fire, and added, distracted: 'I knew the PM later. His name was David Sale, a strange bloke, genuine flawed visionary. I got to like him. He died of a heroin overdose, you know, probably murder by magic, but it was never proved. Magic's hard to prove.'

'You're loaded, aren't you?' said Harry suddenly. 'Both of you?'

The tiger and the wolf grinned, blue eyes meeting brown, in delighted recognition of Harry's acumen. 'Yeah,' said Sage, 'we are totally smashed.'

'It feels like fire,' said Ax, '*Love is like fire* ... I love her lyrics.'

'Me too ... Hey. We must stick to the point.'

'Stick to the point,' repeated the former king of England, nodding fast.

Bereft, vengeful, and out of their fucking heads. Harry did not feel any safer.

'But for the record, Harry,' said Ax, 'I know when I am looking at my girl, and when I am not. Even if she has no face.'

'Ax, we are *past* that. They apologised. An' you're frightening him again.'

'I'm your biggest fan,' breathed Harry. 'I just wanted you in my movie.'

'Oh yeah. That's why you romanced me into bringing Rufus O'Niall's daughter here, so you could give her to the insane war-mongers—'

'Hey, hey, *Ax*. Calm, calm. You know it's not like that.'

'Sorry . . . Sorry, Harry. I know it's not like that.'

'Moving on,' said Sage, 'Harry, you remember the finalé last night?' Harry swallowed, and nodded. 'Well, that's when I saw the stupid hat. I nearly had her, I had the local information space *solved*, an' there she was. Something was in my way, but I came out of it knowing. I saw *a hat*, Mr Loman—'

'I d-don't—' Harry recoiled from a dual *plasma-jet* of blue. 'Okay, okay—'

'I know it's an ironic stupid hat, I knew that all along, but it's still stupid. Of course it meant you. We all have ways of filing things, people, you're the stupid hat kid. So I came back empty; all I had was this image of the hat, but I knew it was all we needed, and I knew we must speak to you with candour.'

'You're n-not making sense—'

The tiger showed his white teeth. 'Yes I am.'

'When she disappeared,' explained Ax, wanting to set things straight, 'our response was fucked up, because of personal things that we have to work out.'

'That we *will* work out.'

'Yes, yes, we will work out . . . personal fuck-ups, and being in an alien land, clouded our judgement. You and the Committee were lying to us, ignoring us, not returning our calls: but you were silently telling us you were on the case and we *must leave it to you*. We should have known that.'

'Actually, we *did* know it,' Sage put in.

'But that's over,' said Ax. 'Now *you* have to leave it to *us*.'

'Look, I don't know why you've brought me here—'

'Yes, you do, Harry. It's obvious. You have to tell us where she is.'

'I can't tell you, I don't know. You'd have to talk to Mr Raine.'

'Bullshit.'

The way they smiled, he knew – if he'd been in doubt – that they knew what would happen to Fiorinda. The National Guard and the serious event response team do a combined operation on a nest of insane terrorists: they shake the young English woman out of the wreckage, dust her down and return her to her friends unharmed? Is it likely? Not even if there was an intention to save her—

'I'm a movie producer. I'm just an errand boy.'

'Really.' Sage's blue eyes narrowed, his smile got wider. 'Okay, then you'll let me check something out. Gimme a thumb.'

Harry recoiled, but the guitar-man's grip had fastened on his wrist. Sage's hollow needle pounced. Harry's blood was taken, was plunged into a clear vial in which a metallic shivering quivered and darted. Sage shook the vial.

'Lo-tech assistance,' he explained. 'This won't take a moment, hang on.'

Oh God—

He watched from a rocketing, expanding distance as they studied the confession written in his blood, inside the white case where he couldn't see.

'Yep,' said Sage, motormouth. 'I've seen this, in his eyes, but I didn't get it. It's harder to decode the unexpected. See, this is snapshot, this is the Harry brand. Don' it line up nice, spike spike squiggle dip spike, what I'd call unequivocal, Sah.'

'Someone should have warned him, snap is not the ideal recreational drug. You might as well try sawing your leg off for the endorphins.'

'I don't b'lieve he was expectin' to have fun. The golden boy has lunatic depths.' Sage looked up. 'Harry, you've been doing neural aligner. Somethen' very like "snapshot" which is the cocktail we used on the Zen Self trail. Now don't tell me you took it in mistake for Tylenol or you bought it from a black lad in a club. Unless you've been playing with the terrorists, which we'd also be interested to know, but I don't think so, the gear came from Vireo Lake. Maybe out the back door, but only from there. Whatever, you see where this is heading. You're a lot closer to the fire than you've been lettin' on.'

Worst case—

—Aerosol-painted metal wall, the two beautiful crazed predators: gone. The déjà vu room was suddenly around him, like a fresh nightmare that you know you have dreamed before. He thought it was a hotel room. He could feel, a blurred mass, the welter of appalling memory that filled the narrow space (no more than weeks, maybe no more than days) left between him and this place. He didn't know why he was naked. He knew the voice that issued the gross and ludicrous command, but he couldn't remember the name, and could not turn his head to see. He heard himself crying, like a little baby: gagging and choking as his tongue reached out, hurting at the roots, getting longer, until he could hold it in his hands and push it, around his balls, into his anus. It was so real, so actual. Stink of shit, taste of shit. Gagging, choking, his tongue is boring into the, going up his spine, through the channel, it hurts blindingly. I'm sucking, licking, I'm going to eat my own brains—

OH GOD OH GOD.

Oh God, oh God it's going to happen. This is how I'm going to die—

'Ah, problem—'

'What is it?'

'Flashback. I think the first-aid kit set him off, bad associations.'

Harry was face-down on the floor, foetal curl, his cheek flattened against urine-smelling grit, whimpering hoarsely, knowing there was nothing but fear left, and the room was still waiting for him, somewhere up ahead . . . He felt hands on him. He was lifted, coaxed like a child. He was being rocked in a man's arms, the first time since he was about three years old: 'Hey, baby, ssh, come out of it. It's only a bad dream—' He'd pissed himself, he couldn't care less . . . Sage had made the fear go away, a relief that was utter bliss, but the room was still there . . .

'No, no, it's real,' he sobbed, clinging, hiding his face. 'It's going to happen—'

'What's going to happen? What did you see?'

'The Fat Boy makes me eat my brains.'

Harry blundered out of the clinch and crouched with his head in his hands.

'I wanted to know, and oh God, now I know. I saw the future.'

Was it unchangeable? When he was there he knew it was unchangeable.

Sage was studying the inside of the white case again. 'Harry, my screen says you took about two hundred mikes of the neuro cocktail, about ten, fifteen days ago: but that was your only time?'

'Yes,' he whispered.

'You haven't seen the future. Snap will give a virgin crackin' special effects, an' they will be nasty, because that drug is intrinsically a bastard: but you won't hardly ever get a trip outside of time. What did you say? Eat your brains? Yeah, tha's typical. The metaphor, word-play, tha's a sure sign you didn't get anywhere.'

'You're wrong,' croaked Harry. 'The rules have changed because we're in the worst case scenario.' He looked up, he faced them. They were so loaded they didn't get it. 'Don't you understand? There *is* a Fat Boy.'

'Okay,' said Ax, bright-eyed. 'Fine. Now tell us where she is.'

They watched him, with such animal calm.

'It was when they started examining the body. It was taken from the Carlsbad morgue before they could autopsy, and the notes you got were ... were fiction. That's when we knew the situation was out of control, and I took the neuronauts' drug. I got it from another younger guy on the Committee, who had access, he supervised. I had grasped the awfulness. I wanted to know whether I was right.'

Harry shuddered, and had to get his breathing back under control.

'And I found out ... oh, God, I found out. I'm sorry you've been treated the way you've been treated. Now you know the reason ... *are you satisfied?*'

'It's all been good stuff,' said Sage. 'But we need to know where she is.'

'She's with the Invisible People. Don't you get it? She's with them.'

'Great. Where are they?'

'I'm not going to talk anymore.'

'C'mon Harry. The time for secrecy is past.'

'The body gave them away ... They have effective magic. There's only one way to deal with them, it was decided long ago and it can't be stopped.'

Ax nodded, patiently. 'We picked up on that. And where is she?'

'I can't. Oh God, please don't make me say this. They did a profile. An abused child, abused children c-can grow up f-feeling they can do no wrong—'

he thought they'd kill him then, but they didn't move—

'If there's a Fat Boy,' said Ax, 'it's not our girl. But no matter who the candidate may be, *if there is one* we're your only hope.'

Harry quailed. 'I'm very, very, sorry, but I'm not going to talk anymore.'

'You think not?' asked Sage. He leaned forward: shining like an archangel come down to earth, to teach an easy lesson. 'Harry, you know the state you were in, ooh, a couple of minutes ago? I can put you back there. I can make it your reality—'

Harry was sweating hard. He could feel the déjà vu room forming, it was crawling out of Sage's white briefcase, a heavy smoke. He couldn't stop the abject whimpering that rose in his throat.

'Ax,' said Sage suddenly. 'This isn't the way!'

The ex-Dictator and his former Minister looked at each other.

'You're right.' said Ax, intently. 'This doesn't do it. Shit, we lost the way. We'll have to find it again. We've finished with him, then. Harry? Let yourself out.'

'Here's your button, Mr Lopez. Call yourself a cab.'

Harry stood up, the padlock key in one hand, his eyesocket button in the other. He took a step and looked back. The king and his minister sat on the scummy floor of this disused drug-bunker, united in alert, silent concentration . . . Their gallantry amazed him. They were not defeated, they would never be defeated, they were just thinking of something else to try. A shock rushed through him, breaking all ties of convention . . . Ax looked up and smiled, as if puzzled to see Harry still there, and he realised he was holding out for no fucking good reason at all—

'Oh, shit. What's the difference? I'll tell you.'

He sat down again. 'She's at a place called Lavoisier, it's a terrorist commune in a ghost town between the Inyo and the Panamint ranges, beyond Owens Valley.'

'Lavoisier,' repeated Ax. 'The Inyo and Panamint ranges, a ghost town full of invisible terrorists. Thank you, Harry, that's all we need.'

'I think you guys are immense. *Immense.* I remember coming to find you on that beach. It was the most romantic, perfect experience of my life. It was magical. Fuck, sorry, not magical, some other word.'

He stood up again. 'I'm leaving now,' and buckled, and fell to the floor.

Ax and Sage looked at the fallen body, laughed, and slapped palms in triumph.

They drove Harry to his house, as he was in no state to be left. The Rat pulled up in front of his movie-star bungalow, fifties-style, except that the yard was planted with desert natives, boojums and ocotillo and *palo adán*.

'How long do you think the waiver will hold them?' asked Ax.

'No time at all,' said Harry, frankly. 'The waiver's their idea of doing things by the book, and they truly wanted you two on board. But it'll go ahead. It's imminent, I don't know when. I genuinly don't. It could be tomorrow.'

'Give me a number I can call.'

'You want to talk to Fred?'

'No, I don't. Give me a number for Colonel Beaufort.'

'I'll talk to Fred. I'll try to get him to hold off. Lavoisier is a little outlaw state, it's not unknown out there. They've been watched but left alone because they were thought harmless, but they're likely to have an apocalyptic arsenal.'

'Thanks.'

The A&R man got out of the car, on shaking legs.

'Harry,' said Sage, gazing through the Rat's windshield. Beyond the house, a row of shock-headed palms stood against a western sky of duck-egg blue. 'We have most of twenty-four hours, let us use it. Then you can try talking to Fred. When you've done that, go and find Lurch.'

'Kathryn hates me,' said Harry. 'She thinks I'm two-faced.'

'Yeah, but go an' find her. Your guru has spoken. So long, fanboy. Take care.'

The idiotic cruelty of Harry's snapshot vision haunted them as they headed into the freeway maze. But they knew Fiorinda was alive, and where to find her.

At Sunset Cape Allie dealt with the studio lawyers, stringing it out; she'd grasped she was stalling for time. So they had got away . . . Rob went up to the Triumvirate suite and found it in disorder, a half-empty tequila bottle and two shot glasses on a table. He had come up here looking for the b-loc. He didn't like the thing, but he'd had to get used to it so he could be with the babies. He found it, and sat on the end of a rumpled bed. The mess brought back the hallucinatory feeling of last night . . . It's tough being in the second rank, when you were the great man's equal at the start. No one recognises your name. But I know who I am, he thought, and I know what I want. Why don't I go for it, the way Ax did? Unilaterally, me. Rise out of the collective. There were only a handful of phones like this in England; one of the people he could reach was Jordan Preston. The mission will succeed or fail, but I will know I did this, and that matters. Okay, Jor. Let's see if you'll accept a call.

Ax Preston and the former Aoxomoxoa arrived at Bighorn, Stu Meredith's dude ranch in Owens Valley, rather late in the evening. They apologised for dropping by, and explained they were on their way to spend a few days in the wilderness before they left the US. They were welcomed, despite the issues Stu had with Sage. Stu's wife of thirty years, Ludmilla Pearson Meredith, had recently lost her beloved mother. She knew that these two hollow-eyed, strung-out young men were in mourning, and she looked on them kindly. Places were laid for them at the family dinner – the Merediths kept late hours, Spanish style, in the hot weather.

'We'd like to see some desert country,' said Ax. 'We were thinking of checking out that ghost town, Lavoisier. D'you know it?'

The dinner table went quiet. Stu's younger daughter had a coughing fit.

'No,' said Stu. 'We don't. Take some potatoes?'

'You'll be staying over,' said Ludmilla, quickly. 'I'll have beds made up in the bunkhouse. It's authentic cowboy accommodation, but it's comfortable. We have plenty of room; there's nobody booked in at the Noise Hotel right now.'

The Noise Hotel was what the family called the famous studio at Bighorn, where favoured artists came to avail themselves of Stu's expertise, in this fabulous setting. Ludmilla had nothing to do with that. She and her older daughter and son-in-law bred horses, for more pleasure than profit.

'Well, thanks,' said Ax. 'By the way, could you not mention our camping trip, if anyone asks? We badly need some privacy. It's been nonstop.'

'The wilderness is a great healer,' said Stu, with a reserved expression.

The rest of the evening was convivial, into the early hours. In the morning Stu took Ax to look at the riding horses. The Noise Hotel was out of sight; the ranch house stood with its big red barn, the bunkhouse and the stables, alone on a wide sweep of sun-crisped pasture, at the foot of the Inyos. Across the great valley, westward, stood the southern massif of the Sierra Nevada, rags of snow still tracing the peaks.

'You must excuse my wife,' said Stu. 'She can't abide drugs in the house.'

Ax had lit a cigarette as soon as he stepped outdoors. 'But it's okay out here?'

'It's a fire risk,' said Stu.

Ax was sure he'd seen John Wayne with a fag in his mouth on many a screen-cowboy classic, but he was not in a position to argue. He sighed, killed the cigarette and put it away. This stopover had seemed an inspired move (everything felt inspired, but he believed he could tell the difference); a gateway to the Owens Valley, a chance to gather information. But Stu's gracious friendship had chilled the moment Lavoisier was mentioned, and Ax was not sure how to broach the subject again.

'You should team up with Sage. He keeps trying to make me quit.'

'I hope you're gonna be careful with those cancer sticks in the wild country.'

'Of course.'

Ten, no, twelve, horses milled about in the corral by the barn. A couple of ranch hands came ambling over, but kept their distance at a look from the boss's husband. 'Expensive pets,' remarked Stu, dryly. 'These are the palace favourites. She has twenty-odd head of breeding stock, and youngsters, also. The whole thing's crazy; we buy feed and truck it to them, three-quarters of the year. Okay, Mr Preston. Pick yourself out a ride.'

'The dark bay, with the white blaze. I like the look of her. But we can't borrow your horses, Stu. Sage doesn't ride, and we couldn't be responsible—'

He'd been reading guides and poring over maps, on paper, not risking the datasphere, while Sage slept. He could have done without playing guitar until after midnight, wasting precious time: but maybe it had been good. When the fingers move, the mind moves, and friendly company is also an aide. He was putting together old Yorkshire routines with the new terrain: borax mines, lava tubes, volcano craters. One thing we do not want to do, however, is ... Stu tugged a Willie Nelson bandanna from his jeans pocket and rubbed it over his palms.

'I had a phonecall.'

Shit ... 'Oh yeah?'

'It was yesterday. This is test-bed country, we're continually harrassed by naval jet pilots who can't read altimeters, buzzing our livestock. The call was a standard disclaimer, don't holler, we're about to run an exercise which may damage sensitive equipment, pull your plugs, take precautions. Funny thing is, I'd heard the jets are grounded, due to adverse atmospherics ... Also, I was talking to an Inyo County Ranger who says the trails are gonna be closed from day after tomorrow, somethen' to do with with an unusual load coming up the valley. That generally means nuclear, but it doesn't generally close the wilderness trails. My lady friend was bitching about our struggling tourism, and the way the military don't give a damn for their neighbours, but I thought there was something going down. Then you two arrived, Mr Ax Preston and his sidekick, mentioning a place called Lavoisier.'

Stu was staring at the barn, and he didn't look around.

'D'you have reason to think there's a connection?'

'Lavoisier has a curious reputation. I slept on it, and now I'm asking you.'

Ax looked within, and rushed on the white light. 'Fiorinda's alive,' he said. 'The FBI have traced her, she'd being held by a . . . some kind of hippy commune, with an arsenal, holed up in your local ghost town.'

Stu nodded, keeping his eyes averted. 'Uhuh. And so?'

'There's going to be a raid. Maybe they're planning a telecoms wipeout likely to affect you. We were told all this just yesterday. We were invited along, but we're afraid she wouldn't survive the frontal attack, so we've made our own plans.'

The Willie Nelson bandanna was getting another working. 'I'm glad to hear your lady's alive, Ax, that's great news. I guess I don't blame you for trying to beat the big guns. Did you come here for help, manpower?'

'No, we're better on our own. But local input's always useful.'

Stu looked around. 'Lavoisier's an armed camp, and worse. You may have heard of the Manson family, uster hang out around here? I don't know, but there are people say the Lavoisiens are their spiritual children. Whatever they mean by that . . . You two are planning to go in *alone*?'

Ax noted that this was a relief to Stu's mind, and was very touched. He would not have dreamed of asking for a posse. 'They've got our babe; we have no other quarrel with them. Maybe we can even negotiate, it's worth a try. What about you? Are you going to make that call?'

'What call?'

'Give me a break.'

'I'm not going to call anyone.'

The rest of the family was coming up, with Sage: Ludmilla, the older daughter, and son-in-law, and Violet, the youngest. There was a boy also, or young man, but he lived in LA. Sage was wearing the mask, and sparking merrily with Violet, a pretty, plump teenager with freckles on her nose. She'd been respectful of the ancient hellraiser last night; today she'd recovered her bounce. 'Maybe you'll get an idea for an immix from this trip.' Violet swung up to sit on the top rail of the fence. 'Horses, mountains, the desert moon—'

'I'll call it "Ghost Riders In The Sky", an' I'll dedicate it to Violet.'

'Oh God. You're kidding.'

'I'm kidding.'

'It must have been *so weird* for you, standing where the Beatles once stood.'

'Hahaha. It may not even have been our first time for that.'

'Did you persuade him?' asked Ludmilla.

Stu gave his wife a 'talk to you later' look, and smiled gravely at Ax. 'Yeah, I persuaded him. Ax is taking Madeleine; I think we'll put Aoxomoxoa on Big Snow. The white one with the spotted behind, Sage. He's a gentle fellow, and very tolerant of children. You keep one of your daddy-long-legs either side, he'll do the rest.'

'Madeleine,' said Ludmilla, taken aback. 'Well, okay ... You like a good horse, Ax? Where are you from, again, in England?'

'Somerset.'

'Is that horse country?'

'Not specially,' he said, caught by unexpected pain, imagining this large, fair-to-grey Californian nonplussed by the miniature landscape, the sodden Levels. 'It's orchard country: and wetter than you people would believe, most winters—'

'When my grandmother's family came to the Owens Valley,' Ludmilla told him, 'this was orchard country; but you must know the story. 1913, they drained us, on some swindle, to fill the swimming pools of Los Angeles—'

'You weren't born nor thought of in 1913, Mom,' said her son-in-law. 'I think you should accept it's time to let go. If they paid us back now, we'd drown.'

The household laughed, placidly, at one of those family jokes that never stales. The ranch hands who'd been kept at bay while Stu had his private word with Ax had come over, interested to add to their rock celebrity collection.

'I could spare Cheyne here,' said Ludmilla. Cheyne was one of the horse-wranglers, the only woman among them. 'She could come with you and handle the horses. You might be wise to take a guide.'

'I'd be fine with that,' said Cheyne, looking pleased.

'They want to be on their own, Ludy. They'll be okay.'

The air was still; the day would be stinking hot. The horses kept milling around: a muffled fusillade of hooves; a whirl of hides like autumn-coloured leaves. 'They're spooked,' remarked Ax. 'Sage, you should take the mask off.'

'They've been like this for days,' said one of the hands. 'The dogs and cats are fussing too. Maybe there's a quake coming.'

The air temperature was still in the low hundreds Fahrenheit when they left Bighorn late in the day. Stu came with them, riding beside the car and trailer as they crossed his fenced pasture at walking pace. They reached the northern boundary, which wasn't far from the house at this point. Sage got out to open the gates: it proved a tussle, his hands were clumsy today. A causeway of packed rubble led north-east, into shadow-painted hills. 'You'll find plenty off-roader trails,' said Stu, impassive, making no move to get down and help. 'Most of 'em aren't marked ... So, you two are going after the man who stole your water.'

'Yeah.'

'I hope you make it. You know, I think I'm more surprised to see that you're in a grown-up relationship than I am about the spiritual awakening.'

The skull mask did *impassive* with a sweet fuck-you. 'They keep me for a pet.'

'You don't really have superpowers, do you?'

'Nah. That's just a story I get my publicist to put out.'

'Watch out for the guy who calls himself Moloch,' said Stu. 'Watch out for the lot of them, bunch of crazy no-knickers Goths and death-wish geeks. You could be right the way you're handling this, but they're not going to be shy of firing first, and I think that Moloch ... I think he's the one. Well, so long.'

A few miles on, they took the Rugrat and trailer off the track and parked them in a roofless cove, backed and walled by scrub-covered hillocks. They led out the horses: Madeleine, Big Snow the Appaloosa gelding, and Paintbrush, the little chestnut-and-white pinto; saddled up Madeleine and the Appaloosa, and erected the ponyfold thing they'd been instructed to use as a holding pen. Sage practised his riding a little, then they settled the animals with feed and water, and unpacked their own kit. The assault rifles, which they had barely had a chance to try, back at Sunset Cape, were easy and solid to assemble, and intuitive in use. (Have to admit, damn sight more fun than the SA/80, an inimitably British weapon, difficult, and proud of it.) They checked over the rest, speaking little, looking at each other with sharp grins. So far so good. They had seen themselves breaking her out of a US government military lab when they amassed this gear. But so far so good: still in phase.

There were no visible livestock, no sign of human presence except for the track; that vanished quickly into sagebrush, whichever way you looked. The hills had turned a rosy caramel with the twilight, the sky shading from colourless pallor to charcoal. Ax remembered a flight he'd taken once, over the Caucasus in a light plane, on one of his 'Ax Preston' journeys, and felt the same stir of wonder, the same irrational tug of longing ... They packed everything again, unloaded fuel from the back of the car and set a fire in a circle of stones. They lit it without using her saltbox, which they carried always; taking it in turns. Neither of them had any appetite. They drank water, and agreed they would eat in the morning.

Here at last the fusion rush dropped them. Stone-cold sober, Ax sat thinking of the ruin that might fall (Anne-Marie's phrase) on Stu Meredith's family; on that chirpy, freckle-faced teenager. Stu knows what we brought on him, so does his wife. They had talked with the seniors alone, after they'd sorted out the horses: in the big, homely kitchen full of horse-memorabilia. Ludmilla was the same as Stu. Mention *Lavoisier*, and people won't meet your eyes ... On the other side of the fire Sage was propped on one elbow, firelight catching gleams in his hair; his face in shadow.

'I wonder what a horse like Madeleine is worth, in dollars.'

'Huh? I'm sorry Ax, I've no idea what fancy horses cost.'

'It doesn't matter. What are we going to do with them? We don't want horses, but we can't just leave them. If we turn them loose they'll head straight home, and then Stu will think we are fucked and call the federales—'

'I've been thinking we're gonna need them, Ax. Our side's obviously planning to fry the enemy's telecoms and digital devices, in case they have any. There'll come a point when we have to dump the Rugrat, before it dies under us ... I think Stu may have called the feds as soon as we were off the premises. He was in two minds.'

Ax sighed. 'You're right, I saw that. Oh, well. It's high summer and we're next door to Death Valley. At least we can rely on the weather.'

'Hahaha. Ax, I wish you had not said that.'

'Sorry. D'you feel like coming over to my side of the fire, at all?'

Sage came over. They sat shoulder to shoulder, watching the flames. Will you let me touch those scars? Ax wondered. I want to touch them every time I see them, I want to kiss them, those knotted strands across your flank that hold your life inside; the idea turns me on, it's perverse, and we won't go into it now: but another time. If there's ever a good time.

'I don't see us getting away with non-violence, bodhisattva.'

'Ha. Doesn't seem likely, my dear.'

Ax had lied to Stu. They had no intention of trying to negotiate, not unless close reconnaissance revealed a very different situation than had been advertised. They talked, going over the plan, not much of a structure, wide-open: the equipment they must take because they might need it, the kit they could discard, now they saw the picture ... The guerrilla mood rose in them, memory building on the shards of euphoria. You never know what's really going to happen on the bridge at midnight; it's fatal to try and lock it into shape. The night grew chill. They spread their sleeping bags and lay down, rifles at hand: putting aside all hope and fear, for a few hours of much-needed oblivion.

They crossed the Inyo range very early, and hit the dirt road that bisected the next valley as the sun rose. They were now within ten or fifteen miles of the ghost town (paper maps varied, and there was no entry on the onboard gazetteer). They were deploying *conceal*: using the 'beaten-up farm truck' (Rugrat had a little repertoire of fun, secret characters). With an incongruously shiny horse-trailer, but that was probably normal enough, and they couldn't drive the AI car naked through this paradoxical landscape, where anything could be hidden and there was nowhere to hide. Sagebrush, grey mudstone washes, red boulders, parched grass shaded into crumpled foothills on either side; the scoured, unearthly peaks of the White Mountains stood in the north. There were no other vehicles. Nothing moved but for the white-rumped flicker of pronghorn taking flight: the jackrabbits, the birds of prey and the piñon jays, and one pallid, trotting fox-like creature. Pockmarked metal signs announced surreal natural attractions, most of them far away in more famous parts of the Great Basin. It was as if someone had tried and failed to launch a tourist industry on a hot version of Mars. No battles, no rich burials, no sermons in stone.

They identified the unmarked turn-off by landmarks and headed east until the town appeared like a mirage above the foothills: a Martian maquette, a cluster of alien right-angles, with a glint or two of glass. Ax drew up and tapped the dash. Through the windshield a pockmarked sign, tiny in the distance, sprang into focus. Lavoisier. They stared, heart-shaken, at the place where she was. There seemed to be earthworks. Was that a rampart and a ditch around the camp, classic style?

'I can feel us pushing our luck,' muttered Ax.

He swung the car around. They drove on and found the auto dump, at the end of a vagrant spur of the paved, but disintegrating, 168, where they would leave the horses. A lopsided white caravan stood derelict among the wrecks. They led the animals out, let them stretch their legs, put them back in the aircon trailbox, then disguised the box with a grimy shroud of black plastic borrowed from a heap of engine blocks. 'We need a third man,' said Ax, depressed that Stu's horses might die of heatstroke if things went wrong. The dump had been recommended to them as covert roadside parking, but it could be days before Stu came looking.

'Or a platoon,' agreed Sage. 'Too bad. We'll have to make do.'

The Rugrat shed its homely mask and became a mirror for the sagebrush. They left the road and headed uphill; the paradoxical emptiness swallowed them.

Lavoisier had been founded in the eighteen fifties, named by a French émigré after the scientist Lavoisier, founder of modern Chemistry, who had lost his head in the Revolution. Manufacturing bath salts, and conceived as a healthful resort above the heat of the valley floor, it had become prosperous, lawless, amazingly violent; and faded into decline. In the late twentieth century it had been revived as a new-age spiritual centre, but the settlers'd had to quit because the water supply had become too alkaline. The no-knickers Goths and death-wish geeks tanked their water in. They'd been in possession for about five years, according to the Merediths. They must have money behind them: they had no land fit for pasture or cultivation, and all the guidebooks and ranger info nowadays warned tourists to stay away. Maybe some of them had city jobs, and commuted. Nobody local had anything to do with the place.

At five in the afternoon they were on foot in a ravine, on the other side of a fold of the Panamints from Lavoisier, dressed for the heat in hats, workshirts and light combats in desert shades of grey and tan, carrying their packs. It was very hot. If there'd ever been a river in this arroyo on a regular basis it had vanished long ago, but there was one of those signs, memorialising a boulder as big as a car, rammed into a crevasse high in the wall by the flashflood of 2003. They stood and looked up at this gravity-defying feat.

'I'm in a constant state of déjà vu,' said Ax. 'I was imprinted on this landscape before I was six, on tv screens, cinema screens, videogames. It's not supposed to be real, and here I am. Fuck, actual *rocks* look familiar. I think this ravine must have featured in an episode of *Star Wars*. Or several episodes of *Star Wars*.'

'If you say so. I always thought those sets were plastic.'

'You must have been a terribly cynical little boy.'

They were alone in the once and future world, naked warriors obeying an oracle. Maybe the people who left the petroglyphs would have understood. 'The first warning we'll get,' said Ax gloomily, 'is when our own digital devices are zapped.'

'We have 'til Friday.'

'We don't know that. Fuck, better just go for it.'

A hundred metres further on they reached the Hole in the Wall: a balcony of red stone, the undercurve weather-carved in a blurred resemblance to swathes of drapery and garlands of flowers. They climbed the steps into an open-fronted cave, where worn tables and chairs stood in the dusk. A counter along one side of the cave held a meagre display of handwoven baskets and polished fossils: a tray of glossy, delicate animal skulls. Behind it a fat bloke was reading a paperback book by the light of a solar-cell lamp. He had a shotgun on the counter. They sat at a table, chugged their own water and ate dried fruit and jerky. The fat bloke came over, frowning, leaving his gun behind.

'Hi. Anything I can do for you?'

'Was this really a notorious outlaw hide-out?' asked Sage.

'Naw, not really. There are holes in walls all over, this one is just a place. Are you guys hiking? This is very bad country for hiking, in the summer time.'

'Backpacking,' said Ax. 'Do you have a bathroom?'

'Uuuh, yeah. Through to the rear of the cavern, and on your right.'

'He doesn't like to sully the environment,' explained Sage as his companion headed into the gloom, taking his pack with him.

'Oh, I agree. The desert isn't a toilet.'

Ax went through the cavern, glancing into shadows, listening intently; finding no unwelcome company. The toilet was as promised: a green painted door set in the rock, with a stencilled inscription, UNISEX TOILET. The passage ended at another, similar door in a larger opening that had been filled with brickwork. He tested the mortar: if they had to get the wall down, it didn't look like a problem. But the lock proved no big deal. He forced it and walked on. The passage became a tongue of stone that reached out like a jetty over a dark lake: looming darkness above, an empty drop on either side and ahead. There must be a way down, but he could make out the dim shapes of boulders, so he went over the edge, landing as quietly as possible. There was a concrete deck, a bed, furniture: a troglodyte living space.

'Hey?' A young, male voice. A figure rose. 'What's going on?'

The cave dweller was not wearing anything on his eyes, but he must have nightsight, because it was fucking dark down here. Ax walked up and dealt him a hard, focused crack to the side of his head. The kid gasped, and his handgun went flying. Ax floored him, and got a line around his throat, which he soon had attached to the kid's hands, lashed behind his back. He took his captive up to the front, where Sage was in a similar position with the fat bloke. 'I got his phone,' said Sage. 'He has nothing internal, did you check yours?'

'What are you doing here?' gargled the kid. 'Who are you?'

The fat bloke said nothing. Sage, the skull mask livid, jumped at the boy, grabbed his shirt and snarled, '*Guess!*'

'I aaarn't see ooo—!'

'He can't see. I smacked his head; his eyesocket gizmo has crashed.' They sat the boy by his partner. 'All you need to know,' said Ax, 'is that we're here for Fiorinda. She's in Lavoisier; you're going to tell us where to find her, and anything else you can offer.'

'We don't have anything to do with those crazed hippies—'

'Bollocks. You're guarding their back door.'

'How many of them up there?' asked Sage. Stu and Ludmilla had estimated maybe a hundred, and whole families, including children.

The fat bloke sweated and stared defiance. 'Fifty, a thousand, it doesn't matter. You won't take them. She's not a prisoner, she's sacred. She's ours now.'

'They keep the witch-queen in the church,' wailed the boy. 'Let me go!'

'He's lying. No one *keeps* her, she's our lady. She'll kill you—'

'Shit, we have a pair of unreliable witnesses, Sage. They're just going to contradict each other. What shall we do with them?'

'I think we should lock them in the toilet.'

They were foiled in locking the toilet; there was no means to do so from the outside, but they dumped the two on the floor in there, trussed like chickens. The kid was terrified, the fat bloke ominously proud and calm. Sage had scanned eye-socket-boy's face and found his button dislodged, giving him nothing but grief: they decided not to try and excavate it. The fat bloke had a bunch of old-style keys (nothing electronic, nothing digital) which opened the doors at the back of the troglodyte deck, revealing a pitch-black opening, about three metres by three. This lava tube had been a useful secret exit in Lavoisier's heyday; later a tourist attraction. It had been closed down in recent years. They assembled the rifles, donned field headsets, rearranged some other kit, pulled down nightsight on the headset screens, and set off.

Shortly, Ax turned to scan the empty tunnel behind them. Since they left the Rugrat, they'd had the persistent conviction that they were not alone. Someone or something walked with them, just out of sight.

'Extra man's a *good* sign,' Sage comforted him. 'As superstition has it. You called him up, you know, back at the auto dump.'

'I could do without that, Sage.'

The tube was about four kilometres long. Near the upper end the Lavoisiens had fitted it with an obstacle course for incoming traffic. They beat the place where the floor slid back, revealing a trough of eye-stinging caustic, by fly-walking along the wall above it, chipping holds in the slick walls of the tube. They dodged a spike trap, jumped the chasm, but had to move very fast to roll under a barbed portcullis that came shooting down from the roof. Luckily they hadn't been planning to leave by this route. 'What fun they had—' remarked Sage, sourly. 'Fucking Peter Pan features—'

'Maybe they've been maligned. Maybe they're just happy hippies.'

They pushed back their headset screens, because natural light was taking over from the darkness. Sage stopped, putting out a hand to halt Ax. Ahead of them a glistening dark stripe had been drawn around the tube, walls and floor and roof. In the centre of the floor, on this dark strip, lay a bundle no bigger than a child's hand.

'Stay back.'

Sage knelt, picked the thing up and tore it into fragments.

'I thought only Fee could do that,' said Ax, uneasily.

'She's not here. You can get by, don't touch any of it; I'll be a moment.'

Ax hunkered down near the entrance of the tunnel and checked the situation outdoors. No e/m in range of his tech. The warm bodies feature was not working too well, air temperature too high (damn); normal vision told him there was nothing moving. The buildings were still a couple of hundred metres away, on the other side of the outer defences. Ramparts and a ditch, yeah. The break in the earthworks where the road came in would be guarded. They knew the best place to cross, after their day's reconnaissance, but that's for later . . . He spotted a gun emplacement. A glint in a window opening, where an upper storey showed over the ramparts: that's a sniper. Sage appeared, and crouched with his back to the wall, head tipped back, eyes closed. He looked sick.

'Was that real?'

'Yeah . . . Quite a kick. There was something in the way, Ax.'

'Are you going to be okay? Anything I can do?'

'If I start acting strangely, shoot me.' Sage laughed, and opened his eyes. He wiped his hands on his combats. 'I'm afraid I tripped an alarm. What's the damage?'

'Don't worry about it. The surprise is what we're going to do to the fuckers, not the fact that we turned up. I can see one sniper indoors,' said Ax, 'and what looks like a gun emplacement in the earthworks, probably part of a ring.'

Sage took out a health pack and reviewed it for restoratives that would not have dire and swift effect on an underage liver. It came down to glucose tablets, ah well. The original psychotropic . . . He split a pack and handed half to Ax. 'We don't have to worry about fixed guns, we're not claiming the hilltop for Colin Powell.'

'Nor snipers, 'cept for getting past them. That's one good thing about an armed camp, they have to hold the perimeter, which cuts the loose numbers down—'

'Fucking wish we *knew* the loose numbers.'

'Fifty, sixty. There's unlikely to be more combatants than that, max, in a community of a hundred. Say at least one gunhole in each quadrant, with two gunners; say at least one sniper. Minimum of twelve tied up there, and the perimeter must be patrolled, that's got to be another dozen. Leaving thirty or so in the bunker area for us to deal with.'

'Hahaha. Estimates are always helpful.'

'You have to start somewhere,' said Ax.

Some will pick up a weapon, some won't . . . You keep telling yourself there have been different times, and they can return, but it gets harder to believe.

'D'you remember when war and violence were being phased out, Sage?'

'Before my time, Sah. I was just shocked when the guns reached *me*.'

'I used to tell myself I was trying to preserve civilised life for her.'

They thought of the little girl, living alone with her cold mother and her crazy gran, devouring the library of twentieth century liberal culture, no idea that her demon father existed. No conception of the world they would all inherit.

'We need a vantage point,' said Ax, at last. 'I favour the saloon. It's two storeys, and has, or had, a cupola on the roof. Shall we check that out?'

'I'm good,' said Sage. 'Let's go.'

They dropped into the ditch and scaled the earthworks. Down the other side, and then a sprint, bent double, to the cover of the wooden buildings. There wasn't much left of the Las Vegas of the gold rush. The splintered wooden sidewalks had hitching rails, and most of the streets had never seen asphalt, but the derelict houses were drably modern, or fairly modern. They went into one, and found a well-preserved room with tables and chairs. Elaborate kabbalistic-type signs covered one wall; a stack of photocopy paper on a table had been used for drawing exercises: fair and poor copies of the wall chart.

Sage turned the pages. 'So this is where you come to be trained as an occult terrorist. Shit, militant fuckin' crystal swingers will rule the world.'

'Maybe they will: but that's not what these characters are planning. Not if they are trying to create the Fat Boy ... D'you recognise anything?'

'Nope. Gibberish to me.' Sage frowned. 'But I don't think we should stare at it too long. Where d'you think they all are?'

'I have a feeling— 'Ax's déjà vu was gaining on him, everything was superimposed; as was the sense of that third man, who must be out in the street, on point, well, fact is there *should* be someone out there ... He was going to say he had a feeling that Lavoisier had wind of the coming raid when instead he knew that he had to spin around. He fired just before the figure that had been blocking the light—

They leapt across the room. The Lavoisien was a young man, with wild yellow-brown dreadlocks, a fresh face, open eyes. Out in the street four more outlaws, clutching rifles, were running to the sound of fire, without any precaution. They got raked with bullets. Three of them dropped. One of them bounced off a wall, belted for cover and started firing back. 'Damn', said Ax. He dropped on one knee and took aim with more care: white face, black shirt, spiked hair, looks like a woman. Before he fired, he saw something moving behind her. A shadow that stooped; and the Goth-girl tumbled. Gone at once, could have been a trick of the light, could be she was hit before, and took her time falling over. Sage and Ax looked at each other, and maybe both decided not to ask, *did you see that?*

The routines take over. You think about nothing, if possible.

'Five down,' said Ax, cold-bloodedly.

'Let's get on,' breathed Sage. 'Long way to go to win this.'

The saloon was on Main Street, which had broken asphalt and even a street sign. They reached it without further incident, and the cupola was still up on the roof. There had been a big fire around the turn of the century, when the last new age settlers were still hanging on. The cavernous bar on the ground floor was a blackened shell, the stairway to the first-floor gallery was gone, but the structure that remained was sound enough. They climbed up, found a smaller flight of stairs and reached their objective: a dusty little octagonal room, windows on every side, most of the glass gone. Sage shucked his pack and initialised the airborne cam and its guidance system. Ax got low and peered out, assessing the steep, shingled roof, it looked solid: an escape route, if they needed one. Lavoisier looked very small: a grid of battered houses, gappy roofs; the rows and sidewalks quickly giving up, long gaps between buildings in the outer sectors. Vehicles in a kind of pound, a water tanker—

'Can you see the church?'

'Yeah. Right in the centre.' There's the Spanish Mission-style church, a dingy pink-washed shoe box in a little square, a squat open-sided belfry rising from one end, lancets down the sides. With binoculars he could see the beam where the bell had hung; no rope hanging from it now. There's the hillside graveyard, with its thickly sown markers, a few crooked trees, outside the ramparts, on the quiet side of town. The defences were less developed over there. He couldn't see the Rat, which was on that hillside by the boneyard: but that's *good*. Fucking thing's going to turn back into a pumpkin, though, he thought. At the worst moment: I know it. Barricades around the church square. Movement on the perimeter, patrols looking antsy, ah well, can't be helped. No noncombatants. Not a one, and nobody *lives* in those houses.

His mouth was dry, and his heart was thumping. Adrenalin's a miracle drug for bursts of action, but hell for the spaces in between. Soon we'll know—

'I know where they are, Sage. They're underground.'

'Oh, fuck. Of course they are.'

'Let's hope the eye-socket kid was telling the truth. If she's in an underground warren for which we don't have a map, the difficulty of this increases.'

'Ready to launch.'

Ax let the binoculars drop and set himself with his back to a strip of wall between two windows, where he could get his rifle trained on the door. He pulled down his headset screen. Sage jumped up and fired the catapult. The camera flew, a vaned, complex sphere the size of a fat spider: over the roofs, into the belfry. Sage ducked down again, tugged the black bar of the headset screen across his eyes and set the control pad on his knees. He applied a touch of motor guidance so the camera dropped, through the hole where the bellrope had left the loft: let it fall, then another touch to make a right angle turn into the body of the church.

'I'm not getting anything. What can you see?'

'With you direc'ly. *Oh, yeah*. We found the people—'

'Got it.' Ax saw a pixelated moving blur that resolved into a view down the church from the west end. Lancet windows foreshortened,

248

dim with evening, naked torchflames in sconces round the walls. About twenty or thirty people were sitting, facing forwards, on the floor: a mixed group, men, women and children, many wearing dark robes of some kind. In front of them a smaller group sat around a table set crossways. It was a scene vaguely reminiscent of the Last Supper, staged for a humble audience of lesser disciples. A glimpse of a railed stairway off to the left, that might lead down to a crypt; a door to the back quarters to the right ... Beyond the high table was the sanctuary of a Christian church, stripped out, a brightly coloured frieze (multicoloured roses?); a sheeny grey shape like a sarcophagus raised on a trestle. Shit, not roses. Brainscans—

'Can you see her? I can't see her. Are you guiding it?'

'It'll guide itself better than I can ... Have you got sound?'

'No. Oh, now I have. Can't make it out, though—'

The flying cam was media-tech, taken over and redesigned for stealthy reconnaissance. It was so light it barely needed motive power to stay in the air, but guidance was fiendishly delicate and costly. It picked up the mean angle of gaze if there was a group of people (or an audience). At default it would drift towards tracking the centre of attention. Their picture broke up, it reformed. They'd lost their overview. They were looking at the high table, focus on the face of a young man in spectral white make-up: hollow eyes, long blue-black hair, a white voile shirt, open to the waist to display a black tattoo of a bat-winged creature, silver chains looping from its snout to nipple rings at the clawed wing tips.

He looked tense, and impatient. He was listening—

Sound became intelligible. The Goth's right-hand neighbour was speaking. *'This was their MO in Yorkshire ... They'd take off together an' rip the shit out of some Islamic position, killing everything that moved. They're fucking psychos.'* The speaker was at least two decades older than the Goth Christ; he had bristle-short brown hair and a crumpled route map of a face. 'I was close to them, for months. I can tell you, it was an education.'

In the cupola, Sage muttered, 'Ever seen him before?'

'Not that I recall.'

'Well, my lady,' the Goth with the bat-winged tattoo raised his voice, and half turned in his chair, 'is this true? Are your boyfriends ruthless killers?'

'I have no idea—' They forgot to breathe. It was her voice. 'If they are, they never used to bring their work home.'

'They got past the Watcher,' shouted somebody from the floor. 'We felt it screaming as it was torn apart. Now we're all going to die for nothing!'

When she spoke the view had shifted towards the sanctuary. It shattered, focused on a stranger's face down in the crowd, shattered again—

'*Shit!*' hissed Ax, agonised.

Back to the high table. A heavy-faced woman to the left of the tattooed Goth was shaking her head in magisterial scorn. She wore brown robes; she had a necklace of animal skulls, knots of feathers, pierced stones. 'No one passes the Watcher. Have no doubt of that. He is hollowed out, his lab-science is rotten wood, he will soon fail.'

'I wouldn't count on it. If I were you, I'd surrender right now. He reached the Zen Self, you dorks. I will try to let them know you're good people deep down, but I warn you I am crap at telepathy.'

'Why the fuck won't they look at her? *Take over!*'

The woman rose from her place, revealing she was sky-clad under the robes. She turned her back to the faithful down in the nave, raised her arms wide and knelt, facing the sanctuary. 'Lady, you know our cause is just. Join our ceremonies. Approve our worship, bless our sacrifice. Help us to defeat the dupes of Babylon.'

'I have considered the worship of the lord and the lady,' said that voice, cool and pure, the crystal vowels of her childhood very distinct. 'I utterly reject it. If you persist in defining me as a Pagan, Elaine, you'll have to put me down as a heretic.'

'*Got it*, but this is eating power. Got about ten seconds—'

The camera pulled back, disclosing a high-backed chair where the Christian altar used to be; and there the witch-queen sat enthroned, flanked by the grey tombs of the cognitive scanners, swathed in white, hieratically still and straight, only her face left bare. Her grey eyes were enormous; she was smiling, her chin up.

'*She's alive*—' breathed Ax.

But she's not a free agent, no way. They could not see how she was bound to that chair, but she had to be a prisoner—

'Why don't we call on our own magician?'

Said the voice of the man with the route-map face—

Brown-robed Elaine turned on him. 'You think we should expose the Fat Boy, to save our lives? You talk up a storm, Moloch, but I sometimes wonder if you've grasped why we're here at all. Let us prepare for worship. The lady will preside. Her power will be with us, though she holds aloof—'

The shot became chaotic, face jostling face, robes falling open from bare bodies, dishes on the table, a child's hand pushing a little toy car over uneven terracotta tiles. A hubbub of voices, a tumble of blurred colour, and black-out.

Ax and Sage shoved back their screens and stared at each other. 'She's alive! She's here!'

Baal, the Black Dragon, had a consult with Moloch, the alleged Islamic Campaign vet. Baal was genuinely into gun control; he didn't allow the citizens to carry weapons unless they were on patrol: but they agreed it was time to break out the home defence. Fiorinda could hear them talking in the robing room beside the sanctuary while Elaine led the prayer meeting in the nave: a clatter of lockers being opened.

'Hold the church, and send out an escape pod,' insisted Moloch, urgently.

'Oh yeah, that's a good idea. And who volunteers to lead that party? Do tell?' The Black Dragon laughed. 'Fiorinda's staying here, and so are we. We are all sanctified. What's the worst that could happen?'

Fiorinda had tried to foster the bad faith between the Goth and his second-in-command. Unfortunately, Baal was capable of darkly suspecting the older man was a traitor, and still hero-worshipping him. That's the trouble with suicide warriors, they just don't fucking care . . . She had a soft spot for Baal, though he was an idiot with a deeply deranged sense of right and wrong. She didn't like Moloch: no chemistry. She couldn't prove it, but she was fucking sure there'd been no US freelances in Yorkshire. He was a bullshitter, and he (sip) *tasted* wrong. She tasted things. She had discovered that she could divert her senses: it helped to make the chair bearable. Shit, what if Baal sends me off in Moloch's custody? He won't do that. He's crazy but he's not stupid—

Time to come out from under the endorphins.

'Hey, Morrigan. Hey, *Elaine.*'

The chief witch left the ritual and came to kneel at the steps. Thick, boned and beaded locks of brown hair fell over her breasts. In life she had been a programmer, a cat lover, a mother, a gentle person: she'd been driven to where she was by sheer despair at the ruin of the living world. She was dead now. It was as well to remember that, when you tried to reason with these people. They were *dead.*

'Let me out of the chair! They haven't come to rescue me. They believe I've joined your cause. They're here to kill me, and then you'll never win me over.'

'You don't know that.'

'Yes I do. Lavoisier is *so full of magic* it's made me prescient.'

'Then you must free yourself,' said the Morrigan, in solemn triumph. 'I knew we would find a way to reach you in the end.'

Damn. Fuck you, fucking logic-chopping geek.

It had been established long ago that Ax can run, but he can't sprint, and Sage can sprint, but he can't run. The man with the endurance muscle does the jogging around, the muscle-bound geek (invincible at close quarters) does the safe breaking. Ax was painfully aware, as he jogged around, that Sage was no longer invincible at close quarters. They were keeping radio silence, but he had a terrible feeling ... He was also aware that he had *company*, that a shadow followed him, and harried his enemies, but he couldn't think about that. The streets were no longer deserted; they were crawling with Lavoisien military, hunting the intruders, while the adepts backed them up (presumably) with ritual. They thought they were hunting both intruders, because Ax had Sage with him, popping up from doorways etc., in hologram form. Ax was just trying to put as many of them as possible out of action, without any heroics. He wasn't fussed whether he killed them or not, as long as they went down. He kept worrying about the e/m pulse. He'd become convinced, as he relied heavily on the hologram Sage, and on the virtual monsters that he sent crawling around the ghost town streets, that his digital tech was going to be fried any moment.

The monsters were immix grafix bots, based on the candy-coloured enemy forces in 'Fiorinda's House': highly illegal toys, ramped up to deliver a burst of irresistible panic fear to anyone who got an eyeful. They weren't so effective now the opposing team knew to look away, but still useful. He had to keep close to the church. He was running round in circles; it was getting very familiar. He jogged down an alley, drawing the latest band of death-wishers after him, dropped behind the stoop with the broken step, and turned, tossing the immix beads like dice. He was nearly out of this ammunition, low on the solid stuff also. Sage had taken both packs, to stash them in case of further need, which had seemed like a good idea, but it meant when Ax was out, he was out ... The fx bots blossomed in the deep gloom (it was almost full dark now); at least two of the bastards caught a hit and fled, wailing. Up comes Ax's rifle, *they are dead*, he told himself, to combat his horror of falling back into killing mode. Not one of them was going to survive the

FBI raid. He jumped for the top of the wall at the end of his alley, one leg over and *there was someone beside him*.

'All done,' said a voice in his ear. 'On my way.'

'See you there.'

He fell over the other side, picked himself up and ran, bent double, seeking cover, not looking for a fight any more, the image of Fergal Kearney's malevolent, grinning face pasted inside his skull: flooded with awful conviction, mirror-image of the manic joy of fusion. He knew this was all wrong, terribly wrong, this was heading straight for hell . . . But ignore it. The western approach to the church was deserted, but for one fallen Lavoisien, who must be dead, because he hadn't moved. Ax arrived back there, still alive, hoping to God the ghost had not followed him. He crouched in the shelter of the barricade at the end of the street.

Sage came over the roofs and dropped from above a few minutes later.

'Hi, soldier.'

'Hi, other soldier. How was that?'

'Not too bad. But there's more than fifty of them, and they keep coming. You?'

'Well, I think we know where they're coming from . . . All set. The back door is wired and ready to blow, I moved the car, an' I've made a hole in the defences on the boneyard side. I don't think they'll get reinforcements, it's a forgotten front this evening. Now we go in, stop the rat-hole, rob the restaurant, deal with any unexpected obstacles *in situ*, and out.'

Blue eyes, smiling, saying *I've been killing people*, help me here.

They're already dead, thought Ax, but he felt this was not an answer.

'I'm glad it's going to be so easy. Ready?'

They stood, together. Sage grabbed the barricade and propelled himself upwards. He reached a hand to Ax, swung him onto the top of the pile and froze, staring. Ax turned his head, chills down his spine, and saw the raw-boned Irishman preternaturally imposed on the gloom: sword on his back and his thumbs in his rifle sling. His eyes were dark flames in his carrion flesh.

'Will yez give me a hand up, fer old times' sake, Sage me darlin'?'

The dead man's hand reached up. Sage reached down. Ax felt a shock as the Irishman brushed past him: a touch like thistledown, a horrifying, *human* glance from the dead eyes. Then he and Sage dropped onto the beaten earth in front of the church, and they were alone again.

*

There were no Lavoisiens visible in the church square. Ax stood guard while Sage applied explosive, delicately, to the big old lock, and the bolts above and below. The last thing they wanted now was a pile of rubble. Back off, duck down. The lock burst, the bolts ripped out. They pushed open the doors and walked in. The Last Supper table had been cleared away. The torches around the walls filled the nave with smoke and flamelight. There was still a crowd of people, but no children left, thank God. The congregation had backed up towards the sanctuary. Ax saw a mass of faces, robes, sky-clad bodies. Not many firearms. The élite rely on magic.

'This is a mistake, Mr Preston,' said the Goth in whiteface with the black tattoo, proud and calm and resolute. 'We have powers you do not dream of. We are the sacrifice, and you are on the wrong side.'

The white-swathed queen sat on her throne, unmoving, her great eyes blank stones in her distant face, blurred by the smoke of the flambeaux.

Ax did crowd control, Sage walked to the stair that led to the crypt. 'Fiorinda!' he called. '*Do* something, babe!' He threw a handful of immix beads down and laid a flashlight on the top step, to keep the barrier of monsters fuelled. Medusas bloomed: nasty-looking coelenterates, a dull pink, apparent height about three metres. Sage and Ax were immune, they had fx blockers in their headset screens. Panic assaulted the adepts like a wrecking ball, charged up as they were with fight-or-flight. It wouldn't last, but they were sliced off at the knees, before conscious control had a chance to engage. They were falling over, fighting each other, rushing for the doors. Ax fought his way through them, without firing a shot. Sage stayed by the stairs, in case reinforcements started coming up. 'Resist! Resist!' yelled Elaine, standing with her arms raised, buffeted by the crowd. 'Close your eyes! Avert your eyes, tell yourselves it isn't real, you—'

Ax paid no attention, he had reached Fiorinda. She did not speak; she kept very still. Her eyes were huge, all pupil. He understood that she could not move, and ripped at the white veiling around her throat. Shit. He had cutters in his belt, but oh, God, this is going to take time. She tipped her head back while he severed the hasp of the collar round her throat. There was another band across her arms. He cut it, dragged the metal apart and heard her whisper, the faintest breath, '*Ax*—!'

'My baby. Be ready. Soon as you're free we're out of here, it's set up, out the back, we have the Rat outside, oh, God, your hands too—'

'*Ax*—'

His heart stopped. He needed to watch what he was doing, and stay aware of the wild rumpus going on behind him, which might erupt this way any moment. But he had to look up. She was looking at him as from an open grave. Everything was so familiar, so often he'd been here before: Fiorinda looking at him like that, he felt sure he was in London, and it was a cold morning, the leaves on the plane trees a faint golden green. *'Elaine the Morrigan,'* whispered Fiorinda. Ax spun around to see the woman in the brown robe, her arms still raised above the calming crowd, like Moses. If he'd realised a moment sooner what he should do, he'd have blown the witch away, but he didn't. She shouted out, very loud, words that ran together into a wordless yell, and Sage dropped like a stone.

Fiorinda leapt from her chair, white veils flying, the last of her shackles tearing like paper. If she reaches fusion, we are done for. The thought slammed into his mind as he ran with her, a superposition of Harry's vision, the black rose in the room with the secret Committee, the fear of death that had filled him today, brimful now and brimming over, not his own death, *a lot* of death ... Fiorinda dived to her knees and grabbed Sage by the shoulders,

'Ax! He's all right! Trust me, come on, get us out of here!'

Sage was trying to stand; it was true, he was only stunned. Ax held him up, half a dead weight, thank God this is the new, slimline Aoxomoxoa ... but could they get to the exit? He would have to fire on the crowd, only held off now by their fear of Fiorinda, but he couldn't get them all. She would have to—

Oh God, no. She must not commit magic, no more, we'll be lost—

'Fiorinda,' he gasped, 'don't do it, whatever you're going to do, *don't do it*—'

She smiled at him, unearthly sweet, and shook her head.

Something took shape at the gates of the sanctuary. It rose like thick, coloured smoke, bordered by flame. A big raw-boned shadow stood there, rifle on his back this time, and his sword naked in his hands. His eyes glowed. 'Git out of here, the three of yez,' he crooned, grinning like a Hallowe'en lantern, tossing back his shining curls. He swung the broadsword up in a salute, and flames shot to the rooftree.

'These darlin's are all mine.'

The monster leapt, with a joyous howl, into the crowd. Ax and Fiorinda, half dragging Sage between them, stumbled for the robing room. Ax fired off the signal, and Sage's charge detonated, (not so delicate, this one), adding a thunderous bass to the Hieronymus Bosch battle going on behind them. Out through the blasted doorway, into the violet night ... 'Which way?' gasped Fiorinda.

'Up here—'

Over the barricade, down a starlit dirt street that ended where the defences rose in a wall of timber, rubble, earth and brushwood. The Rugrat was waiting for them, at the foot of the earthworks, immobilised and concealed, mirroring the surfaces of night in the ghost town. You were gone a long time, it thought, with the little mind that was locked deep inside the code. But I waited. I knew you'd come back.

Ax saw that if the Rat tried its pit-climbing trick on the heap of shit looming over them they'd be buried in landfill. Not sure how that command works, anyway. He swung the car around, gunned it in reverse until its arse hit the barricade at the other end of the street, and went for it. The Rugrat belted up the earthworks in RTE, almost lost it halfway up the concave, tottering slope, bucked like a mule and powered over the top. The back of the car swung around in a lazy arc, the front wheels slid forward. It righted itself, flew over the ditch, landed bouncing and rushed up the boneyard, in a flurry of crunched Wild West memorials of violent death—

'Wait! My saltbox!'

'Yes, yes, saltbox, I have it, it's safe—'

'Give it to me! Stop the car! Ax, please, this is worth doing—'

They'd have given her every star in the sky. She grabbed the saltbox from Sage and jumped out of the car. They leapt after her. Lavoisier was buzzing; there were off-roaders rushing around, people milling in the church square, loud-hailer orders, splashes of light, it looked like trouble—

'I'm afraid Rufus didn't hold them long,' said Fiorinda, ruefully.

She twisted open the wooden apple and swung her arm. An arc of white crystals soared, impossibly far, and landed on an isolated blockhouse in the outer sector. There was an instant, impressive explosion, followed by a rattling cascade of them, a firework display. 'Their big ordnance,' she said, with satisfaction. 'That should keep 'em busy.'

She closed the box and held it to her breast; and stared at them, looking like a ghost in grave-wrappings, barefoot, bewildered as if she'd just woken on this hillside—

'What *happened* to you, Fiorinda?'

'What happened to me? You know how we have Counterculturals? I met the *real* counter culturals. They do things differently in America.

Everything's on a much bigger scale.' And again she stared, like a revenant, lost among the living. 'How did you find me?'

'We didn't,' confessed Sage. 'The FBI found you. Oh, Fee, I lost my mask. I can't believe I lost my *mask*—'

'The FBI found you,' repeated Ax. 'We came to get you out because they know, beyond reasonable doubt, that you have effective magic. They're on their way to annihilate Lavoisier, and you weren't supposed to survive. Come on. We have to get out of sight—'

They reached the autodump and slipped the Rugrat in among the wrecks. Unmasked, it didn't look too out of place: it was filthy, and had suffered a few knocks. They covered it with a groundsheet anyway. Fiorinda laid her palm on the car's flank, be safe, Rugrat ... The trailbox was where they'd left it: they stripped off the dirty black shroud and Ax led out the horses. Fiorinda stood with Sage's arms around her, watching the saddling with huge, doubtful eyes.

'I'll ride if I have to,' she said. 'But I don't want to be in charge of one.'

'You can share mine,' said Sage, stooping over her, inhaling her—

They used the pinto as a pack pony, and Fiorinda rode in front of Sage, Madeleine not being the horse you'd trust to be quiet enough for such a precious burden. They headed into the hills, and at last reached a pan of level ground, hidden by steep bare slopes all around. 'This is where we left our stuff,' said Ax. 'There's a cave. I think we'll be safe here tonight.'

'Ax,' said Sage, 'who is a threat to us? We are safe anywhere. *Look* at her.'

The cave was known locally as the Cow Castle; it had a lick of an underground spring in the back, and a brushwood barrier at the entrance, to dissuade tourists or other vermin. Ax got down and dragged aside the brushwood; they led the horses inside. 'I don't want to be underground,' whispered Fiorinda. 'I've had enough of being underground.'

'Didn't plan to be,' said Ax. 'We'll sleep under the stars.'

He found the camping mattress and the quilt, took them outdoors and shook the mattress to inflate it. Sage brought the nylon stuff-bag full of presents. They sat together, staring at each other, lips parted, awed by the silence, the calm.

'Now, what do we have in here?' said Ax, opening the bag. 'No chocolate ice cream, that's back in the Rat, but we do have—'

'Marmite!' she gasped. 'Oh! You angels, where did you find this!'

'We humbled ourselves, and asked the expats. Give her the Bombay Mix.'

'And here's the Bombay Mix. And the Red Stripe, but it isn't frosty.'

'You can dip the Marmite *in* the Bombay Mix, I m-mean, Bombay Mix in Marmite, and no one will make any remarks—'

Candy corn, liquorice, idiotic toys, a ridiculous dress, old storybooks from Westwood Village ... She sat among her hoard, hugging the foamy, baby-girl party dress, wiping tears from her cheeks. 'Oh, when did you *do* all this?'

'When you went away. We were pitiful. We kept buying things that we thought would tempt you to come back.'

'He thought you'd run off because you were sick of us,' said Ax, perfidious.

'*Sage!*'

'Oh, *he* only thought you were dead. He was totally grown-up and rational.'

Fiorinda drank warm Red Stripe. Ax went to unharness the horses. Sage watched her, smiling, sipping at his own can. 'How is your head?'

'Splitting.' He grimaced experimentally. 'I don't think I'll try getting the button out until morning.'

She wiped her eyes again, sighed, steeled herself, found the end of the bandage with her fingernails, tugged it loose: and unwound it until her naked scalp was revealed, all doodled on by the amateur occult neurologists. Chin up.

'Is that it?' he asked. 'No other depredations?'

'This is it. They cut my hair off, and they kept my head shaved. They kept me in an underground dog kennel, which, to be fair, was no worse than their own cells, and they made me sit in that stupid chair, bound in iron, looking at them, argh, for hours on end. Otherwise they were kindness itself, apart from the fucking scans.' She glared at him. 'Oh, I know it all now, doctor, doctor. All the things that are wrong with me. All the normal wiring I don't have, that I had to invent for myself. But they still couldn't make me do magic, so they were very confused.'

'But *you* are not confused anymore.'

'No, I'm not,' she said. 'I am all right now.'

Ax came back to join them. He knelt beside her, took her hands, and kissed her brow. 'My little cat, my darling, you are so beautiful. Your eyes are so bright.' He didn't know if he should touch her. Maybe he shouldn't touch her, because even to look at her was making him *unbelievably* horny. But he was aware of Sage, lying there watching, peacefully; silently saying go ahead, Sah. Everything's all right. Fiorinda took his face between her hands, whispering Ax, my darling Ax. They lay down together kissing, and he felt himself folded in fire, wrapped in a burning calm, coming home to his own country, after a long voyage on stormy seas; coming back to himself.

∞

Fiorinda's House

Fiorinda woke, curled in the hollow between her lovers' bodies. She reached up to her bumfuzz head to remind herself how bad it was: touched her saltbox and groped for the water bottle. Ah, cool water. She tucked the bottle back under the edge of the mattress and retreated. I have my saltbox, I have water, I have Ax, I have Sage, a warm dry hole to sleep in; and my hair will grow. God, this is *paradise*. I want nothing else, ever. But she needed a piss. Sage stirred and mumbled, 'What is it?'

'I need a piss.'

'I'll come with you.'

Ax was a dim, vulnerable shape, a puddle of dark hair. 'We mustn't leave him on his own,' whispered Fiorinda. 'He might wake and us not be there—'

'We'll keep him in sight.'

In a break between the hills Orion was rising, sideways, over the southern horizon, Betelgeuse just clearing the haze. They crouched on their heels in the sagebrush, watching the glint of familiar stars on two lively dark streams as they hurried to join each other. She remembered a ritual. Long ago, when she and Aoxomoxoa and the Heads were first acquainted, when she was the teenage mascot. An initiation in a freezing cold field somewhere on the Hard Fun Tour: digging like cats and squatting in a row, defecating with these five big men. Ah, communal dumping, it was so important—

'What's funny?'

'The shit fests.'

He laughed, and put his arm around her, tugging her against his breast, resting his chin on her skull. 'I don't like having no hair,' she whispered. 'This is more undressed than I like to get. I feel as if I'm walking about in my bones.'

'Sssh, it won't be for long. It drives me nuts, how fast my hair grows.' Sage fretted if his crop went untrimmed for a week. 'Thank you for talking me up back there, babe,' he said, ruefully. 'I'm sorry I couldn't match the advertising.'

'You did fine. I wish I could have stopped Elaine, but th-that was not the moment for me to take issue with her power-source.'

They considered the unresolved situation. Alas, it's not over yet.

'Do they know about the Hollywood conjecture?'

'They know what could happen,' said Fiorinda. 'It doesn't mean a thing. Their cause is just . . . Sage? I know who the Fat Boy candidate is.'

'So do I.'

She slipped out of his embrace; or maybe Sage withdrew. Fiorinda looked down at her own hands, and her feet, and the myriad reality that glowed through the flesh. The desert night was a cloak she wore. 'I'm sorry,' she whispered.

'Sssh.'

She hugged him, and he hid his face in the hollow of her shoulder, then he looked up and their eyes met, in the starlit dark, for a moment outside time. Sage heaved a sigh, and began to kiss her little breasts, delicious fire: and then Ax, who had quietly come to find them, was there, taking hold of her with the hard, sure touch of his musician's hands, so she could lean back, weightless, soul-kissing with the wolf while the tiger fucked her. Sage carried her back to the mattress, and they changed partners, around and around, until the meat was shared to pieces.

'Hey, Ax?' Sage mumbled, tracing and nuzzling over where her hairline used to be; he was fascinated by this new nakedness, untouched Fiorinda—

'Mm?'

'What d'you say, we persuade her to give this look a fair trial?'

'No,' said Ax firmly, wrapped around her back, sheltering her head as best he could, with his lips, his cheeks, the hollow of his throat—

'Fuck off, Sage. I don't see myself as an elective slaphead, thanks.'

'It could look good. You could wear a very stylish headtie or a hat—'

'Forget it.'

'Leave her alone, big cat. Unrestricted access to the nape of her neck is pretty cool, hm, very horny, but, that's supposed to be our secret—'

'Perverts. I know you're only trying to make me feel better.'

When she woke again a pale blue dawn was well advanced. She could smell woodsmoke and coffee. She lay looking at the broken necklets of pink cloud, scattered over the sky where Orion had been, listening to a curious, mechanical crunching sound. Oh, it's the horses. There was a fire of roots. Ax was watching the blackened coffee pot. Sage was standing beside the big animals, patting them as they tugged mouthfuls of horse-food from a bundle (she felt betrayed. Sage was supposed to be her ally against horses). Three raw-boned rabbits, the size of English hares, with mobile black-tipped ears, were advancing on the group, with more calculation than fear ... 'Did you bring me any clothes beside the party frock?'

'Yep,' said Ax, 'we did. You really think we're idiots, don't you?'

'Bra and pants?'

'Socks and boots, even. I used to run a country, you know.'

Predictably, the underwear was not what Fiorinda would have chosen for being a fugitive in the desert, but never mind. The Cow Castle cave was neither deep nor dark; light came in through cracks. She found her washbag, brushed her teeth and splashed her face, being frugal with the water: tears welling at the thought of them bringing Fiorinda's toothbrush with them on their desperate mission. The cowgirl hat they'd brought for her, however, without the masses of her hair in the way, settled roomily on the bridge of her nose. She borrowed the bandanna Ax had been wearing round his neck and tried to tie it so it could not be mistaken for the *hejab*.

Sage was frying eggs. Ax had disappeared, but before she could be afraid he was coming back through the red rocks, a pair of binoculars round his neck, looking thoughtful. By the fire she found glazed cinnamon buns laid out for her, on a clean square of brown paper from a grocery bag. Sage smiled enigmatically, set the pan of eggs on a stone and popped a tin of self-heating refritos. Memories, campgrounds, wild days, pouring through the fabric of the moment—

'The commando tech's still working,' remarked Ax. 'I just checked.'

Sage nodded. 'What's happening out there in the world?'

'I can't see Lavoisier, but they must have the fire under control, or I'd be able to see the smoke. There's nothing moving around here. How about your damage?'

'I'm okay. Got the button out,' said Sage. 'I have a bizarre headache, sinus feels horrible, fine shiner, and a field defect here—' He circled a finger in the air above and in front of his left eye.

'Have you taken anything for it?'

'Nah, it's not pain exactly. Better not; it'll clear.'

'They won't come after us now,' said Fiorinda. She took a sip of hot coffee and bit into her bun, very aware of the two male animals paying close attention: of the atavistic ritual in these gifts of food, now and last night. The bun was rather stale, but God, *delicious*. 'What are you going to do about the FBI raid?'

Ax sat down beside Sage, with a saddle for a backrest and the pan of eggs between them. He took up a fork. 'Nothing, that I can think of. What do you think we should do? Do you feel like telling us your side of the story yet?' Sage and Ax had babbled in the night, about the Committee and Harry; their troubles and their misdeeds. Fiorinda had said little.

'Oh. Okay.' She put down the bun and thought about this for a moment. 'All right, a summary. I left you, I went down to Silverlode. I walked into the Silver Mule, and I . . . I realised that I was looking at the rendezvous Lazarus had set up. I made contact and went off with them, they took me further up the line, and eventually I ended up here. But I'm making it sound rational, and it wasn't. I left you because . . . that was the day I went completely bonkers. I didn't know what was happening to me, I just knew I had to get through it *myself*. When I walked into the Silver Mule, I was too nuts to know whether I was infiltrating the enemy or, or hallucinating in a padded cell—'

'That was my fault,' broke in Sage, distressed. 'I know I did that to you.'

'Knock it off. Forget it, that's over. We went to Carlsbad, and from there I don't know where . . . They took my clothes, they took my ring, and I didn't realise why, I thought I was being cleansed of Babylon. Oh, shit, but the Rugrat was okay?'

'The car is fine,' said Ax. 'It lost about two weeks of working memory in police custody, that's all.'

'I was afraid they'd find it and kill it. I was so worried about that. When I made contact, I thought I was meeting people who had tried to get near us but been foiled by the studio. I was wrong: the hard core never wanted to meet us. We're the sell-outs. Sage is a labrat, and you've said very mean things about green nazis, Ax. All they wanted was me, because they were sure I had some magic. I went along with them, because I would find out about the Fat Boy. I kept telling them they were wrong about my occult powers, I thought that would cover me, as far as I thought anything coherent. But when I got to Lavoisier they sheared me like a sheep, and they *scanned my brain* the bastards. They decided they had to lock me up in iron, and there was nothing I could do, because I dared not use magic. There was no way I could reach you. I'm sorry. I did *try* telepathy—'

Ax said ruefully, 'We weren't in a very receptive mode.'

'Telepathy sucks,' added Sage. 'It's useless and confusing—'

'Whatever.' She frowned. 'Do the FBI know what Lavoisier is?'

'I think they do,' said Ax. 'They didn't tell us in so many words, but it was there in what they said. Lavoisier is the stronghold of a group called the Invisible People, and a training camp for natural magicians.'

'Hm. Yes, but no. They're not the Invisible People . . . I don't know who the Invisible People are . . . The activist network I met is something else. It's big, a lot of people are involved. Lavoisier's the lunatic fringe or the very hard core, depending on shades of opinion . . . They're the ones who were running the Fat Boy candidate sacrifices. You didn't see the half of it. They do a lot of very weird and gross things in the underground part of that ghost town, in the hope of boosting wannabes to the point where they can make a hex stick.'

'Are they succeeding?'

'Not at all, thank God. Anything effective comes from the candidate, who of course has never been near this place. Vestigal ability stays crap no matter what, and they don't have an idea how to rewire normal brains. They wouldn't want to. That would be lab-magic, which is anathema. They stretched a point with the scanners, but some of them think even that was an awful mistake. When they decided they could see effective magic in me they were thrilled. But conflicted, as you saw.'

She paused, chin on her hands—

'Very conflicted. They were afraid of me, they saw me as a threat, but they longed to worship me, because I was their Holy Grail, and they can't play with their *own* Holy Grail, because the candidate's identity has to be protected. They told me I was dead to the world because they had faked my suicide. I knew they were never going to let me go, I was no nearer to the Fat Boy, and I didn't dare commit magic, for, well, several reasons. So it was an impasse. I *would* have thought of something—'

'Sure you would,' said Ax. 'I knew that. Peter Pan here just got whiney, and scared of being left alone, so we had to come and fetch you.'

'Hahaha.'

The world turned for a little, and the three of them were just breathing, in and out, just glad to have survived the storm, one more time.

'It was when we saw the body that we knew you were alive,' said Ax.

She nodded. 'Yes . . . The volunteer wasn't the best match. They went with her because the willingness is all. They had my hair, they injected her with my DNA (the famous imprinting didn't seem to bother them), and they cooked it all up with pan-occultist ritual. Of course it was the candidate who made it work, in so far as it did ... They're a broad church, did I mention? The Pagans and Satanists share power, because they have the numbers, but there's Voudoun, Aztecs, Vampires, Taoists, all kinds of Native-American; digital-based new religions; Celtics, of course. I didn't have to meet her, I am glad to say. I heard the reports, and gathered it hadn't been a total success. They didn't care. Whatever happened was the right thing to happen, because we're in the endgame now.'

Ax stared. 'The dead woman in your dress had *volunteered*?'

'All the sacrificial victims were volunteers,' said Fiorinda.

'My God.'

'I really believe they were: or they thought they were, doing it for love of Gaia. They'd have been tanked to the eyeballs, I hope.'

'Who did the killing?' asked Sage, quietly.

'Other members of the suicide squad.'

'And Billy the Whizz?'

Fiorinda gave him a straight look. 'I don't know, Sage ... She was a girl who chatted you up at parties. I thought she was okay, but I never talked to her much. I don't know if she was a secret, suicidal eco-warrior. But I've a bad feeling that she wasn't. I think Billy was the exception.'

Sage nodded, and stared at the fire.

Something going on that Ax didn't follow, about poor Billy.

'*Does* iron block magic?' he wondered. 'It's a persistent tradition.'

'Nah. But I wasn't going to do any tricks for them, so it blocked *me* ... Then, two, no, three nights ago, I had a strange dream, involving a techno-wizard and a guitar-man, and some kind of hired orchestra, groovilicious, stadium rock farrago—'

Sage came out of his bleak moment and laughed.

'—at which I'm embarrassed I made a guest appearance.'

'Don't look at me,' said Ax, 'it was all his idea.'

'And I came back from there knowing who the Fat Boy had to be.'

Ax nodded. 'Are you going to tell me?'

Fiorinda gazed into the thin flames, almost invisible in the morning sun. 'Not right now, if you don't mind. Just ... believe me, it isn't a problem any more. I'm not looking forward to what I might have to do, but I can handle it. It's strange. All the time since Baja I was thinking, wow, how can I win another boss fight, if I'm also going crazy? But it was a loop. Because I fell apart, I *had* to sort myself out, which was something I'd been frantically avoiding ... and so now there's no problem. I still don't like magic. I think it will unravel civilisation, if it takes over. But I've made my own peace. I've found my *guai-yi*, Sage. I can live with being me.'

'Very Californian,' said Sage. 'See. I knew this place would suit you.'

'Nyah—'

They pulled faces, while Ax took to heart the things Fiorinda wasn't saying, including the withholding of any detail about the Countercultural Underground. She had to get away from us to heal herself, he thought, and we'll have to live with that. He knew now what the ghost of Rufus had meant; and understood that she had been with him in Lavoisier, sharing the killing mode. Why does she do that? She does it because in a sense *that's Rufus O'Niall*, the unstoppable magician, sitting opposite me, looking like a grey-eyed girl. And Rufus himself? Who knows . . . But these aren't things to talk about. Let them be. He wondered if he was supposed to have guessed the identity of the Fat Boy candidate. Maybe it would come to him when he put the inferences together. In his present state of mind, he wasn't worried. He knew Fiorinda and Sage were on the case. Hey, why am I not touching them? He shifted the frying pan, moved over and kissed the big cat: his soft mouth, his eyes, his golden brows. 'I lost my mask,' Sage recalled, piteously, 'Ax, I lost my *mask*.'

'You've got it on file, haven't you?'

'Yeah, but ancient, I haven't updated it in years—'

'Look on the bright side. You can be a living skull who doesn't look a day over twenty-five. Shall we tell her? What d'you think? Is this the right time?'

'Let's tell her.'

They faced her, nervously. 'Fiorinda,' said Ax, 'maybe. We . . . er, you should know, we found out about the clinic appointment. The folks did some PI work and tracked you down, and Rob talked to the doctor. We know what she said.'

'Oh.' Fiorinda coloured up, carmine through the gold, and twisted her hands together. Her eyes shone, her mouth trembled. 'Oh, then you know. You k-know that horrible woman says I c-can't have a baby until I'm *monstrously* overweight.'

The horses gave up munching and stood quietly. The jackrabbits retreated; a lizard with a very long tail stalked out from under a rock. Ax sought his jacket in the cave, came back and took Fiorinda's hand. He kissed the braided gold ring which they had just returned to her, sat down and started rolling up a spliff, into which he shook a fine powder from a twist of feed-sack paper.

'What's going in there?' asked Sage.

267

'Peyote, I think.'

'Oh yeah? Where'd you get that?'

'Stu's ranch: from Cheyne, the horse-lady.' His eyes were wet, he wiped them with the side of his hand. They'd been getting emotional over the news Fiorinda should have brought them, a long snip in time ago. 'I thought, fuck, think positive. We three might want to do some drugs. Some time.'

The fire burned to white ash. They sat around it at the points of a triangle and smoked the spliff, and then another, and then one more for luck. The sky, above the undulating rim of the red bowl, was a dome so transparent you could see the pinpricks of stars. Fiorinda said, 'Shouldn't you put the horses away, or, er, tie them up?'

'There's water and feed in the cave,' said Ax. 'They know they can retire in there. They seem fairly fixed on us; I don't think they'll wander off.'

The men took on their animal shapes and lay watching her. Their eyes, blue and brown, fused into a steady, greenish gold: the pupils were gleaming vertical slits through which something unknown looked out. The tiger and the wolf, blended into one, with wonderfully soft barred and brindled fur, made a very beautiful animal. She could still see them both, but the mingled beast was dominant. She looked up and saw its muzzle leaning down, covering the dome of the sky like the limb of a giant planet, to take her in its mouth and carry her. The unknown thing that looked through its eyes was now overwhelmingly huge. She spread her thighs and took it inside, all the fifteen dimensions, a web, an atom; and swelled up like a balloon, a thin but unbreakable membrane, interpenetrated by galaxies. I am the thing behind their eyes she realised, and shrank into her body again, like a hermit crab.

Ax sat crosslegged, resting his chin on his hand and his elbow on his knee. I need a shave, he thought. We are some desperadoes. We have set out on a journey that will end God alone knows where, but it won't be in this world. It could even, just about, be literally on another world, another planet, *Insh'allah*, that we finally lay our burdens down, and make the peace. But he didn't like to think of God when he was in any altered state, it seemed to him a form of gatecrashing, and he was too proud to sneak in the back door. I will wait until I'm invited. Yeah, I will wait until I'm invited, and return to the abyss of non-being the old-fashioned way ... He was not surprised to see Sage and Fiorinda had become one person, sitting looking at him across the ring of stones that held the crumbled white ash. He had known that they were one person ... right back when he took Aoxomoxoa's little kid-sister mascot to his bed. Or so it seemed now. But things happen as they must, and there they are, two sides of the same coin. Only their mother could tell them apart. He had an erection, but he was happy to let it simmer, and think about watching them fuck; or watch them do anything, not fussed, and possibly never move again. Yes, this would be dandy, just sitting here thinking about my darlings, for all eternity. He wondered what time it was. He should make them put their hats on; and we should climb higher up the mountains or find some trees or get under the earth. Sage is going to fry.

'Sage,' he said, 'you're going to fry.'

'It's okay, Ax,' said Fiorinda, 'time isn't passing. I think we should visit Vireo Lake. Do you know how to get there?'

'Of course he does,' said Sage. 'He has a map in his head.'

'Yeah, I can get us there. But put your hats on.'

'I want to wear my new party frock.'

Sage beamed, delighted. 'Good idea!'

They had to fetch the Rugrat, but it didn't seem far. Before long they were driving through a different desert, a pale plain covered with golden-toned maquis; more beautiful than the one they'd come to feel was their own. Drifts of poppies, bright as egg-yolk, scattered the verges like harbingers of next year's spring. They drove without music, Ax at the wheel of course and Fiorinda in the middle, through a rushing silence. They had the windows open; Sage leaned his elbow on the rim, smiling. 'I keep thinking I'm listening to music,' said Fiorinda. 'Rock music, not ours, but someone else's. I'm about to recognise the band and then I snap back, like waking up from a microsleep.'

Ax and Sage listened intently, thinking they would name the band for her; it kept eluding them, though the music was extremely familiar. It was one of those glitches where you need to get *past* the moment, so that you can look at it again, and say, oh, yeah, that's what it was. But they could never get past the moment. The silence roared on, like a distant sea. The landscape flew along with them like a magic carpet, getting more barren but austerely beautiful, and they met intersections, at each of which Ax followed the directions on the map in his head. There was still only desert, and they hadn't seen another car, when suddenly the lake was in front of them, a pan of silver they had glimpsed from afar and assumed must be salt.

It was Vireo Lake. They got out of the Rat and walked by the shore. White birds rose from the water. 'Can you drink it?' asked Fiorinda.

'I wouldn't,' said Ax. 'It must be an extremely strange liquid.'

Sage looked up, squinting through his lashes, into a sky that was almost as white as the lake shore. 'It's very clear that we're walking on a seabed.'

'We're where it's impossible for people to be,' said Fiorinda.

'On the cutting edge.'

'At the highest point of the high tide.'

'This is where they're building air for Mars.'

Oh, that long departing roar . . .

They'd passed through the perimeter fence without noticing it: they could now see a car park, bunker-blank buildings, and an artificial oasis of lawn, set with small pine trees, pet trees; economy-size bonsai. They walked in, and walked around the corridors unchallenged, feeling like official visitors – a role they'd endured so often they caught each other smiling falsely, nodding for no reason, and doing needless *how interesting* expressions. It was cool inside the buildings, but not the flamboyant indoor chill they were used to in Los Angeles. Here is one of our neurological labs. Here are the General Electric Gauss 0003/zyg series Cr/t imaging scanners, massively shielded whole-body pods, each worth more than the GNP of a small European state: two short rows of them. Fiorinda and Ax stayed at the door; Fiorinda didn't like the look of those things. Sage walked in, pausing to bow his head slightly at the threshold, like a martial arts student. He stalked around the alien training hall and they saw him raise his eyebrows: he walked out again shaking his head.

'Majestic. You wouldn't have got me into one of those for long, though.'

Olwen's prototype, fusion-detecting realtime cognitive scanners, built by her parent company in Wales, had been on a different evolutionary line; they hadn't needed the massive shielding of the fMRI.

'Did you see anything interesting?'

'They're linked.'

This seemed reasonable to Fiorinda and Ax. Why shouldn't the neuronauts be linked, if they were a team? But Sage was impressed.

They continued their tour, unnoticed, looking for the team, and found them in a cafeteria. As always around these corporate-egalitarian watering holes, there was an obvious caste system. The support staff and technicians sat below the salt; the scientists and the bureaucrats had their special area, lords and ladies of church and state. And then there's the wild cards, the jokers, who have the right to mingle with anyone, but mostly they mingle with each other. They can't help it. Here was another surprise for Sage: there was a woman on the A team. She was number-one cropped, and a bodybuilder with little in the way of breasts, but obviously a woman. The A team were easy to spot. They sat together, a group within the group, and they had an aura: a no-kidding, Anne-Marie Wing, striated halo of coloured light that glowed around them.

'Maybe this was a mistake,' said Fiorinda 'I don't know what to do with these people. I surely don't wish them well, but I don't want to wish them harm.'

'We're tourists,' said Sage. 'We don't wish them anything.'

Outside in the oasis, Fiorinda saw a little grey bird perched on a pine twig. It looked down and sang out a burst of silvery notes as she passed, and she stopped and smiled, holding out her hands. Just because it was a bird, singing in the desert.

> *Rivers of light*
> *Scarlet and white*
> *Sink into the sand*
> *But this is our . . . promised land*

On the drive back from Vireo they made up songs together, something they'd rarely done in the glory days, though they'd collaborated musically, appearing on each other's albums in traditional fashion. There had never been time, and their lives had still been distinct: three different strands, different bands. Working together was very good; it grounded them and made them laugh, it took the rush and raced with it. Sadly none of the songs survived except 'Promised Land'. Sage was the scribe, leaning by that open window, and all the words and music flew away.

They left the Rugrat and headed back to camp, through the landscape that Ax had found so alarmingly familiar. The heat was extraordinary; Ax kept fretting that Sage was going to fry. He'd been taking sunscreen for weeks; his liver was able to deal with those kind of drugs: but however often they told him, Ax forgot this. The trail drifted over a high red plain, scattered with boulder heaps, cactus and twisted Joshua trees. 'How high are we?' asked Fiorinda, holding out her iridescent skirts. The dress was *darker* than anything she'd worn in her punk diva party-frock days: but they'd remembered she hated black. She was a glittering wallflower, a pansy, a bird with smoulder-opal plumage.

With a vulture's bare head, but that can't be helped. It was a token price.

''Bout as high as Ben Nevis, right now.'

'Unbelievable. My eyeballs are on toast. It's like a sauna.'

'You two wait here and I'll fetch the horses.'

'No horses.' Fiorinda quickly thought of an excuse. 'It's too hot for them.'

'You like the dress, Fee?'

'I love it.'

'Let's take a break,' said Sage. They rested in a scoop of black shade behind a boulder-heap and drank water. Ax rolled up a spliff: Sage sat close to him. 'We need to spy out the country we're heading into. D'you want to come up with me?'

'We're good here. If we go up there, whoa, we're in the unknown.'

'You think we might get too far out?' asked Sage.

'Yeah, that worries me.'

'If we get too far out, well, there we'll be.'

'We could go very far,' said Ax. 'Very, very far.'

Sage filled his lungs and leaned over to pour the smoke into Ax's mouth. Fiorinda felt that she was in the way. No girlfriends on manoeuvres, they had private things to discuss. She should assert herself, be independent, and not be a gooseberry (why a gooseberry?). 'I'll keep watch,' she said. She picked up Sage's rifle and went to the side of a tall red boulder, where she could see the trail. Nothing moved. She climbed to the top of the boulder and found a hollow where she could lie, watching over the plain, with the rifle in her arms. She was fascinated by the heavy hard feel of it, and the smell of the greased metal. It gave her images of a dead, horrible, thrusting and stabbing, but she kept smelling it and feeling it until she was convinced it was harmless; though it may kill, this is not a *bad* rifle, this is a friendly rifle.

Free and clear, with her bandanna tugged over her eyes, she spread herself to the sun, and the fire that burns the deserts of California ran easily in her veins. Ah, Babylon, we're not afraid. The great burning, the disaster, is our world where we will live. She had hardly been there any time when she heard scrambling and gormless laughter, and they came up the rock, rock-hard, naked, except for their boots, greased with sweat. 'Why did you go away?' demanded Ax.

'You scared us,' said Sage. 'Don't *ever* go away, don't be out of sight.'

The rock became soft as red milk, continuous with the air, Fiorinda and Ax soul-kissing, Sage between them, the opal frock for bedding, became a flesh machine, and it was endlessly, brutally, working: while the sun raced to and fro over them, burning them to skeletons, fusing them to the rock. 'D'you remember,' asked Sage, when they lay worn out like fossils, hollowed and filled with gritstone, 'once, we were going to stay hornswoggling naked for life?'

'Yeah, because what's the fucking point in being near her any other way?'

'It would have had to be in London, not Tyller Pystri, otherwise not much of a statement, there in the cottage, nobody to appreciate ... What happened to that idea?'

'Let's do it now,' said Ax. 'Let's do it, consecrate ourselves.'

'Mine's still longer. Isn't it Fee? Hey, isn't it?'

'And mine is the tip of an iceberg, fuckface. I'm not getting involved. I know this conversation, and I don't know why you even pretend it is about me—'

'Ah, not by much, and mine is fatter, and that's what counts, heheheh.'

Sage grabbed him and they rolled together until Ax, uppermost, happened to glance over the side. 'Whooo. Er, I suppose we know how to get down from here?'

They were lying in the hollow tip of a red pillar, undercut and smooth, that went vertiginous dizzying down, tall as a house. 'It wasn't like this,' said Fiorinda, worriedly. 'It was *not* like this. It has grown like a beanstalk.'

Sage grinned at the white-pricked furnace overhead. 'I'm going to fry!'

Memo to selves. Climbing up the beanstalk is much, much easier than climbing down, and being naked and under the influence of hallucinogens is no help. Getting back to earth took them a long time: hard work in the heat of the day.

Fiorinda went into the cave in search of supplies. There was the scrape of a spring in the back, where a little water gathered. The horses were there, looming beasts with whiskers on their rubbery lips, and piano-key teeth. They seemed to her malevolent, invidious. She didn't like the way they breathed, or the sense of their great barrel-bodied size in the dark. She brought lager and the bag of Bombay Mix to the front end. She'd changed out of her glittery dress, and Sage and Ax had given up their no-pants ultimatum. They were all dressed and sensible again. The mattress lay where they had left it in the morning, with the cover neatly spread: by Fiorinda. She gave them food and drink, and sat apart.

'The only choice I have,' she said, 'is I can be a monster or I can be property. There's no other way. There is no such thing as an independent artist, I mean, woman. There was another way, but it is shut. Oh, no one's going to abuse me much. If you can bite the heads off live chickens, you're okay. But there's no part for me as a human being in this movie. Fucking typical. Every man that ever looked at me twice has wanted to piss on me some way, except for one who swore he only wanted to be my friend, but *he was lying*.'

'I don't want to own you,' said Sage, miserably. 'You once told me I wanted the Zen Self so I could have the power you have, the spiritual power, not content with the muscle. I *wasn't* just copying you. I *can* have reasons of my own. But it's true I wanted to be with you. To be where you are. All I want is to hold you, and never leave your side. It comes out not the way I meant—'

His hand reached out to her. Fiorinda severed it with a glance, and the five-fingered spider wriggled around, bleeding copiously.

'There's supposed to be a difference between how you react to a male or a female body,' mused Ax, trying to defuse this. 'That's the way you figure your sexual orientation, look at two bodies; which one makes you fire up? Me, I've always been the one saying *no, I'm sorry, I don't see the problem*. I mainly prefer girls, whatever that means, but I don't see the problem.'

'Are you trying to tell me this isn't about sex?' enquired Fiorinda, coldly.

'For me it's about dominance,' said Ax. 'I was born at the bottom of a pit. The people I can feel watching me all the time said, come on Ax, don't be such a loser, you can get out of there. So I climbed as best I could, I tried to be the best I could, and of course the fucking rocks fell on me. So here I am bleeding under these rocks, feeling like a fucking idiot, and so *hurt*, and I can hear the people who watch me all the time saying, well, you can do anything you want to do if you really believe in yourself. It's his own fault, he must have loser genes—'

Shadows had crept over the camping mattress that was their liferaft as the sun went down. It was ironic that they could make themselves so unpleasant, when death and terror and defeat and shame were the great gentle angels standing guard around that bed. But the mean things were in paradise to show that evil cannot be vanquished.

'I want to do something,' said the alpha male white boy, despondently.

'Maybe he wants to teach us to die,' said Ax. 'That's what he did to the folks before we left them: Zen suicide pills; that was our bodhisattva's response to the Fat Boy situation. I thought it was fucking bizarre.'

'It shows you how his mind works.'

'It was what came into my head. And so's this.'

Sage went into the cave. When he came out he hadn't changed his clothes, but they could see he'd tried to spruce himself up. He set Ax's phone on a rock; 'Heart On My Sleeve' began to play from the tiny speakers: annoyingly brash, after the music of the desert silence. The entrance to the cave was his backdrop, the twilight bowl his stage. He smoothed a patch of ground and began to dance. Ax and Fiorinda curled their lips. But they were caught, the way Sage's body in motion always caught their eyes, and then *disbelieving* as the maestro turned his back and began to shimmy his workshirt from his shoulders. Fiorinda laughed. Ax snorted. Before the shirt was off (he took his time) they were both sniggering: succumbing to the ridiculous, eyes on stalks, also undeniably horny. He made it last, he milked them, until they were rolling around helpless—

—and finally dived into their midst, cackling, naked but for one sock.

'You realise,' he warned them, starfish-sprawled, grinning between kisses, 'you realise, if you ever, *ever* tell anyone I can do that, I'll have to kill you both.'

Fiorinda burrowed down to escape the sun and encountered Ax, in the blind world under the covers. 'Hi, sweetheart,' he said, 'how are you this morning?'

'I'm good. Maybe, hm, a *little* bit sore.'

'Me too.'

They hugged each other, giggling. 'I love him,' whispered Ax, 'I *love* him. All my defences are down. Every time I see him I want to hold him—'

'Shouldn't you be telling Sage this? Have you told him?'

'Er, uh.' Ax sat up and started rummaging, in the bed and under the edge of the mattress. 'Not in so many words. It's not a competition, we're past that, that's over: but with Sage, you can't go letting him *know* that you have no defences—'

Actually, hell will freeze over, she thought, before you two stop competing. It didn't seem to her a bad thing, as long as it stayed within bounds. It meant she remained the key between them; and she had tenure. 'What are you looking for?'

'Cigarettes.'

'You finished them. Sage might still have some Maryjanes—'

'Fiorinda, I'm not an utter degenerate. I don't smoke cannabis before breakfast. Are they in his shirt pocket? Pass it over—'

Sage had been tending the horses. He flopped down on the edge of the mattress, exhibited the pack of nicotine-tainted grass cigarillos, scrunched it and lit the last one. 'We have to leave, sad to say. Not only is FBI Armageddon approaching, but we're low on water . . . Ah, well. That was probably some class-A, meet-God spiritual journey powdered cactus, and we blew it on a sex binge. I'm fucking mortified.' He touched Fiorinda's cheek, smiling tenderly. 'Hiya, my brat. Okay?'

'Am I still your stupid brat?'

'Always.'

'Hey, lemme have a hit.' Ax took possession of the cigarillo.

'I assume we still don't want to meet the Federales?' asked Sage.

'You assume right,' said Fiorinda. 'I don't trust the white hats. Not if they find me out here, where nobody's looking.' She got out of bed. 'This is where I have to ride the horse, isn't it? Fuck. I hate riding. I've forgotten how.'

'There's nothen' to it, Fee. You sit there and it walks along.'

'I just think if you really cared, you'd have brought a nice helicopter.'

'Oh yeah, so unobtrusive. And likely to fall out of the sky at any moment.'

They are one person, but they will always need me . . . Ax lay watching the smoke from the cigarillo: feeling like a snake with a new skin, like some kind of desert crustacean with a new shell hardening, a new interface with the world. Ah well, got to get back, no escape from reality.

'Hey.'

They ceased their gentle bitching and turned to him.

'I have to go to Lavoisier.'

'Why?' asked Sage. No side to it, just asking.

Ax handed him the fag end and started putting on his clothes. 'Because those crazy buggers want to die; they probably deserve to die, but that's not the problem.' He sat on the edge of the bed, shaking out his boots. 'You two tell me the Fat Boy apocalypse is cancelled, but I'm thinking, if the monsters of Lavoisier get blasted out of their redoubt by the FBI and the National Guard, it's not going to be a secret. It's going to be eco-warriors as the Manson family. If by some miracle the media don't get hold of it, the people Fiorinda met will fucking know it happened, and this will rebound on an extremely volatile situation here in California, and further afield too, most likely. I heard all those things you didn't say, Fiorinda. So . . . I think I have to try and talk to them, because I'm here: because of who I am, or was.'

He shrugged, embarrassed by their grave attention. 'Oh, okay. I have to do it, same reason as I do everything, to prove I don't have loser genes.'

'You *do not* have loser genes,' said Sage. 'Far fuckin' from it, Mr Preston.'

'You could be right about volatile,' said Fiorinda, dead straight. 'I hate to have to say it, but you should do this.'

They talked as they packed up. It was agreed that Sage and Fiorinda would go north and lose themselves for a night or so. Ax would do his errand, fetch the Rugrat, and they would try to meet at Big Pine, the town at the junction of the 395 and the 168. Fiorinda scrambled into the saddle and walked the little chestnut and white mare around the camp while the men loaded gear onto the Appaloosa. Madeleine didn't get any baggage: they would leave what they couldn't carry. 'Why *did* you get keen on the horse-riding, Ax?' asked Sage. 'I've often wondered. Fiorinda cert'nly didn't hussle you into joining the pony club.'

'Milly,' explained Ax, in an undertone. Milly, the drummer in Ax's original band, had been his girlfriend, before she switched to his brother Jordan; and before Ax met Fiorinda. 'She was the leafy suburban girl; me coloured boy from sink estate. She had her own horse. I decided I had to be into it, and, well, get good. So I did ... I haven't pursued it much. I don't know why it's a problem.' He slung the empty water bags and the collapsible bucket over the saddle horn. Big Snow backed and stamped. 'Can't you hold him still?'

'Sorry. Maybe we won't mention the Milly angle.' It crossed Sage's mind Fiorinda had surely spotted the Milly angle, but he decided not to say this.

'Right,' said Ax, with a flashing grin: thinking, ooh *why* did I hand him that? Fiorinda and Paintbrush came over, horse and rider in reasonable accord. 'Pull to stop, push to start,' she said. 'This saddle's very odd. How do I get down, again?'

'Same as you would off an English saddle.' Ax caught her as she slithered. 'Look, you're fine. I know you are. What's all the fuss?'

'I don't like horses. I don't think they're romantic, I don't think they're sexy. I think they have big teeth and they will bite me.'

'If you take that attitude,' he said, kissing her nose, 'she probably will.'

The ramparts grew in the shimmering heat. The graded road became very broken up before it reached that pockmarked Lavoisier sign. Ax was making his approach by the front door; he'd decided this was more tactful. He thought of islands of civilisation, separated not by scheduled flights and traffic streams but by badlands and desert places, the once and future world. They'd seen him coming. By the time he was within gunshot a reception committee had gathered: two off-roaders and six Lavoisiens standing by them, four men and two women, armed to the teeth.

Ax stopped and waited, with his white flag, which was a pallid feedbag tied to a stick. The Lavoisiens thought about this, then one of the off-roaders came out, down the hill. Madeleine stood her ground. A soft-bellied young man toting a sub-machine-gun got out. He was wearing an I-Systems T-shirt, spiderwired desert camouflage and a black hat with a skull and crossbones on the band.

'What the fuck are you doing here?' he asked, glowering.

Ax dismounted, and held Madeleine close. She was flicking her ears and showing white in her eye, but thankfully didn't act up.

'A parley. I want to talk to someone in charge, that's all. It's quite urgent.'

The kid gave him a smouldering, disgusted look. 'Aw, if it's *quait eurgent*—' He tugged a little mic out of his collar, keeping his other hand on the huge gun, and turned his head to mutter into it. 'Okay,' he said, 'you're to come in.'

Ax was frisked and disarmed. The kid did this, the others stayed in the car; staring. Ax smiled at them, and wondered if he had an aura. Maybe he didn't need one, after the way the commando raid had been concluded. They set off on foot, Ax leading Madeleine, the off-roader lumbering along behind; the second vehicle joined the convoy when they passed it. No one was working outdoors, but he noticed that the gun emplacements had been shored up with more earth and scavenged timber. Barricades in the streets had been reinforced, and gaps between the houses closed with salvage and rubble. He looked for the snipers, and found a couple, same places they'd been before.

'What's your name?'

'It's Simon.'

'Hi, Simon, I'm Ax Preston.'

'I know who the fuck you are.'

'Did you have many casualties, the other night?'

'Some dead ... We had one girl lost an eye. You shot her in the face.'

This appeared to be a personal grudge. 'I'm sorry about that.'

He hoped the bodycount would not affect his chance to get a hearing. Suicide warriors can get unconscionably bitter and worked-up over their dead; he remembered that from Yorkshire. Once they were among the buildings, the fire damage was obvious. The air stank of smoke, explosive and caustics ... They passed through a gap in the church square barricades. The doors had been repaired, a metal patch and a new lock (good discipline, getting that done). Everything had been cleared out from inside, including the scanners. Only the brainscans remained: false-coloured psychedelic roses blooming. 'You can leave your ride here,' said Simon, so he left Madeleine in the charge of a young girl with numb and terrified dark eyes. Lavoisien adepts were drawing a pattern on the tiled floor, using sticks of black wax and a can of red liquid, scattering herbs and chanting as they worked. They gave Ax some sour looks. His escort led the way down the stairs by the sanctuary. The crypt was a field hospital: it was doing brisk business. They walked through, attracting more bitter stares, and Simon opened a door off a passageway beyond.

'You wait in here.'

The room was large, the walls were earth but the floor was brick and there were hospital office furnishings: a desk with a peeling leather top, a balance-bar weighing scale, a photocopier, big chunks of unknown hardware, a trolley of medical supplies. Inside a supermarket freezer cabinet he found a row of glass cannisters with a human head in each, fresh as life, suspended in clear liquid. The neck ends were capped in white binding; he could see stitches on their naked scalps. More volunteers, no doubt ... He thought of Fiorinda, and looked into a dreadful abyss avoided.

Baal the Black Dragon, with his Pagan partner in command, and several other people, arrived after a few minutes. The route-map-faced guy, Moloch, was absent. He didn't recognise anyone besides Baal and Elaine. Getting old, Ax. Time was, you used to note every name and face in a crucial situation, do it in seconds and have them on file. But that was Ax believing his own legend—

The Black Dragon was wearing kohl, and his lips were still glossy black (must be tattooed), but his hair was pulled into a brusque ponytail, and his pallor wasn't make-up. Elaine wore armoured fatigues, with several heavy ankh and tau crosses, like Goth dogtags. Everyone found chairs and sat down, so Ax took a chair himself and drew it up to the desk, facing Baal and Elaine.

'Okay, what do you want?' said Baal. 'You want us to put down the Fat Boy and come out of here with our hands up? You have to be fucking kidding.'

'We know about the raid, Ax,' said Elaine, the Morrigan, one hand clasped around the crosses at her breast. 'We've had intelligence about that. Here we stand.'

'This is our Alamo,' said Baal. 'Everyone's ready to die. There's nothing you can offer us; there is no deal, nothing to discuss. So you have effective magic. We have effective magic, and ours is feeding on blood and pain and terrible sacrifice. Every agonising death we die here will go into the cauldron, which is already *brimful*, and we'll find out what happens when they compete. What are you feeding yours on, sell-out? *Compromise*? MacDisneyfied terrorism? Drowned refugees? Or, hey, *changing the system from within*?'

'Peace and love?' muttered somebody, in deep disgust.

What happens when they compete...oh shit. Oceanic dread brushed him, but he put it aside. Show no fear. The outlaws were in a poisonous mood, but he wouldn't be sitting here if there was no chance. 'Look ... Has anybody got a cigarette to spare, I mean, if it's okay to smoke?'

Baal took out a pack, stone-faced, and pushed them over the table.

'Thanks. Look, it's your legend, not mine, but as I remember, the Alamo was not a victory. It was a massacre of heroic idiots trapped in an indefensible—'

'The battles came afterwards,' said Elaine, smiling. 'With great slaughter. The Alamo did what it set out to do.'

'All right,' said Ax. 'Let's start with, trust me, you have no Fat Boy. It's over.'

The deranged elation in the room did not shift an iota.

He talked with them. He didn't attempt to get closure; he didn't feel very confident he'd achieved anything when he left. They were drunk on the black majesty of sacrifice: the happy prospect of being nerve-gassed in their underground warren, to the man, woman and child. About the only thing he had going for him was that by definition, the people he was talking to had not been in the front of the suicide queue ... At least Madeleine was okay when he returned upstairs, and she'd been given water, though Lavoisier was running dry. They'd pumped out their alkali spring to kill the arsenal fire, but the regular trip to get the drinking water tanker filled was overdue, and nobody was leaving for such a trivial reason now. He got his gun back too, which surprised him.

It was noon before he'd finished with the leaders, and too hot to head for the valley floor, so he spread himself about, talking to anyone who could be bothered to insult him. At last he rode off, found shade in a ravine, called Miriam Beaufort's number and made the case for cancelling. It was much the same as the other conversation ... Nothing solid. When he looked back, he knew this was the way it had always been. Like talking down the maniacs on the Deconstruction Tour, when mob rule, in the name of eco-revolution, was on the rampage through England. You never know if anything's going to stick. As often as not, the moment your back's turned something disgusting happens.

'Madeleine,' he said, 'this is what it feels like to be Ax Preston, with the rocket fuel turned off. When you do the same thing as before, but you no longer believe that you are destiny's child.'

Insh'allah.

He reached the autodump about six ... Nothing had changed. He broke out welcome water supplies, stripped Madeleine, looked her over for dents and scratches, checked her feet, rubbed her down and got her travelling halter on her (to her bared-teeth resentment). He uncovered the trailer, stripped the groundsheet off, backed the Rugrat out and hooked them up: and then sat on the tailgate, looking at the wide pale sky, and the beautiful colours of the desert. The bay mare came and nudged his elbow, bumping her big shapely dark head against his shoulder. 'You're a beauty,' he said. 'You're a handful, but you are a fine creature.'

Alas, how easy it is to fall in love.

He settled her in the box and fastened up. He was about to get into the car (one more gaze, farewell to the crucible) when he heard a sound he recognised all too well, and turned to find himself looking down the barrel of a shotgun, levelled at him by an old bloke in battered overalls with an amazing white beard: who had presumably emerged from the lopsided caravan.

'What's in the trailer?'

'Werewolves,' said Ax.

'Uhuh. Git them off my land.'

'Right away.'

He sat behind the wheel, about to go and meet his darlings, buzzing with reaction after that conference in the crypt, and thought sadly that before long he was going to have to say goodbye to the Toyota Rugrat. You saved our lives, you fat little ride, and I still don't know all you can do. Hm. Do you have a bat out of hell mode, Rat? Nah, Madeleine wouldn't enjoy that. Maybe there'll be another time.

Sage and Fiorinda headed north, into badlands. On horseback, and ignorant of the terrain, they had to stick to the marked trails, which made them uneasy, but they'd been convinced Ax had to have the Rat. He might need to get somewhere, do something, fast; they only had to stay out of the way. There were no signs of the raid. All seemed quiet in the panorama of crumpled red hills that hid Lavoisier. Where they passed, nothing moved except the jackrabbits, the little birds in the sagebrush and the occasional tau cross of some bird of prey above. They found many springs, but the water generally smelled like paintstripper, so they weren't in any danger of poisoning themselves. They spent the night in the open. They didn't have much in the way of food, only the remains of Fiorinda's spoils and some unappealing tins, but they were content with a packet of battered ginger biscuits. Inevitably, they were scared. But Ax had a mystical talent for handling fucked-up confrontations, which they felt they did not share. The presence of either of them at the Lavoisier thing would just have been inflammatory ...

They talked about Fiorinda's horror of effective magic. The actual power might be neutral. It felt to her like unravelling bits of the world, okay, maybe it's not important, world's always ravelling and unravelling itself. But the knock-on, the society that magical thinking would create, was *always* going to be hellish.

He conceded she might be right.

As soon as it was light they headed down the line of the 168, in sight of the road. There was no traffic. They hoped that was just normal for these days, but as they approached civilisation they found Road Closed signs and State Police barricades. Finally they unpacked the baggage from Big Snow. Sage left Fiorinda with Paintbrush and the gear in a fresh and juniper-smelling wilderness of rocks and grasshoppers and rode down to Big Pine. He thought if he kept his hat on he didn't look too weird; or too famous. There's tall, skinny, weather-beaten blonds around. There was no sign of Ax in the little two-street resort town, blighted by economic collapse and fuel costs; suffering on its way to join Lavoisier. He discovered that the trails on the east side of the valley were closed, and the 395 had roadblocks back to Independence. This was looking bad; but at the visitor centre, their default meeting place, he found a secure message waiting on the tourist bulletin board.

He unlocked it with the Triumvirate password, and a poor approximation of the late Stephen Hawking delivered good news. The message was circumspect (never trust the datasphere to be secure), but it told him that the raid had been cancelled, the surviving terrorists were leaving under an amnesty, and Lavoisier was to be thoroughly investigated. Looks like he did it.

The message said, don't come to me, I'll come and find you. They understood this meant that they should lie low for a while longer. They

282

bought supplies in Big Pine, for cash, wary of flashing Digital Artists credit cards, and crossed over to the Sierra side. By nightfall they'd hired a stone-built hut, about eight thousand feet up in the John Muir wilderness, and had the horses accommodated further down. There was a Ranger trail to their cabin, but after the Ranger had delivered the English couple and their gear, there'd be no more vehicles through. They were out of sight, and there was no easy way anyone could take them by surprise. But they weren't expecting trouble.

Tired and sore after two days on horseback – especially Sage, whose previous experience had been nil – they went to bed and played with such of the cable tv as came with the rent. They became enamoured of a women's bowling championship in Arizona, but the affection was unrequited. After they'd declined to buy a gypsy charm bracelet, a dozen red roses fashioned lifesize in porcelain, and a velvet-feel guest room towel set endorsed by Puusi Meera, they were thrown off.

Early in the morning Sage walked down to the Ranger station, where there was a payphone, to see if there was another message. The cabin had running water, but the bathroom smelled of mould and chemical-toilet chemicals. Fiorinda took the dishpan from the kitchenette, dipped water from the North Fork creek, and washed and brushed her teeth outdoors. How quickly the primitive necessities return, and how sweet they are. Icy, icy water, chill morning air, the scent of the forest. A brown squirrel with a yellow throat sat on a boulder and dismembered a large pine cone. One day it won't be from choice that we live this way, she thought, tying Ax's bandanna round her head, and there won't be any cable tv, either ... The great trees made a russet shade, pierced by rays of morning sun. The green water margin was full of flowers: tiger lilies, columbines, blue aconite; this morning, the juniper wilderness, and yesterday the desert. Oh, California, you are an amazing land. The squirrel bounced up the side of a tree, as if on springs. Fiorinda laughed. She saw a big man's shadow, coming along the path. Not Sage: too bulky, not tall enough. He stepped into sunlight. It was Moloch, from Lavoisier.

'Oh, bugger,' muttered Fiorinda. She had totally forgotten about Moloch.

'Good morning, Fiorinda.'

He was disguised as an outdoor pursuits tourist. He had a *map wallet*, the clown. He looked at her in triumph; and with a fearful, unwilling sexual interest. 'Don't be alarmed,' he said. 'I'm not going to hurt you. Shall we go into the cabin?'

'No.' She sat on the squirrel's boulder. 'We can talk here. How did you part with Lavoisier? Did they realise you were an enemy agent? But you don't work for the FBI do you, Mr Moloch? You're somebody else.'

'I found you guys very easily, you know. The Feds could do the same. Or those outlaws, and they were were pissed off as hell. You're right, I'm not the law. I have another agenda, and that's why I'm here now.'

'You were never in Yorkshire, either.'

'Thanks for not busting me,' he said. 'I wondered about that.'

I had my own agenda, thought Fiorinda. She smiled, wondering what to do next. Another shadow was flitting through the trees, and this time it was Sage. He came into the clearing quietly. 'Hi,' she said. 'Look, we have a visitor.'

'I see him. Is this the bloke you reckoned works for the CIA?'

'I don't know who he works for,' said Fiorinda, depressed. 'I don't care.'

'What are you going to do with him?'

'I'm trying to think.'

Moloch was impatient of this exchange. 'Okay,' he said. 'I'm not here to waste time. Fiorinda, you're coming with me. You'll be well treated, your head isn't going to be in a jar. You'll be better off than you were with those bastards in the ghost town, and better off than if the Committee gets its hands on you. Are you going to make it easy, that's the only question.'

Sage was leaning against a tree: an idle stance, no threat.

'You know what really annoys me?' said Fiorinda. 'You know what fucking annoys me? Nobody, not one of you fuckers has tried to *hire* me. Nobody chatted me up, took me to lunch in a fancy restaurant, offered me Ferraris, said, look, Fiorinda, you're a very talented girl, we could do business . . . Oh, no. When you're headhunting me, you come after me with a meat chopper. Nobody ever treated Wernher von Braun like this! I'm not saying I'd have been interested, but it would have been *nice*.'

'I can't help it that you're a person,' said Moloch.

They heard a jeep coming up the Ranger trail. Fiorinda had the faint hope it might be the Ranger, come to offer them firewood or tell them about a campground talk on owls this evening, and defuse the situation. But no, the fuck-up continued. The off-roader was dark and unmarked; the goons who got out were dressed the same as Moloch, but packed an air of professional violence.

Moloch shucked off his backpack. He grabbed the birdboned young woman, slammed her against a tree, and ran his hands briskly, expertly over her body. 'I'm not going to hurt you, Fiorinda—' He kept her jammed against the trunk with the weight of his shoulder and thigh while the goons stopped Sage from intervening. They didn't find this an easy job, but there were four of them, and though Sage was as fit and strong as he would ever be, he wasn't Aoxomoxoa anymore. Those days were gone, and, fatally, he was unarmed. It hadn't occurred to him to take a firearm with him, to use the tourist centre payphone.

'Sage!' screamed Fiorinda, 'Don't! Don't get yourself killed!'

They weren't aiming to kill. Soon the fight was over and Sage had lost. The goons dragged him to a sitting position at the foot of another fir tree, blood streaming from his nose. One of them stood over him with a gun to his head while the other three changed places with their boss. While they held Fiorinda, Moloch opened up his pack and took out equipment that he laid on the ground, carefully in order: like a serial killer arranging the props of his fantasy before the act. Fiorinda could glimpse, out of the corner of her eye, a set of ankle-cuffs, a roll of tape, a black box of hardware: a grey rubbery skullcap with a chinstrap, trailing leads; lumps on its surface. A headscarf, a hypodermic in a case, oh, God, a *straitjacket*—

'I shouldn't have screamed,' she said, 'I made them worse, I'm sorry.'

'I shouldn't have jumped them,' admitted Sage, trying to tip his ringing head back, and swallowing blood. 'Not thinking straight. Uh, okay, start again. Listen, whatsyername, Moloch, you don't know what you're—'

'She won't do anything now we have you at gunpoint. Will you, Fiorinda?'

'You don't get it.'

'No, Fiorinda. You're going to tell me you have no potential, I don't believe it. I know those people had genuine expertise on the new area, wrapped up in their anti-Establishment rhetoric.' Moloch selected the rubbery cap. His route-map face was creased up with fearful satisfaction. He advanced—

'Don't be afraid. I won't hurt you if you take this quietly. You have to come with us, and what happens after that will be … will be negotiated.'

'Let me go,' said Fiorinda.

The goons let go. The one standing over Sage put his gun in its holster and went to join his fellows. Fiorinda met Moloch halfway, and stood looking at him, the morning sunlight making a scarlet aureole around her naked head.

'I know who *you* are,' she said. 'I knew the day I met you. You're that bloke in *Alien* who turns out to be an android. It's your job to see that the evil horrible monster gets delivered to the company so they can develop it. Well? Are you an android? Shall I tear your head off to find out?'

Moloch stared, the skullcap dangling from his hand—

Sage laughed and shook a gout of blood from his nose.

'Go Fiorinda!'

'Sage,' she said, still glaring at the company's spy, 'what shall I do now?'

'Tear the fucker's head off.'

'N-no. I don't think I'll do that.'

'Tear it off and stick it back on again. Give him a fairground ride.'

'Nah. Moloch, watch this.' She went to the mossy boulder and pushed her fist against it. Her hand drove into the stone, and her arm, halfway to the elbow. There was an intense pungency in the air, burning rock, melting granite. Fiorinda withdrew her fist, and the boulder was the way it had been before. 'Was that an illusion?' she asked the spy, 'or was it real? Did I fuck with the world, or with your perception? I will tell you a koan. There's no difference, not where I am. Now you can go. Your goons won't remember much; they didn't see me do that trick. You'll tell your mates at I-Systems, or wherever you come from, that Fiorinda is worthless to them, and you won't tell anyone what happened here. Not until the day you die. Do you get it now?'

Moloch said, carefully, 'I get it.'

'Take your stuff and go.'

He shoved his kit into the backpack; he left, with his goons. They listened to the off-roader driving away; and the cheery voices of a group of early hikers, passing on the trail. 'I wonder how often I'll have to do that in my life,' said Fiorinda. 'Ooh, that was hard.' She nursed her forehead between her hands. 'I was careful; I think I solved it, not just smash and grab, but my brain feels melted and everything is déjà.'

'Maybe not too often.'

She nodded, resignedly, and came and knelt beside him.

'How's your nose?'

'Broken,' said the voice of experience. 'Ah well, I still have both my ears.'

Fiorinda wiped his face with the sleeve of her shirt and crept into his arms. 'Oh, Sage. What a life. Ax should never leave us, we fuck up *instantly*. I *knew* that bloke was unfinished business . . . I wonder who he's really working for?'

'Better not to ask, my sweetheart.'

It's better not to ask. Never blow the whistle, never insist on the truth: you never know who you might need to work with. 'Did you get through?'

'No message. I'll try again later.'

'Shit. All that, and I probably only convinced him to stick around, and wait for the best chance to shoot me with a poison dart.'

They were still sitting against that tree, with the music of the North Fork rushing beside them and the towering grandeur of the Palisade massif above, when a party on horseback came along the path to the cabin. 'Good morning,' said Stu Meredith, looking on the tableau in some amazement. 'Ax told me you were over here, and we should fetch you back to Bighorn. What's been going on?'

'You're a little late,' complained Sage.

The rest of the Bighorn posse gathered behind Stu. Fiorinda stood up: Stu got down, and held out his hand. 'Well, you must be Fiorinda. I'm very pleased to meet you, very pleased indeed. Has this daddy-long-legs fellow been bothering you? I'd offer to give him some lessons in how to treat a lady, but it looks like you have that under control. You pack a punch.'

'We had to deal with some bad guys, leftovers. Sage got into a bit of a fight.'

'Mm. He likes to do that, I recall.'

The ranch hands dismounted; Sage was given first-aid. A pot of coffee was brewed, and breakfast shared: the ranch hands and Stu and the English couple sitting together on the mossy boulders by the creek 'We had a call from Ax,' said Stu. 'He told us you two were in Big Pine, or on your way there, and I should find you and bring you back. He'll meet us at the ranch; he expects to be free by evening. I understand he's discussing your desert trip, Sage.'

'Is he in any trouble over that?' asked Sage, cautiously.

'I don't believe so.' Stu shrugged, and the ranch hands glanced at each other, grinning slightly. They knew enough to feel this was a great story, a worthy addition to their repertoire. 'It's been very quiet since you left, on our side of the Valley.'

The Bighorn ranch was very quiet, late that night. The Noise Hotel was still between bookings. The junior Meredith couple had taken Violet with them to a hell-raising dive in Lone Pine (a much hipper burg, never to be confused with *Big* Pine). Sage and Ax and their hosts sat on the back porch of the house, looking out into a view of stableyards and corrals, and the dim black masses of the mountains against the starry sky. Ludmilla and Stu were drinking bourbon; Ax and Sage preferred tequila, cool but not frosty. A long silence had settled because Fiorinda had decided to go to bed, and for Stu and Ludmilla she had left an unearthly, dazzling space in the company. They would get over it. They'd often shared their daily life with one or other of the real megastars. You talk and laugh and sit down to eat with the idol of billions, a face and voice that have been so *multiplied*; and soon it doesn't bother you. You forget the extraordinary and relate to the person, just as you forget the bizarre miracles that are going on far inside the hardware, and use the machine. But just now, tonight, it was as if a living goddess had risen and walked away from them.

Sage had had his nose taped. He was lying in a long chair with his head tipped back, mouth breathing, occasionally touching the dressing tenderly.

'Your girlfriend's an extraordinary young woman, Ax,' said Ludmilla at last.

'Yeah. Luckily for me, I have Sage to help me keep her in line.'

The seniors nodded politely. They hadn't quite got the hang of the threesome.

Fiorinda walked down past the bunkhouse to where the Rugrat was parked, and leaned on the rail of an empty corral. She liked to see the Rugrat there, but she was homesick for the desert. Memories and impressions rose and drifted on the night breeze. She thought about what the bear had said, and the challenge daunted her. But live for the moment. Right now, all okay.

As she turned to look back at the figures on the lighted verandah a gleam of movement caught her eye, down at her feet. She crouched, very quietly, and saw a small animal with pale fur and black, shining dewdrop eyes. It loped towards her, unafraid, and stood on its hind legs. For a moment Fiorinda and the kangeroo rat, the desert creature than needs no water, looked at each other: a pure encounter with the living world. Then the animal whisked away, and vanished into shadow.

9

Precious Bane

The heat that drenched the forest outside haunted the chill of Mr Eiffrich's study, at Camp Bellevue, where Sage and the President were investigating a legal question. Mr Eiffrich wanted to get a handle on Sage's curious idea about the Vireo Lake project, for himself, before it went any further. He had a couple of law degrees in his portfolio (though he'd never practiced). They were using Bellevue's standalone e-library, and referring to arcane sources Sage had collected through his UCLA contacts, but chiefly they were looking things up in books and weatherbeaten files.

'You're not offended that I couldn't let you guys join the investigators?' wondered Mr Eiffrich. 'It's not that we don't value your expertise—'

'Tha's awrig',' Sage assured him, stacking loose document pages neatly as he scanned through them. He found the schoolmaster glances over the spectacles more intimidating than the Presidential rank. 'We reckon we done Lavoisier.'

'Mmmph.' The fractured syntax comes and goes, thought Fred, likewise the bumpkin vowels. I don't believe Cornish can possibly be his first language: wonder what's going on there? Accents interested him. 'Your captain having applied his telescope to the wrong eye, in a noble tradition of Br— er, English insubordination—'

Sage kept his eyes on the print. 'Telescope? Huh? You lost me.'

The president gave him a schoolmaster look. 'I meant, in matters of United States national security, I thought I was the one giving the orders ... But I'm glad it worked out. And thank God Almighty the worst threat was a bad dream.'

Ax had reported to the Committee that no Fat Boy candidate had ever existed. The ritual murders had been for nothing. There'd never been a chance of the occult training camp producing another Rufus O'Niall. This opinion had been confirmed by the Vireo Lake scientists. What remained was bad enough. Fred didn't know if he was more horrified at the use of magic (a hex that can kill makes a very disconcerting weapon), or the scale of the *respectable* activist network that had emerged.

He laid down his smartboard and contemplated the middle distance for a minute or so. 'Sage, d'you remember, last time you were in this room, you gave me a sample of organic cocaine for investigation?'

'I remember that interview.'

'I have a result for you. You were right; it was from the same vineyard.'

The sample had come from Rufus O'Niall's castle. Mr Eiffrich was reporting that it was chemically identical with cocaine discovered in the possession of Ax's kidnappers, establishing a connection between O'Niall and that hostage-taking.

'I've nothing more to tell you yet, but the case is not closed.'

So you didn't fall, my guitar-man. You were hunted down. The issue no longer seemed vital; Ax had found other ways to leave defeat behind. Sage nodded, not wishing to discuss O'Niall right now. The unfinished business could wait.

'Thanks for letting me know.'

They studied without diversion for a while, Mr Eiffrich unconsciously and naturally using the former Aoxomoxoa as an extension of his reach: search this, copy that for me, fetch me the '97 box; but finding Sage surprisingly adept when they came to a conference. 'You've had some experience in our Intellectual Property law?'

'We spent eight years getting bludgeoned into the ground by Ms Ciccione's lawyers after we quit Maverick.'

'I remember something about that . . . How's the *racial* situation in England since the Dissolution?'

Ooh, and how did we get to English efnic tensions from Madonna? But he answered, placidly, 'Horrible. The Celtic nations have us f— er, surrounded, don't they? The British Resistance are mad dogs, the rural whites are halfway back to the Stone Age. The drop-out hordes have to be kept in camps for their own protection while they do our slave labour, and they're not happy about it. The Boat People drive us all nuts, the hippies are barking, the Islamics think they are God's gift, and the east of the river, the whole fen country from Essex up to Ely, has been a no-go area for years, which isn't something we shout about—'

'*The River* would be the Thames?'

'Yeah. Only one river in England gets called *the river*.'

Mr Eiffrich stored away this tidbit of Englandiana, and made no comment on the lurid catalogue. They continued their search. 'You rockstars should get on well with the black population . . .'

'Nah, that didn't happen, due to historical accident. Back in Dissolution Summer most of the black music scene selected itself out of the famous popstar Think Tank: perceived as too gun-crazy. People make such superficial judgements. The secret rulers had their own plans for violence, see . . ɬ Lookin' at it another way, Allie Marlowe did the paperwork an' she carn' abide hip-hop. Allie's a closet feminist, you know. A very dangerous woman.'

'Don't get too baroque, Sage. I might think you're winding me up.'

'Right.' Sage chewed his thumb-joint, frowning over a stack of withered fanfold documentation for the World Wide Web, University of Hawaii, circa 1994. 'Mr Eiffrich, I need to phone a friend.'

'Who's the friend?'

'My dad. It's going to be reasonably secure.'

This would be Joss Pender, of eks.Photonics, European software baron: one of the awesome few businessmen to thrive in the Crisis. 'Okay.'

Sage tapped his wrist and, for a moment, looked stricken, the cyborg reduced to mere humanity. He slapped his pockets and found a Krypton satellite mobile. Fred Eiffrich listened, with fellow feeling for the man at the other end, overjoyed to be accosted at five a.m., out of the blue, by his vanished, adult child.

'No one can get on with the black politicos,' continued Sage, breaking the connection (voice only, no picture for his old dad, and not a word of open affection, ah, I have been there, thought Fred) and looking around for a previously discarded file. 'They're like Boat People, all f— gangstas: there's no continuity, you talk to some bloke and blam, he's dead, have to start again. Rob gets on best with 'em.' Sage grinned, affectionately. 'Unlike me an' Ax, he can't be a gangsta hisself, as he refuses to pick up a gun. Rob's our genuine radical: non-violence, minimum wage, free education, votes fer women, the whole weird package. He's a throwback.'

'Did you get what you wanted from your dad? I only heard the one side.'

'Yeah. I'll show you in a minute—'

'And the Hindus?'

'Oh, they run the place. All the top suits are Hindu or married into Hindu families. Like the Jews and Hollywood, you know.'

Mr Eiffrich peered over his spectacles. 'Do you do a lot of public speaking?'

'Only in times of acute national emergency. Then I go on the telly and talk about rescuing kittens from trees.' Sage looked up, delivering a jolt of blue and a puckish grin. 'It's okay, Mr President. He keeps me on a short leash.'

Fred took off his eyeglasses, used them for a bookmark (he was examining a tome of IP case reports) and looked around the book-lined room. The western light had mellowed, giving life to the eyes of the dark-haired woman in the portrait over the fireplace. 'It always seems to me to be winter in here,' he murmured. 'Not in a bad way. I mean, there's a feeling of shelter, the fire in the hearth, the blizzard shut outdoors . . .' They had been speaking of the English situation in the present tense and, joking apart, he knew that Ax Preston's Minister understood what was going on.

(the word lover seemed an impertinence, he would leave that aspect alone—)

'Sage, last time we met, I said you were messing with Ax's girl, because I hadn't grasped the situation between you three. I'm personally fond of your boss; I count him a friend, I believe he's a figure of vital influence, and . . . I jumped in too fast. I do that, sometimes. I apologise. Are we square?'

Sage shrugged. 'Of course.'

'Good, because there's something I have to ask. If Ax were to accept the Presidency, would you go with him, and take up that burden again?'

According to the US media, and the imported news from Europe, the English Presidency was settled. Jordan Preston would be taking his brother's place as Ceremonial Head of State, and the delay was just bureaucracy. Sage and the President were better informed. The Second Chamber government knew Fred Eiffrich's preference, and they felt the same. They wanted the legend, not the substitute. They would dump Jordan instantly if they could get Ax.

There was a long silence, Sage frowning, studying the braided gold ring on his left hand. With the damn-your-eyes mischief turned off and the blue eyes lowered, that much-photoed, oddly attractive face looked strained and weary. Ax seemed fine, but the President felt that the Lavoisier adventure had been very tough on this guy, whatever his spiritual resources (another aspect Fred planned to leave alone).

'The trouble with Ax . . . Hm. The trouble with Ax is, he doesn't let the bastards grind him down.'

'And there's no attitude more calculated to get those bastards grinding. Yeah, I hear you. It wouldn't be an easy ride, I know. He'd be no man's puppet, and I see why his friends and, er, anyone close to him as you are would hesitate—'

'What did Fiorinda say?'

'Right now I'm asking *you*.'

'Ax left me, once.' Sage reached for his notepad and turned to look for another of the boxfiles. 'But that was my own fault ... You called me a soldier, last time we met. I didn't like that, but it works. Maybe I signed up for the duration, and Ax is in charge of whatever it is we do, what I signed for. He's far from eager for the job: but yes, I would go with him. I'll never leave him.'

'That's all I wanted to know.' The President recovered his eyeglasses, marked the place with a feather from the jar of owl feathers he kept for this purpose, and said, 'I believe this works. I want to share your idea with some of my staff, let them play Devil's Advocate. Now, a false start is something to avoid at all costs. Will you, *please*, this time, wait until I give you the word?'

'Understood, Mr President.'

Ax and Sage had turned up safe, with Fiorinda. The English were *en fête* and back in favour, shaking their kooky cameraderie all over town. Their avatar lab appointments, which had been in abeyance, were reinstated, bumping rivals and causing grief for other projects. Fiorinda still wasn't going to take another test. She didn't want to. She came to the studio village with the Babes when it was their turn to be dunked (apprehensive as if they were going to have teeth pulled) and went for a walk in the park with Harry Lopez and Kathryn Adams. They bought lunchboxes and took them to a nest of boulders among the trees, overlooking Digital Artists' domain, with the city stretching beyond. It was very hot. Harry was still a little shaky; he seemed almost to lean on Kathryn physically, though they didn't touch. Don't you *dare* hurt my friend, thought Fiorinda, but she knew she wasn't going to interfere.

'You don't have vr tanks in Europe?'

'I don't know,' said Fiorinda. 'I don't hang around amusement arcades.'

'A continent of claustrophobes. Is that what the drop-out movement is about?'

'Nah. That's an instinctive correction for vitamin D deficiency.'

'I had a picnic like this with Ax once,' sighed Kathryn, nostalgic. 'By the Potomac. The squirrels came up, panhandling: I'd never seen them so tame.'

'He's a tamer of all situations,' said Harry. 'He's immense.' He opened his lunchbox and stared into it. His hands were trembling. Rocks and trees, sushi rice with little adornments, a sickening unreality behind which lurked the déjà vu room, rushing towards him, days or hours ... It kept happening, it seemed to happen more, not less: always with the same conviction of an *inescapable* future—

'Fuck, I'm going to have to get out of virtual movies.'

'It's a bruise,' said Kathryn, tough and kind. 'Verlaine told me that. Snapshot blacked your eye, kiddo; don't poke at the place or you'll keep it sore.'

'I think it's a permanent deformity.'

'It'll fade,' Fiorinda assured him. 'Snap needs fuel to burn.'

'Okay,' said the golden boy. 'I get it. I have no capacity for suffering. Go on, be nasty to me. If girls are being nasty to me, I know I'm alive.'

Fiorinda had chosen the laksa package, and regretted it. The pieces of beancurd in her Straits Chinese sauce looked like chunks of sodden doggie-chew.

'Will Janelle let me come and see her?'

Harry shook his head. 'I'm sorry, no. No visitors, no calls, not even Sage. She says she wants to be left the fuck alone. I mean, not rude, she's just concentrating on getting well. Thank God,' he added, candidly, 'she'd finished the qualia-coding.'

Janelle Firdous had a viral pneumonia, twenty-first century flu. She wasn't gravely ill, but she was confined to her cottage. Sadly, this meant the English might not see her again. They'd be leaving California after the reprise of the Hollywood Bowl show; with Fiorinda in person this time. The Few would be going home to England, unless there was some momentous change secretly on their minds. The Triumvirate's plans were uncertain.

'I never really met her,' said Fiorinda. 'She was Sage's friend and I felt ... I didn't want to be pushy. I've regretted that. She sounds like an amazing person.'

Harry nodded. 'She's the queen of the geeky-techies. Alone of all her sex.'

'It's not a problem being a woman in Hollywood,' said Kathryn (she spoke as if 'being a woman' could never be one of her problems). 'You can be huge, and rule, as long as you do it in a woman way, equal but different. People like Janelle, who want to be good as the men at what men do, equal but not different ... they carry the world on their shoulders.'

'Mm.'

'She might be well in time for the gig,' suggested Harry, to lighten the shadow that had fallen on the conversation. 'I don't think it's a bad attack.'

'Let's hope,' said Fiorinda.

The City of the Plain floated in its dirty peachbloom caul of dreams, and the picnic continued, a little quieted and saddened by the thought of parting.

Rob had sold the studio on his idea for getting the Preston family band on stage for the Hollywood Bowl gig. It wouldn't be the first simultaneous broadcast since the end of the data quarantine, but it would be the first use of bi-location tech in this context: a great stunt, if it worked. Jordan wanted to do it. Ax was fine about the *fait accompli*, but he saw no reason why he should talk to his brother. They could meet on the night. He thought he could wing it through a Chosen Few standards set, after all these years. Rob bided his time a few days, until the Lavoisier excitement had calmed down. Then he took Ax out on the town, just the two of them.

They went to a Jamaican restaurant in Leimart Park, they graced a couple of jazz clubs, and settled in a quiet bar. It had been a good evening: Ax with that gleam in his eye, the alert attention for *every single thing around him*, that made hanging out with the guy a privilege, no matter what. Now Rob braced himself. The juice had been turned off, and he was sitting with a cold, hard-eyed stone wall.

He told himself this was years ago; he was the mentor and Ax Preston was the talented guitarist from the sticks, with that ruthless streak Rob was guilty of admiring.

'You know Jordan wants to talk to you, don't you?'

'Yeah, he wants my approval. Fuck that, Rob. If he's idiot enough to let the Second Chamber keep him for a pet, let him do it on his own.'

'That's not what he wants to say, Ax.'

A ball-crushing look from Mr Preston. 'I don't see the problem,' said Ax, and chugged his beer. 'Hey, go ahead, take over. Be the captain of the Reich. Be President yourself, if you want the job. Why do you never follow through, Rob? You start something, then you hang back.'

'I am following through. You said you wanted to be a leader. I'm asking you to go on running the firm, because we need you.'

Ax stared at him: like a trapped animal.

'They tried to burn her.'

Sage was a warm, breathing rock; Fiorinda was propped against pillows, a book slipped from her lax hand, fallen asleep as she waited up. Ax sat on the end of the bed, watching her in the light of one soft lamp, rolling an unlit cigarette between his fingers. A lioness with a shorn mane; how big the orbits of her eyes looked without the mass of hair. How stern, older than old, the set of her young mouth—

There are marks she'll always carry, my baby.

He took his cigarette onto the balcony: might as well respect Californian law for once. Security lights and darkness, the sound of the ocean, the feeling of *strangeness* that he loved. We should take the Rugrat and go, he thought. No direction home. I would never tire of that life. I want to consecrate myself to pleasure.

Fiorinda came out to join him, barefoot; a shawl around her shoulders over the glimmer of her nightdress. 'Hi.'

'Hi, sweetheart.'

'How was that?'

'The restaurant was very good, music so-so. I don't really get on with jazz.'

'*Ax*—'

'I don't want to talk about it.'

'Sorry.' She laid her arms on the rail and looked into the dark.

'Fiorinda . . .' He drew on the cigarette, 'Maybe I'm not supposed to ask, but are you okay to go up against the candidate? I'm scared for you, my baby.'

Touché.

'I can do it. I just don't want to talk about it.'

They smiled at each other, ah, we've been here before. Ax finished his cigarette, they went inside and found Sage was sitting up. 'Don't leave me alone,' he reproached them. 'I *hate* waking up and you're not there.' He hadn't been sleeping; most unusual for Sage, it made him fretful.

'We were only on the balcony.'

They stripped and got into bed, and the three of them made love together. Fiorinda nuzzled into Ax's warm flank: Sage wrapped around her back, drifting in the afterglow. 'Sage? What did you do to Stu Meredith when you were here before?'

'I'd rather not go into that.'

'You beat him up, didn't you?' said Ax. When male persons remember this blond so vividly, there's usually just the one reason.

'Yes.'

'Was it justified?'

'Not fucking remotely. I was rat-arsed. Can we go to sleep?'

When the character avatars had been locked down successfully there was another traditional party, after working hours, in Inventory C. There should have been a screening of the movie, but everything was behind schedule. Harry, mortified, vowed he'd have something ready, a rough cut with the avatars mixed in, for them to see before they left California. The radical rockstars weren't fussed. If you have any kind of brush with tinsel town, there comes a point where you start dreaming that you will be the idol of billions. And then there comes another point, when you realise that was a *ridiculous* idea—

'Digital Artists will have us on file,' remarked Chip to Verlaine as they strolled around, chucking back the champagne and visiting their favourite custom-object areas: the sci-fi horror section; a preposterous oak tree; some of that pus which ends up in the sunset sky. 'If they chop us up small enough they are entitled to recycle the bits. Are you creeped by that?'

'Hollywood seduced us, briefly,' said Verlaine, 'but we leave with our intacta restored, because we leave the seduced parts of us behind.'

'Someday everyone will live like this. A snippet here, a version there.'

'I call it depraved. As if the virtual world wasn't crowded enough.'

Fiorinda sat on the border of a fake parterre of red and yellow tulips, feeling slightly on the defensive because *she* didn't have an avatar, and getting drunk with Lou Branco. She had the size of the money man now. He was like Cack Stannen only without the sweetness; he was a type she'd often met in her work with the drop-out hordes, except he didn't smell and didn't sleep in doorways. Someone who can do one thing freakishly well; all else is whirling chaos, human relationships a mystery. So, he was still a shark and a childish vindictive bastard, but Fiorinda rarely had trouble getting on with the socially disabled.

'What's the deal with Rob, then?' Lou was intrigued by the group marriage, and all the strange English sexual habits. 'Three laydees, one guy. How does that one work? Does he have a rota?'

'Well, no. There's a ritual. Rob leaves his shoes outside his bedroom door—'

'Uhuh?' said Lou, eyes fixed on her face, propping his jowl on one hand.

Fiorinda took a slug of champagne from the bottle they were sharing. 'The Babes come up, and they pee into his shoes, and Rob then sniffs the mixture—'

'They *pee in his shoes?*'

'Yeah. Then he sniffs it, and he can tell from the blend which of them he should spend the night with, or which two of them, or whatever.'

'Uhuh, uhuh. Well, that's . . . He must get through a lot of shoes—'

'It's called "Taking The Piss".'

The toad pondered, with knitted brows. A grin dawned, a guffaw followed. He choked and snorted, and beamed at her. 'You're all right, Fiorinda. I thought you were some snooty, do-gooder, look down your nose, lahdidahdi broad. But you're okay.'

'It's the accent.' Fiorinda stood up. She walked away from him, swiftly. Lou followed, making a short diversion to pick up another bottle.

'You lookin' for someone?'

'I thought I saw Janelle.'

'Ah, she's still sick.' There was a flicker in Lou's eyes, as of someone who knows an illness is diplomatic. 'It's a hell of a thing, the viral pneumonia.'

'I had a friend die of it.'

'I guess she's having the best care. Let's party.'

'Lou, where do the crash-dummies live?'

'They ain't alive, baby.'

'Native English. We say, where does it live, meaning where is it?'

'Oh right, okay. Okay, c'mon that's easy.'

He led her away from the crush, away to the dull part of the vast inventory floor, where no perverse works of creation filled up the spaces between the machines. He stopped by a scanner, the housing sleek and amorphous, a slug the size of a limousine. The flatbed was covered by a shaded dome.

'You want to see them? I know how to do this. I get the safety off, we got no goggles, but it's no big deal ... Look away, now.'

Fiorinda looked away; Lou shaded his eyes with one hand while the lightnings played. When she looked back, the dome was sinking into the floor. The flatbed was like a crowded Underground carriage: or a fishtank room in a brothel, where the whores wait to be chosen on the other side of the one-way glass. The dummies were lifesize, dressed, personality in their eyes, they just didn't move and didn't seem aware of being looked at. They were not taking up enough space; there must be arms and legs overlaying each other, heads and bodies at odd angles, but you couldn't spot where it happened. On the scanner's monitor screens the code teemed away, picking up the angle of her gaze, flipping from one stunning complexity to another—

'I guess you know the story,' said Lou. 'The Screen Actors Guild said Digital Artists had to use real character actors. It was a condition, or they couldn't scan the stars, and that was virtual movies over a barrel, a benchmark case. They picked out these random second-rates, gave them a stingy wad of bucks apiece, and they've never paid a royalty since, not in ten years.'

'No substantial reuse.'

'The studio never *needs* that. Not the way substantial got defined, hehehey! Don't need the fuckin' stars either, but that's a whole other deal ... They call this kinda toybox scan the index. I can animate, I can sort them by ethnics, age, sex, dentistry, you name it. I can make 'em talk, isolate you a characteristic, uh, no, I forgot how to do that. Whaddaya think?'

It was like visiting Vireo Lake; she didn't know how to react. She felt like a savage from the rainforest again, looking at stolen souls.

'There's something called entanglement.'

'Yeah, yeah, yeah. Always hearing about that shit. You prick one of these code-bunnies, some saddo thesp pumping gas in Bakersfield bleeds, and so what? Everything is one, man. I don't go down that route. I stick with my balance sheets.'

'I think they've been used in ways they didn't contract for.'

Lou gave her a sour look: hearing the do-gooder princess after all. 'We all get that, baby.'

'And no one's out of the loop. I'm just drunk. Let's get back to the party.'

The English had done their rehearsing for the Hollywood Bowl reprise in the virtual venue at the studio village: to keep the show under wraps, and because no one was taking any chances with the rescued hostage. Fiorinda hadn't been near the actual place until the evening when she arrived (late) with the crowds, hidden in a shaded limo, backed by armed guards, and was delivered to her trailer. She stepped out of the car, glimpsed the rustling eucalyptus slopes, heard Snake Eyes' big band sound in the distance, *let's get together and feel all right* ... (ooh, I'm late—); and stepped into her gilded cage.

Her slaves-for-the-night were arranging bouquets, funeral-home ranks of them. *Fuck.* How did that get past my radar? She considered throwing a tantrum. *I don't like cut flowers, everyone knows Fiorinda hates dead flowers! Get them out of here!!!*; but nah. I am not psyched-out, this is fucking childish. There was a bunch of long-stemmed pink roses, old-fashioned roses with thorny dark stems. They looked like a memory, a snapshot flash: and then she knew why. Oh, shit. Her father had sent pink roses to her dressing room, one very bad night long ago—

'Who sent all the flowers?'

'I'm not sure, Miss Fiorinda. Everything went through security;

they're still holding the cards and packaging. Would you like me to find out?'

'It doesn't matter.'

No, she thought. I am not psyched-out. You know me, and I know you.

She was being coifed by the wig-person when Puusi Meera swept in, wearing green and gold, and some amazing emeralds. Her entourage filled the trailer, backing Fiorinda's attendants almost into the bathroomette.

'Now, Fiorinda, I know you want to be alone. It's no joke, r-r-revving yourself up to go on stage again, I can imagine, after the ordeals you have been through. And such a big crowd! Do you know, the old Bowl might be genuinely sold out this time? But me, you have to see. Let me look at you!'

Puusi had been a little frosty since her protégée had returned from the dead. Possibly she felt that suicide (which never looks bad on a star's résumé) was enough of a trick, without Fiorinda having the cheek to come back and reap the benefits in person. She took Fiorinda's hands and raised her to her feet, a tinsel town cocktail of malice and genuine sentiment glowing in her great liquid eyes. Fiorinda was then left standing, on the auction block as it were, while Puusi settled, poised and resplendent, in an armchair vacated by the wig-person's assistant.

'Hm. This is one of your famous party frocks.' It was the smouldery-opal dress that Sage and Ax had bought for her. 'Very young, very little girl, which you are *not* quite ... And the wig just like, messy-natural, hm. And then, what else?'

'This is it. I don't do costume changes.'

'That's sweet, and brave, but it's not what the people want; you will be so little and far away, and they will not think they are getting their money's worth.'

'I'll be okay. I have Sage to light me. There will be spectacle.'

'Sage, yes, I had forgotten he does lights. How charming that you people do all your own chores.' Puusi's beautiful brows drew together. 'Is he well? I think he's looking peaky again ... But you have no jewellery.'

'No, I—'

'You were probably going to wear costume jewels. You have no money, and the studio is so stingy. I thought of this, and I have come to the rescue. You will wear the earrings I gave you. Sit down, sit down, I will do it.'

Puusi beckoned, and one of the entourage people produced a casket.

The goddess herself clipped the diamond and ruby falls onto Fiorinda's ears, took up a brush and comb and arranged the borrowed curls so her gift was displayed to best advantage. 'And this necklace, which is valuable and only a loan. I want it back.' She fastened a diamond dog-collar, and shook her head in tender pride. 'Ah, what has happened to the house with the bloodstained walls? Or that skinny yellow-faced girl who came to see me, and told me how she tried and tried but she could not scrub away the dirty shame of the past? You are *free* now, aren't you, Fiorinda?'

'Not right this minute,' said Fiorinda. 'But I plan to be.'

'Good, good. I thought so, I can see it. Now up, stand up again, let everybody see.' The entourage murmured appreciation. Someone opened champagne, and everyone toasted each other. Puusi and Fiorinda moved off camera to one of Fiorinda's sofas. 'You *are* looking well,' said Puusi. 'Very spunky, and your skin is much better. Are you getting a lot of sex?'

'Spunk to my back teeth. Oh, Puusi, would you do something for us? *Can* you persuade the studio not to call the movie Runnymede? Okay, I know it isn't a big deal . . . I wouldn't say this to Harry, but it's only a little virtual biopic, it will come out and nobody will think twice. But Runnymede is going to sound so daft—'

The name change had happened at committee stage. None of the execs had liked *Rivermead*, they didn't think it was historical enough: so the birthplace of the Reich had been moved to Surrey, and was currently located where the Magna Carta had been signed. The English were past caring. Poor Harry was understandably upset.

'Oooh.' Unexpectedly, for a moment, a human being looked out of the goddess's eyes. 'One river, two places, that's *very difficult* for movie folk.' They laughed, and chinked glasses. 'I will do my best!'

Puusi and her entourage departed. Fiorinda discarded the earrings and the collar. Her wig was taken away for finishing touches and the make-up team set to work: buffing and burnishing, smoothing and blending. Your teeth are *fine*, they assured her. You are so natural, these strong brows, so wonderful, just a light, a very light . . . The over-furnished little room reflected in the mirror reminded her of the tiny luxury flat where her father used to fuck her: heaped with the presents that she couldn't ever take home. And to think, once I *wanted* to end up here, cosseted like a queen-grub, Bleggh. It was my whole aim in life. She wondered how much of her revulsion was really down to the horror of becoming a magic psychopath, and how much of it was down to the bitter shame of that twelve-year-old kid, dumped by her grown-up lover—

The trailer had no windows; it had screens instead. The sound was turned off, on her orders, but without moving her head she could see the stage. The big band numbers were over. There was Ax, in his fine red suit with his Fender, playing all by himself: isolated by the lights so he seemed really alone, on the stage that was actually *crawling* with people. He looked very serious. Her stomach clutched. Oh, God, it's not long now.

'Miss Fiorinda? We're all finished.'

'You can call me Fiorinda if you like,' she said, rousing from silence. The face in the mirror, to her disappointment, just looked like Fiorinda with a very high gloss. Damn, I thought they would make me perfect ... 'If you call me Mizz anything, it's *Ms Slater*. I'm not a fucking variety act.'

'I'm sorry, Ms Slater, er, Fiorinda—'

She had put the diamonds back in the casket. She changed her mind, took out the earrings and clipped them on. And I remember everyone who brought me here. I gather them all up, I fill myself, I fuel myself, I'm a holocaust, I'm a firestorm.

Elsewhere, among the dewy planters of a VIP enclosure, with shiny people passing in the background, Allie and Dilip, noncombatants, were talking to tv folk.

'Don't you ever get the feeling that decisions affecting the career of this supergroup are being made in the bedroom?'

'Nah,' said Dilip, grinning. 'We get the distinct impression they have better things to do in the bedroom. Or anywhere else they consider semi-private!' The fragile mixmaster wasn't going on stage, but Fiorinda's return had been a tonic. His eyes had lustre again, he had energy: he might be on his way out, but he wasn't quite knocking on heaven's door.

'They're in charge because we want them to be in charge,' said Allie, keeping it engaged, like this *matters*, but finding the tone hard to maintain, considering what was really going on tonight. 'They are three extraordinary people, and we love where they're taking the band now—'

A big, jowly man journalist had the next turn. 'What do you think of the events in Uzbekistan, Ms Marlowe?'

'It's an appalling tragedy.'

Uzbekistan was where the endless, on and off war between the US and rival oil nations, was currently at its warmest. There'd been an incursion against one of the US-controlled bases on the pipeline, with civilian and technical casualties. Allie didn't miss a beat and didn't elaborate. You can't stop them talking about the war, you just say the most anodyne thing and move on. Dilip (sigh) couldn't leave it there. 'I think it's a squabble on the upper decks of the Titanic,' he said, 'while the ship goes down by the bows. To those of us already in the lifeboats, this behaviour simply looks bizarre, an understandable madness—'

Allie tried to kick him under the table, but—

Cut to the stage, thank God. Intermission over, no more filler required.

Last call. She checked the full-length mirror, and knew that she was having one of those redhead nights. It wasn't the make-up, or the borrowed curls (which felt disgusting), it was an electricity. The dark opal bodice fitted her like a glove; her skirts shimmered glittering embers, smoky feathers; and the cowboy boots, chestnut stitched in aubergine, excellent. Puusi was right. Fiorinda of the party frocks, punk diva all tidied up and glossed, this is so over, so nauseating MOR chanteuse. But it will work, oh yes. *Never in doubt*, she murmured: and was grateful to the goddess for injecting a bracing dose of professional jealousy into this stunt. Well, here I am. From abused child to global star, unfortunately it didn't work out quite the way I hoped, but *here I am*. I made it, Mummy. I made it, Rufus. Aren't you proud of me?

'The men band together,' she said, softly. 'The women are driven apart.'

'You look *great*,' the make-up artist assured her, misunderstanding.

The wig-person gave her a hug, and whispered, 'Puusi's a *bitch*.'

'I didn't mean Puusi. Well, here I go. Thanks for everything.'

She rubbed her bare arms, trembling in shadow just out of sight of the crowd, looking up at the hollow tiers, remembering this place as if she'd visited it in a dream. She was offered something and shook her head impatiently. Someone touched her, *don't fucking touch me*. Who touched me? Oh, it was Sage. But nothing seemed real. She saw her path, out onto the stage, that's where I will walk, yes, guitar where it should be, good. Oh, God, this could be *the last time ever in my life* I stand like this, waiting to go on, looking into all those dark eyes—

Now I will go out there, and we will do what you asked me to do. Fucked-up, twenty-first century normality will be restored, with information-space science throwing up weird tech, but no one will think about the bizarre implications, it'll just be new technology. I will be the only one. I will bury my power, but people like Moloch will come after me. If there are other candidates, then they will have to challenge me. Ah, forget it. Deal with the problem at hand . . . She could not be touched, but she summoned her friends to mind. My pilgrim soul, and my darling guitar-man. Allie and Dilip, Rob and Felice and Cherry and Dora, Chip and Verlaine, Anne-Marie and Hugh; Doug Hutton. And so many others, yes, millions of them, every face, but now it's time.

You won't fold, Fat Boy? You insist on doing this? Let's do it. *Insh'allah.*

The technological marvel was over. The Chosen on stage here, bi-locating from England, had dematerialised. Whee! Just like *Star Trek*! A brief break, then Sage and Ax came back (costume changed into black and white, jeans and singlets), and Fiorinda walked on. She picked up her guitar, donned it and gave the Bowl her calm little wildcat grin. 'Good evening Hollywood!'

'HI, FIORINDA!'

'Be patient with me, I don't speak very good Californian. But you may well believe, I'm EXTREMELY pleased to be here!'

> *Sa, re, ga, ma,*
> *Pa, dha, ni,*
> *Which god is notorious*
> *In the neighbourhood?*
> *Eh, it's the god of fucking*
> *And his sugar cane bow—*
> *Oh, oh, oh,*
> *Sugar cane bow—*

The second concert at the Hollywood Bowl would have mixed reviews. The West Coast music scene had ignored the first event, as they'd more or less ignored the English invasion, reckoning it was nothing to do with them. They took notice of the second show, and elected to find it dirty, fat, and impressive. The big band was the tops, with Anne-Marie Wing and Smelly coming in for a special mention. The industry got off on the tech feat: which was done by I-Systems, who were developing b-loc applications under licence. Some people who saw both shows preferred the first, and spoke of a dullness, a shadow on the second: some people called it a mood of dark intensity. The radical rockstars were *fey*, it was said, both off stage and on. A Celtic term, something about foreseeing your own death. The nineteen thousand people – approximately – in the live audience were polled, in realtime, like all big live audiences. The graphs said they were having a good time (with pockets of resistance); easily as good as the last concert. They peaked when the Chosen materialised, and when Fiorinda walked on and did 'Sugar Cane Bow'. Towards the end of the Triumvirate set (which was basically Fiorinda on this occasion, with her lovers in support), as the material moved from the ballads to the dance tracks, building in energy and passion, the response of the tagged sample went haywire, completely off the scale. At last the three of them came to the front of the stage and stood there, widely spaced, Fiorinda in the centre. Ax had his guitar, the Fender he'd been playing in his solo spot. Sage was empty-handed, leaving his boards to run. The Angelenos yelled approval as they recognised the opening of 'Strange Kisses' from *Yellow Girl*, a favourite dance anthem of this 'English' summer. The Triumvirate sang, the fierce purity of her voice soaring above the bassline: holding out their arms to each other, and to the world out there, *send our defiance . . .*

Strange Kisses

You are so beautiful and strange to me, I can't believe this could be love
If this were heaven I'd be dancing here, There is nothing more I want—

    Send

                  Our

                                      Defiance

    To the

                  World

                                Out There,

There is no chance of dying—

                      In this game,
                        In this game,
                          In this game—

Sage's fx were reduced to a pulse and flow of coloured light, everything was in the rhythm, the voices, and the euphoria that possessed the crowd as it peaked and peaked: until Ax and Sage stepped back and Fiorinda, without a pause, broke into the swinging, sturdy dance that went with 'Chocobo', from her first solo album *Friction*. The crowd didn't know this one so well. It was European trash-taste, absurd lyrics about a big happy bird from a fantasy game; but they were with her.

She danced, while her recorded voice blended with her lovers' backing, rainbows whirling around her, arms and legs like pistons. She just *went on dancing*: while the thousands danced in place, until they could feel the world turning under them, until they never wanted to stop, just let Ax go on playing that guitar, let Fiorinda's beat never stop, let the light and sound and colour never end. Go with it, surrender, totally—

It must have ended somehow.

Somehow the venue must have been cleared. Sober figures in dayglo tabards must have marshalled the crowd. Shards of memory, when she left the stage did she tear off the hateful wig and stamp on it, yelling never, never, never? Were there blurred faces, swelling and shrinking? Was there a car park, black in driving rain? The sound of wind. The fractured galaxies of the freeway lights.

Wake in darkness, naked, shocked and jolted, oh, God, what did I do?

'Oh, God. What did I do?'

'Hush, ssh. You did nothing bad. It's okay, Fee, lie down again.'

'You're safe in bed, my little cat, you're safe with us.'

'It's over,' she whispered. 'It's over now.'

Janelle had said no visitors, but he knew he was expected. At the back of the cottage her car was parked out on the asphalt, debris from last night's rainstorm plastered against the wheels. He unlatched the screen door; the inner door opened when he tried the handle. The blue and white paint in the hallway was peeling, invaded by ocean damp. He walked through the living room, with its seen-better-days good taste: beach sculptures, a stone hearth, black and white landscape photos by major artists. She was in her studio, lying on a couch in the midst of the hardware with a knitted comforter pulled over her, her very professional projector silently running; watching a movie on an irregular shaped décor-screen (the only fashion item in this room). 'Hi,' she said.

'Hi.'

He folded himself down beside her on the rug. The movie was European, from the last century. He remembered that Jan worshipped this director: he even remembered her passionate commentary when they'd watched this very movie together. Things like that stay with you, nineteen-year-old sex vanishes. Subtitles tracked the sonorous, lilting language, words he recognised (Europe's a small place) rising like waveforms . . . We draw the theatre around us, said a young woman in scarlet and gold, The dressing rooms are warm and brightly lit, people sit out there in the dark, liking us—

'D'you know what it is?'

'It's *Fanny and Alexander*.'

'Congratulations, grasshopper. The best movie ever made, bar none, fuck the tech. Hey, the pilgrim's progess of the mind's predicament, what else should art express?' She kept her eyes on the screen. 'So now you know. Sometimes, like when you gave me the lesson on Zen Self, when you told me how you beat Rufus, I was afraid you knew everything and you were just playing with me.'

'I didn't know. I have blindsight. It's not like suspecting the truth. It's like walking in complete darkness, and stepping around things you don't know are there. Fiorinda was looking for a big mean megastar, but I kept coming back here. I kept thinking of you—'

'And I kidded myself it was fond memories.'

'It was fond memories,' he said, and took her hand. Jan was running a fever; her dark skin was dry and hot. She was burning up. 'We were looking for a megastar, and it had to be someone involved with us. You are the star of the virtual movies, Jan. The celebrity faces are just publicity. Those thirty code-people, you're the one who blended them. You were the single mind, giving those fragments meaning, expressing your vision through them.'

'It's what a director does. When did you figure it out?'

'Fiorinda did, when we knew you were the Fat Boy.'

'She's a smart cookie, your girlfriend. Ironic, or what? If Digital Artists had let me make the movies I wanted, I would never have got weaponised. I drowned other people's crap in crude arousal triggers, and the demon juice came gushing into my tanks. I didn't know how it worked. I never heard of the Hollywood Conjecture until near the end. But I guess I knew what I was doing. The code-bunnies tempted me, and I did fall.'

The movie continued, and they watched it for a while—

'I met Rufus once,' said Janelle. 'I met him right here in Hollywood, before you were famous, Aoxomoxoa, at one of those fucking miscegenation rock-movie parties. He looked me dead in the eye, I looked at him, and I got out of that room as fast as I could. I didn't know what the fuck had hit me, I was shitting myself ... He didn't touch me. He just gave me that *I know you* look, and I knew never, never, never go near that guy again. I didn't tell a soul, and he didn't come after me. He wasn't interested,' she added (the wistful tone was chilling). 'I wasn't hot enough.'

'You weren't his daughter.'

'Maybe I was his sister. Like, I was Shakespeare's sister of the occult.

Maybe we were descended from the same Mandingo sorcerer-king. I like to think that magic comes out of blackness, out of negritude, hahaha, to blast the fucking smug white world. That would be my desire.'

'Mm.'

She gripped his hand. 'I don't mean that . . . I don't think like that. I have never used my hidden power for gain, Sage. Well, okay, maybe, gain like, boosting things, fixing parking tickets, high school grades, making people who annoyed me have a shitty day. It was my dirty secret. No one knew: I was smart enough to realise, from when I was a kid, that no one must ever know . . . But I never used it to further my career, because I was proud, and I was honest. I wanted *real* success.'

'What made you decide to work for the Counterculture?'

'Hahaha. I won't try and tell you I started worshipping Gaia—'

He grinned faintly. 'I didn't think so.'

'The environment is fucked to shit, no one has to convince me of that, I live in LA. There is no answer, we're on our way down, and we deserve it. I got approached by Laz Catskill. I don't know how he nailed me for an eco-warrior, but it was very cool. We were this secret club, names that would surprise you. We were behind all the scenes, we were into fusion consciousness, Vireo Lake, the revolution in Europe. We knew what the real news was.'

She sighed. 'They were looking for magic, I had magic. I wouldn't go to the desert, that sounded too fucking weird, and later they didn't want me to, I was to have no association. But I let them persuade me to try the exercises. I didn't know if I was any good, that's the funny thing. The way they talked, I thought shit, they won't be impressed . . . but it was all bullshit. *I was the only one.*'

'Yeah.'

'They had scraps. Auto-suggestion. With me, it was this *geyser* inside me, which I hadn't known was there, and the worse stuff I let them do for me, the better it got; and everything I did for them, fixing their problems, was another taste. So before you know it, I was—' She broke off in mid-sentence, and he felt that something was looking at him, some limitless, hair-trigger malevolence. He turned his head, and she had also turned from the screen: he looked into dark eyes. The blood chilled and stopped in his veins, his balls tried to crawl into his belly, his mouth dried—

'I was a monster.'

'But you're okay now,' he said, gentle and steady.

'Yes. I called destruction on myself, and destruction came.'

She laid her head back. 'I called destruction, but the monster didn't want it. Using the magic opens, oh, God, a pit inside. I was going all the way, last night. I thought I could *win*, for once in my fucking life. But nah, I was screwed . . . I took my medicine, that's what was happening, and I'm glad.' She gripped his hand. A shock swept over her face, as if something behind the flesh would break out: but the spasm passed.

'Hey, bodhisattva, you got a cigarette for an old lady?'

He had none. He found a crumpled pack on her workdesk and sat on the couch beside her while they shared the last one, turn about.

She looked up at him, tears starting, like a little girl.

'They wouldn't let me in, Sage. The bastards *wouldn't let me in*. Because I'm black, because I'm a woman, because I knew I was good and I wasn't going to bow down before the gilded turds. If something was shit, I would say it was shit . . . But the fucking sad thing is, I'm the same as them. I'm their kind. If they would have let me in, I would have bowed down before anything.'

A little later she said, 'I'm dying. Will you come with me? I'm scared.'

'That's what I'm here for, sweetheart.'

It wasn't easy. The thing she'd been trying to become was appalling even in defeat. But he got her past the pit, into the cascade of neurological events that would lead to peace. He returned to find that the children in the Bergman movie had been rescued too; they were safe in the red-shadowed house of curios and marionettes. The old Jew, Isak, read to them.

> *I myself am on my way to the forests and the springs.*
> *I was there once when I was young,*
> *and now I'm trying to find my way back.*

He watched to the end of the scene. Then he left *Fanny and Alexander* to run, left the cottage and went back to Fiorinda and Ax, who had been waiting in the public car park that overlooked the white, tainted sands of the Rosa Peninsula. He got into the Rugrat and they drove away.

It was cancer. The doctors told her she had mild pneumonia, and it was the most awful systemic cancer. Poor Janelle, she was riddled with it. Found by the cleaning lady, isn't that the death we all fear? Virtual Hollywood was cast into mourning and struck by dread, the idols and the money men, golden boys and studio executives, looking in their mirrors and thinking, *that's how it will happen to me*. The former

Aoxomoxoa took a ride in one of those endangered-species silver birds, across the continent to Massachusetts. He had to meet some people, and he couldn't put them off. If you've been granted an audience with the Internet Commissioners, you turn up or forget it. They do not get messed around.

By tradition there were sixteen of them. When one of their number had cause to drop out, the team chose and appointed a replacement. Repeated attempts had been made to suborn this process, by government, military or business interests, without success. They brooked no interference. Their ages at present ranged from seventy to twenty-four, sexuality various; there were two women and fourteen men. By their own standards they were riven by huge ideological differences, generation gaps, theory feuds. To the rest of the world they were a hive-mind.

They liked to meet in person (which tells you something). They were indifferent to terrorist threats, and the expense of travel was not a concern. The case of some hermit nethead who belonged on this team but travelled by bicycle was theoretically possible, but it hadn't arisen yet. They weren't paid for being Internet Commissioners, but they were all in the extremely high income bracket, one way or another. They moved around, sometimes meeting in Seattle, sometimes in New York State, or Texas: at the moment it was the Sprawl.

Outdoors, in this select node of Boston's silicon valley, the trees pressed like rampant weeds around clearings hacked for digital business, and suburban dwellings. Humidity was so high you could take a handful of air and wring water out of it, and the heat was scalding. The conference room, on the upper floor of a blank, gold glass blockhouse, was dry and austere, bathed in cool neutral light. The netheads sat around a large oval table. The table and their persons were snootily devoid of visible tech, but Sage wore the living skull. It was the right touch. Some of the Commissioners knew him as the renegade son of one of their own; all of them knew Aoxomoxoa, at least by repute. Now is not the time to try out new material.

He told them they were going to have to call a halt to the experiments at Vireo Lake because the government-paid scientists were using code from *Morpho*, the first immersion album in the world, which Sage Pender had authored, seventeen years ago. Then he sat back.

They took his news as a joke in poor taste.

'I'm personally opposed to remote-controlled weapons of mass destruction,' said the chairperson, at last; a gigantically obese fellow in a floppy pale suit, with a leonine head of curly grey hair. 'Of any variety.

But open source is something I hold sacred. What the hell are you talking about, Sage? You made immersion code public domain. Are you trying to have us claw it back for you? It's a long time too late for that, young man.'

'I'm not trying anything.' said Sage. 'It's your rules. Morpho code was used in creating the Ivan/Lara virus. The Internet Commission bans the use of any scrap of live viral material, in any public-funded application, an' as yer may recall, Ivan/Lara was the bug that killed the European net.'

There was a gratifying silence.

'So, this is what Fred's come up with,' mused the chairperson.

'Did he fuck. This is *my* idea. I thought of it all by myself.'

The razor-cut, nose-to-ear-chain biker lady next to the chairperson rolled her eyes and groaned. 'C'mon, Sage. Don't bullshit us. We know that desert nest was a sideshow. We know Fred Eiffrich hired you guys to help him screw the Pentagon.'

'How is Ax? Is he going to take the English President job?'

'How's he planning to deal with the Second Chamber?'

'Will he hold democratic elections?'

Sage sat back from the table and folded his arms, the living skull disgusted. 'I'm not here to talk about Ax Preston. If you want me to divulge politically sensitive information it will cost you, an' you can see me after. I want to talk about *my idea*.'

'Me, fucking me. You haven't changed.'

'When Ax last came over, you bastards shoved him off to a subcommittee, just to insult him, until Fred kicked you into line. I've got no time for your personal comments. Are you interested or are you not? I can leave. I can walk out now.'

They were interested. Sage showed them (everyone had implants, or eyesocket tech) what he was talking about: code he had authored, so long ago, and the indisputable role it had played in the virus that had come near to destroying modern civilisation. The demonstration itself raised a *frisson* of dread: Ivan/Lara had been the doomspell of all doomspells.

'I mention this in passing,' said one of the youngest Commissioners, a slender fashion victim, Japanese eyejob. 'Not that I give a shit, but you happen to know, line by line, the software our top-secret weapons developers are using?'

'Of course I do,' said the living skull. 'Use yer head, Dino. This is neuroscience, not the fucking recipe for Coca Cola. The labrats have to be trained on immersions. That's how you get the neuronal architecture for handling multiple virtual worlds, an' you have to have that in place, or you carn' get anything from hitting information space, which is the set of all virtual worlds including this here. That's why me and my mates got into the Zen Self. We had the onboard equipment that Olwen Devi needed in her test pilots.'

'You're admitting your stuff really does burn people's brains?'

'Sure. So does learning to read. Your point is?'

The netheads were not fully informed on fusion consciousness. A couple of people around the table became abstracted, glazing over while they went after a crash course in the privacy of their heads. One of them came out of his trance, impressed, but shaking his head. 'Sage, okay, how can I put this, have you talked to the band? You're already on the index in fifteen states. Now you want to announce to the world that classic immersion code contains the seed of a deadly virus?'

'It's Morpho, not immersion code. We don't care what happens to Morpho. We lost the rights, remember? Like anyone in Europe knows, I re-authored, and everything after Morpho is in Mark II. But the evidence is the Vireo Lake project is using Mark I, which is tainted. I don't know why it would be a public scandal. I'd think it'd be something kept very quiet. But if the word got out, an' our sales took a dip, we can weather it.'

He didn't explain it would mainly be the Second Chamber government's loss.

The leonine chairperson said, thoughtfully, 'Can it be argued that this viral infringement happens *specifically* at Vireo Lake?'

The living skull smirked. Well, of course. We don't want to pick a fight with any other users, like the virtual movie industry; or medicine. The time he'd spent with Fred Eiffrich had been spent laboriously tracing, right from evolutionary sources, a path that would single out the weapons developers. 'The lawyers in the President's camp say a case can be made for that.'

The chairperson nodded. 'Mm.'

'Immersion code was never my property, see. All I did was figure out what I needed, went looking for it, picked it from the bough, made it do my will. I didn't nick anything, besides crunching time, which I was siphoning off my dad's machines at eks, without his knowledge—'

'You can't still believe Joss didn't know what you were doing,' someone broke in. 'Grow up, Sage. You have to get past this emotional block you have.'

'Shit, I'm sorry. I didn't know this was the Joss Pender fanclub.'

'Your dad was caring for you. He was giving you what you needed most, the only way that you would let him—'

The living skull turned on the speaker with a hideous glare. '**Fuck. Off.**'

'Three chillies,' said the meeting's acting secretary. 'One more of those, Sage, and you are out of the room.'

'Fer fuck's sake, I only told him to fuck off.'

'It's the tone of voice. You can call Andrew a brown-nosed interfering little cunt with stupid hair, and I wouldn't argue. But you don't look at him like that and you don't use that tone. We do emotion control, and we do gentleness, Sage, and don't you fucking cross the line again.'

'*As I was saying*. I didn't nick anything, I didn't create anything. I got there first, which was very cool, and me an' the Heads then made a stack of profit, but I put the code back in the public domain because that's where I found it. I had no control over its use; I didn't make Ivan/ Lara happen. But I feel responsible, and that's why, having realised this situation, I decided I had to come to you.'

The Commissioners conferred, silently, but he didn't need to know what they were saying. He knew they were sold. He knew they hated the fusion consciousness weapon, or there'd have been no point in trying this. No love lost between net-lovers and icky grey matter research. Better than that, it was their psychology. These were sixteen of the smartest, best informed and most successful people in the entire world, but all geeks are mischief-makers at heart.

'They'll have an answer,' said the second woman Commissioner and deputy chair, a NASA information systems chief, with regret. No love lost between inner space and outer space. 'They'll prove they're clean.'

'Maybe,' said someone else, gravely. 'But we'll have to check it out. Very carefully. It's complex. It could take years to come to a decision.'

'Yay! Let's pull the plug on the buggers! Awesome!'

'You're the firemen,' said Sage, limpidly. 'You can do whatever you like.'

He was dismissed, and left the building with Dino Logothetis. The weight of several overheated atmospheres fell on them as they stepped outdoors. Californians are from Mars, Sprawlers are from Venus.

Dino looked at Sage, suddenly curious. 'Have you changed the mask?'

The living skull would have raised its eyebrows, if it had any. 'Not recently.'

'You look different somehow—'

'I had my hair cut yesterday.'

'Hahaha, that must be it. Share a taxi?'

'No. I hate sharing taxis.'

At Logan International, he ran the gauntlet of civil unrest. One of the things that middle-class Americans don't tell you is that the price of aviation fuel is only part of it. Airports are where the poor gather, picketing, hustling. The security's horrible; it's just a miserable experience. Safe inside the echoing, melancholy halls he found a bar, collapsed there, and tugged the mask button from his eyesocket. The button was new, the mask he'd been able to download from England, thank God. He couldn't have done that pitch barefaced. It's been confirmed, I'm not Aoxomoxoa anymore. Letting exhaustion rise, he thought of the woman whose bitter brilliance had been extinguished. *Tonight it doth inherit, The vasty hall of Death.* He was very tired, ominously tired. He picked up the tiny button and held it on his fingertip. Shall I chuck this? Nah, I would only buy another one next week.

Know thyself.

The President had been spending too much time at his beloved Bellevue this summer. His detractors were bitching; but they were going to have to shut up when the Lavoisier affair was revealed to them, so he could afford one more weekend. He held a quiet dinner party, to which Ax and Fiorinda were invited: kind of an apology, he said, for the way he'd missed both their Bowl concerts. The hostess was Cleonce Sherville, the lady very quietly known to be the President's *maîtresse du titre*. Ax noted the compliment with something like dread. The meal was late, Spanish-style. Coffee and liqueurs were served outdoors. Ax and the President strolled on the Japanese terrace: moonlight shone on forested ridges, stretching away forever. 'I hate to leave this view,' sighed Fred. 'I dream about it. How's the big guy?'

'He's okay. He won't take care of himself, that's all. *What can I do* with a man who had his liver replaced a year ago, and insists on drinking alcohol?'

'You could try accepting that he's a grown-up.'

'I'll hold that one in reserve,' said Ax, gloomily.

'What are your plans, the three of you? Where are you heading?'

'I have plans,' said Ax, with a hunted look, muscles knotting at the angle of his jaw. 'Someone has to look after Sage, he keeps forgetting he's not superman, and Fiorinda won't do it; he has her hypnotised. I badly need to see more of the world; and I'm thinking I might learn to sail. I have to get those two to appreciate the Blues, that's very important. And there's Beethoven. I have to convince Fiorinda to give Beethoven a second chance. She has the – the superficial idea that he's some kind of shallow, megalomaniac tyrant—'

'I have something for you. Shall we go along to my study?'

They walked around the overgrown log cabin, shadows following them. Even here, in the heart of this armed camp, the secret service minders were within arm's reach. The President opened the French doors, shut them again behind his friend, and drew the curtains. The lamps were lit. On a table by the hearth stood a silver tray bearing bourbon, ice and glasses.

'Let me see—'

Mr Eiffrich rifled neat stacks of papers on his desk. 'Is that Vireo Lake?' said Ax, looking at a glossy colour photo that lay on top of the Morpho boxfile. Sleek blockhouses, little bonsai pines in green lawns, all set in an unreal white plain—

'Yeah.'

Well, well, thought Ax. That peyote was good stuff.

'What happened to the faithful protestors?'

'They don't get beyond the perimeter fence. Nobody does, except authorised personnel. You want to pay them an official visit? I could fix that up.'

'No thanks.'

'Get it while you can, Ax. The place will be shutting down very shortly. And before they get out from under the moratorium, I'll have disclosures I can make about the Lavoisier affair that will outlaw research of that kind forever. Fusion consciousness science may be the coming thing. Human weapons development in the USA is down the tubes. And that means forever, I hope.' He gave Ax a warm, firm smile. 'For which I am eternally grateful, to you, and your lady; and to Sage.' He'd found what he was looking for. It was a dark red plush box, like a jewel case. What's in there? A present for Fiorinda?

'Yeah,' said Ax, looking at the red case. 'Think nothing of it.'

'Shall we sit down? Will you take that drink, this time?'

'No thanks.'

They went over to the hearth and sat in opposite armchairs. The President poured himself a little bourbon. 'Ax, all this time, I haven't said a word to you about English politics, or the situation with the Presidency—'

Ax nodded. 'I noticed, and I was grateful.'

315

'I saw the ambassador, in Washington last week. Do you know the guy, James Spencer-Mehta? He has a great respect for you.'

'I've never met him.'

'They want you back.'

Ax shrugged, his mouth tight. 'I gather. Why not? I'm decorative.'

Mr Eiffrich looked into his glass, and sighed. 'How did it happen, Ax? How did England fall? Of all the states in Europe—'

'The mother of all stock market crashes, and a mountain of consumer debt. That's how it happened. Millions of people living one paycheque away from ruin, a governing class slipping into tyranny and corruption; and then ruin came. That was the situation that brought the fall, and empowered the green revolution.' Ax's eyes flashed. 'We did a good job, Fred. When we took over we made that revolution work: for a while, marginally, smoke and mirrors. But it was a shambles that I directed, and I always knew it. You know what that means? It means a slaughterhouse. What was slaughtered was a civilised nation. It's gone. And the venal idiots who find that situation comfortable and profitable are the ones who have ended up in charge.'

Mr Eiffrich looked guiltily alarmed for a moment—

Ax laughed. 'Oh, don't worry. That's not in the movie. Practically the only on-screen casualty will be the truth.'

'That's good.'

Soon, thought Ax, you'll spot that your eco-warriors *don't* have effective magic. There was only one, and she's dead, may the Compassionate have mercy on her. But before you know that, you'll listen. You'll engage. So will others, who would never, never have listened before. I think that's a result.

'I talked with Spencer-Mehta, and he gave me this. Ax, your brother himself knows he's not the man for the position; and I know you've talked to him.'

Ax had talked to Jordan. He'd had the pep talk from Rob. He wondered if these people knew they were hammering on an open door. To go back, to try again, and this time *without* the corruption of absolute, arbitrary power, which he'd always known was the wrong way ... It wasn't something he didn't want. It was an unbearable temptation. Mr Eiffrich had put the jewel case in front of Ax. He had to open it. Inside, on a bed of velvet, lay a gleaming leaf-shape of green stone, as long as a man's hand.

'It's the Falmouth Jade,' said the President. 'To replace the stone axe that was lost when you quit the dictatorship. They really want you back, Ax.'

'I don't think they know what they're asking for.'

'Fiorinda will go with you. She wants to look after her drop-outs. Sage will go with you, and you could have no wiser friend.'

You think I'll be useful in Europe, he thought. The Westminster government wants to trade on the legend, and my darlings want to go home. They know we can't live in England unless I take the Presidency. It would be Ax Preston lurking down in Cornwall, no fixed role, a focus for every plot and conspiracy. How long could that last? 'Are we talking terms? Let's talk about the way the oil wars are making the Islamic populations of Europe, including England, impossible to govern—'

The President leaned forward, elbows on his knees, the bourbon glass in his hands. 'I'm not a fool, Ax. I know what the USA looks like from Crisis Europe. I know people over there see me – maybe even you see me – as the puppet of the callous super-rich of the richest nation on earth. I can only tell you, it's not true. It's true I have to obey the secret rulers, like every head of state, and I have no choice about who those rulers are; my country's history makes that choice. But I have a mandate, and I intend to use it to do everything in my power to get the world out of this very frightening tailspin we are in. But I will not fight battles I can't win, and the war in the Middle East is not something I can mess with. There's things I can do for you, and there's things I can't do for you. Will you go back?'

They stared at each other, and it was Ax who broke away. He stood up, without a word, and walked out of the room. Fred stayed by the empty hearth. He raised his glass to the dark-haired woman above the fireplace: and grinned, as at a point well gained, in a long and still doubtful game.

'Turned him!'

* * *

The English said goodbye to Emilia and the house at Sunset Cape and moved into the Alisal, a historic (well, repro) Art Deco hotel in town. The day before the Few were due to leave, by H-train, for New York and the voyage home (they were going by sea), they did a live group interview for a mass-market movie-news channel. Harry had sprung this on them without notice, just to prove he was still Harry, and they'd said yes, for old times' sake. The interview was a circus. It was conducted in the Triumvirate suite; there were far too many people, most of them there for no good reason, and the interviewers, who modelled their style on DeeDee and Bob, the software bots, treated the

Few like filler, barely even pretending to include them; which did not endear them to anyone.

Interviewer: 'What's it like living with three laydees, Rob? Aren't you everlastingly catching hell about the toilet seat?'

Felice: (Unintelligible, sound cone whisked away.)

Interviewer: 'I just can't get over the bisexual Aoxomoxoa, Sage. Don't you find that a lot of your male fans are kind of ooooh, woooo, about that?'

Sage: 'Who are you calling *bisexual*? I'm not bisexual! *He's* bisexual, I'm perfectly normal, there's nothing wrong with me—'

Interviewer: (merrily) 'Ax, why the fuck do you tolerate him?'

Ax: 'I get off on being publicly humiliated. When I was dictator I used to meet workers in the sex industry on railway concourses, and pay them to reveal disgusting details of my sexual habits to the tabloids. But they always let me down—'

Fiorinda: 'He didn't pay them enough. He's incredibly stingy.'

Ax: 'They could have revealed I was incredibly stingy, couldn't they?'

Anonymous party boy: Ax, are you going to hold democratic elections?

And so on. The interviewees stuck it for about twenty minutes, then retired to the lobby bar, a beautiful space, the walls built from granite boulders, huge naked beams overhead, leaving the circus to carry on without them. They emptied the miniature pretzels out of the crystal miniature pretzel bowl and made a pile of the cheques they had received as their movie fees after the Second Chamber government's deductions.

Possibly the price of a nice cup of coffee in Tokyo, if they shared it.

You have to admire the guy, thought Sage. He was going to see us in hell, for all eternity, and torture us to death beforehand, but he still took the time to wreak havoc on our finance. Now that is *thorough*. He sat back on a sleek Alisal sofa, stuck his hands in his pockets and laughed. 'Hey, if we stay on a few weeks, I bet I can get a gig doing a *Don't call me baby* set in Vegas somewhere.'

'I'd pay to see that,' grinned Ax. He poked at the cheques. 'We should set fire to them. I think we owe Harry a minor rock and roll behaviour incident—'

Harry had not turned up for the circus.

Fiorinda slipped off her shoes and tucked up her feet on her comfy armchair. 'Get it while you can. We're servants of the people again next week.'

The Few glanced at Ax, with whom the decision was still a sensitive point.

'I've been finding out about Lavoisier,' he remarked, leaning back beside his big cat. 'Did you know, as well as inventing modern chemistry, naming oxygen and God knows what else, he discovered that breathing is a form of combustion? And he once had his father carry a bowl of goldfish across France for him, not sure why. He used to get on with his dad, they were good friends—'

'Is that a chip memory?' asked Sage. He worried about the way the archive from Ax's long-deceased implant kept turning up, in fragments.

Ax shrugged. 'Yeah, probably. But life is fire, it burns, and we can't breathe air without fire in it; that's not a chip memory. I knew that.'

'D'you know the story about him at the guillotine?' asked Rob.

'Everyone knows,' said Verlaine. 'He told a friend of his to watch and he would blink as often as he could after his head was chopped off. It's a meme, or one of those things. I forget, a marker of something, if you know it—'

'Trivia wiring.'

'Yeah. It was eleven times,' said Allie.

'I thought it was fifteen times,' countered Dora. 'You get about twenty seconds, apparently.'

'Twenty seconds,' said Chip. 'Woo. A lot can happen in twenty seconds.'

'Couldn't possibly comment,' mumured Verlaine.

'My father lasted longer than that,' remarked Fiorinda. 'He lasted all the way home from Ireland, and then some. I thought about it a lot, when I was scared I was going to be a head in a jar. I was wondering if I could beat my dad's record.'

Her friends were silenced, stilled. Gallows humour on this topic was no accident; it was one of those things that happens, it was natural to them. For a moment the banter became *not funny at all*, so that no one knew how to recover, and Ax was appalled that he'd started this. But it was too much. They cracked up, all of them, in a manic fit of irony. Fiorinda raised her glass, grinning. 'Long live the revolution!'

'**Long live the revolution!**'

Heads turned. Ax and Sage's sofa took a little jump, and so did the rest of the furniture. The Few glanced around, comically puzzled: hey, who's doing this? Fiorinda swallowed the rest of her drink, to protect it from being spilled. 'There's something about getting in a doorway . . .' said Ax, calmly. The lobby of the Alisal shifted again, lifting and flopping down, like a sailing boat bouncing over choppy swell. The other people in the bar had begun to mill around and there were voices raised, but no alarm bells went off. The granite boulder walls stood firm.

'What are we supposed to do?' wondered Dora.

'There'll be storm shelters, earthquake drill, they're used to this, um—'

'I think we should get outdoors,' said Fiorinda. 'Now. Quickly.'

A lot of people had the same idea. Outside, the traffic had all backed up, sirens were wailing, the air was full of red dust. The sky through the reddish cast was white, a negative white, full of dancing sundogs, a storm of naked energies, without any wrapping of rain or wind. The third shock hit; buildings shook like jelly. Ax and Sage got either side of Fiorinda, but the others had disappeared, gone in the mêlée. There was a sound like thunder, a roaring like the sea in a shell, and they realised that what they could see coming over the horizon was a tall wall of brown, churning water rushing down the Pasadena Freeway—

Two hundred miles away, in the Anza-Borrego desert, the Vireo Lake A team had come on line.

As Sage had once remarked, the Zen Self programme had traits in common with nuclear fission physics, a sudden breaking of barriers, an explosive release of energy. The Vireo Lake project had taken a route more genuinely analogous to fusion. The neuronauts had indeed been selected for latent psi ability, after being vetted for the usual right stuff criteria. Their test programme had been based on a concept known as sympathetic magic in the occult world (the same concept Sage had used for locating Fiorinda). They were attempting to visualise the molecular composition of crude oil, make a change, and transfer (or superimpose) that change onto a tank of the stuff, buried under the desert. The reservoir was shielded as if it was a trap for neutrinos, the researchers were prepared to measure 'fusion' effects in parts per trillion. After the first successful test, which would have been the last test before the Internet Commissioners shut the lab down, they didn't have to go that far. It was obvious at once that they had a tank full of hopelessly disordered slime. But the A team were dead. They had died, under the scanners, about the same time as the change.

There was no smoking gun in the fault lines, linking the LA quake to the location of the underground tank, but nobody really believed there was no connection. Nevertheless, as analysis of the slime went into overdrive, the Vireo Lake scientists knew they had a staggering vindication of their work. In spite of the human tragedy, and the devastation, they were triumphant. A week later a note, which might be construed as a joint suicide note, was found. It had been hidden so that it would only be discovered in the course of this kind of investigation. It began IN THE NAME OF ALLAH, THE COMPASSIONATE, THE MERCIFUL, (none of the neuronauts had been Muslims); it ended THE LORD GIVETH AND THE LORD TAKETH AWAY, BLESSED BE THE NAME OF THE LORD. It declared they had acted for the good of humanity, and that the human weapon building should never be repeated. The note was suppressed. The neurological data was re-examined. It was established that the neuronauts might have reached the Fat Boy state together, for an instant, at the moment of their death.

By that time, a handful of people already knew what the A team had done.

The rest of the world would find out by degrees, as the ruin spread.

CODA

At The Gate Of The Year

It was the end of October, and a cool, rainy day in Washington DC. In California the Los Angelenos were rebuilding, with what aid their state and nation could muster. Not many lives had been lost in the quake, but treasured landmarks were gone, food and water were in short supply and a lot of people had been left homeless. The Few were back in England. The Triumvirate had stayed in California, where Fiorinda had managed to turn the balance at 110lb, more than she'd ever weighed before in her life, counting when she was pregnant. In the midst of that chaos, she'd had the treatment to reverse the sterilisation. Ax had been in talks, meanwhile, with the Federal and State governments, and the people running the secret networks that she had encountered. They were visiting Washington, finally on their way home.

Ax was doing a live tv appearance from the White House with Fred Eiffrich, a morale-booster for the frightened, and very frightening, new world out there, in the USA and around the earth. The White House Media Office had been surprised to find they couldn't have the other two members of the Triumvirate to complete the picture: but you have to draw a line and stick to it. It had been established long ago that Ax does this sort of thing on his own. Fiorinda went with Sage to the Rock Creek Cemetery. He wanted to visit the Adams Memorial, the setting of the scene Jan had shown him from her dreamchild movie.

Janelle Firdous had been cremated, quickly and privately, after her sudden death; without any religious rite, as had been her wish. Ax had been at the cremation, with Harry. There'd been a big memorial service later, after the quake, and Jan would have said, *be proud*, because in spite of the situation, everybody who mattered had turned out. Sage and Fiorinda had stayed away from both ceremonies. This was the place where they would pay their respects. They found their way to the lonely arbour, where a young woman called Eleanor Roosevelt had struggled with her broken heart, more than a hundred years ago, and sat on a bench facing the statue called *Grief*. The shrouded figure, head bowed in the sombre peace of exhaustion, held their gaze and quieted them. They sat in silence until another, lone woman visitor arrived; then they walked away.

'Did you know,' said Sage, 'there's a demographic time bomb ticking in the US? When choosing the sex of your child became routine, the middle classes all started voting for daughters. It's like China reversed, and it'll hit the executive ranks in the next few years. The glass ceiling is finally toast.'

'Meanwhile, the ghettos fill up with angry dispossessed young men. Great.'

'Oh,' he said, crestfallen.

Fiorinda slipped her arm in his and leaned close against his side. 'We drop the subject. Now is not the time to debate sexual politics: leave it to the mills of God.'

'May I quote you?'

'Hahaha. If you feel lucky.'

They dismissed their cab and walked beside the Tidal Basin. Red and yellow rags of leaves fluttered on the famous cherry trees. Fiorinda got up on the barrier wall and sat crosslegged: Sage leaning beside her. The sky was grey and low, scattering cool drops that beat on the dark pewter mirror of the water. So far, so good. Fiorinda had a working womb, a menstrual cycle, and one functioning ovary. Dr Trigos had warned her, at their final interview, she should *forget* about natural childbirth, owing to the cervical scarring, for which she didn't recommend rebuild surgery. This warning kept returning to her, with a shiver down her spine. If she says that, she really thinks I could get pregnant.

'Fee?'

'Mm?'

'What was your baby called, the little boy who died? I don't remember.'

'You don't remember because I never told you, or Ax, for a good reason. I was a pre-teen Aoxomoxoa and the Heads fan, remember? I named him Stephen, Sage. After you.'

'Oh.' He stared at the water. 'I'm glad I didn't know that when—'

'When you killed his father.' Fiorinda sighed. 'Shit. Maybe dysfunctional rockstars with hideous family backgrounds shouldn't try to have children. Only Ax is even partly normal, out of the three of us, and he's a megalomaniac.'

'Mm. I've been thinking . . . Maybe it's pure superstition saying this, but your child and mine might be very, very strange.'

'I've been thinking that too. On the plus side, she probably won't be alone. In the world she'll live in, she could seem quite normal.'

'If there is a world. If we aren't all soup by next week.'

For ten weeks they'd been living as if in the shadow of the asteroid strike – the one that will not be announced because there's nothing to be done. In this case (if they lived where global village media had survived the Crisis), the people knew what had happened . . . But so far, things had been quiet. The world was still in shock. Where would the collapse end? No one knew, and no one had yet dared to try and reverse the process. Not even in a test tube . . . Neuroscientists in the tiny, global, fusion community were furiously analysing the data from the Vireo Lake event, trying to establish the A team's precise intentionality. If what they found was bad news, they wouldn't necessarily make it public. Is *oxygen* a fossil fuel?

Nothing to do but wait, and live. Every moment.

'There's an easy answer,' said Sage. 'Only Ax gets unsterilised.'

'Don't be such a wuss. One for each of you, we agreed.'

'If we're lucky. Many people aren't, these days. And for you?'

She shook her head. 'I had my baby, my little baby. Two's enough.'

He turned, struck by a sudden realisation. Fiorinda's hair clustered over her head in springy little corkscrews, the colour of a copper beech in April. Her skin glowed fallow-gold, her eyes were calm and bright. She looked *amazing*.

'What's the matter?'

'You said "she"? I thought we were going to leave that to chance.'

'Yes, of course we are. Oh. I did, didn't I?' She frowned, and then grinned, ravishing sweet. 'Nah, doesn't mean anything. Come on, let's go and find Ax.'

Leaving the USA in wartime, on one of the last transatlantic jet flights for the foreseeable future. Last time he'd flown out of Dulles Ax been oblivious. This time, as he said goodbye to Fred and Harry, and once more extracted from Kathryn the solemn promise that she would *never sell the Rat*, he had a feeling of valediction. The Atlantic's only four days wide (shit. Will we still be able to crack water?) but I have a very strong feeling I'm never coming back here.

Their plane, borrowed from the Presidential fleet, rose up and headed into a cracking set of electrical storms. Gusts of wind buffeted them, rain hammered, and there's the interesting possibility that the fuel in our tanks will collapse. But nah, that's not going to happen. The experts say that's *not* going to happen, and I have two of those experts sitting here beside me. This silver bird will touch down safe in John Lennon airport. And above us only sky . . .

They had the cabin to themselves. Fiorinda's nose was pressed to the window. Sage, on Ax's other side, had already contrived to fall asleep. Ax set about scanning through the stack of English newspapers, e-format, that he'd picked up from an airport callpoint (yep, I'm doing my homework on the bus, *I did not have time*.) An AI car can keep going, theoretically, for ninety or a hundred years, but they don't forget. They don't have that feature. It'll remember us, if we come back when we're pensioners. If . . . He put the plane-safe reader down: future shock. This gadget in my hands, this plane I'm sitting in, all these things may pass away, not over decades, not replaced by similar models, but *wham, gone*. And where is she, the ice-cold little girl, implacably decent and honourable, that I first took to my bed? Where is my friend, the drunken, brainy, skull-headed clown? They are gone. I will never see them again.

That's the lesson of faithful love. You keep losing the same people, over and over, and it teaches you: nothing lasts. The silver bird bucked and bounced. A chime, and a voice in his ear said, warm and confident, 'Hi, this is your captain. I thought I should tell you guys, since you may not have travelled by air in a storm for a while, don't worry about the lightning. The plane itself is a lightning conductor, we'll come to no harm . . .' What lightning? He peered over Fiorinda's shoulder and saw a magical thing, in the howling dark out there: wave on wave of rose-coloured, liquid light, flowing and colliding, standing up like shimmering frost flowers, across the complex surface of the wing.

'Isn't it *beautiful*?' whispered Fiorinda.

'Yeah.' A shock of joy went through him. Some time soon, I'm going to be fucking, armed and dangerous, for the first time in my entire life! How bad can the Green Presidency be?